SPIRIT HUNTER

SPIRIT HUNTER

VICTOR OF TUCSON ‡ BOOK THREE

PLUM PARROT

Podium

This is a work of fiction. Names, characters, places, and incidents are either products of the author's imagination or used fictitiously. Any resemblance to actual events, locales, or persons, living, dead, or undead, is entirely coincidental.

Cover design by Podium Publishing

ISBN: 978-1-0394-3333-5

Published in 2023 by Podium Publishing, ULC
www.podiumaudio.com

Podium

To Andy,

thanks for reading so much of my stuff

and for all the inspiration along the way

SPIRIT HUNTER

1

AFTERMATH

Victor sat in the shadows of the ready room holding Lifedrinker's cold metal against his forehead, desperately wishing he could hear her voice again. Though the handle was warm and she seemed to vibrate ever so gently against his flesh, no lilting feminine voice sounded in his head, and he said, "I'm sorry. I'm so sorry, *chica*. I'll make it up to you, I promise. I'll wake you up again."

A shadowy figure approached down the long hallway leading to the pit. At the same time, the door to the stairway leading up to the grounds opened. Thayla burst through the door, Captain Lam right behind her, and she charged over to Victor, grabbing him into a tight hug. He was sitting while she stood to the side, arms around his neck, smashing his head into her stomach. "You scared us to death, Victor!"

"Ungh," he grunted, reaching up to gently push her away so she'd loosen her death grip on his neck. "I didn't mean to scare you. I thought I was dead, too, to be honest."

"How'd you come back from those wounds? It seemed she'd pretty much gotten you to spend all your Energy," Lam said, coming to stand before him.

Victor was about to answer, but the shadow coming down the passageway resolved into the form of the arbiter. He strode forward into the ready room and held out his hand. Victor's belongings were arrayed there in his palm, Gorz hanging from one of his fingers. "I already gave Rellia her belongings. Some part of me wondered if you were bringing her down here to finish her off. I was pleased to find her sitting alone in the passage."

Victor reached out to take his rings, pouch, and necklace, then said, "You think she'll mess with me?"

"You showed her a great mercy," Captain Lam said. "Rellia can be a cold bitch, but she's known for her honor—well, her pride, at least. It's one of the reasons she felt she had to punish you—for her family's so-called honor. I can't predict how she will respond to this loss."

"Your friend is right," said the arbiter from the depths of his hood. "The ap'Yensha clan holds a grudge, but they also honor a debt. Rellia owes you a great debt, and along with that, she no longer has the Empire's laws on her side."

"Thanks, Arbiter," Victor said, holding up his fistful of jewelry, then he started putting on his rings.

"You're welcome, Victor. Congratulations. I'll leave you to your celebrations." He turned and walked through the door instead of the tunnel. Apparently, he was done with his officiating and wanted to leave. Victor didn't blame him.

"Well, how did you do it?" Lam pressed as soon as the door closed.

Victor lifted Lifedrinker and started to answer, "I didn't," he had to stop because his throat got thick, and his eyes began filling with moisture. He looked down and took a deep, shaky breath. "Lifedrinker," he started, but again his throat closed up, and he shook his head, staring at the floor.

Thayla reached out and rubbed the back of his neck, her warm, strong fingers smoothing out some of his tension. "It's all right. You don't have to talk about it right now."

Victor took another shuddering breath then cleared his throat, spitting a wad of bloody phlegm onto the stone floor. "Sorry," he said when he realized how gross it was. Then he said, "Lifedrinker saved me. She gave me most of the Energy she'd been gathering to make herself conscious." He cleared his throat again and rubbed at his eyes with one hand, the other refusing to let go of Lifedrinker.

"Really?" Lam asked. "I didn't even know that was possible."

"She spoke to me," Victor started then shook his head, rubbing at his eyes again. "I'll tell you guys more later. Can I please wash some of this blood off now?"

"Damn right, you can! You've achieved something amazing tonight, Victor. With or without your axe's help. Thayla's daughter should be in my coach by now. Let's head out, and then we'll go back to my estate to celebrate." Lam held out a long, pale hand, and Victor took it, letting her haul him to his feet.

Despite her lean figure, she was strong and solid, and he admired how her fingers wrapped around his wrist like a band of iron.

"How's it feel?" Thayla asked, taking hold of his other arm.

"What?" Victor asked, looking over his body. Had one of his wounds not healed when he went berserk?

"To be free! To not have anyone hunting you!" They walked together to the door and started up the steps as Victor answered.

"I'm glad I'm free, but there's still plenty to worry about. That asshole from Persi Gables that sent his goons after me? Remember? Belikot? All the people I've met that are still fucking slaves? And then there's Lifedrinker—I don't feel like I can celebrate."

"That's shit, and you know it," Lam said, turning back to look at the two of them. "You helped Thayla get free. You helped her find her daughter. You earned your freedom and dealt with a serious threat tonight. You need to take the wins when you get them, Victor."

"Yeah," Victor said, considering her words, and nodded. "Yeah, I guess so. Still, I just want a bath and a bed tonight. You guys celebrate for me, all right?" They'd reached the top of the stairs and, as Lam opened the door, were greeted by a crowd of people who seemed to have been waiting for him. They burst into cheers, and Victor, standing behind Lam with Thayla still holding onto his arm, frowned, drawing his dark eyebrows down in a glower.

"I didn't know they'd be here," Thayla said. "When we came through, it was empty."

Victor grunted, still glowering around, but Lam held up her hand for quiet. When the crowd settled, waiting to see what they'd say, Lam spoke loudly and clearly. "Victor appreciates your adulation, but he's had a very hard-fought victory. He's not up for a celebration. Feel free to call upon him at my estate!" She waved then grasped Victor's hand, pulling him through the crowd and out onto the lawn where more people milled about. "Really!" Lam hissed. "The magistrate needs to have an easier path out of this place!"

Lam pushed her way through the crowd, and Victor and Thayla followed in her wake. Victor kept his eyes down, finding it easy to ignore the cheerful, boisterous people if he simply didn't make eye contact. Soon they were past the bulk of the party, and Lam led the two of them over the dimly lit lawns to the gates where her coach was waiting. Victor hadn't seen it before, and it wasn't what he'd expected.

The coach was white with blue trim, and it was long, shaped more like a van than the stagecoach he'd imagined. It had six wheels with glittering metal spokes and tires made of something he couldn't guess at, but they were thick and blue, and looked more pliable than a car's tires. Strangest of all were the animals pulling it—tall, red-furred, stag-like creatures. There were three of them, and they each sported a pair of long spiral horns. "Nice," he said, his earlier stress momentarily forgotten.

"I won this coach in a dungeon, believe it or not," Captain Lam said. "It's enchanted to fold in on itself. If I wanted, I could pack it up and slip it into a backpack."

"Seriously?" Lam nodded, and Victor continued, "That's pretty damn cool. What about those antelopes?" He gestured to the horned creatures.

"Oh, I bought those. They don't fold up with the coach, unfortunately." While she spoke, a coachman came out from behind the vehicle and opened a door in its side. Three steps folded out as the door opened, and Thayla hurried into the coach, eager to see her daughter.

"What are they called?" Victor asked.

"What?" Lam asked, one foot already on the steps.

"Those animals," Victor gestured toward them again.

"Oh, they're called vidanii. They're from the plains far, far to the north of here." With that, Lam hoisted herself into the coach, and Victor was left standing outside with the coachman. He stood there for a minute, breathing in the night air, still not a hundred percent sure that he was alive. Hadn't he pretty much died in the fight? Was all this some kind of dream? He moved a hand to rest on Lifedrinker, remembering the sound of her voice in his head and the way she'd shown him her love and trust.

"Sir?" the coachman asked.

"Yeah?"

"Will you be joining the captain inside?"

"Right," he grunted and pulled himself up the steps and into the dim interior.

"Victor!" a small, high voice called. Victor followed the sound to see Deyni sitting on her mom's lap. Another woman sat next to Thayla—a yellow-haired Ardeni with bright matching eyes, a long sharp nose, and thick full lips. She was beautiful in a way, though she had deep frown lines around her eyes, and Victor could tell she'd had a tough life. She held one of Deyni's hands in a tight fist and regarded Victor with a suspicious brow.

"Hey, kiddo," Victor said, climbing the rest of the way into the coach and sort of falling into a seat next to Captain Lam, facing Thayla and her friend.

"It's a fast, comfortable coach but not really made for people as tall as we," Lam said to him with a wry grin.

"Told you he wasn't in jail," Thayla said to her daughter and smiled at Victor.

"That's right, *niñita.*" Victor smiled at the little girl, suddenly conscious of all the dried blood on his face. "Sorry, I'm a mess right now."

"He needs a bath, Mommy," Deyni said, and Victor was surprised to see she spoke to the other woman. Thayla tried to cover it, but he saw the frown that touched her lips. He tried to make eye contact and let her know he understood how frustrating that must be, but she hid the emotion too quickly, looking toward Deyni to avoid his eyes.

"He sure does," the woman said, then she looked at Victor and said, "I'm Rhessa. I've been looking after Deyni for Thayla while she was, um, away."

"While she was traveling!" Deyni said.

"Right, sweetie," Rhessa said.

"I've heard a lot about you. Nice to meet you." Victor started to reach out a hand, but then Lam shifted impatiently next to him.

"What's going on with this coach?" she asked, pulling a cord on the ceiling. A little door opened near the front of the coach, and the coachman's face appeared in a window.

"Ma'am?" he asked.

"Why aren't we moving yet?" Lam's voice was sharp, almost angry.

"There's a gentleman here, trying to impose his presence on your guest. I'm working on getting him to leave." The coachman, a middle-aged-looking Shadeni, spoke with perfect poise, not the least stressed by Lam or, apparently, whatever was happening outside.

"Which guest? What's the man's name?"

"He's claiming to be the brother of Rellia ap'Yensha, and he wants to speak to your guest, Mr. Sandoval."

"Open the door," Lam said. The window closed, and Victor could hear the coachman moving out of the driver's compartment. "Do you want to speak to him?" Lam asked, looking at Victor.

"Not really, but if it gets things moving, I guess I can."

"I can talk to him if you want . . ." Lam started, but Victor was already getting up and moving back to the door, stooped over to keep from smashing his head. A moment later, it opened, and he crouch-walked down the steps back to the flagstones. The coachman ducked his head in a show of respect, and Victor stood up straight, once again breathing deeply in the clean air.

After he'd filled his lungs, he looked down at the Ardeni man that stood, his free hand fidgeting with his lapel, a folded envelope in the other, waiting for Victor's acknowledgment.

Victor could see the man's resemblance to Rellia. He looked older, though, softer, and his eyes weren't nearly as sharp. He cleared his throat and held out the envelope. "My sister insisted I give you this before you leave. I think she's afraid you'll disappear into the universe before she gets a chance to contact you again. Quite a show you put on there. Thank you, by the way, for not killing my sister. Oh, dear! My name is Roth. Roth ap'Yensha."

Victor reached out and took the envelope. "Right. Got it. That all?"

"That's all! Sorry to hold you up. Please pass my apologies on to Captain Lam." The man actually bowed slightly and backed away. Victor didn't reply but turned and climbed back into the coach, clutching the envelope tightly in one fist. When he fell into his seat next to Lam, he turned to her.

"He's sorry for holding you up." As he said the words, the coach lurched and started moving.

"Well? What did the little twit want?"

"To give me this," Victor said, holding up the slightly crumpled envelope.

"Did you read it?" Lam asked.

"Not yet." Victor looked around the coach. Deyni looked as if she was asleep in Rhessa's arms, and Thayla sat staring at Victor, though her eyes were a million miles away. He turned back to Lam and said, "Should I?"

"Yes! Ancestors know what someone like Rellia thought was so important!"

"All right," Victor said, peeling the wad of pressed green wax away from the envelope's flap. He pulled it open to reveal a handwritten note.

Victor,

My missing foot throbs terribly as I write this to you from my room at Magistrate Thiv-dak's estate. I don't say that as any sort of accusation but just as an illustration of the state of my mind—how can a foot that no longer exists throb so?

You showed me two kindnesses tonight. One, you allowed me to live. Two, you lifted me from that pit of shame and shielded me from the eyes of my peers. The first I could imagine you did because you might be weak, foolish, or misguided. The second, Victor, the second could only mean that I've been very wrong about you.

My honor will not allow me to live with the debt you've placed me in. I beg of you: please come to see me when you've had time to rest. I'll be at my estate in Gelica until the month's end. I trust you to allow my obsequious, sentimental letter, written in pain and humiliation, to remain between us.

With gratitude and ever in your debt,
Rellia ap'Yensha

"That's fucking weird," Victor said, folding the letter closed and stuffing it back into the envelope.

"What did she say?" Lam asked, her bright, glittering green eyes boring into his.

"She wants me to come see her. Says she's in my debt and needs to make things even." He shrugged and slipped the envelope into his ring. It seemed to him that Rellia had asked him to keep the tone of her letter between them, and he didn't have a problem with that. At least not yet.

"This could be very good, Victor. Having such a powerful family feel like they owe you something is a boon." Lam turned away from him and was staring up at the ceiling of the gently bouncing coach, clearly fantasizing about what he, and she through him, could get out of Rellia.

"I don't like it," Thayla said. Victor looked at her and saw that she'd focused her attention on him, whatever she'd been brooding about forgotten for the moment.

"Well, I don't much like it either. That bitch almost killed me."

"Just remember that if you go see her," Thayla said. "Speaking of seeing people, are you still going to travel with me to see Oynalla? I think it will be good for me and Deyni to spend time with Tellen's people."

"Yeah, of course. Nothing's changed as far as that goes. C'mon, Thayla, cheer up." He could see she was irritable, and if he had to guess, he'd say she was bothered about how close Deyni was with Rhessa and how the girl treated Thayla like a visiting relative, not her long-lost mother.

"And me?" Rhessa asked over Deyni's head. "Will these Shadeni hunters be welcoming to an ex-criminal Ardeni?"

"Yes, I'm sure they would. We can talk about this later, though. I'm sorry I brought it up—I'm not sure where my head was." Thayla sighed heavily and looked toward the window at the rear of the coach, eyes going distant again.

"We've had a rough day. Sure, Victor is the one who did the fighting, but everyone was on edge all day, some of us more than a day. I think we'll all do better after some rest," Lam said, affecting a much different tone than when she'd suggested a celebration just a short while ago.

"Truth," Victor said, leaning his head back in the comfortable seat, letting his eyes close.

The rest of the coach ride passed by in a blur for Victor. He drifted in and out of sleep, and no one else spoke. Deyni's soft breathing served to lull him deeper and deeper into his own slumber, and he was somewhat startled when he heard the door being opened and felt Lam stirring next to him. He exited the coach to find Edeya standing with six of Lam's house guards. She held a spear, and her soldiers were warily watching the shadows of the tree line near the wall of Lam's estate.

"Congratulations, Victor!" Edeya said with a bright smile, moving past him to help Rhessa and Deyni down from the coach.

"Thanks. What's with the high alert?"

"I told her to have the house on battle footing. I didn't know how certain people would respond to the fight," Lam said, then turned to the guards and continued, "Move to your patrols. There's no current threat."

"Huh. All right, well, I'm going to my room. That cool?"

Lam looked at him with an amused smile and an arched eyebrow and said, "I'm beginning to understand your slang, I think. Yes, that would be cool, Victor. Go and get yourself cleaned up and have a much deserved rest."

"Thanks." Victor turned to Thayla, who'd reclaimed her slumbering daughter from Rhessa. "Come talk to me in the morning, okay?"

"Sure. We'll come by for breakfast, all right?"

"Perfect, but not too early!" Victor smiled at her, then turned, waving to everyone gathered around the coach, and made his way up the cobbled path to the front entrance of Lam's estate. Servants held the doors open, the lights were on, and Victor could see waitstaff lurking in the side hallways. He wondered if they were ready to throw a party if that's what Victor had wanted. "Not tonight," he said, reaching up to rub at the crusty blood in his hair, massaging his temple.

Victor bathed, fell into his bed, Lifedrinker in one hand next to him, and slept. His slumber was fitful at first, and he kept waking with weird impressions of dreams he couldn't remember. After a few hours of tossing, though, he eventually found deeper sleep and didn't stir until the sun was bright on his face, shining through the open curtains of his balcony.

He dressed, opting for one of his new pairs of pants and a blue button-up shirt he'd bought while shopping with Thayla. They'd been a handful of Energy beads, but just like his favorite black pants, they were self-cleaning and self-repairing. Moreover, the tailor who'd sold them swore his enchantments were superior to those on Victor's old pants. Victor didn't care if they were superior; he'd just been asking to make sure they were as good—he couldn't imagine any pants going through more than his original pair, and they were still holding up fine.

His nose alerted him to company before he heard the knock at his door. The unmistakable aroma of bacon was wafting under the door when he approached and opened it. Thayla stood in the hallway with Deyni and one of the house staff. A cart laden with breakfast foods drew his immediate attention, though, and he smiled, licking his lips. "Damn, that smells good. Get in here!" He opened the door wide, and Thayla came through, tugging Deyni along.

"You talk funny, Victor," Deyni said as they waited for the Ardeni woman with Lam's household uniform to push the cart over to the table. The woman started to set the table, putting out silverware and arranging the food trays.

"I do talk funny, Deyni! I've heard that from a lot of people! Excuse me, miss. You don't need to set the table. We'll take it from here." Victor smiled and opened the door for the servant, who looked a little disturbed, as if she was breaking some sort of rule, but she nodded and hurried out of the room. Victor closed the door, sat at the table, and started stuffing his face straight from the platters.

"Ancestors! Deyni, don't learn your manners from Victor!" Thayla laughed. She didn't sit down right away; instead, she looked around the room, and her eyes lingered on Victor's bed for a moment. Victor followed her gaze and realized he'd left Lifedrinker on the mattress. He grunted and stood, hurrying over to pick her up and slip her into the loop on his belt. "You slept with your axe?"

"Don't start," Victor said, unwilling to endure any teasing about Lifedrinker.

"I'm sorry, Victor. I wasn't thinking."

"No worries. Sit down and eat, or I'm going to eat your portion. Come on, Deyni! Get up here and eat some bacon!" Victor picked up the little girl, plopped her into a chair, then sat down and folded an entire piece of buttered toast into his mouth. Deyni didn't need much encouragement. For some reason, she watched Victor and mimicked his choices—when he slathered jam on some toast, she followed suit. When he picked up a sausage and ate it with his fingers, so did she. Thayla watched the two of them with bemused resignation.

"Eat some fruit," Thayla said to Deyni, giving Victor a pointed look.

"Mmm, fruit!" Victor said, scooping some of the cubed melon onto his plate. Deyni reached for the bowl, doing the same. "*Madre*! I wish they had some *chorizo* and *tortillas*, though!"

"Are you going to see Rellia?" Thayla asked, kind of startling Victor with the abrupt topic change.

"Yeah. I don't know why, but I want to hear what she has to say. You know, if she's being real. Like, if she really wants to pay me back for sparing her, maybe she can help with Lifedrinker somehow." Victor shrugged, sitting back in his chair and patting his stomach. "Damn, that was just what I needed!"

"You look better than last night," Deyni said, smiling at him around a mouthful of melon. She had long black hair like her mother, but hers wasn't braided. Instead, it was held in two pigtails on the sides of her head. Victor thought she was the cutest person he'd met on Fanwath. He reached forward and very gently pressed her button nose with one of his big fingers.

"I had a bath, cutie." Victor smiled and rubbed a hand through his rough, short hair.

"Do you feel like you can talk about that a little more?" Thayla asked, like a dog with a bone, refusing to change the subject. "I'm curious how it went with Lifedrinker. One minute you looked—" Thayla glanced at Deyni, then continued. "Out of it. The next minute you were glowing like a red torch and, you know, berserking again."

"Yeah, don't worry; I'm not as emotional as last night. I mean, the feelings are still there if I think about it, but I'm good. Well, Lifedrinker gathers Energy from things I fight. You know that, right? She'd been gaining a lot, and you could see how she was changing. She'd even spoken to me a couple of times. She gave up a lot of that for me—let me pull it into myself, and I healed with it, enough to cast Manifest Spirit and Berserk and finish things." He lifted Lifedrinker out of the loop at his belt, holding her so her black metal head was visible to Thayla.

"She insisted. I tried to resist, but she—" Despite his earlier bravado, Victor felt his throat tightening and his eyes getting watery, and he finished quickly. "She said she loved me, and she trusted me to help her recover." He put Lifedrinker back into her loop and covered his emotions by stuffing another sausage into his mouth.

"She gains Energy only from, you know, things you fight?" Thayla asked, clearly trying to avoid talking about killing things in front of Deyni.

"That's right. I can channel Energy into her, but it's just a temporary boost—it makes her do more damage to things I chop."

"All right, well, when you go speak to Rellia, Deyni and I will do some shopping. I know of a pretty good Artificer I can speak to. Maybe there's a way to speed things up with Lifedrinker. You know, a way to help her gain Energy without you having to . . ." Again she glanced at Deyni. ". . . chop so many things."

"That would be cool. Thanks, Thayla."

"Cool. Cool? Cool, cool," Deyni said softly, scooping up another piece of fruit and shoving it into her mouth.

"See what you're doing?" Thayla asked, an arched eyebrow aimed at Victor.

2

RELLIA

Victor stepped out of the coach, stretching his back and squinting in the bright midday sun. Two days had passed since his duel, and he felt rested—so much so that he was feeling antsy, as if he should be going somewhere. He'd decided to get things started by visiting Rellia. Thayla had tried to talk him out of it, and when that hadn't worked, she'd tried to come along with him. Victor had insisted he needed to face this alone, though. He wasn't sure why, but it felt right, and a small part of him just wanted to do something on his own, even if it might be stupid.

Victor noticed the coachman standing nearby, and he nodded, handing the man a few Energy beads. Edeya had ordered the ride for him and advised him what to pay the driver to stick around for his return trip. "I don't think I'll be very long," he said.

"Never you worry, sir. I'll be right here when you're ready to depart." The coachman nodded curtly, then turned to climb back onto his driver's bench. The coach was much more like what Victor had imagined Lam's would be like. It was small, black, and pulled by two roladii. It hadn't been nearly as comfortable as Lam's, either in its appointments or in the smoothness of its ride. The large, spring-shocked wheels did their best, but Victor had been jostled and jounced rather severely during the short trip through town.

He nodded and turned to regard the ap'Yensha estate. It sat in a wooded copse, not unlike Captain Lam's, though it was significantly smaller and newer looking. "Damn, Lam wasn't kidding about how great her place was," he muttered as he walked toward the gates. A liveried footman approached, spear in hand, his partner watching his back from the closed, white-painted, rolling gate. Victor could see more guardsmen up the drive and near the doors to the whitewashed villa.

"Your business with the ap'Yensha?" the footman asked, speaking in a strange, lilting accent that Victor hadn't heard before.

"I'm here to see Lady Rellia. I'm Victor Sandoval." He strode forward, not stopping or flinching away from the guard.

"Of course, sir. I've standing orders to show you through," the guard said, quickly lifting his spear and standing aside. He nodded to the guard by the gate, who pulled it to the side, opening it at least twice as far as Victor would have needed in order to walk through comfortably.

"Thanks," Victor said as he passed by. He strode up the cobbled drive to the door, wondering if he should have had the coach drop him inside the gate—he supposed they would have waved it through when he announced his name. "Ah, fuck it. I can walk a bit."

Victor kicked a nut or fruit pit or something off the cobbles, sending it skittering into the shrubs lining the drive. He glanced up, wondering where it came from, and saw a tree with branches arching over the cobbles, some sort of red plum-like fruit hanging from it. On an impulse, he jumped up and snatched one of the fruits. He wiped it on his gray shirt sleeve and then took a deep sniff of it. It smelled tangy and sugary, and he shrugged, taking a bite.

Juice sluiced out of the fruit at his bite, dripping down his chin, and the tart but sugary meat crunched under his teeth, very much like a plum indeed. Victor grinned at the unexpected treat and chewed the rest of the meat off the pit while he walked. He wiped his chin on his sleeve, trusting the material to clean itself, and tossed the pit into the shrubs as he nodded to the servants standing at either side of the double doors. "Hello, men," he said.

"Hello, sir. Might I inquire as to your destination in the estate?" the Ghelli on the left asked. Victor gave him a good look, wondering at his pink skin and tiny wings. Was he a Ghelli? He knew there was a lot for him to learn about this world, but it felt as if every time he started to get a grip on things, he realized there were ten more things he didn't know.

"I'm here to see Rellia."

"The lady is resting, sir. She sustained an injury recently," the guard said, pulling off a face that perfectly said, "I hear what you want, and I'm very sorry, but you can't have it."

"I'm Victor Sandoval. She asked me to come." Victor rested a hand on Lifedrinker, though he kept a neutral expression.

"Ahh! I should have realized! My apologies, sir! Please follow me, and I'll show you directly to Lady ap'Yensha." The guard looked like he'd swallowed a frog, his face turned so red, standing out brightly over his pale pink neck. Victor almost felt sorry for the guy, so he nodded his head and smiled genuinely.

"Don't worry, man. I won't say anything." Victor glanced at the other guard, an older, Ardeni with dark blue skin and gray-flecked red hair, and said, "Your buddy won't either. Right?"

"About what, sir?" the Ardeni asked, winking at his companion.

"Nice." Victor held out a fist, but the Ardeni just looked at it and he put it down. "All right," he said to the first guard, "let's go."

"Sir!" the man said, pulling the door open and waiting for Victor to step through. The interior of the ap'Yensha estate was very richly appointed but in a different style than Captain Lam's estate. While Lam favored marble and plaster, the ap'Yensha home had dark hardwoods on the floors of high-traffic areas with thick plush carpeting in the rooms that Victor could see. The walls were covered with art, some of it eye-catching in its depiction of nude men and women. Victor wondered if they were real people—relatives or friends of the family, or if they were simple depictions of beautiful bodies.

The guard moved quickly past him and said, "Please follow me, sir!"

Victor nodded and followed the man up a flight of stairs, through a long hallway, and then down another hallway which, if his mental image of the exterior was correct, took them into one of the wings of the estate. The guard moved quickly but constantly checked over his shoulder to ensure Victor kept pace. He stopped in front of a pair of glass-paneled, French-style doors and tapped delicately on the glass with a ring he wore. He put his hands behind his back then and waited, turning to nod nervously at Victor.

A moment later, Victor saw a woman approach through the glass. She opened one of the doors, poked her head out, and said, "Yes? She's resting."

"I have Victor Sandoval here," the guard said, nodding to Victor, who smiled at the girl. She was young; he could see that much, though she wore a neat uniform that looked almost as if it belonged in some sort of military. Her long-sleeved white shirt was buttoned severely at the neck, and her trim black pants had a blue stripe that ran down the sides. Her boots were polished to a brilliant sheen, and her sea-foam hair was tied back in a very tight bun. She turned her matching eyes on Victor and nodded.

"You may go, cadet," she said to the guard, and Victor did a double take. Was she the boss? "Come in, Mr. Sandoval. The lady has been waiting for you." She stepped back and pulled the door open wide.

"Oh, uh, thanks," Victor said and strode into the room. He'd been able to tell from the exterior that it was brightly lit, but now that he was inside, he could see the curved windows surrounding the room and the open glass doors leading out to a sunlit balcony. The room held a lot of furniture, but most of it was covered with sheets.

"Excuse the room, please; it's closed for the season, but Lady Rellia wanted to take advantage of the unseasonably warm weather. She's sitting just outside."

"Um, thanks," Victor said, looking at the woman, at her light-blue skin and frowning face. "I guess I don't know your name."

"Captain Valla. I'll be here. If I'm needed." She spoke in clipped, short phrases and sounded simultaneously polite and threatening.

"Right. Thanks, then, Captain Valla," Victor said and walked toward the open doors and into the sunlight. While his eyes adjusted, he held a hand out to block the sun and looked around. He saw Rellia right away, reclining on a wooden-slat lounge chair. His eyes went directly to her foot, some part of him wondering how she'd dealt with the injury. Her silky white pant leg was pinned up over the stump, and the other foot was naked, with no shoe or sock.

Rellia had a matching white shirt tucked into her pants. Her red hair hung down one side of her head in a ponytail, and a white hat shielded her face from the sun. She sat up when Victor strode onto the balcony and smiled at him. When he studied her face, he couldn't see any signs of malice or deception—the smile was natural and seemed to be reflected in her eyes. "Hello, Victor. Thank you for coming."

"Well, I had my doubts. I had some friends tell me I was crazy to come here, but I figured you and I had a connection they couldn't understand. We've both held each other's lives in our hands, haven't we? I don't feel like you're going to do something to me, at least right now." Victor took a step toward her, wondering if he should feel some rage at the sight of her. Nothing stirred in his gut, though.

Rellia frowned slightly, perhaps taken aback by Victor's lack of niceties. "We have, Victor. The only difference is that I tried to take yours, and you let me live. My shame had started to fade, but now I feel it again, freshly surging. Would you please sit down? There's a chair against the wall there; pull it over. My neck hurts looking up at you."

"Sure." He glanced where she'd indicated and saw a handcrafted wooden wheelchair sitting next to stacked patio chairs. Victor walked over, picked up one of the chairs, a matching piece of slatted wood furniture, and carried it over to Rellia's side, turning it so that he faced her when he sat down. The chair creaked, straining under his bulk, but held up. He leaned back, admiring how the slats contoured to his form, pressing into his lower back. "Comfortable," he said, giving her a crooked grin.

"They ought to be, for what we paid. The craftsman is something of a local celebrity. He made my wheeled chair there, as well." She paused, appeared to gather her thoughts, and then looked at Victor, her head resting comfortably now that he was sitting down. "How are you, Victor? That fight couldn't have gone easily for you. I'm sure you have allies that are angry that you spared my life."

"Well, they might be angry, but none of them have given me any shit about it yet." Victor cringed at his words and wanted to slap himself on the head, but instead, he kept talking and resolved to try not to sound like a street kid for once in his life. "I mean to say that no one has objected to my decision."

"That's surprising," Rellia said, smiling at Victor's choice of words.

"You seem different than when I imagined this conversation," Victor said, shifting, trying to get Lifedrinker's haft to lay along his leg so that her head wouldn't dig into his side. He finally gave up, lifted her free of his belt, and rested her on the ground, haft leaning against his chair.

"How did you imagine things?" Rellia asked, watching him struggle with his axe.

"I didn't think you'd be exactly friendly or smiling." He gestured to her foot. "You know, after everything. I'm actually surprised I don't feel some rage right now. I'm looking at you there, and, if I don't dwell on the shit you put me through, you know, sending hunters after me, making me fight you in that pit, and all that was lost because of it—" He paused, took a deep breath, staring at her, and noted the way her faced scrunched and her smile faded. "Well, if I don't dwell on it, I can almost look at you and not feel any anger." He huffed out a big breath, trying to even out his heartbeat, which had sped up.

"I'm sorry, Victor," Rellia said, her voice soft and her red eyes staring at him, trying to get him to look into them. Victor complied, staring into those ruby irises, and he could see doubt, worry, sadness, and a little fear, but he didn't see any lies. This wasn't the Rellia ap'Yensha he'd been imagining. She wasn't at all like people said she was. For that matter, she wasn't much like the woman who'd menaced him with a rapier just a few nights ago.

"The fuck is going on?" he asked before he could stop himself. "Who are you?" He didn't mean the question literally, and Rellia knew it. She frowned, her happy demeanor falling away, and she spoke, her eyes starting to grow watery.

"I'm Rellia ap'Yensha, the head of an ancient household, and I have a thousand kinfolk who expect me to act, speak, and live a certain way. I had ten uncles and aunts hounding me to track you down and regain the honor of our family because you killed my nephew. A nephew pursuing his own illicit venture without my backing or knowledge, I should add!"

"I heard he was your favorite nephew," Victor said, watching her face.

Rellia's scowl deepened, and she spoke so forcefully that spittle flecked her lips. "Lies! I hardly knew the fool, and when I did see him at family functions, he couldn't make eye contact with me, let alone earn my favor!" Victor wasn't a human lie detector like someone in a bad VR, and his experience with reading people was limited by his young age, but he'd had quite a few people screw him over, and he felt that he was getting a feel for when someone was fucking him. Right now, he felt as if Rellia was trying to be honest.

"So your hands were tied? You were acting on behalf of your family? You're an innocent victim?" Victor asked, gesturing to her foot.

"I didn't say that, Victor. Didn't I say I was sorry? When I went into that arena, I wanted to humiliate you the way you'd humiliated me! Do you have any idea the hell my Uncle Tam put me through when you killed the expensive bounty hunter I hired? Or when I'd announced to the family that you'd been captured by that old fool Vodkin, only to never hear from him again?" She paused, breathing rapidly, glancing around, perhaps searching for the right words.

"I thought I was hunting down a mad dog, mind you. I thought you'd slaughtered my nephew in an escape attempt—only yesterday did I hear the real story from Captain Lam. Ancestors! I wish I'd spoken to her sooner. You know, she tried to contact me on your behalf several times. What a fool I was!" A tear slid down one of her cheeks, and she swiped it away angrily, as though her eye had betrayed her.

"What are we doing here?" Victor asked after several moments passed, the silence beginning to fill the air awkwardly. "Are you trying to make me see your side? Are you trying to make me your friend? I don't think that's going to happen, Rellia. You and I are from the polar opposites of society, and I don't think I could ever get along with someone who runs slaves and hires bounty hunters and whatever other kinds of shit you get up to."

"Slaves? Do you mean the contracts we buy? The people in the mine? Listen, Victor, I . . ." She paused, then shook her head. "You're right. I could spend the whole day trying to explain the pressures I'm under and the lessons I was raised with. I could make a million excuses, but it boils down to me being born into a family with far too much. Not only that, but I was raised to run a large portion of it, maintain it, and grow it. It's not a clean business, and I won't lie to you anymore. There are things I've approved that I'm not proud of. Victor, don't you see? You've given me a chance to do something right for a change. Something good!" She leaned forward, both of her hands reaching out for his left hand.

Victor started to pull his hand back, but he stopped, imagining for some damned reason what it would be like if someone did that to him. He let his hand rest still, and she grasped it with both of her smaller, blue hands, her fingers surprisingly gentle and warm. He looked her in the eyes again and said, "What do you mean?"

"Because of your victory and because you showed me such mercy, I was able to meet with Captain Lam without losing any face. Yesterday, after I spoke to her, I figured it out. I figured out who the liars in my family were. At least with regard to this situation. For the first time in a long while, I have some leverage over some of the older, 'silent' powers in my clan. My uncle Tam is on the run, metaphorically at least, and several of the Old Powers in Tharcray have taken my side and given me leave to do some house cleaning. They've also given me permission to reward you, Victor."

She still held his hand in hers and squeezed gently while she spoke, emphasizing her enthusiasm. Victor couldn't lie to himself—he liked how her hands felt on his, and he was worried she was charming him or something, so he pulled it away, a slight frown marring his face and his heavy black brows narrowing. "Old Powers? Tharcray? You'll need to explain a bit more."

"I'm sorry, Victor, I forget about your history. It was only yesterday that I learned about how you came to this world. Tharcray is the capital of the Ridonne Empire. It's thousands of miles to the east and north, and when I say 'Old Powers,' it's a name that only people of my political class would understand—they're members of my family that have distanced themselves from the day-to-day of our existence. Most of them are very old, some would say ancient, and they spend much of their time away, either in the capital or off-world."

"Huh. So there's you and your aunts and uncles who run things. Then there are the older, 'silent' members of your family, and, finally, there are the, um, 'Old Powers?'"

"You see what I have to contend with? The world sees me as the head of this clan, but it's more like a public face than an actual head. Enough about my family, though, Victor. I've wanted to ask you this since you carried me into the tunnel after our fight: why didn't you kill me?" The sudden change in topic, to one so grim and fraught with emotion, caught Victor off guard, and his eyes narrowed further as he began to wonder if that had been her intention.

"Do I have to have a reason?" he asked, enjoying the show of being obstinate.

"Please, Victor? Who else can you talk with about this? I'm alive because you chose not to act like me. You fought through your rage to stay your axe. Why?"

Victor picked up Lifedrinker and held her crossways in front of him. He ran a hand over her warm, living, hickory handle. Little glimmers of light seemed to flare to life in the path of his hand, brightening the dark wood. "She used to be conscious," he said, indicating the axe.

"It's an impressive weapon. Beautiful, even," Rellia said, clearly feeling that she was indulging some sort of distraction.

"When you cut my throat, she gave herself to me. Filled me with her Energy and her love. It cost her almost everything she'd gained, her consciousness." He paused, tapping the side of his head, and stared hard at Rellia, looking into her red irises and trying to see a reaction. Rellia, for her part, narrowed her eyes, clearly trying to understand what he was saying but perhaps not grasping the full import of his words.

"So that's why you didn't die?"

"Yeah, and looking back, logically, I feel like I should have been even angrier at you when Lifedrinker"—he patted the axe—"lost so much to save me from what you'd done. Still, in the moment, I blamed myself. I took from her. I drained her to keep myself alive. She'd given so much, she'd shown me how she felt, and I was overwhelmed by the selfless love she felt for me. I didn't—I don't—deserve it." Again, he paused, looking up at the pale blue sky and taking a deep breath.

"So that's half the reason I didn't kill you—the emotions I felt because of Lifedrinker's sacrifice. The other half is that when you were crawling, gasping, bleeding out into the sand, you reminded me of a woman that showed me genuine kindness. She was the first to do so in this world, and I couldn't tarnish her memory by butchering you. Rellia? I'm being honest with you. I'm sharing something that I feel like I couldn't tell anyone else. Don't betray it."

"I won't, Victor! I swear, on my Ancestors, I have only the desire to repay you. I want to make amends for what I've done. What my family has done. Now that I know your story and see what you've been through in this world, I can't find any ill will toward you, no matter how deeply I search my heart. Do you believe me?"

"I do, but I've been a fool before. I hope you won't make me one again." Victor managed a crooked smile, inhaling deeply through his nose.

Rellia smiled back at him and held out a hand, "Could you help me up and pull that wheeled chair over? I'd like to show you how I'm going to repay you."

"Sure," Victor stood, slipping Lifedrinker into her loop, then reached down to pull Rellia into a sitting position. He knew damn well she didn't need his help to sit up, but he figured she was just playing a part. Once she was sitting with her feet over the side of the lounge chair, he pulled over her wheelchair and held it steady while she stood on her good foot and pivoted to sit down.

"Captain Valla will be apoplectic that I didn't call her for help, but just smile and nod as we go by. The room we're heading to is just out of this one down the hallway."

"Isn't there some sort of magical remedy for your foot?" Victor asked as he wheeled her toward the open doors.

"Yes, don't worry about that. I have a clan Artificer working to make me a silver foot as we speak. It's a temporary fix, I hope—if I can advance my race a few more times, I'll grow a new one."

"Well, that's good, I guess. Silver, huh?"

"Naturally," Rellia said with a chuckle. As they moved between the sheet-covered sunroom furniture, Victor saw Captain Valla stand up from a small table she was working at and stride over. She did indeed look angry, her green eyebrows drawn together in a deep scowl.

"Lady! I was available! To help you!"

"Yes, of course, Captain. Go back to your books, please. Victor will aid me for now." Rellia waved toward the little table where the captain had been sitting. Victor smiled at the woman and nodded, wondering how she managed to keep her clothing so perfectly wrinkle free.

"Very well, lady. May I ask? Where you'll be?"

"The map room, Valla, just down the hallway. I'll scream should something untoward happen." Rellia wore a wry smile, and Victor realized she was teasing the uptight captain. "Straight ahead, Victor, through the doors, please."

Victor followed Rellia's directions out of the room and down to a set of doors that opened into a high-walled room. Each wall was covered in maps, and a table at the center had another huge topographical map built into its top. *"Gorz,"* Victor said in his head, speaking to his amulet for the first time in quite a while, *"can you take in these maps?"*

"Yes, I can. I'll study them while you continue to speak to the lady, Victor."

"Thanks, Gorz," Victor thought, annoyed at himself for forgetting about the spirit until he'd wanted something from it.

"Please wheel me over to the map table, Victor," Rellia said. Victor complied, and when he pulled her chair up to one side of the table, Rellia stood, hopping on her good foot and leaning on the table. "Stand beside me, please, so I can show you where to look."

"All right," Victor said, moving next to her, trying to take in the massive map, following the blue lines of rivers with his eyes, and wanting to reach out and feel the bumpy mountain ranges.

"Look here; this is Gelica," Rellia said, pointing to a black dot next to a long, thick blue line. "This river is the Rill Catcher. It flows from the World Breaker Mountains in the north, all the way to the Great Western Sea." She traced the line of the river in illustration. "We're on the western edge of the Ridonne Empire," she continued. "If you follow an imaginary line straight east from here, you'll pass through, roughly, the center of the Empire and end up here." Again she pointed, this time to a body of water about the size of her palm. "At the Starfall Sea."

"Okay . . ." Victor said, not sure why he was getting a geography lesson.

"South of the Starfall Sea and the city-states around it, you'll come to another mountain range, the Granite Gates. They're called that because they border the Empire, shielding it from the frontier lands known as the Untamed Marches. Ridonne claims the right of sovereignty over the Marches, but no one, at least no one civilized, lives there." Rellia tapped a section of the map beyond a high, raised mountain range, shaded in dark green and extending away for nearly half again the area depicted by the Empire.

"So, what's this got to do with me?" Victor asked, feeling like a cliché.

Rellia, still leaning on the table, pushed herself straight and turned to face Victor, smiling. "About a hundred years ago, the Emperor decided he should make efforts to expand the Empire's sphere of influence into the Marches. He chose a hundred noble families and gave each a Writ of Conquest—legal authority to go into the Marches and claim their own sovereign land, requiring only a de facto trade and mutual defense agreement with the Empire."

"And your family was one to get a Writ?" Victor guessed.

"That's right, and that's where you come in. Victor, I've been given permission to give you a fifty percent stake in our Writ. Any land you conquer—you will personally own half of it!" She slapped the table in emphasis, her breath quick with excitement.

"Hold on, Rellia. I don't know shit about conquering lands in some distant frontier, and I have to ask the obvious question: If it's such a good deal, why haven't any of the hundred families done it yet?"

"You're asking the same questions I've asked ever since I was a little girl and I learned about the Marches! Why haven't we moved in? We could be far removed from the Empire, free from the burden of its taxes, and living in a country of our own making! My father told me before he died that the families didn't have the stomach for it. He'd explain that the expense of moving a large force through the Granite Gates was prohibitive alone and that pushing into the jungles of the Marches was a suicidal errand in futility."

"Huh." Victor studied the map, not speaking more.

"And that's only half of it—if the rumors are to be believed, the System itself will challenge any conquering force that moves in that direction."

"The System? Why?"

"I don't know. A rite of passage? A way to force us to prove we're worthy of taking on the stewardship of those lands? A chance to force us to grow stronger, killing each other and feeding it Energy? My father believed that the System would send armies from another world there to fight any people that came to claim those lands."

Victor started to say something but just grunted, imagining tall mountains with narrow passes and jungles filled with monsters and hostile armies. "At least you aren't holding anything back," he said, staring at the vast green expanse of the Untamed Marches on the map. "Are you?" He turned his gaze to her and narrowed his eyes.

"I want to help fund an expedition. I want you to lead it, and, as I said, you'll become lord of your own lands if you have any success at all." Rellia reached out a hand, grasping Victor above his elbow, and stared into his eyes. "You're a conquerer, Victor. You can do this if any man could. I have soldiers who want to seek you out and swear fealty to you just because of the accounts of your fights spreading through the city's taverns. Imagine how people will flock to our banner once you've fought some real battles in the field!"

"Our banner?"

"This would be a joint venture, Victor. Like I said, you'll get half, but house ap'Yensha will claim the other half. You'll have an ally in the Marches, someone who will stand with you against the untamed borders and, should you need it, against the Empire." Her voice was hushed as she said the last, as though she feared to speak out against the Empire, even in her own home.

"Really? You have a problem with the Empire?" he asked, letting his eyes drift over the large black-bordered section of the map that represented Ridonne.

"This isn't the best place to speak of such things, but, yes, Victor. I'm placing my life in your hands by saying this, you know. If one of the Imperial Inquisitors caught wind of my . . . discontent, they'd haul me away for questioning. Victor, there's a rot in Tharcray, the insidious disease of corruption that spreads through the rulership of our people. I want to take land in the Marches because war is coming, and I'd rather our clan wasn't at the center of it."

3

A PLATE FULL OF PROBLEMS

"Rellia, this is a lot," Victor said, his mind trying to take in everything he and Rellia had spoken about—her family, her motives, the Empire, the map, the Marches, and the Writ of Conquest. He felt that every time he started to wrap his head around things, she would add another piece to the puzzle. Now she was talking about war with the Empire? Or was it just war in the Empire, and she wanted to be out of it?

"I know," she said, still leaning on the map table, still looking at him with eager, bright eyes.

"Look, just an hour ago, I was wondering if you would try to kill me. I was wondering if I should want to kill you! I'm still raw about everything, and you're still involved in some things that I think are plain evil. Now you want me to go to war with you? To travel into some unknown wilderness and 'conquer' it? It's just too damn much."

"Victor, I—" She paused and gathered herself, standing up straighter and breathing deeply through her nose, the smile fading from her face. "I understand you. I understand your reservations. I'm trying to plan for an eventuality that most of my family thinks will never come. When I've spoken to the ones I trust, the few, about what I think we should do, they put me off. They treat me like I'm paranoid. They point to the age of the Empire. They mention the Old Powers and how they don't seem concerned.

"Those are the more benign reactions. Others in my family think war in the Empire would benefit us. They see it as a chance to grab power, snuff out other families, and take what was theirs. Mind you, these are just the opinions of the very few whom I trust enough to share my doubts, to whom I dare mention the corruption in Tharcray. When I've tried to propose a plan, creating a haven for our family using our Writ of Conquest, I've never had support. Only because of you and the schemes of my uncle and his supporters have a few of the Old Powers given me their blessing."

"Yeah? How does that change any of my concerns?"

"Victor, I don't think the Old Powers would interfere, would even consider the expense I'm anticipating, if they disagreed with me. They're in Tharcray—they know things that none of my peers in the family do. Something is happening in the Empire, and I think the time to prepare is slipping away."

"Right, Rellia, I get how this is important to you. I don't get how it's important to *me*. Sure, I can gain some lands and whatever that entails, but do I even want that? I'm young, and I've hardly had a chance to live in this world. I have plans of my own—things I want to do and accomplish. I mean, I was going to go spend the winter with some hunters out on the plains, learning more about my Core."

"We wouldn't launch a campaign like this in the winter anyway, Victor. Won't you please tell me you'll at least consider my offer? I can't make it happen without you. My excuse for using the Writ is that I'm repaying our clan's honor by sharing it with you. You'd need to be seen as the one driving the expedition." Her face had fallen, and her earlier excitement was replaced by a more sober, almost pleading tone. Victor had to admire that she was being so honest with him about how she was basically using him. It didn't mean he had to like it, though.

"Do you love anyone in your family?" he asked, the thought coming to him rather suddenly.

"What?" For once, he'd caught her off guard.

"The way you talk about them makes me wonder why you're making these efforts. Are they redeemable? Think about the evil your clan has committed to remain in power."

"Victor, I do love people in my family! There are hundreds of children completely removed from our family's business. They're truly innocent. There are hundreds of people in my family involved in very benign industries. Only a few dozen are like me, with hands sullied by things like indentured contracts, industrial sabotage, and—oh, Ancestors! Am I confessing all my sins today?"

"If you expect me to go into this venture with you, I want to know what's going on in here." Victor reached out and poked Rellia in the chest, trying to indicate her heart, and he felt she got the message. She didn't pull away, and she nodded.

"I want to change. I want to change how things at this level in my clan operate. I don't like the corruption and dishonesty. I don't like the guilt. I don't think about the people whose contracts we buy because I'd never sleep if I did. I push them all into a corner of my mind and label them 'criminals paying their dues.' Victor, if you help me, I'll start divesting our family of those sorts of businesses. I'll say I'm raising funds for the campaign. I have the influence right now, and once I start us down that road, it would be impossible for my detractors to derail us, not until we fail, which is what they'll be counting on." She had tears in her eyes again, and Victor could feel the emotion in her voice.

He tried to keep focused on all the suffering that he and others had been through as a result of this woman's actions, but even then, Victor couldn't help believing she was sincere and knew he had to get out of there before agreeing to something he might regret. "Listen, I think I believe you, Rellia, and part of me wants to help you. Part of me wants to agree right now, but another part of me, the part that's been screwed over and nearly killed a dozen times, is telling me to get out of here." He took a step away from the table, nodding as if to confirm his conviction to himself.

"Wait, Victor," she said, using the table to hop around to a bureau of drawers against a nearby wall. "That's fair. I want you to be sure, and I hope you'll go and talk to the people you trust. Tell them what we spoke about, but please leave my comments on the Empire and Tharcray out. I want to send something with you, though. I want to give you something solid that illustrates my conviction, my intentions." She opened one of the drawers and pulled out a polished silver scroll case, densely packed with golden filigrees and purple ribbons hanging from each end.

"This is my family's Writ of Conquest. I want you to hold it. Take it with you, and think about what I've proposed. I'll return to Persi Gables at the end of the month—I always winter there. I'm going to start laying the groundwork for this venture. I'll take this time to prove to you that I am sincere.

"If you come to me in two months, you'll find I've sold off our stake in the Greatbone Mine and cleared all our balance sheets of indentures. I'll be surrounded by furious family members, but as I said, they won't move against me unless our venture fails. They'll kill me if it does. My life is, once again, in your hands, Victor." She held the scroll case out to him, and Victor grimaced.

"Goddamn! You'll lay that shit on me? If I decide I don't want to do this, you're gonna die? Why not try to conquer some of the Marches without me?"

"My approval from the Old Powers is dependent upon your participation. Victor, you asked me to change how my family does business. I will do as you asked, but there will be a price. We can pay the cost with a successful conquest or with my head. I'm willing to risk everything to do what you asked." She saw the storm clouds building in Victor's eyes and added, "I know it's the right thing to do, Victor. You aren't responsible."

"*Puta madre*!" Victor swore, taking the scroll case, "Fucking hell! You really tied me up here, Rellia!"

"I'm on borrowed time, Victor. If you never show up—if this plan of mine blows up in my face, I'll consider this winter a bonus. I should have died in that pit when we fought, and you know it." She held out a hand as if she wanted a handshake, and Victor looked at it, then stared hard at her, looking into her eyes. He wished he had some sort of superpower that let him read people's minds, but he didn't, and he couldn't see any deception there.

"All right, then. I won't leave you hanging—I'll let you know one way or another. Let me talk to my friends and spend some time figuring shit out, and then I'll get word to you." He took her hand, and she wrapped her surprisingly long fingers around his palm, squeezing firmly. He found himself reluctant to let go, but he did, then he pulled her chair closer to where she'd hopped. "You good? I can find the way out."

"I'm fine, Victor. Thank you for hearing me out and for accepting my trust. I hope I hear from you soon."

"And you took it?" Thayla asked, incredulous.

"Yeah, I mean, what else could I do? She was laying everything on the line." He glanced from Thayla's outraged face to Lam's gleeful one to Edeya, standing by the door, doing her best to remain impassive. They were in Lam's front parlor, going over the news, Victor sitting in a chair facing Thayla and Lam as they lounged on a couch.

"This is a wonderful opportunity!" Lam said. "Victor, you have to let me help with the venture! I can raise several companies! Get me into a meeting with Rellia, and I'll negotiate for a portion of her piece, not yours. I'm sure I can get that out of her!"

"Oh, Ancestors!" Thayla huffed. "Lam, aren't you going to try to talk any sense into him? Rellia ap'Yensha? Turning a new leaf? Do you really believe this nonsense?"

"I know I'm not explaining things perfectly, but Thayla, you had to be there. She's either the world's greatest saleswoman and liar, or she truly wants to make some changes. It should be pretty easy to see if she's sincere, right, Lam? We'll be able to check if she really sells out of the mine and gets out of the indentured servant business, won't we?"

"Of course! It will be trivial to find out if she follows through. Even if she doesn't, though, this is a fantastic opportunity, Thayla."

"Of course you would say that, Captain!" Thayla said, scowling from Lam to Victor. She kicked a foot against the coffee table, pushed herself farther back on the couch, and crossed her arms in front of her chest.

"Why? Because I know a good opportunity when I see one? Because I know that these Writs of Conquest are worth a fortune? Even though none of the families have taken advantage of them, at least publicly, I know that deals are brokered for them at the top levels of society all the time. Some families have collected ten or more of these Writs, trying to squash future competition. Something tells me the Marches won't remain vacant forever, and Rellia knows it."

"Let me guess," Thayla said. "You've been trying to buy one?"

"Of course! They're impossible to get ahold of for an upstart like me, though, despite my wealth."

"Well, I don't know what to do about any of this," Victor said, rubbing his hands through his hair, scrubbing at his scalp as if he were trying to stimulate his brain.

"What do you *want* to do?" Lam asked, and Thayla grew quiet, staring at Victor to hear his answer.

"I don't know. I kind of want to just fucking disappear. You know, go with Deyni and Thayla, find Tellen's camp, and spend some time with them. I'd like to learn a thing or two from Oynalla. I'd like to do some real adventuring and exploring."

He took a deep breath, exhaling through his nose, then he continued. "I think of those things, and then I remember I've got all kinds of shit I'm responsible for, still. I have to do something about Belikot—something I was going to talk to you about, Captain. I need to visit the Wagon Wheel in Persi Gables and put Yund out of business." He paused to glare around, waiting for someone to tell him not to worry about that. He hadn't voiced that desire aloud, at least not so clearly before.

"And there's a certain minor noble, at least I think he's minor, living near there that I need to deal with. He's the asshole that tried to wreck my Core and sent some hunters after us here." He paused, then added, "I mean, let's not forget about Lifedrinker. If I'm being honest, that's what I want to do more than anything right now—help her recover from the sacrifice she made for me."

Lam started to say something, opening her mouth but then closing it and shaking her head. Victor stared at her a few seconds, then turned to Thayla, saw how she'd started to frown, perhaps sympathetically matching his own expression, and said, "Am I missing anything?"

"Probably, but that's enough to stress about right now," Thayla said, reaching out to pat his knee, her earlier scowl softening.

"I can't think of a better place to adventure and explore than the Marches," Lam said, giving him a sly smile.

"God, you're not going to let me get out of this, are you?" Victor sighed, trying to resist Lam's smile but finding his lips creeping up at the corners in response.

"I'll be with you every step of the way, Victor. Now, tell me about this Belikot situation. If we're going to go along with Rellia's campaign, I think we should get your plate of problems cleared off a bit." She sat back, folding her hands with a smug smile, and once again, Victor found himself wanting to trust her. Hadn't she tried to help him at every turn? She'd given him Lifedrinker, bought out their contracts, sheltered them, and spoken on their behalf to the Magistrate. She'd fought with them, too, in the depths.

Victor thought about when he'd seen Lam soaring out of the high tunnel to smash amongst the swarm of beetle riders. She'd saved them that day. Though now that he thought about it, they'd been in that battle because of her. She was the one who'd brought them down there. She was the one who'd told them to guard that spot while she hunted treasures. Suddenly Victor realized what had been bothering him, a thought that had been scratching at his subconscious mind since he'd come back to Lam's estate. He looked at Lam and said, "How many indentured workers do you own the contracts of?"

"What? How's that important right now, Victor?" Lam didn't frown, she didn't scowl, she maintained an impassive expression, but Victor could see his question had bothered her. He stared at her green eyes, beautiful as they were, and frowned.

"Come on, Lam. Answer the question. If Rellia's willing to stop doing business that way, shouldn't everyone involved in the campaign at least be honest about it?" He leaned forward, resting an elbow on his knee as he kept eye contact with the captain. He couldn't tell what Thayla was thinking, but she shifted uncomfortably in his peripheral vision.

"Are you really that ungrateful?" Lam asked, allowing some of her anger to show. "Everything I've done for you, and you bring this up? I own some contracts, but I'm good to my people, Victor, even the indentured ones. You know I didn't own any contracts among the delvers, right? I'm done with the mine—sure, I made some profits there, but I won't do business with them anymore. Is that what you want to hear?"

"It's a start, but I'd like you to stop buying indentured contracts, too. Just fucking hire people to work for you, Lam. Is it that hard? If we're going to be working to make a new start, to build something new, let's fucking do it right. Can you get on board with that? If you can't get Rellia to share some of her split, I'll share some of mine. It's worth it to me if you'll agree to do things without slavery. That's what those contracts amount to most of the time; you realize that, right?"

Lam sat back and licked her lips, looking into the space over Victor's head, clearly thinking things through. Just as the silence was starting to feel awkward, and Victor was trying to think of something more to say, she looked at him, brushed some of her silvery blonde hair behind one of her ears, and said, "It'll cost me, but not terribly. I appreciate your convictions, Victor, and I know you have good reason to feel the way you do. If I can manage a twenty percent stake in this venture, I'll sell off all my indentures immediately. If you or Rellia don't want to give me that much, I'll stop buying indentures and work to clear my books more naturally as the contracts expire. Deal?"

Victor smiled and held out a hand. Lam took it and squeezed, her fingers like iron bands around his much larger palm. Victor grinned and squeezed back, almost laughing as her eyes bulged a little. He let go and said, "Thanks, Lam. I know you're not one of the bad guys, but that's been bugging me in the back of my mind for a long time."

"Now that you two worked that out, can we tell her about Belikot, Victor?" Thayla asked. "You're stressing out about him because you promised me you'd deal with him. Maybe that's not really necessary anymore?"

"I think I'll feel better having his situation resolved," Victor said, turning to Thayla and offering a slight shrug. "He might leave us alone, leave you alone, but we don't know for sure, right?"

"Who the rotten roots is Belikot?" Lam asked with a growl.

"All right, let me explain," Victor said, and that's what he did. He told

Lam about Thayla finding the skull in the dungeon and about how it tricked her. He told her about how he'd won the phylactery from the dungeon boss and how he'd noticed its tether to Belikot in Thayla's body. Lam asked questions throughout, and Victor had to explain Gorz to her, and then they had to have a whole side conversation bout how Victor had lied to her when he'd told her about the map he'd seen showing the route to the dungeon.

"So anyway," he continued after apologizing for not trusting her completely when he and Thayla had first gone to her for help. "Gorz helped me follow the tether, and I ambushed Belikot, forcing him back into his skull and helping Thayla to get back into her body. That's when we met Oynalla—she's the Spirit Caster for Tellen's clan. She kinda guided me with the process of getting Belikot out of Thayla."

"So, what's the problem?" Lam asked. Victor noticed that Edeya had come closer, enjoying the story. He didn't look at her, though, because he didn't want Lam to yell at her for moving away from her post.

"The Belikot that tricked me was just a small fragment of the real Belikot. We found out he lives in a dungeon in a ruined town called Gel Harra. Lam, there are Naghelli in there—real ones," Thayla answered, perhaps afraid Victor would be too long-winded with his explanation.

"Naghelli? I think you must be mistaken. They were probably dungeon constructs." Lam sat back with a snort.

"Nah, they were real, Lam," Victor said. "I killed one, and his wife came to thank me for giving him an honorable death in combat. They spoke about leaving the dungeon soon and continuing Belikot's 'great work.'" Victor shrugged as if to say "none of it makes sense to me either."

"They stole the phylactery from Victor while he protected me. I'm not a match for them, Lam." Thayla shook her head, eyes distant, clearly remembering the battle.

"You're Tier Two, Thayla?" Lam asked. She knew the answer but seemed to want to confirm something.

"Yes, I think the Naghelli were Tier Four. Victor was still Tier Two at the time, but, well, he's Victor."

"Yeah, so I told Thayla I'd go back and sort things out with Belikot. You know, after she and her daughter were safe. I figured maybe I could get some help here in Gelica 'cause, well, who wants a crazy necromancer to come out of a dungeon with a bunch of Naghelli and start up some kind of evil plan?"

"You're sure it's evil?" Edeya asked, lifting a hand to her mouth as if she hadn't meant to speak. Lam looked at her, raised an eyebrow, and snorted.

"Well, come and sit down, then, Edeya. I think the guards outside the door are enough," Lam said, surprising Victor.

"We don't know their plan, but the Naghelli spoke about some kind of new empire, and they said that since we brought them the phylactery, they'd make us some of their top servants or some bullshit." Victor grinned at his summary, then sat back, rubbing at the stubble on his chin. He didn't grow enough facial hair to manage a beard, but he did get some thin, wiry stubble around his chin. He figured he was due for a shave.

"The fragment of Belikot we met was duplicitous and cruel, and the way he treated me when he stole my body tells me that anything he's planning will not be good for people who aren't among his followers," Thayla said, glaring at Victor.

"What?" he asked.

"Well, you either say too much or too little! Don't you think mentioning what Belikot is like was a good idea?"

"Damn, Thayla! I figured we were both here, and we could both explain shit."

"All right, all right. Here's what we'll do; I'll come with you to the dungeon, Victor, and I'll bring a few old friends, like Polo Vosh. We'll deal with this Belikot fellow. Meanwhile, Edeya and some of my troops can escort Thayla to your friend Tellen's camp. After we deal with Belikot, you can go visit. Near the end of winter, we'll make our way, you, me, and the troops I've raised, to Persi Gables, and before we join up with Rellia, you can sort out your problems around that city. I'll help if you need it." Lam sat back with a satisfied grin, and Victor and Thayla stared at her with open mouths.

Victor closed his mouth and started to speak, "I, well, shit, Lam! You make it all sound easy!"

"I've always been good at organizing. Edeya, fetch my lap desk; I want to write a message to Rellia."

"What are you going to say?" Victor asked.

"I'm going to tell her that we'll be working together, that you'll be unavailable for a few months, but that you'll see her in Persi Gables come springtime. I'll also let her know that we'll need to borrow a Tier Four or Five from her personal guard for a short mission—something important to keep her in your good graces." Lam smiled at him smugly.

"You think we'll be able to handle it? Belikot seemed very powerful—the Naghelli were afraid of him," Victor asked, frowning at the memory.

"If you could hold off a pack of Naghelli, even though they were higher rank than you, then a group of us should be able to settle things well enough."

"You know how strong Lam is, Victor. Polo Vosh and a few others will make you a force to be reckoned with. I think you can do it," Thayla added.

"All right. Shit, Lam, I feel a lot better having sorted out my problems and having a plan to go after them all."

"Victor, it's a fundamental skill that officers in the Imperial Legion are drilled with: list out problems and prioritize based on severity, distance, and urgency. Stick with me, Berserker, and you'll learn a thing or two." She favored him with a brilliant smile, and Victor remembered his old crush on her. He wanted to go back in time and slap his old self upside the head.

Lam was so much more than beautiful. She was strong, intelligent, an incredible leader, and a savvy politician. She was ambitious and experienced, and the thought of trying to pursue her romantically made Victor want to run and hide. He'd rather face down a thousand giant river rats than try even to hold Lam's hand.

"Thanks, Captain Lam," he said, leaning forward earnestly. "Thanks for everything, especially respecting my feelings about indentured servants."

"If Rellia ap'Yensha can do it, so can I," Lam scoffed. "Edeya! Hurry! Get my desk while I still have a few amusing quips at the tip of my tongue!"

"Yes, Captain," Edeya said and hurried out of the parlor, barking at the guards outside the door to get out of her way.

"Come on, Victor. I think this would be a good time for me to take you to meet the Artificer that Deyni and I visited. He has some ideas for your axe." Thayla stood and motioned toward the door.

"Really? Right on! Thanks, Thayla! All right, Captain, let me know when you have a plan. I mean, like when we're leaving and who will be coming." Victor stood and began to follow Thayla.

"I will, Victor. You'll have a plan of action to read through before breakfast tomorrow," Lam said distractedly. She'd produced a quill and paper and was already writing down some notes. "I have some clever remarks for Rellia, and I want to write them out before I forget them."

Victor shook his head with a grin on his face and followed Thayla to the main foyer. He felt immensely better now that he'd shared all of his problems with someone other than just Thayla. It was as if the more people who knew about them, the lighter they felt. On top of that, it felt good to know there was a plan of action and not just an amorphous cloud of concerns circling around the back of his mind.

"You seem happy," Thayla said.

"Well, shit, that went well, don't you think?" Victor asked, joining her by the doors.

"Yes. Lam's a captain, and she knows how to make things happen. She earned that rank, you know—people outside the Legion don't get to call themselves military ranks without having served. At least not in the Empire. Now, let's take advantage of this calm before the storm she's about to stir up. Ready to see if we can help Lifedrinker?"

"Hell, yes!" Victor put his arm around Thayla's shoulders, and the two of them strode out of Lam's estate.

4

FESTIVAL

Let's not take a coach," Thayla said as they passed through the gates of Lam's estate. "I want to talk a bit while we walk."

"All right. I could use the fresh air," Victor said, and he meant it. As the evening darkened the skies, the breeze blowing in from the north had brought a crisp chill to the air, and he was enjoying it. He was used to heat, used to the sweltering sun, but he always loved it around November in Tucson when the mornings would have a bit of bite to the air and he'd smell mesquite burning on the breeze.

No one he knew had a fireplace, but there were a few houses he would walk by on his way to a friend's house or up to the restaurant where he'd worked when he was sixteen—they loved any excuse at all to burn some mesquite, and a chilly morning seemed to be cause enough. He could smell woodsmoke now, but it was different. Still, it reminded him of November and family gatherings and good food.

"With magic and shit, I'm surprised people need to burn wood for heat," he said, sniffing the air.

"Energy at the levels you have isn't that common, Victor. Not everyone can afford Energy furnaces either, and if they could, not everyone can recharge them. It takes longer to charge a power stone than it does to craft an Energy bead, and you've seen how long that can take. Oh, dead uncle! I forgot to tell you! You're rich! At least compared to a lot of people. I staked your beads for you, and you were a fifty-to-one underdog."

"Dead uncle?"

"It's a curse! Is that the only thing you heard?"

"No, I heard the rest. That's great, Thayla. You have some weird curse words, though."

"Victor! Not very many people have fifty thousand Energy beads!" Thayla shook her head in exasperation, giving him a shove as they walked.

"Well, half of those are yours, right?" He nudged her shoulder with his fist, returning the favor.

"If you insist!" She laughed. "I'll give you your half when we get back to the estate, all right?"

"Yeah, that's cool." He kicked at a fallen branch, clearing it off the brick walkway.

"You know Lam's using you again, right?" Thayla's eyes grew serious, and her smile faded.

"Yeah. I'm not stupid, you know? I know everyone has their own reasons for doing things. That doesn't mean she's bad, though. She wants a chance to gain power and influence, and this whole thing gives her a shot at gaining some land of her own—outside the Empire. I mean, Rellia's after the same thing."

"Yeah, as long as your eyes are open to it." Thayla shrugged, then she changed the subject. "What about Belikot? I thought you were going to let things go with him. You were pretty sure he was busy with his own problems. Why the change of heart?"

"You know better than anyone that I tend to give people too much credit. When he warned me about my spirit wandering and said I should learn that Tether Spirit spell, my instinct was to give him a whole lot of credit—you know, a powerful necromancer showing me some mercy, letting me go, and warning me at the same time. I've thought about it since then, though, and something just felt off about it. I think he was afraid of me." Victor paused and looked at Thayla, and she raised one of her dark eyebrows.

"Somehow, my spirit was wandering in his proximity—what if I found him? What if I came upon him on the spirit plane? I might be new to that whole thing, but my spirit is strong, Thayla. My will is fucking high. I might just be able to beat his ass in that realm. So what does he do? He warns me, 'Oh, look out; you're wandering in dangerous areas, better tether your spirit down, don't let your subconscious guide you to me!'"

"You think that's what was happening? Your subconscious was seeking him out?"

"Maybe! I mean, fuck, I'd been thinking about him nonstop for days and days. I was worried about him, but I also wanted to confront him. Anyway, I've been thinking about this, and I won't be cool leaving him alone. I need to at least talk to him and see what his deal is. You weren't wrong when you said he's not a nice guy, though. I'm willing to hear out those Naghelli, but they did attack us first, and there was something pretty creepy about them."

"Turn here," Thayla said, and Victor realized they'd made their way back into the city while they were talking. The streets were fairly quiet, but a lot of noise and light came from further in. Victor followed Thayla's directions and turned up a side street, and the light fell away behind them.

"What's going on back there?" he asked.

"It's still Harvest Fest time. There'll be a celebration in the main square for a few more nights."

"What kind of celebration?"

"Music, food, games, things like that." Thayla shrugged.

"What the hell, Thayla? Let's get Deyni and go there!"

"Really? You want to go?"

"Hell, yes! I can count the fun things I've done in this world on one hand—half a fucking hand!"

Thayla laughed, and Victor loved the way it sounded. She'd been so serious since his fight—he was glad to see her let loose a little. "I'll get Deyni while you're talking to Ganjoon."

"Ganjoon?"

"The Artificer I told you about. That's with a capital *a*, by the way. He's a real Artificer, as in that's his Class."

"Oh, cool. I haven't heard a name like his. Is he Ardeni or what?"

"He's an Ilyathi, like that bounty hunter you fought on the bridge. Quite a different type of person, though," she chuckled. "We're not far now, just up at the corner." She led the way to the shop, a corner store with window cases displaying all sorts of items with descriptive hanging tags. He saw everything from self-cleaning glassware to an entire suit of red plate armor densely inscribed with silvery runes. The sign above the door simply read, "Corner Artifice."

"Huh," Victor said, reading the rather bland name.

"He told me his work speaks for itself when I asked him about the name," Thayla said, noting his gaze. "C'mon, I'll introduce you, then I'll go get Deyni."

"Okay," Victor said, and the two entered the shop. A bird trill accompanied the door opening, and Victor smiled, wondering where the sound came from. He knew it was some sort of enchantment, but shouldn't it need a speaker or something? He snorted; he knew Energy didn't work like tech, but he still wondered how it did something like make a bird sound. Was it like a spell pattern but written into the door?

"Hello! Thayla, I'm glad to see you again!" A warm tenor voice interrupted Victor's musings, and he turned to the sound.

A tall, thin man with a smooth gray head and wide black eyes smiled at him from behind a counter. He looked similar to the bounty hunter, but Victor could see the differences, especially in the warmth of his smile and the laughter lines around his eyes. The sides of his head were covered in tattoos depicting runes and sigils that meant nothing to Victor, though he thought they looked cool. The shopkeeper wore a plain green shirt but had a leather toolbelt buckled around his waist with dozens of slender tools poking up from pockets. "This the friend you told me about?"

"Yes, Ganjoon, this is Victor." Thayla stepped forward and gestured back to Victor while she moved to clasp the man's hand.

"I see. Yes, I doubt he could be anyone else," the shopkeeper said as Victor came out from behind a display and stepped toward the counter.

"Yeah, not many like him around," Thayla chuckled.

"All right, all right, go get your daughter before you get into your joke material about my size," Victor groused, nudging Thayla aside so that he could reach out for Ganjoon's hand. The man gave him a firm handshake, smiling all the while. Thayla grunted and gave Victor a shove, putting her shoulder into it as if he were a boulder she was pushing up a hill. When he barely budged, she sighed heavily and turned back to the door.

"I'll be back in about twenty minutes—we'll get a coach on the way back."

"Sounds good," Victor said, waving as she stepped out.

"So, warrior, let me see the lovely lady," Ganjoon said, gesturing to Lifedrinker hanging from his belt. Victor didn't lift Lifedrinker free right away, though. Instead, he took a deep breath through his nose and looked around the shop. He knew Thayla liked this guy, and she'd told him a thing or two about Victor and Lifedrinker, but that didn't mean that he had to trust him instantly. He wanted to get a feel for Ganjoon, so he walked over to the nearest display. It was a glass-shelved case of rings and bracelets.

"Do you make the items in here or just enchant them?" he asked, leaning over to study the jewelry. They were all quite beautiful as far as he was concerned, clearly crafted from precious metals and gemstones. Some were carved intricately, with little symbols or tiny flowers and animals. Some were plain but gave off a luster that hinted at their fineness.

"I do both, Victor," Ganjoon said, clearly taking the hint that Victor was feeling him out. "I started my career as an Enchanter. At Tier Two, I refined my class to something called an Energy Tinkerer, and at Tier Three, I was lucky enough to gain the Artificer class."

"You made all this?" Victor gestured around the shop to the myriad items from jewelry to weapons to household goods.

"Heavens, no! The items with yellow tags were crafted by me, the ones with blue tags were only enchanted by me, and the white tags are simply on consignment—items I thought were worth a spot in my shop."

Victor nodded, pulling Lifedrinker from her loop and walking back to the man's counter. He gently laid her on the wood, resting his palms nearby as though reluctant to let her out of reach. Ganjoon leaned forward, producing a lens, something like a magnifying glass, but with an opaque glass that sparkled with little lights when Victor tried to see what it showed. Ganjoon scrutinized every part of Lifedrinker, from the knob of her haft to the edge of her blade. When he straightened up, he had a grin on his face.

"Lovely, lovely weapon, she is! Sleeping gods, but I'd have liked to see her before the, well, the incident. Thayla told me about it, you see."

Victor wanted to ask him about the "sleeping gods" interjection but instead said, "You know anything I can do to help her come back to me faster? I had to kill a shitload of monsters, and some powerful ones, at that, to wake her up the first time."

"She has a Heart Silver Core, which allowed her to come alive. You know that, right?" Victor nodded, and he continued, "Somehow, the Heart Silver was embedded in an alloy primarily comprised of cobalt. Some serious artificing went into the construction of that axe-head! I can see the tracery of the Heart Silver's growth here." He ran a finger along the slightly discolored black metal of the axe-head where the bright silvery veins had been growing.

"Yeah, before she saved me," Victor said quietly, looking at Lifedrinker as though he'd committed a crime.

"Lad," Ganjoon said, shaking his head, "you don't need to feel bad about that! She wouldn't have done it if she didn't want to. Waking up Heart Silver isn't easy, I'll have you know! It's not just a matter of gathering a lot of Energy—the metal, shaped into a purposeful tool, has to feel a connection to another soul. It's like it has to catch a spark from that soul, and it won't do that for just anyone. Nah, she wanted to help you, and it filled a sort of purpose for her. She'll be even stronger when she comes back, mark my words."

Victor felt emotion constricting his chest as he stared hard into the mysterious depths of Ganjoon's eyes. "Really?" he asked with a thick throat.

"Really! I have texts on this subject. There are only a handful of accounts of someone actually waking up their Heart Silver weapon or tool, despite the hundreds, nay, thousands crafted every few years. I can feel her stirring in there. You can, too, right?"

"Yeah, she's not like when I first got her. She didn't give up everything."

"Right! So you don't have to worry; the hard part is done, and the spark is struck! Just help her recover, give her Energy."

"Is there any other way to do that? Other than killing things?" Victor asked, clearing his throat and straightening up, feeling as if a weight had been taken from him.

"Well, sure. She's an axe, though, and she's grown accustomed to feeding a certain way, hasn't she?" he asked, and Victor nodded with a wry grin. "Well, that's always going to be the easiest way for her to gain strength and to grow. Pure Energy forms, created to spur growth in the consumer, will work for her, too, particularly those the System gives as rewards. Have you ever seen an advancement orb?"

"Nope," Victor said.

"Well, sometimes the System gives them out as rewards. They're like balls of Energy, but you can't cultivate them or even move them—the first person to touch them will gain enough Energy to advance a level. They're rather rare, but you can find them, not too uncommonly, in dungeons or for completing System-generated quests. I think that Lifedrinker could consume such an orb."

"All right," Victor said, nodding, "that's cool. Anything else?"

"I'm sure there are natural treasures that might offer her some advancement. Certain fruits with the power to improve a person's Core are often filled with easily digested Energy. Most importantly, Victor, you need to keep using her. Treat her as the wonderful weapon she's always been. Speak to her, and remind her that you're waiting for her." He gave Victor a long, hard look, then asked bluntly, "Do you love her, Victor?"

"What?" Victor asked, surprised. He started to deny it, to say something like "hell no!" but he looked down at the axe lying on the bench and clamped his mouth shut. How could he say something like that in front of her? After everything she'd done for him? She'd shown him her love, and if he were honest and not trying to seem like a macho idiot, he'd admit that it had sparked deep emotions in him. He cared about Lifedrinker and wanted her to be all right. Did he love her? He wasn't sure that was the right word, and if it was, it certainly wasn't romantic—he didn't want to marry his *pinche* axe!

He cleared his throat and said, "I care about her, man. I want her to be all right because she's the best friend I could ever ask for." Victor paused and reached out to put a heavy hand on Ganjoon's shoulder and added, "You better not repeat that to Thayla! I mean, Thayla's my best friend with two legs, but fuck, Lifedrinker's been through hell with me." He reached out and gently caressed the warm haft, and Lifedrinker rewarded him with a vibrating buzz on Ganjoon's countertop.

"Wow!" the shopkeeper said. "She's listening to you! You know, I've had the luck to inspect a few intelligent weapons in my time, and I never saw one actually move itself! I saw a sword that would glow and pulse with light when its wielder spoke to it, but this is the first time I've seen something like that!"

"Yeah, she's something special," Victor said, lifting Lifedrinker from the counter and slipping her into her loop. "Thanks for your advice, Ganjoon. I'm glad I met you."

"Likewise, Victor! Can I interest you in any items while you're here?" Victor thought about it and realized Ganjoon had spent a lot of time with Thayla and with him, talking about an axe with no profit in mind. It made him want to help the man's business.

"Yeah, why not? You got anything for kids? Any cool magical toys?"

Ganjoon looked at him with a puzzled expression for a moment but nodded to cover his bafflement at Victor's strange turn of phrase and said, "Of course! Could you describe the child in question?"

"She's Thayla's daughter. Um, I think she's six, but she's a real *coyotita*—she's clever and bold and loves her mama."

"Six, hmm? I bet you'd also like to please Thayla with this gift, eh?"

"Sure! Something for them both would be *perfecto*!"

"I have an idea," said Ganjoon, walking to a cabinet at the corner of his shop. He rummaged through one of the shelves for a moment and returned to Victor holding something that seemed to be made of glass in his hand. When he held out his palm, Victor saw two necklaces with silver chains. Each had a crystal pendant attached, shaped roughly like an elephant, though they differed in that these animals had delicately carved manes of feathers around their necks and six legs.

"Pretty," Victor said. "Do they do something?"

"Of course! This is Corner Artifice, is it not?" He handed one of the crystal elephant-like pendants to Victor and said, "Watch." He walked back behind his counter and through the swinging door leading to his shop's back room. A moment later, Victor's pendant began to pulse with purple-blue light, and a tiny voice came out of it.

"Victor?" the little elephant creature said, its trunk moving up and down. "If you hold the amulet tightly and speak, your voice will come out of the other one!"

"Oh, cool!" Victor said, recognizing Ganjoon's voice, though it was higher and had a faintly sharp quality. Ganjoon came out of his back room wearing a broad smile.

"Don't you think they'd like this gift?" Ganjoon asked.

"Of course! How far away can they be from each other?"

"Oh, anywhere around the same house—a few hundred meters at most."

"Ahh, still, that's fucking cool. Do you have any with a longer range?"

"Not presently, but I sometimes get requests for such. They're popular with the military and adventurers, though quite costly. These short-range crystal bolisii are four hundred beads, for instance. If you want some that can reach much further, say a few miles, they would require a material that can hold Energy more densely, and even then, each use would require a day or so of recharging."

"Well, even then, I could imagine some uses. I'll keep it in mind, Ganjoon. For now, let me buy these little elephants." Victor held up the necklace in his hand.

"Elephants?"

"Oh, um, what did you call these animals? They look like something called an elephant where I'm from."

"Ah. They're called bolisii. They're large, mild-tempered beasts that are often used for labor on farms and such. Will the price be any problem?" Ganjoon smiled warmly, and Victor wondered what he'd say if Victor said yes.

"Nah, it's fine." Victor stepped over to the counter and pulled out one of his sacks of beads, spending a few minutes sorting and counting out enough to give Ganjoon the requested four hundred. When he was finished, Ganjoon nodded and scooped the beads into a dimensional container of his own.

"I'll wrap these for you," the shopkeeper said then, and he took the two pendants over to another table where he worked on boxing and wrapping the gift.

Victor started to peruse the shop again while he waited, but the door opened, a bird sang out, and then Deyni charged at him, wrapping her little arms around his knees. Victor laughed and scooped her up, holding her on one of his hips and looking to the door where Thayla was just stepping into the shop. "Hey, *niñita*, ready to go play some games and get some treats?" he asked Deyni, poking her little nose.

"I am, Victor!" Deyni said, carefully articulating her words. "My mom, Thayla, says they have sugar crisps, and I can win prizes!"

Victor smiled and looked at Thayla, and she shrugged. He looked back at Deyni and said, "Deyni, I know your mom's name. You can just say 'mom,' okay?"

"Okay, Victor!" She reached out to touch his cheek, and Victor wasn't sure what she was doing. He looked at her, bemused, but then he realized she was running her tiny fingers along the sparse stubble growing there.

"Gah!" he said. "I need to shave, hmm?"

"Victor?" Victor turned back to see Ganjoon approaching, holding out a small box wrapped in shiny silver paper with a delicate, beautifully tied pale blue ribbon. "Here's your package."

"Thanks, Ganjoon," Victor said, handing the package to Deyni. "This is a present for you and your mommy. You guys can open it later, okay?"

"Victor!" Thayla said, stepping forward. "Why are you getting us presents?"

"It's really for Deyni. Don't get yourself all worked up," Victor said, chuckling. "Here, I'll hold onto it till we're back at the estate." He took the package, giving Deyni a wink, and put it into his ring. Then, still carrying the little girl, he walked toward the door, calling over his shoulder, "Ganjoon, I'll be back if I need anything magical. See you soon, I'm sure."

"Farewell, Victor. Good luck with your lady axe."

Out on the street, Thayla walked up beside Victor, rubbing her hands in the brisk night air, and said, "Lady axe?"

"'Bout time someone else gave her the respect she deserves." Victor grinned, turning to start walking toward the festival.

"Oh, Ancestors! Did he offer you any help?"

"Not exactly, but he gave me a lot of information about Heart Silver and how it works. He's sure Lifedrinker's going to be okay, though, and that made me feel a lot better. Come on, now, Thayla! Let's go have some fun." He picked up his pace, still holding Deyni, and the little girl giggled as Thayla had to almost jog to keep up.

"Hurry, Mommy!" she called, giggling at her mother's breath pluming out.

"Do I need to carry you too, Thayla?" Victor laughed, slowing to a normal pace. She just sighed and reached up to pinch her daughter's cheek, and they continued on their way. It wasn't long before Victor started to smell the food and hear the music from the festival, and soon they were pushing their way through crowds, and Victor had to struggle to keep his mouth closed as he took in the bright lights strung through the sky, and the colorful, amazingly diverse crowd.

Most everyone dressed normally, like Victor and Thayla, though some wore costumes. He figured they were like clowns in this world because they had painted faces with exaggerated expressions and brightly colored robes and cloaks, and they moved through the crowd handing treats to children. Thayla called them "harvest spirits," though, and explained that they represented the people's ancestors, handing out "blessings" to the children, ensuring their good fortune for the year to come.

The celebration took place in two market squares and the streets between them, and all the businesses lining the markets were open, providing more space for the festivities. Victor insisted on sampling food from nearly every cart they passed, enjoying his stomach's ability to appear bottomless. He bought sweet treats for Deyni and himself, which Thayla usually refused, and he ate several different types of marinated meat skewers.

Victor enjoyed everything but couldn't help wishing there was even one good taco stand. He came upon a cart that offered a kind of sandwich with thin, chewy bread stuffed with meat and vegetables soaked in a creamy, spicy sauce, and it almost scratched his itch for a good burrito, though.

They played all sorts of games, and they reminded Victor of carnival games he'd seen people playing in VRs about small towns where the weather changed a lot more than in Tucson. He helped Deyni win a handmade doll at a booth where you had to throw beanbags through holes. It was easy, and he almost wondered how the people made any money, then realized he'd paid more for the chance to throw the bags than the dolls probably cost.

Throughout the evening, the air was inundated with music from bands that played in the corners of the squares. The music reminded Victor of his time at Steampool Vale and at the Red Roladii with Thayla. He didn't dance, but he bounced along with the music, usually when he was carrying Deyni, and her giggles and bright eyes made him want to clown it up even more.

Victor found the entire experience to be more fun than anything he could remember doing. He was sure he'd had more fun at some point growing up, but his life on Earth was so distant in his mind that it almost seemed like a dream, and the festival that night seemed more real, more solid, than the distant memories of wrestling tournaments or parties at his cousins' houses, or even when he'd made out with his girlfriend after a school dance.

Deyni got sleepy after a few hours, and Thayla and Victor walked back to Lam's estate together, with the little girl sleeping on Victor's shoulder the whole way. As they approached the gates, Victor fished around in his ring and pulled out his present, handing it to Thayla. "Open that when you guys wake up tomorrow. It's just a little something for Deyni and you."

"Thank you, Victor. I wish I had something for you," she said, grabbing onto his arm as they walked, kind of leaning into him.

"You don't have to give me anything, Thayla. I'm just glad I have you and Deyni. If it weren't for you, I'd just have Lam and Rellia to deal with, and, well, they're more interested in how they can use me than they are in me. You know what I mean?"

"I know exactly what you mean, Victor," Thayla said, squeezing his arm and leaning her head against his shoulder. "Exactly."

5

RUNNING WITH THE PACK

Victor had found that when he cast Tether Spirit before sleeping, it seemed to calm his dreams quite a lot. It made him wonder just how much he was dreaming and how much his spirit was wandering and encountering strange things. After saying good night to Thayla and Deyni, he'd returned to his rooms, prepared to get a long night of rest after the mentally straining, emotional couple of days he'd had.

When he stood there, naked except for his underwear which was how he liked to sleep, staring at his bed, he had the thought that maybe he wouldn't cast Tether Spirit. Hadn't he just said to Thayla that he thought Belikot might have been tricking him, might have been trying to keep Victor out of his hair by getting him to tie his spirit down? He struggled with the impulse, shaking his head, and wondering if he was being stupid.

Part of his problem with the spell was that he didn't like the idea that he had to restrain himself. He didn't want anyone tying him down, not with collars and chains, not with control rods, not with spells. Why should he do it to himself? Oynalla hadn't mentioned anything like that, had she? She'd cautioned him about spirit walking carelessly, saying there were dangerous people he could encounter that way. Was his spirit wandering while he slept the same sort of thing? "Why don't I just ask her?"

He looked around his bedroom, wondering if he felt safe enough to spirit walk without getting someone to watch his back. He moved to his door and locked it, then shoved the heavy five-drawer dresser in front of it. The windows were another matter—they opened with a crank, each large enough to allow a person through. He cranked the little handle in front of them each until they were closed, then looked around the room for something to barricade them.

Victor hoisted the armoire on the far wall, carrying it over to block up one window. Then he picked up his mattress, a fluffy, feather-filled thing that bent and wobbled as he carried it, and plopped it upright in front of the other window. Frowning at the wobbly barricade, he reached into his storage ring and pulled out a few of the spears he'd taken from the skeletons in the dungeon. Apologizing silently to Captain Lam, he propped the mattress upright with the spears, jamming their blades into the hardwood floor to hold them in place.

Victor nodded to himself, looking around the room. Nobody would easily gain entry, and if they created enough racket to get past his barricades, he was sure the guards in the hallway would come running. Still, he moved into the en suite bathroom, closed the door, and jammed another spear into the vanity to bar it shut. Then, Victor sat down on the cool tile floor and cleared his mind. As he was getting ready to cast his spell, another thought occurred to him, and he said, "Hey, Gorz, you there?"

"Hello, Victor."

"Gorz, I'm sorry I haven't been much of a friend. The truth is you're so quiet all the time unless I'm talking to you that I forget you're there half the time. I know that's shitty, and I hope you aren't feeling messed up about it."

"I appreciate the sentiment, but I don't feel bothered at all. It's the nature of my enchantment. Unless I'm addressed or working on a task, I don't generally notice the passage of time the way living creatures or some differently enchanted spirits do."

"Did your old master make you that way on purpose?"

"I'm not sure, Victor. I'm just a fragment of my original self, you know. It's possible that there wasn't enough of me to be more . . . aware."

"If I ask you to watch out for trouble while I cast Spirit Walk, do you think you could do that? Could you scream into my mind if something bad was happening?"

"I believe so! If I have a task, such as watching the tether when you were hunting Belikot, then I seem able to focus on it."

"Awesome!" Victor looked to Lifedrinker, where she leaned against the nearby counter, and shook his head, pulling her over to rest across his knees. "All right, Gorz. I'm casting it. Please watch over me."

"I will endeavor to stay as vigilant as possible."

"Right." Victor rested his hands on Lifedrinker's haft and cast Spirit Walk. When he stood up, surrounded by the lightly wooded grassy plains around Gelica, he realized his hands weren't empty; they held a spirit version of Lifedrinker, her haft dark like the night sky but filled with a billion twinkling motes of silvery light. Her axe-head, always dark in reality, was brightly shimmering like the surface of a lake as the wind stirred its waters to reflect the moonlight.

"Hey, you never came with me before!" he said, lifting the weapon to look better at the bright, shimmering blade. "Well, thanks, Lifedrinker; I'm glad to have you along." He held her hard, cold metal to his forehead for a moment, but though he felt a buzz of Energy and warmth, no voice sounded in his head. He rested her on his shoulder and started striding forward, thinking about Oynalla, and wondering if she'd be waiting for him or if his efforts to speak to her would be in vain.

He strode between trees and out into a seemingly endless plain, the enormous night sky with its countless stars making him feel small yet part of something vast and amazing. He glanced left and right as he walked, always keeping Oynalla in his mind, but after just a few steps, he stopped. Not far away to his left, he saw a brightly flickering fountain of lights that reminded him of fireworks—something like a giant sparkler. He debated ignoring the phenomenon, but something inside him was too curious, so he turned and walked over to it.

As he drew near, Victor saw his analogy become more and more appropriate. The sparkling lights looked more and more like a fountain of sparks erupting from some unseen object. Soon he was standing before the spray, and he felt the Energy pouring out of it, and he realized the differently colored sparks were various types of attuned Energy. He strained but couldn't tell what sorts of Energy they were—none of them resonated with his two affinities.

Victor knelt and examined the fountain's source, but all he could see was a blurry distortion in the air. When he tentatively reached out a hand to see if he could feel anything, it felt as if he was sticking his hand into thick, warm syrup, but when he pulled it back, it was completely clean—just his slightly glowing spirit fingers.

"Strange, isn't it?" Oynalla asked from right behind him. Victor jumped, literally, and rolled forward into the grass, coming up with Lifedrinker between him and the old woman.

"You scared the shit out of me!" he growled.

"Ha!" Oynalla said, then she started to chuckle and then laugh, and it sounded strange to Victor's ears because her spirit self had a pleasing trill of a laugh, not the cackle he'd grown to expect.

"Well, since you're here, tell me what this thing is!" Victor gestured to the phenomenon, struggling to hold back the surge of anger at being made to look a fool.

"Relax, warrior," Oynalla said, smiling, beautiful, and youthful. She glided, graceful in her movements, to the fountain and studied its spray of Energies. When she turned to look at Victor again, her eyes were distant and unfocused. "If you found this spot on the physical plane, you'd be in the presence of a powerful artifact. Something that could change a person's life." Her eyes refocused, staring into Victor's face, and she said, "Come, it's not safe to linger here. Take my hand."

"All right," Victor said, moving closer, and then Oynalla recoiled.

"Careful with that weapon, warrior; don't let her touch me! I can feel her hunger from here!"

"Really?" Victor lifted Lifedrinker, and a grin spread on his face. "No wonder she came along—she *is* hungry!" He rested her back on his shoulder and said, "Hopefully we'll find something to feed you, but leave Oynalla alone, please." He grinned to himself, enjoying the discomfort the old Spirit Caster had shown, then he stepped closer to her and reached out a hand, and the old-young woman tentatively took it.

"Walk with me," she said, striding into the endless ocean of purple, starlit grass. Victor matched her pace, and she continued, "I was with Thayla just a little while ago. She thought you might seek me out tonight. She knows you well, doesn't she?"

"I guess so," Victor said, wondering how Thayla might have guessed his intentions and annoyed with himself for not considering or even wondering how often Thayla and Oynalla had been meeting on the spirit plane.

"I'll speak to you about an important matter before discussing why you sought me out. Will that be all right?" Oynalla asked, lifting his hand that she held and gently patting the back of it with her other.

"Sure, Oynalla," Victor said.

"Thayla has an important role to play with my clan, and I believe you have important things to do and see in very distant places. Can you understand that?"

"Uh, sure, but I don't know if you're right—about me, at least."

"Victor, you've been very kind to Thayla and her daughter. She's told me about her time with you since your great victory and before it. She loves you like a brother and begins to wonder if she should think of you as more. I don't want you to hurt her, Victor. You are young and foolish and can't see past your two feet, but I see more and farther, and I'm certain you won't be staying with our clan. Do you believe me?"

The point of this strange conversation suddenly smacked Victor in the face, and he realized what Oynalla wanted him to say. "Oynalla, I care about Thayla a lot, but I'm not sure how far those feelings go. Yeah, I figure you're probably right; I'm not looking to settle down with a clan of hunters, even if I do like your people an awful lot. I won't push things with Thayla, all right? I'm happy thinking of her as a friend—family, even."

"Good, warrior," Oynalla said, patting his hand again. "Now, why did you seek Oynalla out?"

"Do you tether your spirit when you sleep?" Victor looked down at the much smaller woman, watching for her reaction.

"Why would I do that?" She squinted her eyes in puzzlement, then looked up at his face and continued, "When I sleep, if my spirit wanders, it's only partially walking on this plane. It, no, *I* have one foot on the physical plane and one foot here. Any harm that came to me would send me scurrying back to my body, which I still have contact with, waking me up instantly."

"What's the point of that spell, then? Tether Spirit, I mean."

"I suppose someone with a weak will could be snatched away if their spirit wandered near a powerful Spirit Caster. None in my clan ever had a problem with such a thing, though. Perhaps others in large cities have an affinity or curse . . . maybe a class that causes such things. You shouldn't worry, Victor. Your will is like an iron spike embedded in the footings of a mountain. No one will move your spirit against your will."

"Goddamn it," Victor said, shaking his head.

"What is it, warrior?" Oynalla turned to look at him, holding his hand with both of hers. He realized they'd stopped walking a while ago and now stood in a small wooded depression, a stream babbling nearby. He glanced toward the sound and saw that the water looked like liquid moonlight, and as it cascaded over the rocks in its path, it threw up a mist that made rainbows in the twilight of the spirit plane.

"This is a beautiful spot," he said, temporarily forgetting their conversation.

"Yes. This is near my birthplace. My mother showed me the spirit plane for the first time here. Now, why do you berate yourself with the curses of a distant god?"

"Bel . . . the spirit that we dealt with, the one that was in Thayla's body. He spoke to me while I dreamed, told me to learn to tether my spirit, and that he was doing me a favor. I fucking listened to him and have been casting that damn spell every night before I sleep."

"Ha! There is real danger here, from creatures like him, even, but not for one such as you if you're only dream walking. Perhaps he feared you wandering upon him while he performed his dark works. Death Casters use this realm, too, you know. Here, we're very close to the veil." She stopped talking for a moment and looked hard at Victor and at Lifedrinker, then said, "Warrior, he may well have feared you. This one you speak of, he's no Spirit Caster. I felt his fragment when you drove it out of Thayla and into that skull. Death Casters, even strong ones, are not a match for a strong Spirit Caster in this realm."

"I had that thought but wondered if I was being too cocky. You know, too, uh, full of myself."

"You've manifested your weapon here. You did so without trying, hmm? She's a smart one, though, not a plain old axe . . . still, that's not something easily done for even an experienced Spirit Caster. I can feel your Core blazing from across the plains, though mostly because I know what to look for. Hmm, no, I think, in this realm, the one whose name you fear to speak should be the one with fear in his heart."

"Really?" Victor asked, and a wild, slightly insane impulse flared to life inside him. Oynalla, perhaps, saw the look in his eyes, and she opened her mouth to speak but stopped herself, cackling instead, and this time it was the sound the older woman made in the real world.

"Really, warrior! Now do what your heart calls for you to do!" Again she cackled, and Victor felt his mouth responding with a maniac's grin. He dropped Lifedrinker from his shoulder, holding her in both hands, and started striding out of Oynalla's grove, his mind focusing on Belikot. He pictured Belikot's skull, he pictured the figure that came to him in his dream, and he focused on the sound of that deep, self-important voice. He could hear it echoing in his mind, hear the words Belikot had spoken in his dream. When he had the image solidly in his mind, he picked up his pace, moving into a jog.

While he ran, Victor cast Manifest Spirit, and suddenly he was running with his pack, five red-tinged, yipping, barking fragments of his spirit keeping pace with him. "Let's hunt!" he called, and they answered him with barks, howls, and their ever-present yapping chatter. They coursed over the plains, and Victor felt a thrill in his heart, and he pushed himself even faster, stretching his long legs and really letting his improved body loose, sprinting for everything he was worth and laughing at the rush of the ghostly wind whistling past his spirit form's ears.

He continued to concentrate on his mental image of Belikot, hoping that the Death Caster was out on the spirit plane, hoping he could catch him unawares. A wild, mad grin was on his face, and he knew it was because he was acting—Victor was doing what he wanted to do and not following the instructions of one of the many people in his life who felt they needed to direct his every move. Some part of his brain knew that wasn't fair, knew that he'd asked for help from a lot of those people. Still, it felt glorious to do something spontaneous, dangerous, and decidedly what he wanted to do.

As he ran, he began to fear that Belikot wasn't out, that whatever business he had on the spirit plane was done. He frowned and focused, and this time he remembered how Belikot's cold, slippery Energy had felt as he'd tugged it out of Thayla and pushed it into the skull. Suddenly his surroundings changed, and he and his pack were coursing up a steep hill littered with broken black stones.

When they came to the crest of the hill, Victor saw that they'd climbed to the rim of a black crater and at its center was a brightly shimmering, blue, misty rip in the air. A robed figure stood before the flickering tear at the head of a long line of dim, stooped, humanoid spirits bound by blazing blue chains. Victor turned to his pack and held a finger to his lips, and amazingly, they stopped their yipping, crouching low as if they were stalking a rabbit.

When he turned back to the scene at the bottom of the crater, perhaps a hundred yards down the slope, he saw the robed figure, undoubtedly Belikot, pull one of the bound spirits to him. Belikot put a hand on the spirit and, reaching out with his other hand, began to siphon Energy out of the captive and into the rip in the air. Victor grunted in disbelief and anger and started charging down the slope.

Belikot's back was to him, and he seemed deeply engrossed in his efforts. Victor wanted to yell, wanted to holler a war cry, but he kept silent, and his pack did the same. As he charged down the strange black crater wall, he lifted Lifedrinker and used Sovereign Will to boost his strength, dimly wondering how the spell even worked on the spirit plane. When he hit flat ground and was only fifteen paces from Belikot, he launched himself into the air and used Channel Spirit to flood Lifedrinker with rage-attuned Energy.

At the last minute, Belikot turned, eyes wide, mouth open in dismay, and then Lifedrinker split his head like a cleaver through a ripe cantaloupe and buried herself deep in his chest. "Drink that fucker up, *hermosa*!" he growled, driving Belikot's spirit form to the ground and pressing Lifedrinker down on the thrashing body.

It said a lot, in Victor's mind, that the Death Caster was still thrashing and fighting, but Lifedrinker wasn't letting go. Though Victor could feel the spirit tugging and pulling, he reached out with his mind, almost like when he cultivated Energy, and pulled on it, locking Belikot down while Lifedrinker did her work.

Belikot's thrashing grew more intense, and black tendrils started to writhe up out of the soil, reaching for Victor and his axe, but Victor held his ground, and as they snaked toward him, his pack jumped into the fray, biting the tendrils of evil Energy and ripping them apart, shaking their heads like terriers with rats. "No, fucker!" Victor growled, watching as thick rivulets of blue and frosty Energy surged through the spirit form into Lifedrinker. "You're done, *cabrón*!"

Lifedrinker drank from Belikot's spirit for what felt like a very long time, and as the currents of Energy she was drawing grew thin and then trickled away to nothing, his form dissipated into a fine mist and was gone. Victor looked around and saw the shimmering blue rip in the air and the bound, faintly luminescent spirits swaying nearby.

Close as he was now, Victor could see the faces on the figures—they were all Shadeni and Ardeni, and they looked weak and wan, their eyes haunted and filled with pain. The one closest to Victor held up his chained hands, a questioning look on his face.

"Can you speak?" he asked.

In answer, the spirit shook its head and held up its hands again. Victor nodded and lifted Lifedrinker, charging her with inspiration-attuned Energy. He brought her down on the exposed links between the man's wrists, and she sliced through them with just a slight tug of resistance. When the chains were severed, the spirit's face relaxed, much of the pain leaving his eyes, and he started to dissipate into a fine mist. An echoing, distant voice said, "Thank you," as the mist dispersed.

The other spirits began to crowd forward, holding up their chains, and Victor repeated the process more than a dozen times, severing the bonds that

Belikot had put upon them and watching as they all disappeared in a cloud of faintly luminescent mist. Victor stood there, surrounded by his coyote pack, now licking each other and yipping quietly. He looked around the black crater, then up at the shimmering blue rip in the air, wondering if there was anything he could do about it, when he felt a familiar presence at his back.

"Hey, Oynalla," he said, depriving her of the chance to startle him again.

"Warrior, you seem to have caught your quarry. I watched from yonder rim." She pointed up at the lip of the crater.

"Did I kill him? Could it really be that easy?" Victor felt good but had a strange twist in his gut, as if he'd cheated or something.

"Aye, warrior. He's dead. I've never seen a spirit so thoroughly destroyed. Your axe is throbbing with the Energy she consumed." Oynalla continued to walk forward, closing the distance between them.

Victor hefted Lifedrinker, feeling the warmth of her handle, and said, "Good. She deserves it. What were those spirits, the ones with the chains?"

"Victims of Belikot. He caught them here or killed their bodies to trap and bring their spirits to this place. He was using them to further rip this gateway through the veil." She gestured at the tear Belikot had been making.

"Can we do something about it?" Victor asked, squinting at the weird blue hole in the air.

"Perhaps, if we knew the right spells. Don't worry; the veil will mend itself, given time and without Belikot's efforts to the contrary." She smiled at Victor then and said, "Why didn't you tell me about your pack here?" She gestured to the slightly luminescent red coyotes.

"I didn't have a chance, I guess. I learned a new spell called Manifest Spirit—they're a little piece of me."

"You're going to surpass my abilities soon, Victor. You're already stronger than I ever was. I can still teach you a thing or two, though, should you come to visit me. Even if you don't!" She gestured around, indicating the spirit plane.

"Yeah, I guess if we can talk here, you can teach me here, huh?" Oynalla nodded, and he continued, "I'd still like to visit you. I'd like to see you and your clan in person."

"Of course, of course," she chuckled, reaching out to grab Victor's arm. Strangely, at that exact moment, Victor became aware of someone grabbing his real, physical shoulder and shaking him.

Then he heard a distant echo of Gorz's voice in his mind, *"Victor! Your friend Edeya is here!"*

"I think someone's trying to wake me up. I'm going to go back to my body now, Oynalla. Thank you for your advice!"

"Ha! Of course, warrior. When you're ready to talk more, seek me out. I'll be here." She nodded as though to affirm what she'd said, and Victor didn't doubt that the old Spirit Caster would somehow know when to meet him.

He took the hand she'd put on his shoulder and gently squeezed it, then ended his Spirit Walk spell. "Victor!" Edeya said, shaking his shoulder again. He opened his eyes and smiled at her.

"What?" He grunted and heaved himself to his feet, looking around. His bathroom door had been broken in half; the part with this spear barring it was still in the frame, though the other half was in pieces.

"The guards patrolling the garden saw the barricades in front of your windows and came to get me. We were afraid something had happened . . ." Edeya trailed off, looking around the bathroom and then back toward his bedroom. Victor followed her gaze and realized it did look as though it had been ransacked. Still, Edeya knew about his spirit walking.

"Hey, I was on a spirit walk. What if I didn't want to be woken up?" He gave her shoulder a nudge, smiling to soften the words.

"In that case, you need to tell someone what the depths you're doing!"

"Yeah, I didn't want to wake anyone. What time is it, anyway?"

"I don't know. An hour before dawn? What were you doing? Is everything all right?" Edeya was dressed in her uniform, though the buttons were misaligned on her coat and her hair was wild. She must have been sleeping when the guards woke her. Victor felt a twinge of guilt, realizing she was working harder than anyone he knew, probably because she felt some massive debt to Lam for turning her life around in the mines.

"Hey, everything's fine. I'm sorry you got woken up like that. Listen, I have some good news you can report to Lam." He paused and waited for her frustrated snarl, indicating he needed to hurry up. "I just killed Belikot . . . what the fuck?" Victor cut himself off as he saw bright golden and purple lights burst through the walls of his bedroom, and then a stream of Energy surged into his chest, lifting him off the ground and flooding his pathways. Euphoria filled his mind, and he laughed, spreading his arms out and enjoying the weightlessness.

*****Congratulations! You have achieved level 31 Spirit Carver, gained 10 will and 10 vitality, and have 8 attribute points to allocate.*****

6

CAMPING IN STYLE

Victor sat in Lam's kitchens, Edeya, Thayla, and Captain Lam on the bench across from him, and, between huge bites of food, explained what he'd done while spirit walking. He mentioned meeting Oynalla and his hunt and finished with a brief description of how he had surprised Belikot and killed him before he could hardly retaliate.

"So, I don't need to gather my old friends? We don't need to go and confront this Belikot fellow?" Lam asked after chewing on a bite of bacon thoughtfully for a few moments.

"No, Oynalla was pretty damn sure I killed him." Victor shrugged and drank down a full glass of milk.

"What about the phylactery? His soul shards? He's not so easy to kill, Victor," Thayla said. She'd been frowning for most of his retelling, and now he realized why.

"Look, the only other shard we know of is in my dimensional bag. As far as the phylactery goes, we know it increased his strength, and maybe it was a way to help him jump his soul around, but Thayla, I had his fucking soul on the spirit plane. I watched Lifedrinker drain it away!" He lifted the axe and showed them the Heart Silver veins that had started to spread through the dark cobalt axe-head. "I don't know how he could recover from that, and if he did, if some piece of him is still out there, then it's a shadow of what he was."

"A shadow with a grudge," Edeya said, nodding to Thayla.

"Oh, God." Victor sighed and rubbed his temples. He knew they were right, in a way, to still be wary of Belikot, but couldn't they take a fucking win when he handed it to them? "The point is, if he's pissed at anyone, it's me. If he tries to mess with me on the spirit plane, I'll whip his ass again, and if he comes at me in the real world, then I'll deal with it. This isn't a problem for 'us' anymore, all right? You all can let it go." He couldn't help the growl that had entered his voice or the scowl on his face as he roughly wiped his mouth with a napkin.

"I'm not trying to downplay what you did, Victor," Thayla said and opened her mouth to continue, but Victor shook his head and held up a hand.

"It's not that! It's just . . . well, it's just that I'm sick of having to run my plans and actions through some kind of fucking committee. I just want to, you know, live for a while."

"Victor, people are depending on you . . ." Lam started, but again Victor spoke over her.

"Yeah, I know, Lam. I know you have a lot riding on the campaign in the Marches, and I know Rellia's life depends on it. I'm not backing out of that. I'll meet you guys in Persi Gables in the spring, and we'll get shit going, all right? For now, though, I want to escort Thayla and Deyni to Tellen's camp, spend some time visiting with Oynalla, and from there, I'll see what grabs my interest. Is that all right with everyone?" He glared around the table, scowling down at everyone but Captain Lam, who met his eyes with a strangely open expression.

"That's good, Victor. I can respect those sentiments." She glanced around the table, her face pensive as if she was trying to decide if she would continue, but she pressed her lips into a firm line and gave a short nod as though giving herself permission. "My family made a lot of demands of me. They paid for schooling and expected me to stay in Twilight Home and continue forging my father's business empire. I ran away." She said the last part quietly, and her eyes fell.

"You just ran?" Edeya asked, her voice soft and her eyes wide with awe.

"Yes. I didn't want to face my parents. I didn't want to make my wishes clear like Victor just did. To me, it was easier just to erase my past from my mind and move toward my goal, so I went to Tharcray and joined the Legion."

"Damn," Victor said. "And your family? Did you ever let them know what you got up to? I bet they're proud of what you've done now, huh?"

"I wrote to them a few times. My mother wrote back and told me to stop. She said my father had disowned me and that it was too painful to hear from the 'ghost' of their daughter." Lam dug at the wooden table with her thumbnail while she spoke, perhaps unaware of the action, and Victor had the urge to reach out and take her hand. He didn't, though, and he inwardly railed at his cowardice.

"Lam, that sucks. Thanks for sharing that with me, though." Victor looked around the table and said, "I mean us. It means a lot."

"Well!" Lam said, shaking her head and thumping her palms flat on the table. "When will you two be leaving?"

Victor glanced at Thayla, saw her slight shrug, and said, "Soon, I guess. Maybe today."

Lam nodded, quick and informal, and said, "I have a map for you. I had one of my secretaries do a little research into Tellen's clan. He mapped out the shortest routes to their fall and winter camps. You've got money now, Victor." She turned to include Thayla in the discussion. "Buy yourselves some mounts or a coach or something. You don't want Deyni walking all that way, do you?"

"No, that's a good point, Captain," Victor said, nodding.

"Also, let's invest in a proper pair of Far Scribe books." Lam nodded to Edeya, adding, "Will you give Victor two thousand beads from the campaign account? That should cover much of the expense, but you can cover the rest, Victor. It's good for you to have some stake in the operation, too."

"Yeah, no problem. Those are books that let us see what the other writes?" He was sort of guessing, but he vaguely remembered someone describing the process to him. He couldn't remember who. Unsure if it had been someone in the mine or the pits or if it was one of the three women sitting with him now, he decided not to act completely clueless.

"That's right. Edeya will shop with you and bring me back my copy. I suppose this is farewell, then. I pray the Trees and Roots watch you, Victor. I pray they guide you to Persi Gables in the spring, for all our sakes." She stood and reached out a long slender hand, and Victor stood up to shake it. As always, he liked the feel of her grip, the way her fingers closed on his meaty hands like bands of warm iron. He gripped her back and smiled, pulling her so she leaned over the table, and clasped her into a partial hug with his other arm. He was surprised when she pulled him in tight with her free arm, returning the gesture.

"I'll be there, Lam," he said as they hugged, then he let her go. "Well, Thayla, how about getting that runt of yours out of bed, and we can do some shopping!"

Thayla smiled and said, "Watch this." Then she pulled on the silver chain at her neck, lifting out the crystal pendant Victor had bought her. Holding it tightly in her hand, she said, "Deyni! Get dressed; Victor is taking us shopping for animals!" Her eyes squinting from her broad smile, Thayla let go and held the amulet up in the palm of her hand, watching it expectantly.

"Okay, Mom!" a high, tinny version of Deyni's voice piped up out of the amulet as it flashed pink very briefly.

"Neat!" Edeya laughed. "Well, go get her, Thayla. Victor and I will meet you at the gate."

Not long after that, Victor, Thayla, Edeya, and Deyni walked into town. Three guards in Lam's livery kept pace a short way behind them. Victor turned, frowned at their escort, and said, "What's with the guards, Edeya?"

"Captain Lam's just being overcautious. You ruffled a lot of feathers with your duel, and word is spreading about your agreement with Rellia. She has her own set of enemies that might want to mess with you. Things will be better when you're out of the city and moving swiftly."

"This place is like a rattlesnake nest," Victor said, shaking his head.

"Gelica is worse than a lot of cities. It's on the edge of the Empire, and many families conduct things past the line of what you'd call 'legal' out here. Persi Gables is nicer, in some regards, because it's an independent city, but they have some rules and laws that don't sit well with me," Edeya said.

"Oh, you mean like allowing creepy wizards to kidnap people from other worlds and force them to fight in a pit?" Victor scoffed.

"Well, technically, I don't think that's legal," Edeya laughed. "Let's say the laws are loosely enforced in that city, but at least it's not directly under the influence of the Empire."

"Right," Victor said, kicking a loose stone over the cobbles. Once again, his thoughts drifted back to his time at the Wagon Wheel and his dissatisfied feelings of betrayal, anger, horror, and injustice. He thought of Vullu and wondered if he'd ever see him again. His steps grew slow, and his sensations of the world around him dimmed as he thought about Yrella. So many times, the memory of her death had come to haunt him, but now he thought about her life—her beauty, laughter, and kindness.

"Victor?" Thayla said, and her tone indicated it wasn't the first time.

"Yeah," he asked, rubbing his head as if to rub away his thoughts.

"Edeya wants to know if you have an Artificer you prefer. I told her you seemed to like Ganjoon."

"Yeah, Ganjoon's cool. Let's go there." Victor reached down, hoisted Deyni to his shoulders, and picked up the pace. "C'mon, slowpokes!" he said, causing Deyni to giggle and look back at Thayla and Edeya.

"Yeah! Slow pokers!" the little girl said, and Victor laughed.

Ganjoon was happy to see them, and when Edeya told him they needed a Far Scribe book with a lot of pages, he was delighted to provide some options. Each of his books was handsomely bound in leather, though they varied in size considerably. The least expensive was only fifty beads, but it had a mere ten small pages. His most costly book was large, something like an old-school encyclopedia or dictionary, and had five hundred pages. "This one will cost you thirty-five hundred beads," he said with a self-satisfied pat on the heavy tome.

"Really, Ganjoon?" Victor asked. "No discount for friends?"

"Friends, hmm?" He let his eyes shift down toward Lifedrinker, and they widened in surprise. "Your lady axe looks better already! What did you do, Victor?"

"He'll tell you about it for a discount," Thayla said, grinning as she put her hand on Victor's shoulder.

"Well, are you going to buy anything else?" Ganjoon asked, a calculating look on his face.

"Yeah, we're leaving town and need to pick up a few things. Hey! Do you happen to have any kind of magical chariots? You know, like Captain Lam has?" He gestured vaguely in the direction of Lam's estate. "Something that folds up or drives itself or some other cool shit?"

Thayla slapped him on the back of the head and said, "He means he's open to hearing about any sort of magical transport you have."

"Now you're talking about truly expensive items. Expensive to buy and to maintain, at least as far as the object I have for sale goes." He gave Victor another appraising look, and then his eyes moved to Thayla, Edeya, and even little Deyni, who sat on a stool playing with a set of enchanted dice at the front counter. "I'll show you something, but I fear it's beyond your means. I've been unable to sell it since I won it from an imperial contract nearly eight years ago." He stepped behind his counter and into his back room.

"What's this, you reckon?" Thayla asked.

"No idea. Maybe a coach like the captain's," Edeya said.

Victor just shrugged, and then Ganjoon returned, carrying a heavy-looking carpet roll. He unfurled it in front of the counter on the show space floor, and Victor caught his breath at its beauty. It was about five feet by eight and shimmered in the shop's lighting. It was spun from two different colors of thread in an intricate pattern of interlocking squares and rectangles.

The threads glimmered metallically, one a luminescent orange-yellow and the other a shimmering silver.

"This carpet can fly faster than a roladii can run. It's spun from pure amber ore and starsteel. It could hold the weight of four people and fly for a day. If you have the personal Energy for it, you could recharge it in a few hours or let it sit in the sun for a day, and it will be ready to go again."

"A fucking flying carpet?" Victor asked, reaching down to feel the heavy, rich weave.

"That's right. I'm afraid I couldn't let it go for less than a hundred thousand beads."

"Any wiggle room?" Victor asked, standing up and shaking his head ruefully. "Nah, never mind. Even if you'd take half that much, I wouldn't want to spend that amount. Maybe someday, Ganjoon. Maybe someday."

"Thanks for showing it to us, though," Thayla added, and Victor realized she was right—Ganjoon was showing a lot of faith, putting an item this expensive on display for them.

"When you've made your fortune, come back! I'm sure I'll still have it," Ganjoon said, rolling up the carpet with a laugh. "I'm sorry I don't carry many transport items, but I have a friend who can surely help you out. How about I give you his name? He'll treat you right if you say I sent you."

"Fair enough, Ganjoon. We'll buy that book. I'll pay fifteen hundred, and Edeya will cover the rest. Don't worry—she's paying with Lam's money." Victor chuckled and started fishing through his ring for one of the heavy sacks of beads Thayla had given him from their winnings.

While Edeya doled out her portion, Victor said, "Anyway, Lifedrinker had a big night. She and I did a little spirit walk, and I ran into a Death Caster that I had some history with. Lifedrinker got a good, long drink from him."

"He must have had quite a powerful Core. It looks like she drew a lot of Energy in! One of those Heart Silver veins is almost fully regrown, and the others have started out from her edge as well!"

"Yep! I'm looking forward to seeing her continue to advance," Victor said and noticed Thayla leaning against the counter, staring at the two of them as they talked with Lifedrinker on the counter between them. "What?" he asked.

"You know 'she's' an axe, right?"

"Oh, God, not this again!" Victor sighed and slipped Lifedrinker into the loop on his belt. "At least Ganjoon knows how to respect her properly!"

"Yes, she's developing quite a spirit." Ganjoon nodded. "Don't get on her bad side with prejudice, Thayla!"

"Prejudice?" Thayla's voice was high in disbelief.

"Yeah," Victor nodded. "You're anti-axe!"

"I'm *not* anti-axe! I'm sorry I said anything! Fawn over *her* all you want!" Thayla violently crossed her arms in front of her chest and turned to regard her daughter.

"Here you go," Edeya said, pushing a pile of glittering Energy beads toward Ganjoon.

"Right! Here's your copy, Victor, and the one for Captain Lam, I presume," he said, holding out a thick volume to Edeya and shoving the other toward Victor. When they'd each stowed their books away, he said, "Now, go see my friend Bernale. He sells transport animals and vehicles near the south gate. His business is easy to spot, 'Bernale's Beasts.' It's a large wooden structure with an enormous attached barn. It takes up nearly a block on Vine Street."

"All right, Ganjoon. Thanks for your help—I'm sure we'll see you again, but it might be a while. We're heading out today." He turned toward Thayla, who was still staring dourly at the counter where Deyni was tossing the dice, her thoughts clearly far away. "Come on, Thayla. Quit sulking," Victor said, then hurried toward the door as she made to smack him.

"Safe travels," Ganjoon said, "May the Father of Winds bless your skies." The serious tone and the formality of his words made Victor stop messing with Thayla for a minute, and he turned to regard Ganjoon again.

"Thank you, Ganjoon. That means a lot." He nodded his head, trying to show respect to the strange-looking, gray-skinned man, and then stepped out of his shop.

When Thayla, carrying Deyni, and Edeya joined him on the sidewalk, Thayla said, "Do you have to make me look bad like that? I wasn't trying to insult your axe!"

"I was teasing, Thayla; relax. Ganjoon knows you didn't mean anything." He reached out his hands for Deyni and said, "Come here, monkey. I'll put you on my shoulders again."

"Monkey!" Deyni echoed and allowed Victor to lift her away from her mom.

"Well? Edeya, you don't have to come with us; I know you probably have stuff to do back at Lam's."

"Actually, Edeya, could you do me a favor?" Thayla asked.

"Um, sure," Edeya said.

"We left in kind of a hurry. Could you tell Rhessa to get her things and meet us by the south gate?" Thayla reached out a hand to Edeya's slender shoulder.

"I can, sure. I guess that means you guys are really leaving today? It feels sudden. I'd thought Victor and the Captain would go hunting that Death Caster, and I'd get some more time with you all. I'm going to miss you—I hope I see you again soon!" She lunged forward, wrapping her arms around Thayla.

"Oh, hush," Thayla said softly, stroking the girl's hair. "We'll see each other again soon. You know where Deyni and I will be! Tellen's clan stops by Gelica a few times a year, and if I want, I can always come here on my own." She glanced at her daughter. "With Deyni, of course."

"Yeah, and I'll probably see you in the spring. I have a feeling Captain Lam will bring you along to Persi Gables," Victor added.

"Come here, you thunderak," Edeya said, letting go of Thayla and grabbing Victor around his midriff, burying her head in his chest.

"Thunderak?" Victor asked.

"Big lizard," Deyni said with a giggle.

"Oh, nice," Victor laughed and gently patted Edeya's back, avoiding her fragile-looking wings while Deyni reworked her grip in his thick black hair.

After a few more exchanges of hugs and promises to visit each other soon, Edeya hurried off toward Lam's estate, promising to send Rhessa to the south gate. Victor watched her leave, noting her confident pose with straight shoulders and the way her boots glinted in the morning light, and he almost couldn't picture the scrawny, dirty waif whom he'd met back in the mines. "Come on," he said to Thayla, nudging her in the direction of the south gate. She looked up at him and Deyni and smiled, and the three of them made their way through town.

When they came to Vine Street, they both had their eyes peeled for Bernale's place of business. It was Deyni, still perched on Victor's shoulders, who bounced up and down, pointing ahead to the left, and said, "Look at those animals!"

"That's it!" Thayla said and led the way across the street. Victor followed her, eyes on the line of sectioned-off pens that hugged the city wall for, just as Ganjoon had said, more than a city block. He could smell the animal dung and the hay-like scent of feed. The various noises of the creatures reminded him more of a zoo than a stable.

He saw animals that had to be the living versions of the elephant-like thing on Thayla's pendant, swaying their big heads and trumpeting. Before he could think about going over to see the fantastic creatures up close, Victor's attention was stolen by a lizard nearly as large, flopping around in the dust of its pen and flicking out a tongue as big as Victor's arm. Thayla tugged him toward the office building on the far side of the lot, and they passed by pens with huge birds, horse-sized antlered creatures, roladii, and some animals that looked very much like horses but with brightly colored fur and feathered manes.

When they entered the office, Victor was surprised by how clean and well-appointed it was. A Cadwalli man sat at a polished desk speaking quietly to an Ardeni couple, and when Victor and Thayla stepped onto the plush rug, and the heavy door clicked shut behind them, he looked up and said, "Please wait there." He gestured to a sitting area off to the side. "I'll be with you soon. In the meantime, please have some tea."

"Thank you," Thayla said, pulling Victor over to one of the couches. He'd taken Deyni off his shoulders to get through the doorway, and now he set her on the couch next to her mom. Before he sat down, Victor went over to the sideboard and poured himself a cup of tea, and picked up the tray of thin sugar cookies he found next to the kettle. When he sat down next to Deyni, he put the cookies on the coffee table in front of the couch and winked at her.

"Have a snack," he said.

"You're spoiling her," Thayla said, but she reached down, faster than Deyni, and snatched a cookie.

They didn't have to wait long before the Ardeni man and woman stood up with the Cadwalli, and they all shook hands. As the Cadwalli led them to the door, Victor heard him say, "I'll have that wagon ready for you in just a few days. I've got my top man, Ornuf, applying the lacquer tomorrow!" After he'd closed the door behind his customers, he turned to Victor and Thayla and said, with a strange goat-faced smile, "I'm Bernale! Welcome to my shop. Would you come sit by my desk? The little one is welcome to stay there and eat more cookies."

Victor stood up and walked to the desk while Thayla spoke quietly to Deyni. "It's good to meet you, Bernale. Ganjoon sent us your way. I'm Victor, and that's Thayla." The chair was comfortable, if a bit narrow for Victor's frame. He wiggled back and forth to get settled, and the wood squeaked alarmingly.

"Oh? Ganjoon? What a great man, a great man! I'll be sure to thank him at our next thrampo game," the stocky little man said as he moved behind his desk. Victor knew it wasn't cool to laugh at a person for how they looked, but something about seeing a pudgy little goat man in a tight, gray, maroon-striped suit almost pulled a giggle out of him, especially as the man sat down and the buttons on his suit strained and tufts of fur poked out through the gaps.

"Thrampo?" Victor asked, clearing his throat to cover his amused expression.

"It's a dice game, Victor," Thayla said, sitting beside him.

"Well, what can I do for you today, fine folks? If Ganjoon sent you, I can only assume you're looking for something special!"

"We'll be traveling over the plains for a week or so, and, at some point, he'll be going further still." Thayla gestured to Victor, then continued, "We'd like sturdy conveyance that's comfortable for a child." Thayla nodded toward Deyni, then added, "But we'd like it to be swift. Ganjoon said your prices were reasonable and that you wouldn't try to cheat friends of his." Victor was glad Thayla had spoken up and just nodded his agreement.

Bernale leaned forward, gripping his two hairy hands together before him, and said, "Dear me! That implies that I might cheat someone who wasn't a friend! I would never! I'm as honest as they come. Why, just ask any of my former clients, of which there are many. Many!"

"I didn't mean to imply . . ." Thayla started.

"No, no. Nothing to worry about. No offense taken. Let's see here. I have quite a few vehicles that might suit you, and as you saw when you approached my office, I have the beasts to pull them! Would you mind answering a few questions so that I might narrow down my recommendations?"

"Sure," Victor said.

"Excellent! Firstly, will the three of you want to sleep within? Would you like the interior to be equipped with some necessities of comfort? I mean things such as a stovetop, cupboards, or a cold-cabinet? Why, I even have wagons with bathing facilities!"

Thayla looked at Victor and raised her eyebrows. "I didn't even think of all that," she said. "I think you need to make these decisions because, when you leave, you'll be taking it with you."

"Why are you so sure of that? You'll need a way to move with the clan when they go from camp to camp." Victor leaned back and studied Thayla's face. Was she acting strange about him leaving, or was it in his head?

"Well, that's true, but I'm sure we'll have a tent, and they rely on roladii, and I don't want Deyni and me to stand out." Thayla frowned, and Victor noticed she'd painted her lips black. He knew she'd done that back in the mines, but it seemed like a while since he'd noticed it.

Looking at her face, a strange memory came to him from when he'd first met her, and he'd thought the angle of her eyes made her look angry all the time. Looking at her now, he felt her eyes made her look clever and inquisitive. Her irises, deep red, almost purple, were full of mystery and depth, and he found himself looking away quickly, as if he'd been caught staring at something he shouldn't.

Victor cleared his throat and said, "Well, uh, Mr. Berlane . . ."

"Bernale, if you please," the little Cadwalli corrected.

"Oh, right, sorry about that. Well, I think we'd like something with those sorts of comforts, and of course, if it needs animals to pull it, we'll need those too. Can you give us an idea of the cost? Could you show us something without those, um, features and then something with all the cool shit?" Victor grimaced and said, "I mean all the extra stuff like stovetops and bathrooms."

"Naturally, naturally," Bernale said, then turned and lifted an empty picture from the shelf behind his chair. He placed it on his desk, facing Victor and Thayla, and said, "Look here at this frame, and I'll show you some of the conveyances I have in my warehouse." Victor felt a soft pulse of Energy, and then an image began to take shape in the picture frame. It was like looking through a window with a very faint tint of sepia. Nonetheless, a clear image of a classic black coach with big wheels and a bench for a driver appeared in the frame.

"This is a basic but very high-end coach. It's sturdy, self-repairing, and has Energy-driven compression pads between the axle and the passenger compartment, ensuring a smooth, comfortable ride. This coach will cost you an even two thousand beads. For a pair of roladii to pull it, add another two hundred beads." Victor watched as the image in the frame panned around the coach, showing all the angles, and then an image of the coach's interior appeared, showing off the two comfortable bench seats covered in plush red upholstery.

"All right. What else do you have?" Victor prompted, and then he and Thayla and Deyni, who came to sit on Thayla's lap, watched as the little salesman went through a series of ever-increasingly expensive coaches and wagons that appeared in the frame. Victor started to get bored after the third or fourth coach that was only slightly more ornate or had a few more minor enchantments, but when they got to larger wagons, he started to perk up. As Bernale began to show them wagons enchanted with dimensional magic to be bigger on the inside than the outside, his eyes began to bug out as he saw house-sized interiors for wagons that were just a bit larger than the first coach.

"What about dimensional containers? Can I go inside those wagons with my ring?" He gestured to one of his storage rings.

"Naturally! That's part of the expense. If we weren't trying to avoid such conflicts, we could make wagons with interiors the size of a royal palace!" Bernale said with an excited grin.

"All right," Victor said, glancing at Thayla and seeing some eagerness in her eyes. "You've got our interest. Show us a wagon like that, with most of the things you'd need to live comfortably on the road, but leave out all the extra ornate materials, filigrees, and shit."

"Things," Thayla said. "He means and 'things.'"

"I think I know just what you're looking for, Victor," Bernale said and channeled a bit of Energy into the frame. The view resolved into the shape of a wagon just a bit larger than a regular coach but more rectangular and painted in two-tone lacquer—the top half was royal blue which gradually darkened to black on the bottom half. "Beautiful, isn't it? It's very sturdy, too. Just like the coaches we sell, it's enchanted to self-repair and has Energy-driven compression pads. You'll hardly notice the bumps in the road! The interior has just what you're looking for, I think."

The image changed to the wagon's interior, and Victor smiled when he saw an ample space with two big beds on one end, separated by a curtain from a bathing area, complete with a brass bathtub and a nearby toilet. The center of the space held a long wooden table with two matching benches, and on the other side of that was a kitchen, complete with a long wooden counter lined with cupboards, an oven and stove, and a large cold-cabinet.

"Where does the toilet flush? What about the bath? Where's the water?"

"You'll love this, Victor," Bernale said. "The water is stored in a dimensional container attached outside the living space. It's very densely enchanted and can hold many thousands of gallons. The toilet flushes into a similar, smaller space with an outlet into an incineration chamber. All waste is dispersed as smoke, but only when the wagon travels at speed."

"That is fucking cool," Victor said softly, leaning forward to admire the image in the frame again. "All right, Bernale. What's this going to cost?"

"This wagon, with the bare-bones interior and the simple two-tone lacquer exterior, costs thirteen thousand beads," Bernale said, his voice quiet and his eyes slightly downcast as though he didn't expect his customers to be excited about the price.

"Hmm," Victor said, rubbing at his chin. "All right, and what about some animals to pull it? I know roladii are two hundred, right? Isn't that what he said, Thayla?" She nodded, and Bernale did as well. "How about something faster than roladii? Lam has some kind of antelope pulling her coach."

"Those are vidanii, Victor," Thayla said, shaking her head.

"Right! Anything like that, Bernale?"

"Well, yes, and they are fabulous animals, quite pleasant in demeanor and fast. I'd happily sell you a pair of them for only two thousand beads!" Bernale leaned forward, clearly starting to feel that he was about to make a big sale.

"Ten times as much as a roladii?" Thayla asked, shaking her head.

"It does seem like a big jump," Victor added.

"The vidanii cannot be bred in captivity! Each one has to be taken in the wild, and they don't run anywhere near here. I'm sorry, but the price is fair."

"You have this ready to go now?" Victor asked.

"Victor! That's a lot of money," Thayla said.

"I certainly do," Bernale said at the same time.

"Give us a minute alone, please, Bernale," Thayla said, shifting Deyni in her lap. The little girl was sitting there, staring into the crystal of her necklace, either bored or tired. Victor couldn't tell.

"Oh, yes. Of course, of course." Bernale stood up and started to move around his desk toward the door, but he glanced nervously at Thayla and said, "If I might ask, did you mention that you know Captain Lam?"

"That's right," Victor said.

"Well, I sold her those vidanii, and, well, if you're friends with the captain, I'd love to offer you a ten percent discount. Please keep that in mind while you deliberate." He sketched a bow, and Victor almost lost his cool again, seeing the pudgy little goat-like man bend and imagining the strain on his tight striped slacks. When he'd stepped out of the office, Thayla started to speak at the same time as Victor.

"I think that wagon is cool as hell . . ." he said.

"I hope you're not buying this to prove something . . ." Thayla said.

"Prove what?" he asked with a frown.

"I don't know," Thayla said. "I guess that was stupid."

"I really do just think it's cool. That room in the wagon is as big as my *abuela's* house! How cool would it be to just cruise along in our wagon, and when we decide to call it a day, we just go inside, and we're in there?" He pointed at the image still in the picture frame.

"I think it's very nice, Victor, but do you really need something like that? Or are you, I don't know, doing it for Deyni and me?"

"Nah, relax, Thayla. I don't have some kind of hidden motive here. I just think it'll be nice to go camping in style for a change."

Thayla looked into Victor's eyes for a long moment, and he enjoyed the opportunity to look in the depths of hers, noting all the interesting patterns and colors within. Then she sighed and said, "Well, I guess we're going to have a fun trip out to the Shadeni camp, Deyni." Thayla grinned and kissed the top of her daughter's head.

"That's the spirit," Victor said, smiling. "Hey, Bernale!" he called. "Come in here! Let's talk about that discount . . ."

7

ONE WAY OR ANOTHER

Victor couldn't help the grin on his face as he drove his new wagon down the southern road out of Gelica. The vidanii were fast when he gave them their head, and the wagon was smooth as butter on the dirt road despite its big, old-fashioned-looking wheels. The Energy-powered shock absorbers the salesman had raved about were working hard to prove he hadn't been full of shit.

Even more pleasing to Victor, the driver's bench was designed much more like a luxury auto seat than an old-timey coach bench. The leather-clad seat wrapped around his prodigious frame comfortably, supporting his back and providing plenty of room for him to stretch his legs forward. Though to get entirely comfortable, he found himself alternating feet up over the box-like enclosure, so he tended to have one leg stretched out and hanging in the breeze.

It wasn't like driving a car—he figured the wagon topped out at around thirty miles per hour, and most of the time, he took it quite a lot slower than that. Still, it beat the hell out of walking, and the vidanii had endurance that bordered on the mythical. Bernale had sold Victor a dimensional bag filled with feed for the animals and shown him a built-in drinking trough that pulled out from the front of the wagon. The trough was fed from the same reservoir dimensional container as the rest of the facilities on the wagon's interior. Bernale insisted it would be years before Victor had to fill it again.

They'd picked up Rhessa just outside the southern gate. She'd been sitting on a short stone wall surrounding a message board covered with flyers describing jobs and special sales and everything else you might find in a newspaper. When Victor saw it, he'd thought about how different life was in a place with no internet or instant messaging, and then he wondered if some Energy-powered alternative could be developed. He'd decided that it was a problem too big for his plate at the moment, but an interesting thing to think about nonetheless.

Rhessa had looked irritated and wore a heavy scowl when Victor rolled up in the wagon. When he told her that Thayla and Deyni were inside waiting for her, she'd slapped a rolled-up parchment in his hand with a huff and gone inside. The parchment had proven to be a map to Tellen's campsites, and Victor had studied it briefly before storing it away.

The sound of the hatch opening behind him brought Victor back into the present, and he looked around to see Thayla poking her head out. Victor knew she was standing on a ladder near the living compartment's kitchen, and he grinned at her when she hollered, "Are you going to drive all day, or would you like a break?"

"I'm not tired yet," he laughed.

"Well, if you want a break, let me know. I could use one. A break, I mean," she said more quietly.

"Oh? Your friend seemed grumpy. Is she giving you shit about something?" Part of Victor heard his words and how uncouth he was and cringed, and another part just laughed and said, "this is who I am." He felt he'd gone a long way over the last months to speak more clearly and with a broader vocabulary. Still, he also happened to enjoy saying certain words and phrases and wondered why he should change everything about himself, especially when he was with people who cared about him.

"She's upset that we left Gelica in such a hurry. She was enjoying Lam's estate. Now I'm dragging her to a campground to live with roving hunters." Thayla's face was pained, and Victor figured she'd been getting an earful for the last few hours while he drove.

"Sorry, Thayla. That sucks." He shrugged—what else could he say?

"Very helpful." She snorted and descended back into the wagon's interior, letting the lacquered wooden hatch fall with a satisfying *thunk*.

Victor drove the wagon through the farmlands south of Gelica for most of the afternoon, and when he came to a crossroads that led away to the east on a much narrower, more overgrown road, he turned that way. According to the map from Lam, Tellen's autumn camp was in that direction, and if he were right, this was the road he'd need to follow for a day or two before turning south again on a much smaller road still—on the map, it was just a faint dotted line.

He'd stopped twice in the afternoon to water the vidanii and brush their sweaty fur under their harnesses. Bernale had insisted that the animals were much more evolved than roladii and that they sustained themselves on ambient Energy to a much greater degree, much like higher-level people. Bernale had nodded to Victor as though he were an example of the phenomenon, and it had given Victor pause—how obvious was it that he'd advanced his race and achieved Tier Three with his level?

A bump jostled him and brought his thoughts back to the present, and he realized he'd just driven through a deep rut—one that the magical shocks couldn't fully compensate for. He smiled, thinking about how awesome the wagon was, which opened a whole other can of worms in his mind. Why had he spent such a chunk of his fortune on a fucking wagon? He knew Thayla thought he was trying to impress her or Deyni, but Victor didn't think that was it. No, he'd wanted it when he'd seen the inside—how comfortable and secure it had seemed.

When he thought about that feeling, he came to the conclusion that he'd been homeless since he arrived in this world, and this wagon gave him a sort of home, mobile though it was. Victor had been forced to sleep in cots, on the ground, in filthy, bloodstained hay. He'd shared a home with other captives, slept on the run, in dungeons, under the sky, or around campfires. The idea of having a place of his own was tremendously appealing, despite its cost and potential impracticality. No, he hadn't done this for Thayla.

The sun was starting to dip low in the west when he saw a copse of short, bushy, blue-leafed trees not far from the track, and he decided to pull the wagon into their cover for the night. Thin ruts through the grass told the tale of other travelers with similar ideas in the past. Victor followed the old trail around the clump of trees and then into a cleared area at the center. A ring of stones surrounding some ashes occupied the center of the clearing, with dried and cracked logs spread about, probably once used for seating.

Victor pulled on the reins, bringing the vidanii to a halt, and hopped down from the driver's bench. Bernale had taken the time to explain the harnesses and hitches for the big, docile creatures, and Victor followed his instructions painstakingly, using Gorz as a cheat. He wasn't sure he'd remember which buckles to remove first, where to stand to avoid a kick or stomp, how to operate the feeding trough, where to hook their leads for the night, and every other little detail without the amulet's help. "Thanks for the help, Gorz."

"It's what I'm here for," the amulet said, managing to sound rather put out, even with his inability to modulate his tone.

"You mad about something, Gorz?" Victor asked.

"No, Victor. I'm just sorry to see us fleeing civilization again without my having read even one book."

"Yeah, I guess I kinda fucked that up, didn't I? I should have bought some books to keep in the wagon. Maps, too. I promise I'll work on acquiring some of those sorts of things soon, all right?"

"I'll look forward to it," the amulet replied, and Victor thought it sounded a little less peeved, but he figured ninety percent of the emotion he heard from Gorz was due to his own projecting.

"We're stopping?" Thayla asked, head poking out through the main wagon door.

"Yeah, unless you want to really hurry and travel through the night . . ." Victor let his thought trail off, hoping Thayla took the hint that he didn't want to do that.

"No, this is good. Why don't you come in and get some rest? Rhessa is making soup. I'll watch the wagon for a few hours." Thayla hopped down and walked toward the front of the wagon, where Victor gently brushed one of the vidanii as it snuffled around in its feeding trough. Her head barely came up to the animal's shoulder as she reached up and scratched her nails through its short rust-red fur. The animal snuffled and stamped, enjoying the sensation, at least as far as Victor could tell.

"Think we should name them?" he asked.

"Why not? People name their roladii."

"Well, while you're on watch, try to come up with some ideas. Maybe Deyni will come out and give you some help." Victor held the brush out to Thayla, and when she took it, he started toward the door to the wagon.

"Wait! Why should we think of the names? They're your beasts!" Thayla asked, moving to the other vidanii and starting to brush its sweat-lathered rump.

"I've only ever had dogs and cats as pets. These things ain't no *perritos*! I've no idea what to call an animal this size!" He laughed, shaking his head as he climbed inside. The wagon's interior was fairly bare-bones, just as Bernale had said, though the materials used in its construction were rich and warm, and Victor felt his smile spreading as he looked around and breathed in the scent of homemade soup.

Lightly stained hardwood floors, white-painted wainscoting, and plaster walls gave the space an airy, beach cabin sort of feel, and the sparse furniture made it more spacious than it really was. The coolest thing, in Victor's mind, were the windows and skylights that let in a lot of the light from outside. The tricky thing about them was that they appeared much smaller on the wagon's exterior, and the glass was so dark that you couldn't see through it.

Deyni was sprawled on one of the two beds, drawing in a leather-bound notebook, and Rhessa turned to him with a smile, saying, "Hey, about time you took a break! Soup soon." Victor wanted to remark about her change of demeanor but figured it wouldn't be wise to bring up how she'd been crabby earlier.

After he'd eaten some soup—a deliciously rich sausage and root vegetable affair, seasoned with herbs Victor couldn't even name—he decided to try to take a nap. He heard Deyni go outside to hang out with her mother, and he saw Rhessa doing some sort of needlework at the table, and then he was out, more tired than he'd realized.

When he woke, some hours later, Rhessa and Deyni were sleeping in the other bed, and the Energy lamps were turned down to just a dim glow. Victor stood, picked up Lifedrinker, and quietly made his way outside. For some reason, he was feeling some dread, and he felt an unreasonable amount of relief when he saw Thayla sitting on a log near a small, flickering fire she'd built in the old campsite. "Hey," he said. "What time is it?"

"I'm not sure, but somewhere around midnight, I'd guess. You drove all day. If you want to keep sleeping, that's fine," Thayla said, poking a stick around in the coals of the fire.

"Nah, I feel great. You should get some sleep!"

"If you're sure, I will. Hey, Deyni and I came up with some names for your beasts, but you have to hear them from her. She has a few ideas for you to choose from!" Thayla said, standing up and brushing the dust from her butt.

"Ha, hell yeah. I knew she'd have a good idea or two. Your friend made some good soup. Did you get a bowl?"

"Yes. I think she's forgiven me for uprooting her life with Deyni. We had a good talk, and when I told her more about my plans and about Oynalla, she started to see how it would be good for Deyni." Thayla had moved closer to Victor as she spoke, and he was surprised when she stepped even closer and pulled him into a hug, resting her head against his chest. "Thanks for everything, Victor," she said softly. "Good night." She gave him another squeeze and then hurriedly climbed the steps into the wagon.

"Night . . ." Victor called after her as she disappeared within. Oynalla's words from his spirit walk came back to him, and he wondered if he was doing something wrong. He definitely had feelings for Thayla, but Oynalla was right—he didn't want to settle down with the hunters, and he didn't want to hurt Thayla by starting something he wasn't going to stick around to finish. "Fuck," he muttered as he moved over to the fire and sat down on the log Thayla had vacated. He picked up the stick she'd dropped and poked at the coals in frustration.

"Trouble, warrior?" asked a silky, feminine voice from the shadows of the nearby trees. Victor exploded into action, leaping to his feet, ripping Lifedrinker through her loop and into his hands, and casting Globe of Insight, overcharging it with Energy so that it illuminated the clearing like a floodlight. The rich white light blasted the shadows away from the trees and revealed a Ghelli, hunched down, shielding her eyes from the blazing orb. Her entire form was bathed white from the light, so, as Victor studied her, it took him a moment to realize he was wrong—she was a Naghelli.

Victor glared around the clearing, wondering if more of them were lurking around, but he didn't see anything in the sparsely wooded grove. The woman before him was crouched low, still shielding her eyes, when she said, "There's no need for that axe, warrior. I'm only here to talk. Please, if you wouldn't mind dimming that light a bit, I'd appreciate it."

"Make it quick, Naghelli," Victor said, pulling back on the surge of Energy he was pouring into his orb. It dimmed significantly, more like a floating lamp than a stadium floodlight, and the woman sighed in relief, standing up and lowering her hand. Victor immediately recognized her—she was the Naghelli who'd spoken to him as he was about to leave Belikot's dungeon. The one whose husband he'd split with Lifedrinker. He held his axe firmly in his hands, watching her warily.

"Do you remember me, warrior?" She, perhaps self-consciously, reached a hand up to the glittering ruby necklace that hung in the deep, open neckline of her silky black blouse.

"Yeah," Victor said, alert in the light of his orb, straining to hear or sense any sort of ambush that might be coming. The woman was staring at him, her dark eyes hard to read, but the flesh around them expressive enough. She looked tired and stressed, the bluish tint around her eyes dark and more like a bruise than a hint of color. Her silver hair, still long and shimmering in his light, looked frazzled and slightly unkempt. Perhaps the most significant sign of her distress could be seen in her wings—when Victor had last seen her, the orange spots on their gossamer surface had blazed and glowed, but they now appeared dull.

"Vellia," she said, nodding, "and you are Victor. I haven't forgotten."

"Vellia," Victor repeated, unable to think of anything other than how like Rellia it sounded. He shook his head, "Well? What do you want?"

"May I sit?" She gestured to a log on her side of the fire.

Victor nodded, but he cast Inspiring Presence. He knew it would be evident to her that he did it, but he didn't care. He wanted to be alert and ready in case something sneaky was going on. As the inspiration-attuned Energy poured forth into his pathways and affected his mind, everything, as always, seemed clearer. He felt as if he could see further into the shadows around the camp, even with his light dimmed down. He noticed how Vellia limped slightly as she stepped to the log, but more than that, he saw how she inhaled deeply and seemed to relax when she felt the effects of his spell—she was benefiting from his aura.

"Thank you," she said, as though he'd done it to help her. "I feel much better. Victor, I've had a harrowing journey and a difficult time finding you. I know you've no reason to feel sympathy for me, but I want you to know that I'm here, not to cause you trouble, but to ask for your help."

"Huh. Seems like asking someone for help can cause plenty of trouble." He still loomed over her, standing near the coals of the fire, Lifedrinker menacingly hanging before him.

"Warrior, our master has been slain." She said it as if it was something that should shock him or bring him to his knees. So full of desperation was her voice that Victor did feel a little twinge of sympathy, but his overall reaction was to snort.

"Belikot?" he asked, remembering how the Naghelli had freaked out when he said the name in the dungeon. She flinched, but she didn't caution him this time. "Well? What do you want me to do?"

"We Naghelli are under a geas placed upon us by Belikot centuries ago." She looked small and pitiful. Though she tried to look into Victor's eyes, he could see that it was difficult for her to look up at him with his orb floating behind him. He took some pity and sat down on a log across from her, still holding Lifedrinker over his knees.

"Go on," he said.

"It's our fault—mine, my sisters, and my brothers—those of us who served him. He forged the contract, but we signed it. We put our Energy into it and allowed it to happen. We gained much from Belikot at first—power, victories, and a haven after the war. Still, his demands became more and more difficult to bear. I won't . . . I can't go into it all, Victor, but even people who've done wrong, who've hurt others, don't deserve to have some evils visited upon them. Can you see?"

Her dark eyes had pooled with liquid, and Victor realized she was about to start crying. Victor was having a hard time even understanding what she was talking about. Was she saying that Belikot abused the Naghelli? "Look, I'm sorry for your trouble, but what do you want, exactly?"

"Though Belikot perished, the geas still holds. There must be fragments of his soul still lingering in the world. We feel . . . compelled to find and help him, though we have no way to do so. It's killing us, Victor!"

"How do you know he died?" Victor asked, wondering how she'd react if she realized he was the one that had done him in.

"He was spirit walking—seven of us were chosen, as usual, to guard his body. You see, when he performed a spirit walk, he'd often be vulnerable like that for many hours, and so we stood, weapons drawn, ready to defend him, locked deep in his sanctum. He'd been gone many hours when his body began to thrash. It was like watching a person drown. We did everything we could, Victor, but his spirit never returned, and though we poured healing draughts down his throat, his heart stopped beating, his breathing ceased, and his body died.

Still, we didn't give up on him. We kept his body cold, waiting for his spirit to find its way back, but it never did. We all felt compelled to help him. We feel the *need* to find him somehow, to heal him, and none of us know how! Are we supposed to find his other spirit shards? Are there any more? We thought he'd gathered them back to himself!"

"Um, how long ago did this happen? Why did you come to me?"

"I marked you well, Victor, just as your little Shadeni friend told me to. I used an artifact of Belikot's, one that he'd flay me alive for touching, to see past the ward that you wear, the one that blocks out scrying. I had one chance to come to you, Victor, because the artifact had but one use. With dangerous potions fueling me, keeping me running, swifter even than your vidanii, I ran to you."

"Yeah, but why?" Victor repeated.

"When you parted ways with me, you said you didn't think you'd be fond of Belikot because of the 'versions of my master' you'd met."

"Ahh, shit. I was exaggerating, Vellia—I only met one version of him. The one that took over Thayla's body for a while. I, uh, expelled him."

"To where, Victor? Where is that shard of his soul?" She clasped her hands before her and stared at him, something like hope mixed with despair in her eyes.

"Vellia, how many Naghelli serve Belikot?" Victor asked, his mind racing furiously, trying to figure out how to handle the situation. He didn't think it would go well for anyone if he gave the Naghelli the fucked-up shard of Belikot that he had in his dimensional bag. "What about his phylactery—could that have something to do with your, um, what do you call it? Geas?"

"There are thirty-seven of us left, Victor. Please! Tell me what you know of the shard! The phylactery is of no use! Belikot took the shards from it and reabsorbed them—that's how he was able to start spirit walking again."

"So you guys feel compelled? Like you have to find his missing shard or shards?"

"Yes! The geas begins to affect our ability to absorb Energy. We'll wither and die if we don't figure out what to do!"

"What about if Belikot had died like you thought he did? Would the, um, agreement be over?"

"It should be, yes. The fact that we all still suffer tells us that some remnant of Belikot lingers, and we must find a way to help him! Will you please tell me where you left the shard?" Victor looked at her pleading face, the pain in her eyes, and he grunted and stood up. He turned and began to pace back and forth between the wagon and the fire, glancing at Vellia every few steps.

A big part of him wanted to help her. He didn't know why, though the cynic in him thought it had something to do with her pretty face and how her blouse exposed more of her chest than he was used to seeing. He allowed his mind to wander down the path of possibilities.

If he gave her the insane, cruel Belikot shard in the skull, and they somehow managed to get him into his old body or a new one, what then? That shard of the Death Caster definitely didn't like Victor, but it didn't know that he had killed the greater version of itself. Not even Vellia knew that. Would it be so terrible if this little group of Naghelli had a weakened version of their master back?

He paced back and forth a few more times, glowering at Vellia, and she remained silent, apparently able to discern that he was wrestling with a dilemma and not wanting to sway him in the wrong direction. Finally, he growled, shifted Lifedrinker into just his right hand, and said, "I'm about to show you something. If you want my help, you have to promise to stay seated and not try anything. Use your words only. Got it?"

"I swear it, warrior!" she breathed, her eyes suddenly hopeful. Victor reached into the dimensional bag tied to his belt and took out Belikot's skull. He stared into the eye sockets, daring the weakened spirit within to try something, but they stared back at him, lifeless, with no blue flames announcing Belikot's presence. Still, Vellia gasped, and he saw her tense and start to stand.

"Stay fucking seated!" he growled, allowing some rage-attuned Energy to flare forth. She dropped back onto the log, but her eyes tracked the skull like a terrier watching a rat. "This what you're looking for?" he asked, setting the skull on the log where he'd been sitting.

"Yes! I can feel it! He's in there! Let me take it, Victor. Please! You won't hear from us again."

"This thing's been in my dimensional container for weeks. Belikot was already an asshole; how do you think he's going to be as an insane asshole?"

Vellia flinched at his words, and he saw a shadow flit behind her eyes, but she said softly, "It doesn't matter, Victor. If we don't try to help him, we'll suffer and die."

"Now that you see this in front of you, you know what to do? To satisfy the geas thing, I mean?"

"Yes! I feel compelled to help this shard of Belikot. To help it recover as much of its former self as possible . . ." she trailed off, her eyes going wide as Victor lifted Lifedrinker high. "What are you doing?" she screamed as he brought the axe down on the skull, not as hard as he could—he didn't want to split the skull and send the halves flying. No, he wanted Lifedrinker to get a good long drink, and he didn't want to give that bit of spirit an easy way out.

"I'm helping you, one way or another," Victor grunted as Lifedrinker sank effortlessly into the smooth yellow bone of the skull. He grinned, feeling her vibrate hungrily as thin blue veins of Energy began to spread along the split halves of bone toward her blade. Movement from Vellia caught his eye, and he cast Project Spirit, pushing twisted inspiration Energy at her, and growling, "Sit down!"

Vellia sobbed and fell forward on her hands and knees, and Victor saw the long, onyx-handled dagger clutched in her hand, though she made no move to swing it. She seemed defeated and broken, sobbing in the dirt, inches from the hot embers of the fire. As Lifedrinker shuddered, finished with her feast, and the yellow skull began to crumble into dust, Vellia ceased her shuddering sobs and collapsed the rest of the way to the ground. Though she barely breathed, Victor saw that the orange spots on her wings had begun to glow, ever so faintly, once again.

8

TO HUNT THE HUNTERS

It wasn't long before Vellia started to stir. Victor hadn't touched her or the knife still loosely clasped in her hand, though he sat and watched her closely, Lifedrinker still resting on his knees. He'd noted, with pleasure, that the axe had recovered part of one of her old Heart Silver veins from her recent feast. He figured she was about halfway back to her old glory already, and he knew that if he got a chance to do some real fighting, she'd bounce back even faster.

Vellia grunted, slowly pushing herself up so she could pull her knees under herself, sitting there next to the cold firepit, looking around in a bit of a daze. When her eyes fell on Victor and his axe, they narrowed in understanding. "You . . ." she started, then cleared her throat and tried again. "You could have been wrong. What if there'd been another shard? I'd have been no closer to solving my problem—the delay could have killed me and my kin."

"Well, there was no way I was giving you and your 'kin' the insane shard I had. I guess we lucked out, huh?" Vellia glanced down at her hand, still gripping her knife, and suddenly it was gone—stowed into some dimensional container, no doubt. Victor smiled and stood, slipping Lifedrinker into her loop. He held out a hand for Vellia, and the woman took it, allowing him to pull her to her feet. "What will you do now?"

"I don't know. My life has revolved around Belikot for so long . . . I'm too nervous about it to say I'm free. I suppose I must see what my brothers and sisters will do."

"Are they? I mean, are they really your brothers and sisters?"

"No. I use the term loosely—we consider each other family because there are so few of us. Some are related to me, though. Nephews or cousins . . . one niece. Horol and I had no children, and now he's gone . . ." she trailed off, eyes down, apparently not wanting to look at her husband's killer at that moment.

Victor sighed and said, "I'm sorry, Vellia, but I didn't start that fight."

"I know. I . . . we were foolish and cruel to attack you that way. We're not good people, Victor." Her eyes pooled with tears, and she shook her head, taking a step away from him. "We've done so many things in Belikot's service, so many things that were wrong. Some of us felt trapped and wanted a way out, but some enjoyed it. I fear there will be a reckoning—it's going to come to blows when we regather. My people are spread to the four winds, looking for a solution to our problem, but as they feel what I just felt, when they realize Belikot is no more, they'll return to the pocket realm, and I fear our numbers will dwindle even more."

"Really? Let me guess: you're one of the good Naghelli, one of the ones that hated working for Belikot?" Victor snorted, unable to keep a bit of a snarl out of his voice.

"No, Victor. Not good. Perhaps not evil, though. I swear to you: my freedom will be spent atoning. I'm going to take this chance you've given me, and I'm going to help those Naghelli who feel as I do to slay the others, and then we're going to spend the next hundred years mending our souls." She wiped her eyes and performed a bow, so formal and elegant that Victor felt the scowl leave his face, and he nodded to her.

"Well, I wish you luck, Vellia. I hope there are more 'not evil' Naghelli than the other kind, and I hope you can think of a way to do some good in this world."

"I'll tell you now, Victor; we will win. Kethelket is among the Naghelli that feel as I do, and he's the greatest swordsman to walk this world in three hundred years." She reached up to her neck and unfastened her necklace, holding the silver chain and the ruby as large as Victor's thumbnail out to him. "Please take this," she said.

"You don't need to give me anything." Victor kept his hands by his sides.

"Please! I'm attuned to this gem, Victor. Should you need to find me for any reason, simply hold it in your hand and think of me. It will connect us—you'll sense where I am, and I'll sense that you're looking for me."

"Uh, and what about the other way around? Can you find me as long as I have this thing?"

"No! I wouldn't give a gift with thorns." Vellia scowled, her purple-stained lips pressed in a thin line. "It won't work unless you hold it and activate it as I described. It's inert otherwise. If you don't trust me, have the witch among the Shadeni examine it."

"How do you know about Oynalla?" Victor took a step back.

"I lingered here, watching your friend and her daughter while I waited for you to come out of the wagon. I heard many things about your plans." Vellia shrugged, still holding out the ruby.

"All right, give it here," Victor grunted, reaching out and snatching the necklace. Vellia smiled, her face lighting up with the expression. Victor thought she looked a hundred percent better already than when she'd first come out of the shadows to speak to him.

"You're looking better. Your wings are glowing again."

"Thank you, Victor! I won't forget this debt I owe you. I hope we meet again soon, but if we don't, I wish you bright moons and a swift blade." She bowed again, and then, to Victor's amazement, she seemed to shimmer, and then she was gone, another shadow among the trees, flitting away faster than his eyes could track.

"Neat trick, that," Victor grunted, tucking the ruby necklace into a pocket under his ringmail vest.

When the eastern sky lightened, Victor hitched up the vidanii and resumed his travel toward the sunrise. He'd been on the road for nearly an hour before Thayla popped her head out of the top hatch and asked, "Didn't want to have some breakfast together? Why don't you pull over and come in? Rhessa cooked up some eggs, and I opened a jar of fermented veggies I bought in Gelica."

"Fermented veggies?" Victor pulled a face, but when Thayla just nodded, smiling, he shrugged and pulled the wagon to the side of the road, really just a slightly grassier spot without the ruts he'd been following. After applying the brake and softly telling the vidanii he'd be right back, he climbed through the hatch after Thayla.

The fermented veggies turned out to be peppers and root vegetables that tasted like spicy pickles to Victor. Rhessa was quick to point out that they weren't pickled, though, saying the fermentation made them taste that way but was a lot healthier. Victor shrugged, eating quite a load of them with his eggs. "Not bad," he said halfway through. "I feel like I could eat pretty much anything and be healthy, though, what with my attribute enhancements and everything."

"Probably," Thayla said. "Not everyone has as many racial advancements as you do, though. Some of us need to be careful about the junk we put into our bodies!" She glared at him pointedly, nodding toward Deyni, who, as usual, was copying Victor bite for bite.

"Right! I always eat what's good for me because it helps me grow big and strong!" Victor flexed an enormous arm and made a snarling face at Deyni. She giggled and copied him, growling fiercely. "That's a girl! Eat those eggs, and soon you'll be bigger than your mama!" Rhessa laughed from the kitchen, where she was washing some plates. "Hey, Deyni, I heard you had some names for my vidanii! Lay 'em on me!"

"Lay 'em . . ." Thayla started to say, but Deyni caught Victor's meaning and interrupted.

"I have four names! You have to pick two!"

"All right. I'm ready!" Victor took a massive bite of eggs and chewed them noisily while staring at Deyni.

"Cloud, Starlight, Thistle, and Swiftwind!" Deyni said, speaking softly, almost reverently.

"Oh, my!" Victor said, rubbing at his chin. "Those are great names! I have a question, though, that might help me decide."

"What?" Deyni asked, her voice hushed to match Victor's conspiratorial tone.

"Do you know if they're boys or girls?"

"Ancestors!" Thayla laughed, shaking her head. "Victor! One of them is a boy, and one is a girl! Even Deyni saw that!"

"Well, excuse me for not checking out the animals' equipment right away!"

"Hush, mama!" Deyni said. "Victor, now you know, what names do you like?"

"Well, for the girl, I absolutely think Starlight is the way to go. As for the boy, I think Thistle fits. Starlight and Thistle! What a pair!" Victor didn't think any of the names were bad, but he did think those two had a nice ring.

"I knew he'd pick Starlight," Thayla said, nudging Deyni.

"It was my favorite name for the girl! I saw how the stars were reflected in her big eyes!" Deyni smiled to herself and resumed eating her breakfast.

As they traveled over the plains, ever eastward, Victor saw fewer and fewer stands of trees, and they hardly passed any other travelers. Every now and then, though, he'd come upon some people walking on foot, sometimes leading pack animals. Very few of them seemed interested in any small talk, and the most he tended to get out of them was a "safe travels" or some commentary on the weather or the state of the road. Toward midafternoon he came to a narrow, barely discernable track peeling away to the south, and he stopped the wagon to consult his map.

Victor couldn't be sure—he'd passed quite a few dirt tracks that didn't seem to go anywhere—but this one was roughly in the right area, if he was gauging their speed correctly, so he turned down it, following it as it skirted the slope of a low but massive hill. When they finally rounded the hump of the hill, and its far slope fell away before them, Victor stopped the wagon again to take in the breathtaking view.

The grass changed in hue, from pale green to more of a blue as the elevation fell away, and beneath the gray skies, filled with clouds and late afternoon light, it was easy to imagine he was looking at an ocean of water, not a grassland. He thought he saw, far in the distance, almost impossibly thin and faint, a darker line that might be a forest. "Or it might be some kind of mirage, like you see in the desert, for all I know," he said to the vidanii as they snuffled at the cool air. "What's that you say, Starlight? Did Thistle fart again? You're a naughty boy, Thistle!" He laughed and gave the reins a light switch, getting the animals moving again.

They traveled over those grassy plains for two more days, stopping early on the second day to wait out a storm from inside the wagon. As the fat rain droplets had begun to fall, Victor had unhitched the vidanii and hooked them each to long leads so they could move about and graze—Bernale had extolled the animals' toughness, saying they could weather almost any sort of storm, be it rain or snow, so he didn't worry too much about them while he and the others sat in comfort within the wagon, eating soup and playing dice games.

After the storm, Victor savored the brisk fresh air when he drove the wagon out. He'd brushed the vidanii, smoothing out their rough short hair and making sure it was dry, and they hadn't appeared any worse for the wear. The animals seemed invigorated by the weather, and Victor decided to give them their head, urging them on with gentle switches of the reins and whooping exuberantly as the wind rushed through his hair and past his ears.

It was during that morning sprint when Victor made first contact with Tellen's clan. He was barreling down the barely visible track, laughing and bouncing, when two figures stood up from the grass, not a hundred yards distant, bows with arrows knocked and drawn.

"Whoa!" Victor called, pulling on the reins, and the big vidanii snorted and began to slow but still moved too fast for the wagon to be stopped before he arrived at the bow-wielding hunters. "Whoa!" Victor called again, pulling harder on the reins and squeezing the wagon's brake handle. This time the animals dug in their heels, ripping up the soft grassy soil and sliding to a halt a good twenty yards before the hunters.

"Hello!" Victor called. He was reasonably sure they were Tellen's people—they wore the beaded leather and had their long black hair pulled into braids as he'd seen on his earlier visit. "Like Thayla," he said, snorting at the obvious observation.

"You're riding into our territory, traveler," said the wiry Shadeni man on the right.

"Yeah, that's the idea. I'm Victor. I'm here to see Tellen and Oynalla." As Victor spoke, the hunters lowered their bows, and the woman on the left laughed.

"I told you, Geng! How many pale people the size of a giant do you think there are?"

"Hey now," Victor said. "I'm not that pale!"

"She means you aren't red or blue; you're like a big Ghelli . . ." the man started to say, but Victor interrupted with a laugh.

"Nah, I know what you mean. No worries. So, is the camp nearby?" As he was speaking, Thayla poked her head out of the hatch.

"Why'd we stop?"

"I think we're almost there," Victor said, gesturing to the two hunters.

"Yes, Victor, friend of Tellen. I'll guide you in," the man named Geng said, whistling shrilly. A moment later, a roladii, fat and gray and maned with orange and red feathers, came charging out of the tall grass to the west. The hunter mounted and started trotting the funny two-legged bird-lizard off to the east. "Come, follow me if that wagon can handle a few bumps!"

Victor glanced back at Thayla with a grin. "Better hold on!" he said, then he clicked the reins and started the wagon through the grass, chasing after Geng and his roladii. The two vidanii had no trouble matching the rolling gait of the roladii, and Victor actually had to pull back on the reins a couple of times to keep the spirited animals from trying to overtake it. They ran like that for fifteen or twenty minutes, then Geng slowed down, and Victor saw why—they'd reached a secondary watch line, and several hunters stood up from the grass to wave them through, and at least one of them recognized Victor because he whooped out a hello.

It wasn't long after that when the tents came into view, and their telltale smoke lines drifted into the blue sky. Victor drove the wagon to the edge of the camp, then set the brake and hopped down, smiling at the small crowd of Shadeni that had gathered around. He saw quite a few children who seemed excited by his appearance and the sight of the wagon and the vidanii. Victor figured any chance to see some animals other than roladii was a special time for the kids.

"Victor!" said a scratchy but cheerful woman's voice, and he looked over the crowd to see Chandri making her way toward him. Meanwhile, the wagon's door had opened, and Thayla climbed down the steps, Deyni in her arms. "Thayla!" Chandri called as she pushed into the little clearing at the center of the crowd. "What's this? Some sort of Ardeni wagon? Come, Thayla, you know the Shadeni don't need such things!" Her smile and twinkling eyes gave away the fact that she was just teasing, but Thayla bristled nonetheless.

"Blame Victor! I tried to talk him out of it!"

"I like the wagon, Mommy!" Deyni said, squirming to be let down.

"Who's this then?" Chandri asked, squatting in her colorful leather clothing to get a better look at Deyni.

"Deyni!" the little girl said, thumping her chest proudly.

"That's my Berserker apprentice," Victor said with a chuckle.

"Oh? I see! Fierce!" Chandri said, grinning and holding out a fist for Deyni to punch. "My father is hunting," Chandri said, and Victor thought he saw some unease in her eyes as she glanced around, but then it clicked—she'd called Tellen 'father,' and that was new. She was probably still nervous about using the term openly.

"When do you expect him?" Victor asked.

"Oh, tomorrow or the next day. Oynalla waits for you, though. She told me to be sure you bring your daughter, Thayla."

"All right, can you show me where to park the wagon? I'm going to be staying a little while, I think." Victor gestured behind him at the shiny lacquered blue and black wagon and realized it stood out like a sore thumb in the camp of canvas tents and mud-bricked buildings. Still, he grinned and said, "She's beautiful, isn't she?" He turned to Chandri and winked.

"Oh, sure! Beautiful, Victor, beautiful." She turned to the crowd and laughed, saying more loudly, "Isn't Victor's wagon pretty, everyone? Make sure you tell him how pretty it is!" Suddenly everyone was smiling and laughing, coming closer so they could look up at Victor and pat him on the shoulders, saying how lovely his wagon was. Victor laughed along with them, then hopped up into the driver's seat.

"Wait!" Thayla said. "Rhessa is coming out in a minute."

"Victor!" Chandri called. "Go around to the west edge of the camp, behind the sweat lodge. You'll see some spots between the other tents there. Also, even though your wagon is silly, I love your vidanii! Those are some wonderful beasts!" Chandri laughed and hoisted Deyni up into her arms and walked over toward Starlight, and Victor could hear Deyni telling her about the vidanii and how she'd named them. He heard the wagon door thud a moment later as Rhessa climbed out and closed it.

When Victor looked toward the motion and saw Thayla's friend, he was surprised to see the blue-skinned Ardeni wearing a leather vest, pants, and boots. More than that, her long, bright red hair was braided into plaits, much like Thayla's. She glanced around nervously, and Thayla said, "This is my good friend, Rhessa. She'll be staying with me—she's like another mother to Deyni."

Chandri smiled and reached out to clasp Rhessa's wrist, "Hello, cousin! It's been a while since we've had one of the Dreamer's children with us." Victor had no idea what that meant, and when he looked at Thayla with a questioning expression, she didn't notice him. He decided to ask about it later and clicked his tongue, just barely twitching the vidanii's reins.

The animals started up, moving gently toward the crowd, and the gathered people split, allowing him through. "I'll meet you by the sweat lodge and guide you to Oynalla's tent!" Chandri called after him. He waved acknowledgment, then flicked the reins again, letting the vidanii show off a little as they pulled him out into the grass and around the scattered tents.

He circled the camp, coming up on the far side, and the sweat lodge was easy to spot—a squat, broad, mud-bricked building with a central smokestack. It looked just like the one in the other camp. Victor found a wide open space between a couple of tents and parked the wagon.

While he waited for Chandri, he unhitched the vidanii and tethered them on long leads. He'd just finished up when the young Shadeni woman called out, her scratchy voice unmistakable, from near the sweat lodge, "This way, Victor." He gave Thistle a final pat and started toward her, and Chandri continued, "Thayla's already with Oynalla, but I got an earful for not bringing you right away. I don't know what's got her all worked up, but I haven't had her chase me with a stick like that since I was younger than Chala!"

"Oh, really?" Victor hurried his steps, falling in beside Chandri as she led him on a meandering path through the tents.

"Yes! It's funny because she acts like she knew you'd be here today. Did you speak to her spirit?" The way Chandri mentioned "speaking to her spirit" so nonchalantly caught Victor by surprise, but he figured it must be a difference in cultures. Here, in this camp, they respected Oynalla and her skills with spirit magic. It made sense that the Old Mother might have mentioned Victor's abilities—especially to Chandri, who treated the woman as a mother figure.

"A few days ago, but I didn't say anything about when we were coming." Victor shrugged.

"Well, she sees things. Don't think too much about it. There it is," Chandri said, pointing to the familiar red and yellow stained canvas tent. "I'll see you later, Victor." She paused and directed Victor's gaze between two tents toward the center of the camp. "If you go straight that way from Oynalla's tent, you'll find ours. Come to our fire tonight if you want—I'll cook something good."

"All right, thanks, Chandri. I guess it depends on what Oynalla has in store for me, but I'll try to come by."

"Good!" She smiled, her little animal tattoos crinkling around her eyes, and then she walked off with a short wave. Victor walked toward Oynalla's tent, and he wasn't surprised when the flap opened at his arrival and the old woman stood scowling at him.

"Hurry up, warrior! We have much to discuss and little time." She waved a hand, gesturing for him to come inside, and Victor quickened his pace, ducking low to slip through the opening.

"What's the emergency? How'd you know we were going to be here? I thought the wards we bought blocked your scrying!"

"Hush! Sit down! Let Oynalla speak!" She gestured to the furs piled around the center of her tent, and Victor saw that Thayla, Deyni, and Rhessa were already inside, though sitting together on a different pile of furs in the far corner of the space.

"Hi, Victor!" Deyni called out and nearly spilled a small wooden cup of steamy liquid she held. Thayla quickly steadied her hand, then touched a finger to her lips in the universal signal to be quiet.

"Yes, hush, for now, child," Oynalla said. "I have to speak to this warrior and send him on his way—he has an important quest."

"What?" Victor said, feeling a twinge of alarm.

"Sit, Victor!" Oynalla said, trying to push him toward the furs nearby but only succeeding in making herself grunt comically. Victor didn't want to antagonize her, so he sat down and waited for her to explain herself. "Good!" she said, heaving a deep breath and sitting down across from him with a loud grunt. "I didn't scry you, warrior. I have rituals to see portents. They're usually vague and hint at the weather, the movements of the herds, or some other mundane thing, but two nights ago, I had a very clear, very dire vision!" She paused to stare at him, perhaps to ensure he was listening.

"Go on!" he said. "I'm listening!"

"I saw Tellen and his band hunting something strange—a beast they didn't know. I watched them from the spirit plane, and I saw that they were fooled! The hunters were being hunted! Then I saw you coming to the camp, warrior, and I knew what must be done. You must find Tellen and make him see his folly. You must become the third hunter in the chain!"

"Oynalla, I want to do what you ask. I want to help, but how can I find Tellen? I'm not a tracker." Victor frowned, feeling agitated, as if he had to act immediately, but he had no idea what to do. Should he just charge off in the direction Tellen had gone hunting and hope for the best? "Do I just hope to get lucky?"

"Victor, if you would hush, you'd hear all of Oynalla's vision. I saw you, unmistakable figure that you are, hunting for Tellen, and you rode a great horned creature. At your back was one of ours, the girl, Chandri. She can track her father, warrior."

9

ANIMAL TAMING

When Oynalla said she'd "seen" him hunting Tellen from the back of a great horned beast, the first image that came to his mind was of Starlight and Thistle as he'd last seen them, quietly munching from their feeding trough. "I came here with a wagon pulled by two vidanii," Victor said quickly. "Did the horned creature I was riding look like that?"

"Show me," Oynalla said, climbing stiffly to her feet with several grunts of exertion. Victor tried to help her, but she swatted his hand away. "I need to work at it, warrior! If I don't do it on my own, will you be here to help me stand whenever I need?" She smiled at him, softening the words, and Victor backed up toward the tent flap, nodding. "Thayla, leave your girl here for now and go find Chandri. Bring her to Victor's wagon."

"She went to Tellen's tent," Victor said as Thayla ducked through the tent flap. "That way." He pointed in the direction Chandri had shown him.

"All right. Are you okay, Victor? This is all really sudden . . ." Thayla started to ask, but Oynalla was close on her heels and cut her off.

"Hush, daughter. He's meant for this sort of thing; don't put your worries onto him. Now hurry, get that little huntress!" She made a shooing gesture to Thayla and then took hold of Victor's elbow. "Take me to these vidanii of yours, Victor."

"Right," Victor said, turning and walking, as quickly as Oynalla's much smaller steps would allow, toward his wagon. When they came around the tent blocking the view of his little plot, and Oynalla laid eyes on the vidanii, she cackled, and her grip on his arm tightened significantly.

"That one!" she crowed, pointing to Thistle. "I recognize the white socks on his front feet!"

"You really saw me riding him?" Victor asked, looking at the big horned animal in a new light. He was bigger than any horse Victor had seen up close, but that wasn't saying much. In fact, when he thought about it, he realized he'd never seen a horse in person, only in VR. Still, Thistle's shoulders were almost as high as Victor was tall, and he knew he was pushing seven feet. "Do people do that? Ride vidanii?"

"You do!" Oynalla cackled. She let go of Victor's elbow and walked closer to the animals, and when she laid her hand on Thistle's rump and drew it along his side, he turned and snorted at her with his big, moist, black nose. "You're a big boy, aren't you? He's rich in Energy, Victor. The hunters here would do much for a mount like him. I warrant he's much faster than any roladii."

"Oh, they're fast, all right." Victor walked up beside her and rested his hand on the short rough fur of the animal. Thistle was almost uniformly rust-colored, though around his ears and horns it was darker, with little black hairs mixed in. Looking down at the animals' feet, he saw that Thistle's front feet were, indeed, the only ones with white fur. "His name's Thistle," Victor said, giving the animal a good scratch.

"You're off to a good start with him," Oynalla said. "He likes you, and he likes his name."

"Well, actually, I didn't . . ." Victor started to say, but Chandri's voice rang out in greeting, and Victor turned to see her and Thayla jogging toward the wagon.

"Good! Chandri, you and Victor must hunt for your father and his band. I've had a vision, and it's important that you leave soon."

"I'll get Boog," Chandri said, turning.

"Wait, girl!" Oynalla said, shaking her head and walking toward the two women. "I saw you riding with Victor on this beast, not your roladii," she said, pointing to Thistle.

"Really? Do you have riding tack for him, Victor?" Chandri walked toward Thistle, rubbing her chin. "I think I could ride him," she said, nodding.

"No, Victor was in control of the beast. You were riding behind him."

"Uh," Victor said, stepping closer to Chandri and Oynalla. "That's kind of going to be a problem. No, I don't have any riding tack, and I don't even know how to ride. I've never ridden a pony, let alone a *pinche* giant antelope!"

To Victor's amusement, Oynalla snorted in laughter, shaking her head. "It doesn't matter what you know. What matters is what I *saw*, warrior." She turned back to Chandri and said, "Thayla and I will go talk to Berset-dak about a saddle. You teach this giant how to ride." She smiled as Chandri nodded, clearly biting off a complaint by tightly pressing her lips closed. Chandri had dark burgundy, almost purple eyes like Oynalla, though hers seemed brighter, and when they squinted in annoyance, it was all too easy to read.

"Well," Chandri said, her scratchy voice low as she watched Oynalla and Thayla walk away between two tents, "tell me you at least have some Animal Taming."

"What? Not really—my *abuela* had two *perritos*, but I just played fetch with them now and then. They mostly slept and barked at me when I came home from school."

"No, the skill. Do you have any ranks in Animal Taming?"

Understanding dawned on Victor, and he shook his head. "No, Chandri. I've only been in this world a few months, and most of that time was spent fighting or traveling. I guess I could have learned at some point, but I didn't. I didn't even know it was a thing."

"Ancestors," Chandri said softly, and Victor couldn't tell if she was cursing or asking them for help. "Have you been taking care of these?" She pointed to the vidanii.

"Yes! I'm the one that's been feeding them and brushing them, well, for the most part." He felt he had to qualify the statement because Thayla and Deyni had also spent some time with the animals.

"That's a good start, at least. What do they like to eat?" Chandri moved over to the big animals. "Do you know which one you want to ride?"

"The male, um, Thistle." Victor ran a hand over Thistle's back and scratched at it gently. "They like their feed—I bought a ton of it, and they look forward to it every day."

"Good. Take his lead and move over there, away from the other, out into the grass." Chandri started walking to the area she'd gestured toward, and Victor turned back to Thistle.

"All right, boy, I don't know what's in store for us, but I think I might be about to learn to ride you. Be cool, all right?" he said, keeping his voice low as he untied his lead and started walking away from the wagon. Thistle followed him obediently, hardly needing any pressure on the loop of rope tied around his neck.

"It's good that you speak to him. Use his name as much as you can—it helps to trigger the skill."

"Trigger the skill?"

"Yes, have you learned any skills in this world? I think you must have, or you'd be dead."

"Yeah, lots of weapon skills and, I guess, my cultivation drill."

"Well, when you learned your weapon skills, were you eating soup?" Chandri's voice, scratchy as always, held a touch of humor.

"No, I was using the weapon—practicing with it. I get what you mean now." Victor smiled. He knew Chandri was irritated to have someone so clueless to teach, and he knew she was teasing him, but he didn't mind. He'd always been like that, though—some people might say he was too willing to take shit from girls, and he figured it was true. He'd been in plenty of fist-fights with smartass dudes, so why was he so chill when a girl was messing with him?

"Something to do with nature, I guess," he said, grinning at Chandri's puzzled look. To throw her further off guard, he said, "Hey, I love how you use turquoise and other beads to brighten up your leather. You think you could teach me to do something like that?" He slapped a hand against his black ringmail shirt.

"I don't think . . ." she started to say, then shook her head. "No messing around, Victor! My father may need us to hurry!"

Victor suddenly realized she wasn't so much irritated at his cluelessness as she was worried about her father. "Right, sorry. So what's next?"

"Well, the beast—I'm not using his name on purpose because I want him to feel more familiar with you—is very docile around you. That's good. He follows you nicely and seems relaxed. He has horns and those big black hooves for a reason, believe me! He could probably fight off a boyii pack by himself, yet he acts like a holbyis around you." It took a minute for Victor to remember what a holbyis was, then it clicked—they were the colorful sheep-like animals.

"Right, so that's all good. What next?"

"Hand me his lead, then get some of his feed out of your container." Chandri held out her hand, and Victor noted she had about ten different rings on her fingers. He wanted to ask her about them but didn't want to irritate her further, so he put it off. He handed her the rope and pulled a handful of the vidanii feed from his dimensional pouch. "Good. Now stand about ten feet away and call to him, using his name. Let him sniff at the feed first."

Victor did as she said, holding his closed fist full of grain up to Thistle's snout and allowing him to snuff at it. He started to try to pry Victor's fingers open with his fuzzy black lips, and Victor laughed. "Not yet, boy," he said as he started to walk away. Chandri had to haul on the rope to keep Thistle from walking with him.

"Good! He already wants to go with you," she grunted.

When Victor was ten or fifteen feet away, he turned and opened his hand full of grain and called out, "Come here, Thistle!" The big animal dug in his hooves, and Chandri laughed as he dragged her over to Victor, gobbling up the handful of feed in just a pair of seconds. "*Tienes hambre*, Thistle?" Victor softly asked, scratching between the vidanii's horns as it snuffed up the food.

"I'd say he's already an expert at coming when you call him. That's good, but it might make the next part harder. You have to teach him to wait until you call. I'll help at first, holding him as a reminder, but we want him to learn to stand still until you call him, too. You should use the same command with him each time—something like 'stay' or 'wait.'"

"All right," Victor said.

"So, show him the treat, say your command a couple of times, and if he starts to follow, I'll tug on the lead. If he keeps coming, you must walk him back, without giving him the treat, and then tell him the command again. This might take some work . . ." Chandri said, her voice trailing off and her smile fading as she remembered why they were doing this.

To Victor's glee and Chandri's relief, it didn't take long at all. Victor only had to correct the vidanii two times before Thistle waited to be called, then he repeated the trick several times. "I think he gets it!" Victor said, unable to keep from smiling as Thistle slobbered the grain out of his palm.

"No skill yet, though?" Chandri asked.

"Nothing yet."

"All right, try it a few more times without me involved. This time call him but don't give him the treat. Make him do it a few times before you reward him." Chandri walked back toward Victor's wagon, and he did as she said. The first time, when he got Thistle to come to him but didn't reward him right away, the animal kept nudging his huge nose into his shoulder, trying to lift his hand with the feed in it, snorting and shaking his head as though to figure out what was going on.

"Good boy, Thistle. Good boy! One more time, now. Wait, Thistle! Wait!" he said as he backed away. Every few steps, when the animal's leg moved as though to take a step toward him, he'd say, "Wait, Thistle!" When he stopped, a good twenty paces distant, he stared at the big vidanii for several seconds before saying, "Come, Thistle!"

Thistle practically charged over the grass to him, sliding to a halt in a shower of torn-up grass and rich, dark soil. Victor fed him his treat and then whooped as a message appeared in his vision:

*****Congratulations! You have learned the skill: Animal Taming, Basic.*****

"I got it!" he called out to Chandri just as a small swarm of little golden Energy bubbles materialized in the air and surged into him.

"Yes!" Chandri whooped in return, dancing in a circle with her fist in the air. Victor realized she'd been pretty stressed about this process, probably fearing it would take him a lot longer. She ran over to him and Thistle and said, "Now look into your mind, think about your skill, and see if you can realize everything the System just gave you!"

"I . . ." Victor started, but then he understood what she meant, that he *did* feel he knew a lot about animals that he hadn't before. He knew what sorts of food different types of animals would like to eat. Some of it was stuff he'd known before—he'd known about carnivores and herbivores, but Victor had the names of grains in his head, for instance, which he was sure he'd never seen. He pulled out a handful of the vidanii feed, and he knew it was a mixture of oats, something called winter grain, and chopped bits of "blue tundra grass."

More than that, he knew all sorts of sounds that common domesticated animals liked. He could click his tongue in a way that might calm down a skittish roladii. He knew sounds to make for his vidanii, too, and as he thought about it, the depth of knowledge started to freak him out. "Fucking A, it's like I've got a wiki about animals in my head."

"Don't try to think about it all at once. Sorry, I shouldn't have told you to do that—it can be overwhelming, huh? Just let the knowledge come out as you need it. If you continue to improve your Animal Taming skill, the System will begin to focus on the animals you work with. For now, do me a favor and think about riding your vidanii." She looked up at him, her eyes squinting against the afternoon glare of the sun, and her breath held expectantly.

Victor did as she said, thinking about riding Thistle, and he was suddenly aware of all sorts of understanding. He knew the optimum setup for his riding gear—that he'd need a saddle blanket, saddle, stirrups, reins, and a bridle. He knew that if he tried to use a bit with a vidanii, it wouldn't go well. More than that, he knew what to do with his legs and knees. He knew the kinds of sounds he should make when trying to get the animal to turn or speed up or stop. He knew he'd probably be very sore for the first few days, but if he had a high vitality attribute, it wouldn't be too bad.

"I'm going to need some riding gear," Victor said.

"Good! You think you know what to do now?"

"Yes, and I think it will go well—I can boost my vitality to around one eighty."

"Oh, Ancestors!" Chandri laughed. "Most Shadeni learn before they're even Tier One, so something more like ten or twenty vitality. You'll be fine! As for your gear—" She gestured back toward his wagon in the distance. He hadn't realized just how far they'd wandered away from it in his efforts to train with Thistle, nor had he realized that a small crowd had gathered around the blue and black vehicle.

"I see Thayla, Oynalla, Rhessa, Deyni, and a few others. I suppose this is what goes for entertainment around here?" Victor took Thistle's lead and started walking toward the crowd.

"Of course! They're hoping to see a giant ride a great horned plains runner from the distant north. Wouldn't you want to see such a sight?" Chandri laughed. "See that man on the blanket with all the leather and scraps? That's Berset-dak—he's probably the best leatherworker in the clan, and I'm sure Oynalla has enlisted him to make your riding tackle."

"Will it take him long? I think we should try to get started today, don't you?" Victor asked as they walked toward the little crowd sitting in the grass near his wagon.

"Yes, I'd like to leave as soon as possible! I don't know everything Old Mother saw, but if she thinks we need to seek out Tellen, I'm sure it's important. As for your saddle, I doubt it will take Berset-dak long. He's probably altering parts for a roladii saddle. I'm not certain, though. My leatherworking talents only extend as far as my own vests. She gestured to her tasseled, beaded vest and continued, "I don't even tan the hides—Shivena does it for me."

"That's cool," Victor said absently, his mind wandering as he thought about what Oynalla had said about Tellen—something was trying to make him its prey. He glanced at Chandri, saw her glance away as if he'd caught her looking at him surreptitiously, and he smiled, bumping her shoulder with his elbow. "Hey, we'll find him."

"Warrior!" Oynalla's unmistakable voice called out as they came close enough to speak. "Come! Let Berset-dak take some final measurements. He was able to start work based on your beast's sister animal."

"He measured Starlight!" Deyni called, running forward to take Thistle's lead. She looked up to Victor, eyes wide with excitement, and asked, "Are you really going to ride Thistle? Do you think I could learn to ride Starlight?"

"I'm sure you could!" Victor said, picking up one of her long black braids and tickling her nose with the end of it. "You can learn anything you want, munchkin. The sky's the limit." He glanced up and then back at her with a grin. "Or maybe it isn't!"

"You've a strange way of speaking, Victor," Chandri said.

"That's not the first time I've heard that. Didn't you tell me that already?" He laughed, and before Chandri could reply, an older, grizzled hunter had walked over with a long flexible strip of leather. It was marked with tiny lines, and Victor assumed he used it for measuring. Victor held out his hand and said, "Nice to meet you. I'm Victor."

"Hmm," Berset-dak said, "we've met. I was at the Ban-tok's fire when you first came to our camp. Please hold this beast still while I make some measurements."

"Right, sorry. That night's a bit of a blur," Victor said, then he pulled Thistle's nose down toward his shoulder and scratched him around his horns and ears. He seemed to love that more than any other kind of scratching, and he pressed his head into Victor, grunting and huffing out big steamy breaths while Victor scratched. Berset-dak nodded and began to move around the vidanii, taking the various measurements he'd need to get Victor's riding tack right.

"Just a little larger than the female. The buckles will be fine. Let me measure you for the stirrups, Victor," he said, coming over and holding his leather measuring tape against his hip and down his leg. "Hmm, I'll charge Oynalla extra for all the leather I'll need!" He laughed and then went back to his blanket, stacked with beautifully tanned leather, and Victor could see that he'd already finished the saddle and was just making some final adjustments to the straps.

Victor followed after him and said, "I'll pay for this! No need for Oynalla to . . ."

"Nonsense, warrior," Oynalla said. "He was only teasing you—you go to save our Ban-tok and his hunters. We'd give you a dozen saddles for such a service."

"All right," Victor said, nodding. "I appreciate it."

While Thayla and Rhessa talked to Chandri about animal taming, and Deyni begged her for lessons, Victor squatted near Berset-dak's blanket and watched the man work. His hair was very short, peppered with gray, just like his beard, and Victor thought he looked as though he'd spent most of his life outdoors. Victor shook his head at how obvious that observation was, glancing around the camp and the great expanse of the sky overhead. Berset-dak's long wiry fingers expertly pushed the hooked needle he used to stitch the leather, and Victor could feel little surges of Energy from the process.

"Are you using a spell or a skill or something?"

"Aye, of course. I'm a Leather Artisan, and I have some class skills that make my work more durable and, of course, increase the speed with which I can craft things. If you tried to make a saddle like this, I think you'd be at it for weeks, even with my guidance. I can do one in a day."

"Pretty fuckin' cool," Victor said, under his breath, admiring the rich dark leather. It had an undertone of red, and the stitchwork was beautiful, straight, and even with tiny seams. "What kind of leather is that? It looks kind of red."

"This is from some huldii Tellen hunted up in the hills around Greatbone. They were small, but Tellen said they moved fast and had more fur than the huldii down by the forest. No matter, though, Shivena scraped it all off when she treated the hides." Berset-dak finished a stitch, cut the leather cord with a small hooked knife, and then tied it off. "That should do it; let's see how it all fits! You carry the saddle."

Victor picked up the heavy, richly oiled leather seat, noticing that Berset-dak had made it longer than a standard riding saddle with a secondary set of shorter stirrups, no doubt anticipating Victor's need to take Chandri with him. Marveling at the quality of the leatherwork, he turned back to Thistle. As he started toward the animal, though, a youthful, familiar voice called out, "Wait, Victor! I have your saddle blanket!" He turned to see Chala, Chandri's little sister, running toward him with a bundle in her arms.

"It's a custom," Oynalla said, walking close to Victor and steadying herself by holding onto his elbow again. "In our clan, when a hunter goes on her first hunt, a friend gifts her with a saddle blanket she made."

"*Her* first hunt?" Victor asked.

"Or *his*, warrior! Open your mind!" Oynalla tsked.

"I made this blanket last summer, Victor!" Chala said, between gasps, as she came running up. Her face was painted fiercely in white and blue angles, and Victor leaned down to look into her eyes. They were lighter than

Chandri's, more pink than maroon, and had tiny blue flecks in a spiral pattern around her pupils.

"Thank you, Chala! This will bring us a lot of luck. I'm sure of it!" He took the offered bundle, and when he held up the blanket, dark gray with blue and white concentric squares, he whistled. "It's beautiful!"

The girl beamed at the praise and said, "Please take care of my sister!"

"Are you kidding? She's the one taking care of me!" He held out a fist, and when she looked at him quizzically, he said, "Pound it. With your fist, silly."

"Ahh!" Chala made a fist and punched his knuckles, grinning when he mock-winced at the pain.

"Nice one! *Chica feroz*!" He laughed and, using knowledge he couldn't explain, put his new saddle blanket on Thistle's back.

When the blanket was nice, smooth, and even, Victor lifted the saddle he'd set down and put it on top of it, applying the cinch straps and the breast collar, speaking softly to Thistle the entire time. When he was done with that, he turned to Berset-dak and took the bridle and reins he was holding, carefully securing them to Thistle's head.

"See the loop I made you for your axe?" Berset-dak asked, pointing to the ring of thick worked leather near the back of the saddle.

"Oh, nice! Thank you, Berset-dak." Victor pulled Lifedrinker from his belt and slipped her into the one on the saddle. Then he turned and looked around the gathered people. "I feel like Chandri and I need to go now. Isn't that right, Oynalla?" Victor felt some urgency, deep in his belly, and he wasn't sure if it was because of what Oynalla had told him about her vision or if it was truly his gut speaking to him. Either way, he wouldn't be able to relax until he and Chandri were making their way toward Tellen.

"You're right, warrior. Come, all, make a circle," Oynalla said, motioning for the small crowd to gather around Victor and Chandri, who'd stepped forward and stood next to him. When Oynalla, Thayla, Rhessa, Deyni, Chala, and even Berset-dak had linked hands around them, Oynalla spoke again, "Ancestors!" Suddenly Victor felt a surge of Energy, powerful spirit Energy that reminded him of inspiration, but it was more focused, more pointed. It came from Oynalla, surging into the air around Victor and Chandri, and she said, "Guide these hunters to their quarry! Bless their arrows and blades, and bring them home!"

The Energy seemed to seep into his pathways, and Victor allowed it, fearing nothing malicious from Oynalla. As it filled him, he felt driven, ready, and sure that he could accomplish the quest she'd set before him. He grinned somewhat wolfishly and said, "Thank you. See you all soon!" Then, Victor turned, put his foot into the stirrup, set perfectly for his height, and hoisted himself into the saddle. He reached down, took Chandri's hand, and effortlessly lifted her up behind him.

"Good luck, Victor!" Deyni called.

Victor smiled at her, then locked eyes with Thayla, and she clearly mouthed, "Be careful!" He nodded to her, then turned, flicked the reins, and clicked his tongue, and Thistle started trotting off into the grass. "Go east," Chandri said into his ear. She was leaning against his back, arms around his waist, and Victor could tell she was under the influence of Oynalla's spell, just as he was, because she hissed, "Fast!" and squeezed her arms tight.

"Hold on, then!" Victor yelled and leaned forward, touching his heels to Thistle's flank and flicking the reins again. Thistle didn't have any trouble knowing what he wanted, and suddenly the great animal surged forward. The wind was racing through Victor's hair, blowing tears out the corners of his eyes, and he and Chandri were bouncing, trying to match their up-and-down motion with the animal's heaving, rolling stride. Victor knew that if he didn't do so, he'd have one hell of a sore ass in a short while.

"Ancestors!" Chandri screamed with glee. "He's twice as fast as a roladii!" She gripped Victor's stomach tightly, and he felt her motion as she lifted herself in her stirrups and let herself down as the beast moved. Trusting in her experience, Victor tried to match her movements, and soon the ride became much more bearable. He laughed as the wind continued to howl past his ears, and the grasslands flew by in a blur.

10

STORIES

Chandri moved carefully through the scrub on the low hillside, searching for signs of Tellen's hunting party. This was the fourth area she'd led Victor to, hoping to pick up a trace of the hunters' roladii or evidence of them camping. She knew most of the general areas where the clan liked to hunt at that time of year and insisted once she picked up the tracks, she'd be able to find them without any problem.

"How does it work? Your tracking? I mean, are you looking for footprints or flattened grass or what?" Victor asked, still sitting atop Thistle's back. The vidanii had proven to be a tireless runner, and during their travel, Chandri had started to verbalize plans to acquire a breeding pair for her clan. When Victor had told her about them not breeding in captivity, she'd seen it as only a setback and begun to devise plans to take a yearly trip to the north where she was sure she'd be able to capture some live animals.

"It's a skill, like Animal Taming. I learned it the way all our people do—I was left to fend for myself when I earned Level Five. If the System senses your need and intent while you hunt for food, you have a good chance of gaining the skill. It's tough for people with higher Energy levels to learn because you're rarely truly in need when it comes to tracking game."

"What about tracking people, like we're trying to do? Do you think I could learn the skill by trying to find tracks?"

"It's possible, but I've never heard of any of our people learning it that way. I think the System views it differently when you're starving and desperate to find a feyris for the fire."

"Feyris—that's the name for the little rodent animals in the grass?"

"Yes, and other small game animals. It's sort of a general term." Chandri straightened and looked around the hollow. They'd spent a day riding at a breakneck pace to the east and, just that morning, started climbing into the hilly lands that led toward tall, dark, jagged mountain peaks that stood out starkly against the gray-blue sky. Chandri called the mountains Starfall Ridge and said that if he and she crossed them or followed them to the northeast, they'd come upon the Starfall Sea.

"Nothing?" Victor asked, watching Chandri huff in exasperation.

"No. Let's try a bit further south. They hunt these hills often, and I think we'll have a good chance of picking up their trail if we meander through them."

"Right. Walking? Or . . ." Victor eyed the saddle behind him.

"Walking. Just let your beast have a break! I can only imagine having a man your size riding on my back . . ." Chandri clamped her mouth shut and quickly turned away, busily studying the ground as she began climbing between two hills. Victor started to chuckle, then shook his head and stifled it. He clambered out of Thistle's saddle, deciding to ignore the, in his opinion, hilarious opportunity for teasing. He paused a moment, giving Chandri a bit of space, and gave Thistle a good long drink from one of the small casks of water he had in his storage pouch.

"Good boy," he said. After a few minutes, he started after Chandri, leading Thistle behind him, and when he crossed the ridge and saw her a short ways ahead, he called out, "Hey, why do they call it the Starfall Sea?"

Chandri turned to him, her eyes magenta in the bright light, and regarded his face for a moment. He thought he saw the hint of a smile and a nod, then she said, "We have a story about it. Do you want to hear?"

"Yeah, sure. Tell it to me while you hunt for tracks." Victor gestured around the hills as he came closer to her.

"I will, but you keep your eyes out, too. You might spot something I miss!"

"Right." Victor nodded.

"Well," she said as she turned back to the little gully between hills and started walking, "a long time ago, when Fanwath was new, and the people of the four worlds still fought for their places in it, it's said that there was a great city where the sea now rests. It was a city built by a third people from Alurath—the homeworld of the Shadeni and Ardeni."

"Oh, is that why you called Rhessa 'cousin?'" Victor asked while Chandri paused to inspect a small gully to their left.

"That's right. We're closely related. Some people think that Shadeni and Ardeni are the same people, that we simply have a predominance of different bloodline traits."

"Huh," Victor said, his mind busy imagining, not for the first time, that this world was once four different worlds.

"It is said the people who built the city were the Ordeni, and they were brilliant people, very gifted with Energy use, and they embraced the System and its lessons after it merged the worlds. They gathered there on a great plain and built their vast city-state, and began to develop Energy in ways the other peoples thrown into chaos by the world-merging couldn't fathom.

There was one group of people, though, the Yovashi, who didn't like the System and wanted everyone to rage against its implicit control. They were from a different world—Kthella, also the homeworld of the Ilyathi and Ghelli."

"Yovashi! I've met one!" Victor exclaimed.

"Really?" Chandri stopped her chant-like tale and turned to him with wide eyes. "There aren't many of them left in this world."

"Yeah, I was tortured by one, but it was being controlled, I think, by an Ardeni—a lord near Persi Gables."

"The nobility in the cities are known for their corruption, and Oynalla says it's because they've lost track of the old ways." Chandri nodded as though that explained everything and then returned to her tale. "The Yovashi were strong Energy users before the System came to their world. They had learned about it and harnessed it, and they were the dominant people on their planet. They were not kind to the other races—to this day, the Ghelli and Ilyathi bear a terrible hatred for them. The Yovashi saw the System as an interloper, ruining their position in what they viewed as a natural hierarchy."

"I'm listening," Victor said when Chandri paused and looked back at him.

"I'm sorry—I'm giving you more history than usually goes with this story, and I was afraid it was boring. I know you're new here, though." She smiled at him, her black-stained lips curling up and revealing her long canines.

"I know you get the tattoos for your hunts, but does your face paint mean anything? I noticed your sister always has her whole face painted . . ." Victor gestured to his face as he trailed off, afraid he'd overstepped.

"It's just tradition, Victor. Some of us think the old ways are fun, especially the makeup! Chala does her makeup like she's going to war, and I only go about halfway. If you look, you'll see many younger men and women in the clan do similar things. Oynalla teases us about it, saying we should hope never to see a time where the warpaint is truly called for." Chandri turned and kept scanning the hills. Perhaps she'd reminded herself that they weren't out on a hunt for fun but to find her father, who might be in danger.

"Well? What happened with the Yovashi and those other people?" Victor prodded after a few moments.

"Oh, right. Well, during that time, the System was still working on our world—especially our moons. It's said that great rings of rocks and pieces of the four planets' original moons circled Fanwath and that the System was building our current moons out of them. The Yovashi, using their brand of Energy-work, performed a great ritual. It's said that they sacrificed a hundred thousand slaves and harnessed the blood and death-attuned Energy to reach into the sky, pulling down a mountain-sized piece of rock, directing it to fall on the Ordeni city."

"*Madre*," Victor hissed.

"Yes, Great Mother, indeed! Our story describes the falling mountain like a tremendous falling star, streaking through the sky and visible to everyone who lived at that time. The Ordeni were all but wiped out; only a handful who'd been traveling survived, and they've since mingled their bloodline with the Shadeni and Ardeni." She paused, perhaps used to the storytellers in her clan doing so at that point. Then she said, "From that moment on, the civilized peoples of Fanwath united against the Yovashi, and all of our leaders swore never to allow anyone to commit such an atrocity."

"Fuck, man. Do you think the whole story is true? Do you think that's really where those mountains came from? The impact pushed them up?" Victor pointed over the hills to the distant, jagged peaks.

"I believe it to be true, aye. Oynalla would tell me if it were fantasy."

"Yeah, Oynalla's not a bullshitter, is she?"

Chandri laughed and shook her head, "I understood part of that, and no, Oynalla doesn't speak shit!" She held up a hand before Victor could respond, then she trotted down a slight depression into a narrow gully between two hills. "I see tracks!"

When Victor caught up, she scanned the ground around the sparse clumps of grass in the gully and carefully moved deeper into the narrow cleft between hills. "What is it?"

"It's Genn, one of Tellen's hunters. He was moving like he was stalking something. I don't see any roladii tracks."

"You can tell which hunter it was?" Victor asked softly, trying to match her steps.

"Yes, the skill shows me. I have my tracking up to Improved." She continued, crouching and moving as if she, too, was stalking something, and after a few minutes, she stopped and studied the hillside to their right. "The rest of the hunting party came this way down the hill and followed after Genn's tracks!"

"What about their roladii?"

"No, they were all on foot! Perhaps they were trying to be stealthy . . ."

"Can you see how old the tracks are?" Victor asked, imagining how valuable such a skill would be.

"Sort of, but only if I know a person's normal tracks. The images I see are brighter based on the residual Energy of the person or animal that left them, and they fade with time. I don't know all these hunters' normal tracks well enough to judge, but Tellen's . . . Tellen's are about two days old." She continued down the gully, Victor close behind. Something seemed to tickle the back of his neck, and Victor found himself holding Lifedrinker in his free hand, the other still leading Thistle.

"I feel like something's watching us," he said, glaring up and down the scrub-covered hillsides and back over his shoulder. He didn't see anything move, but that was strange in itself—earlier, he and Chandri had remarked about the abundant small game and the birds warbling from the dense clumps of scrub. He was busy looking for a mysterious attacker when Chandri took in a hissing breath and stumbled back toward him. Victor caught her, dropping Thistle's lead, and looked over her head.

The gully widened ahead into a stone-floored miniature box canyon between three hills. Rubble and scree covered the ground, and Victor figured the stones had fallen from the hillsides over the years, resulting in the jumbled mess ahead. That explained the rocks, but it didn't explain the blanket of blood covering a dozen gray stones and thickly sprayed over the ground. The blood was nearly black and very dry, but the stench of copper still tainted the air, and Victor was no longer surprised that the local wildlife had departed the area.

"Oh, Ancestors!" Chandri hissed, moving forward. "I see so many tracks. All the hunters were here, but—" She moved around the bloody spot at the center of the clearing and continued, "Eight left that way, climbing over those stones, and Genn's end at that mess."

Victor was warily looking around the canyon walls, Lifedrinker held crossways in both hands, and growled, "Well, do you see the tracks of whatever did that?"

"I don't, Victor. It doesn't make sense, though I suppose there are ways to obscure your tracks. I've never heard of an animal doing so." She was squatting near the blood splatter, shaking her head. "Nothing left of him."

"Well, don't you think your father and the hunters would have gathered his remains? Shit, maybe he wasn't dead, and they were carrying him!"

"It's so much blood. Could he have lived?" Chandri shook her head and said, her voice small, "I don't think so, Victor. Maybe. Maybe if Tellen was close behind and gave him a powerful draught . . ." She stood and warily looked around the surrounding hills, slowly scanning as if she could force whatever was out there to reveal itself to her.

"I don't like this place, Chandri. Let's get after Tellen's tracks—he'll be able to explain what happened." Victor moved toward the piled boulders and scree, scanning the blockage for the most probable path.

"Right. You're right, Victor. Let's hurry!" She hurried past him and climbed the first, largest boulder, and then Victor grabbed her hand.

"Hold up," he said and pointed at Thistle.

"Oh!" she sighed, sliding down from the rock. "We might have to work our way round this hill and then pick up the track again."

"Yeah, it's that, or I can start moving rocks. What do you think will be faster?"

"Let's give Thistle a chance to show us what he can do. I bet we can round this hill and pick up the next gully in just a few minutes," Chandri said, moving over to the big animal. "He's not even skittish around this blood. He'd be a wonderful mount to take on a real hunt."

"Yeah, he's a good boy, didn't even pull back on the reins when I led him in here. Maybe he knows something we don't," Victor said, climbing into his saddle and pulling Chandri up behind him.

"What do you mean," she asked the back of his neck as they started back the way they'd come.

"I mean, maybe he's good at sensing danger and didn't feel anything here. I mean, either that or he's really bad at it!" Victor laughed, then touched Thistle's sides with his heels, pushing him into a trot. Chandri chuckled at his attempt at humor, squeezing his sides to hold on, and Victor continued to urge more speed from Thistle.

Over the last couple of days, he'd gotten quite comfortable with the animal. Still, he didn't fool himself—he knew that ninety percent of his riding skill was based on his knowledge of the Animal Taming skill and his body's superhuman attributes. He was stronger, healed faster, and was far more agile than a normal person. Shit, if he were taking stock, he was smarter too. He laughed at that—he definitely wasn't smarter than some of the people he'd known back on Earth, even now. Intelligence must have more to do with Energy use or how quickly your brain works. It didn't make you a rocket scientist by magic.

"Maybe it has something to do with what kinds of skills and spells you can learn," he said, having lost track of his reality while his mind wandered.

"What?" Chandri asked.

"Nothing," Victor said as he steered Thistle around the big hill to the right, already halfway back to the gully if he were correct in his estimate. He figured he should probably speak to Gorz and get the amulet's take on his mental attributes and how they affected him outside of Energy use. He'd made a little effort to talk to the amulet now and then, but he found the conversations dry and very one-sided, and he wondered just how much of a personality the trapped spirit really had.

"Watch out!" Chandri cried, and Victor realized they were riding right toward a deep fissure that split the side of the hill and the ground across their path. Almost instinctively, he clicked his tongue and twitched the reins, and Thistle surged forward to leap the crack. Chandri whooped, and Victor laughed as they came down well clear of the obstacle.

"Good boy!" Victor cheered, patting the animal's neck, and then they were rounding the last corner of the hill and riding straight for the gully the landslide had blocked. Victor pulled up on the reins as Thistle trotted between the hills, and Chandri dropped out of the saddle. She spent a minute scanning the ground and then pointed further east, where the gully grew into an actual canyon between two very large hills. Victor figured if they continued that way for very long, they'd eventually come to the mountains of Starfall Ridge.

"Now that I have the tracks, I can see them from Thistle's back. Let's make up some ground!" she said, reaching up for Victor to pull her into the saddle. Victor nodded and steered Thistle in the right direction, and soon they were trotting over the rough ground, moving ever deeper into the long, shadow-filled canyon between the hills. He had to slow down before long because their makeshift path grew more and more rough, with fallen rocks and loose stones making footing treacherous, even for the nimble vidanii.

While Victor didn't mind getting the sun off his neck, the shadows also sobered up their charging pace, and soon he had to let Thistle walk, trotting when there was a stretch of clear ground. Still, his steady gait was much faster than he and Chandri could have moved on foot. The tracks led directly between the towering hills, and it wasn't long before Victor and Chandri realized they were in a dried-up riverbed, the long, high-walled canyon stretching to the east, seemingly endlessly.

"Maybe this river flowed before the worlds merged," Chandri said at one point, but Victor had another idea.

"I bet it was a river that passed by that city the Yovashi destroyed. When the falling 'star' smashed into the ground and pushed up those mountains, it blocked the river. That's probably why there's a sea on the other side."

"Ahh! Victor, you're smart!" Chandri said, giving his ear a tweak.

"Hey!" he laughed, ducking his head to the side. "Sometimes I guess the right answer, that's all." He was about to say something about how he'd also done plenty of guessing in school, but then he saw something ahead. "Shit," he breathed, pulling on the reins, slowing Thistle to a stop. Chandri leaned into his back, standing in the stirrups so her chin rose above Victor's shoulder.

"No!" she hissed, leaping from the vidanii. Victor jumped down after her, yanking Lifedrinker from her loop on the saddle, and followed her into the scene of carnage. It was much like the one they'd found earlier, where the unfortunate hunter Genn's tracks had ended. Though here, it looked as though two or three people had been bled of every drop of blood. Splash marks marred the stone of the canyon walls to the north, and the ground was painted with deep puddles, still tacky and moist.

Chandri slowly walked around the horrific scene, silently pointing to pieces of flesh and shredded clothing and leather. This slaughter hadn't been picked clean like the previous one. Still, no large body parts, dead people, or animals could be seen, and Chandri breathed a sigh that sounded relieved to Victor, saying, "Seven sets of tracks continue; only poor Jeggit's end here. Something else must have died with him, don't you think, Victor? It's too much blood for one man!"

"Well, something died with him, or something bled a hell of a lot. You still don't see any tracks from whatever it was?"

"No, I don't!" Chandri balled her fists in frustration, then returned to Victor and the vidanii. "Let's hurry! I think we've gained a lot of ground—they must have been moving slowly!" Victor nodded, and they remounted, continuing into the canyon. It wasn't long before they realized the source of some of the blood—significant drops and little puddles mixed in with the tracks Chandri was following. "They're hurt, Victor. You can see they had to rest frequently; look to where the blood puddles."

"Yeah, I get it," Victor said, jaw clenched, worried that Tellen, one of the few friends he'd made in this world who hadn't tried to manipulate him, might be hurt or dying. "Or dead," he muttered, too softly for Chandri to hear. He urged Thistle to move a bit faster than he felt was safe, but as they covered the ground, he was happy to see the blood drops and pools start to get smaller and less frequent.

"I think they managed to slow the bleeding—Tellen's band of hunters are all Tier Two or higher. Given time, I'm sure most of them would heal from cuts," Chandri said when he pointed out his observation. He nodded, some relief seeping into his thoughts as they continued to hurry up the canyon.

The shadows were long, and the sky was starting to go from steel gray and cloudy to dark gray and foreboding when they came upon a rocky path that led up the northern side of the canyon to a ruined stone building—an ancient keep of some sort. Victor could see, from the jagged remnants of walls, that it had once stood imposingly over the canyon, but now it was little more than one story of crumbling gray stone blocks.

Chandri said the tracks led up toward the keep, so Victor turned Thistle up the loose, stone-covered path that switchbacked up the steep hillside, and they'd made it to the first turn when a male voice called out from above them, "Stop! There are traps!"

Victor peered up the hill and saw a Shadeni wearing the usual leathers of Chandri's clan, waving from a higher level of the trail, just beyond the next switchback. "Visha?" Chandri called out.

"Aye, Chandri! Tellen is above, but he won't be happy to see you. Wait for me to guide you past the traps!" The lanky man, more a shadow than a defined person in the gloomy late-afternoon light, started to make his way toward them. He moved quickly but clearly avoided some parts of the path and occasionally stopped to fiddle with something behind a rock or hidden in a scraggly shrub. "Here we are," he said as he strode up. Victor immediately noticed that the man was missing several fingers and bore a long, freshly scabbed-over scar across his cheek and down over his chin.

"Visha! What happened to you!" Chandri said, sliding out of the saddle and rushing to hug the slender man.

"Something terrible is out here, 'Dree. We need to hurry up to the keep before the sun's gone. Gimme the lead to that beast, Victor, and I'll guide you past the traps."

"All right." Victor did as he was asked, not surprised that Visha knew him, or at least knew of him—he'd met, in passing, a lot of Tellen's hunters. Visha led them, Chandri walking behind him, up the path, pausing and returning to reset things that looked like trip wires to Victor. It took them fifteen minutes or so to slowly make their way up to the flat area near the top of the hillside where the ruined keep sat.

When they rounded the last turn of the trail and came into sight of the keep's entrance, two more hunters came running over and exchanged hugs with Chandri and greetings with Victor. They also bore terrible scars and fresh scabs, and Victor wondered how the rest of the hunters looked if these were the ones chosen to keep watch.

"You shouldn't be here, Chandri! This place is cursed!" the second hunter cried when Chandri pulled him into a hug, carefully avoiding his left arm's bandaged, bloody stump.

"Hush, Kolo. Oynalla sent us—she had a vision." Suddenly hope bloomed in the defeated hunter's dark red eyes, and he looked at Victor, still sitting atop the tall vidanii.

"Maybe . . ." he gulped visibly and looked at the other two hunters. "Do you think the Ancestors haven't abandoned us?"

"Of course, they haven't!" Chandri said, taking his good hand and walking toward the keep. "Take me to my father."

The hunters seemed reluctant, but they did as she asked, guiding her and Victor up the stone steps and into a broken-walled courtyard. Victor tied Thistle to an old petrified beam sticking up among some stones. They all waited while he set up Thistle's feed bag and put out a barrel of water, which the animal thirstily began to drink.

When he was finished, the hunter named Kolo tapped his short, javelin-like spear against the piled barricade at the keep's entrance, and a moment later, Victor could hear things being dragged away from the opening. When the last sizeable wooden barrier, an old table, if Victor wasn't mistaken, was pulled aside, it was Tellen that stood before them. The Ban-tok of the clan was better off than the hunters Victor had seen so far, still sporting all of his appendages, though his leather armor was in tatters, and he bore the signs of many recent injuries.

"Ancestors! Chandri! No! Why would you come here?"

"Not you too, Father!" Chandri cried, rushing to hug the tall, wiry hunter. "I'm here because Oynalla had a vision, and she sent me to find you. To bring Victor to you."

"Um, hello, Tellen," Victor said, taking the last step into the doorway. He loomed over the hunter as he held out his hand in greeting.

"Come in!" Tellen said, backing up. "Help me put this barricade back up!" He looked at the three hunters who had greeted Victor and Chandri and said, "You should come in now. It's dark soon." They didn't argue, hurrying in, pushing past Victor, and then, almost before Victor and Chandri could get out of the way, they started piling the barricade back into place.

"What the fuck's going on?" Victor finally asked.

"We're cursed, Victor! I wish you hadn't come! I wish you hadn't brought my daughter!" Tellen said, shaking his head and moving further into the ruined hall. Victor followed him and looked around. The ceiling wasn't fully intact, though it looked as if Tellen and his hunters had worked to barricade the larger holes. The doorways out of the hall were similarly blocked off with ancient wood, furniture, and piled stones. Victor even thought he saw a stone statue tipped over to block a doorway, though it was partially covered with rubble, obscuring most of it from view.

A fire burned in an ancient stone fireplace, and several figures were laid out before it, wrapped in blankets and seemingly unconscious. "What kind of fucking curse?" Victor asked, resting a hand on Lifedrinker.

"Something hunts us, Victor. Something fast and strong and unrelenting. It toys with us, cutting us apart, slaying us, and then departing when it could have finished us all. Each night it comes, and each night it kills or maims one of my hunters." Tellen shook his head, despair in his eyes as they fell upon Chandri again.

"Why didn't you ride home, Father? Why did you track it?"

"Ha! We didn't track it, child. We camped atop a hill, and Genn was on watch. We think he heard a noise and investigated, but when the morning came and he was nowhere to be found, we tracked him to the scene of his slaughter. While most of us searched the area for tracks, trying to figure out what beast did this, Ulena went back for the roladii. She found them slaughtered."

"So you gathered up Genn and then continued into the canyon? Why?" Chandri pressed.

"We were hot with rage! We thought if we stayed together, we could find the devilish beast that did this and slay it!"

"You were sure it was a beast?" Victor asked, something tickling the back of his mind.

"The way it killed—Genn was ripped apart. The roladii were disemboweled. I thought it a great saber-cat that had gone mad. Ulena said it looked like a mad terror bear had come upon the roladii."

"Terror bear?" Victor asked.

"You don't want to meet one, Victor," Chandri said, reaching up to gently squeeze Tellen's arm above his elbow.

"Well, I'll need to switch places with my vidanii," Victor said, surprising everyone. Tellen looked at him as if he'd lost his mind.

"Yeah, I mean, if we're going to put out bait, I'd rather it wasn't Thistle. This whole thing reminded me of a story I know, a story that happens to be one of the five or ten things I remember from English class. Seems like too big of a coincidence not to mean something; I think your ancestors have a job for me."

"A story, Victor?" Chandri asked, and when Victor nodded to her, looking around at the hunters, he saw hope in their eyes. He figured it was because he'd mentioned their ancestors. Still, when he saw their broken bodies and their desperate desire to believe him, when he saw Chandri and the pride in her eyes when she heard his words, he knew he was right—he had to face whatever it was that tormented them. These poor hunters weren't up for it.

"Yeah, it's about a monster named Grendel and the badass, *pinche* warrior that ruins his day."

11

MONSTER OR HERO

Victor sat on a flat stone block in the middle of the ruined courtyard, watching the dark clouds as they alternately obscured and revealed the enormous ringed moon and her little round sister. Outwardly, he looked relaxed and vulnerable, but he was quite alert. He'd boosted his agility with Sovereign Will and had Inspiring Presence primed in his pathways, and though his body seemed reclined, leaning back, bracing on his left hand, his right hand rested on Lifedrinker's haft, and he held his core tense, ready to spring.

Tellen had tried to talk him out of his plan, tried to get him to hunker down for the night and then flee with Chandri, making haste on Thistle's swift hooves. The other hunters, those who could rouse themselves to consciousness, had remained silent, though, and Victor could see the desperate hope in their eyes. Chandri had only wished him luck on his hunt, and it had been her confidence and, strangely, pride in him that had really solidified Victor's determination to stand watch alone—to face the demon that had so tormented Tellen and his hunters.

Sitting in the dark, waiting for the monster to come, Victor wondered at the lack of fear in his chest. He felt ready, almost pumped, as he would be before a big match. He had some nervous energy that was difficult to mask, but he didn't feel fear or trepidation. He felt damn good, in fact, as though he were doing something he was meant for.

The way Victor saw it, if he was growing into some kind of killing machine, a monster of sorts, then wasn't it right and good that he spent his efforts fighting other monsters? Shouldn't he defend the people he cared about? It was very fucking easy to put himself out in this dark courtyard, waiting for a bloody fight to the death, when he imagined Tellen or Chandri getting cut to pieces like the hunters this "demon" had already slain.

Every now and then, if he let it, his mind would start to wonder at the surreal nature of his situation. Just a week ago, he'd been sitting in a massive bathtub, enjoying the fancy soaps that Captain Lam had provided. Now he was dirty from days of travel, sitting on a hard stone in the moonlight, waiting for this world's version of Grendel.

Was part of the reason he was out here waiting because he'd rather think of himself as someone like Beowulf than a monster like Grendel? Beowulf had been a badass, that was sure, and he didn't take any shit, but he also was a hero—a man who fought the monsters weaker men couldn't face.

Victor momentarily recalled his crisis of conscience back when he and Thayla had killed the soldiers sent by ap'Horrin. He remembered how Lifedrinker had spoken to him, brought him back to himself, and helped him see that he wasn't wholly to blame. He was a wolf, and those that hunt wolves need to fear the fang. "Isn't that what you said, *chica*?" He gently caressed the warm wood of the axe haft with his thumb, and he was sure she vibrated gently in response.

A loose bit of stone fell from the high crumbling walls, and Victor ceased his introspection to listen and feel, trying to surmise if it had been the wind or gravity finally winning an ages-long battle or if something had disturbed the stone. Nothing else stirred, and his gut told him it wasn't anything to worry about. Victor had begun to trust his gut more and more, and he wondered if it was a product of his attributes, Class, or even his bloodline—whatever it was, he felt more connected to his instincts.

Instincts—could they be responsible for his quick acceptance of Oynalla's quest? He hadn't argued, hadn't sought different solutions, hadn't expressed any concern for his or Chandri's well-being. He'd simply accepted her vision at face value and gone along. He didn't feel used, though. He'd wanted to go. His gut had said, "Let's hurry and help Tellen as fast as fucking possible." Should he feel used if his own wishes coincided with what other people wanted him to do? "I don't think so," he said, "especially if I like those people."

He wasn't worried about being quiet and didn't want to seem as if he was waiting for a fight, so he figured talking to himself was A-OK. His mind drifted back to when he'd brought Thistle into the hall with the hunters and begun to head back out. He remembered how Tellen had gripped his wrist and thanked him, having given up on talking Victor out of his "mad" plan. He remembered how Tellen had walked away, leaving him with Chandri for a moment, and then he remembered her hug and how it had been different from any hug he'd ever gotten from Thayla.

She'd folded into him, her arms under his, and her fingers had gently caressed his back when she'd said, speaking into his chest, "I can feel your heart; it thumps like a mighty drum. Ancestors pity the creature that tries to take you tonight, Victor. When you bring its head back to us, I'll help you mark this hunt with ink." Though he'd stood several paces away, Victor had seen Tellen's look of concern—the way he shook his head slightly in dismay, and he knew that Chandri was alone in her confidence. She'd never seen the "demon," after all.

Another clatter of stones, this one from the wall near the broken gateway, brought Victor back to the present. His thoughts of Chandri's gentle touch and how her body felt so warm as it pressed against his snapped away as though someone had thrown ice water over his head. He feigned a wide yawn, making noise to signal his boredom as he used to do when his *abuela* made him play old board games. Using the act of stretching as cover, he took a glance around the courtyard, and his fist tightened on Lifedrinker's haft when he saw a dark shadow slipping purposefully through the gap in the walls.

Victor braced himself, every muscle primed to move, and waited, trying to stay still and look like a victim. "C'mon, you *pinche monstruo feo*!" he hissed under his breath. Suddenly the hairs on the back of his neck stood up, and he knew it was time to move. He erupted into motion, veritably flying into the air, simultaneously casting Inspiring Presence and whipping Lifedrinker in a flat arc at the space behind the stone on which he'd been reclining.

As the spell took effect, the shadows fell away from the courtyard, and the moons' light, even obscured by the clouds, seemed more luminescent and sanguine. As Lifedrinker's razor sharp, gleaming edge ripped through the air, Victor's teeth bared in a feral grin of amusement when he saw she was cutting straight for the shoulder of his quarry. "Gotcha, asshole!"

The "demon" was certainly deserving of the moniker the hunters had given it. Victor's Grendel was bipedal and tall, with long lanky limbs covered in knobby gray flesh. The creature's head was hairless and adorned with a ring of short black horns that almost looked like a crown. Of its face, Victor only had time to notice angular, gleaming orange eyes and wicked, sharp teeth in jaws wide open, ready to bite. As his axe crunched into the monster's shoulder, and Victor felt the reverberation all the way up to his elbows, as if he'd struck a steel beam, he noticed that the "monster" was wearing a sleek black jumper with a broad silvery belt.

"This prey has a tooth, hmm?" it hissed as Lifedrinker rebounded, and Victor sidestepped, moving like an enormous ballet dancer, hunched and ready. He held his center of gravity low and trained his eyes on the creature's waist. He brought Lifedrinker into a two-handed grip and cast Channel Spirit, flooding her with rage-attuned Energy, granting her a red, furious nimbus.

The monster's voice reminded Victor of a hacksaw cutting tin, and as he circled it, he saw that its long fingers weren't as long as he thought—four-inch claws tipped the six digits on each of its wide, splayed hands. They gleamed in the moonlight, and Victor knew they weren't natural but weapons this being had grafted to itself.

"You can speak, fucker?" he growled, ready for the deadly speed this thing had shown the hunters. They'd barely been able to describe the monster as bipedal with razor sharp claws, unable to get a good look at it as it ripped through them, blending with the shadows.

"The simple creature wonders if I can speak?" A low chuckle followed the grating words, and then it was gone, disappearing from Victor's sight, and a bloom of pain erupted on his thigh. Five long, deep gashes had opened on his right thigh as if by magic. He hadn't even seen the creature's attack. The low, grating chuckle continued, this time from behind him, and Victor whirled to face his attacker. His leg moved just fine, and he had a disturbing thought as blood soaked his pants and ran into his boot: had this "demon" avoided crippling him to draw out his suffering?

The hunters had told him how fast the monster was. They'd told him how they couldn't strike it, let alone avoid its claws, but something had stood out to Victor when they'd described their encounters. Each time it came around to kill or maim, it was a flurry—a lightning attack of cuts and stabs that seemed to come from nowhere. The creature would laugh and roar, and in a matter of seconds, it was gone, leaving them bleeding and despairing.

When Victor heard their accounts, he'd had a suspicion, one born of experience fighting fast people. What if the "demon" couldn't maintain such speed? What if he could outlast it? If there was anything he was good at, it was soaking up damage. Realizing he was no match for the monster's quickness, even boosting his agility, Victor redirected his Sovereign Will to his vitality. He smiled as the attribute jumped to nearly two hundred, and the pain in his leg immediately started to dull.

"What's your deal?" he asked the creature, watching as it circled him. One of its long arms dragged the razored claws along the stone in a show of red sparks. He hoped to stall the next attack, giving his vitality a chance to close up his leg wound. He knew he could hit the monster, having done so once, but it would take some luck, and he'd need to catch it off guard.

"My deal? I hunt. I sharpen my skills. Why do you kill?" Its chuckle echoed in the darkness as it once again disappeared from Victor's view, and as he braced himself for another strike, Victor cast Dauntless Radiance, sending a surge of courage-attuned Energy into the air around him, and just as the rings of his armor on his left shoulder clanged and burst apart, a bright golden light filled the air. Victor stumbled forward at the impact, and he knew the claws had cut more than his armor when his left arm protested and wouldn't properly move when he tried to whip Lifedrinker around in another cutting arc.

Still, the red-gold glow of his spell filled him with confidence, and he shrugged off the injury, knowing his body could take it. As he circled, scanning for any sign of his elusive enemy, he said, "I can tell you I don't hunt down people weaker than I am. I don't torment people and butcher them as they cower. How does that sharpen your skills? Sounds like a fucking *puta* move to me!"

"Interesting Energy, prey," the grating voice echoed out of the shadows, seeming to come from all the corners of the courtyard at once. "You make my cultivation difficult. Shall I just finish you and feed upon those cowering within that ruin?"

"You have a name, fucker?" The words of the creature had sparked some understanding in Victor. None of the hunters had mentioned it "feeding" on them. If Victor's courage-attuned Energy made its "feeding" difficult, perhaps it hungered for their fear or despair, or something else the courage nullified.

"You wish to know who slew you? Jikrak is my name, and you shouldn't despair at a death by my hand—one day, this weakling world will call me lord. You are but one of my early victims." Victor finally laid eyes on him as he spoke, standing just outside the light of his spell, lurking in the darker shadows near the gateway. Victor smiled grimly and primed his next spell, staring at the dark figure, focusing on the glint of his shimmering, metallic belt—the only bright spot in the shadows.

"Jikrak, huh? So you aren't from this world? Got chased out by stronger guys?" Victor taunted, switching his vitality boost to agility and loosening his grip on Lifedrinker, though he still held her in front of himself.

"Yes, prey, I think I'll end you quickly. You're no good to feast upon," Jikrak said sharply, his grinding, sharp voice ripping through the night. Victor stared at that glinting metallic belt, and as soon as he saw it wink out of existence, he whirled, casting Project Spirit, launching a wave of sickly, yellow-black, twisted inspiration-attuned Energy into the darkness. Each time Jikrak had struck him, it had been from his flank, and Victor knew the cone of his Project Spirit was wide enough to catch him, especially as he backpedaled, widening its arc of influence.

The unusual spell knocked Jikrak off guard, pulling him out of whatever ability allowed him to move so fast. His falter was brief but long enough for Victor to release Lifedrinker and reach out to grab the wrist attached to the long claws that ripped into his armored belly. As the claws punched home, barely slowed by his armor, Victor grasped the monster's knobby, rough appendage with both hands and bore down with all his might, squeezing as if his life depended on it. It did, after all.

Jikrak fought back against the disorienting effect of Victor's projection, and in just seconds, Victor felt the monster's will assert itself. As Victor wrestled with the creature's surprisingly prodigious strength, barely able to hold onto the wrist with both hands, Jikrak started to slash at him with the other hand. He ripped long deep ribbons in Victor's arm and tore long grooves in his side, sending chunks of black enamel and shattered metal rings flying with each terrible gash. As blood soaked Victor's arm and hands, he felt the monster begin to slip free.

"Fuck this!" Victor growled in furious agony. Forgetting about his plan to try to outlast the creature's speed, he cast Berserk. Victor had been waiting, saving his ace for when he had the monster on the ropes, or at least had ahold of it. He'd wanted to be sure he didn't cast the spell too early and burn up all his rage-attuned Energy while the monster avoided contact with him.

So many plans had been in his mind—how he might use his coyotes to surround the creature or chase it down if he caused it to flee, how he would try to win this fight without Berserk entirely, winning with a clever plan and raw skill. Those thoughts went out of his mind, though, as he felt Jikrak start to slip out of his grip.

When the spell triggered, and rage started to flood out of his Core and into his pathways, Victor urged it out, pushing it with his will. When the red fury washed over his vision and the pain of his ribboned flesh faded to just an itch, he laughed and bore down on the monster's wrist. His fingers, larger and longer and horribly strong, squeezed that thin gray appendage until he felt the satisfying crunch of bones faltering and shattering under the pressure.

As he grew and healed, and his mad laughter turned into a roar that echoed off the walls, shaking rubble loose all around them, Jikrak's confident slashing attacks turned to panicked thrashing. Victor's voice, deep, loud, and inexorable like waves grinding against the shore, rumbled from his chest as he said, "Am I prey now, manling? What fool are you to challenge the Quinametzin?" His eyes were red with fury, and he hunched over the thrashing panicked Jikrak, his shoulders and neck hulking and bunched with thick cables of muscle.

Jikrak's ineffectual stabs and clawing cuts were nothing more than an annoyance as he continued to stab and hack at Victor's shoulder. Irritated that the little man hadn't answered, Victor released Jikrak's shattered wrist with one hand and snatched the attacking arm by the biceps, lifting Jikrak into the air, so he was forced to look him in the face. "Am I prey?" he roared again, just an inch from the orange predator eyes of the "demon."

Jikrak didn't answer, but Victor saw his eyes gloss over as he tried to concentrate, and then the flesh under his mighty fingers started to turn slippery, and it felt as if Jikrak was falling through his grip, as though he were turning to air. A glint of triumph appeared in his enemy's eyes.

When he felt his insolent attacker start to slip away, the rage in Victor's mind surged to new heights, and he lost, momentarily, his cognizance. In a blind madness, he lifted Jikrak above his head and smashed him to the stone ground with enough force to liquefy an ordinary creature. Jikrak had been in the midst of some sort of spell, making himself incorporeal, and when Victor madly threw him down, his semi-solid body sank into the stone, leaving him half in and half out of the flagstones.

The impact had ruined Jikrak's concentration, spoiling his spell, and as the horror of his demise registered, Jikrak's orange eyes bulged out, and he opened his mouth, but only blood cascaded forth, no words. Victor roared in mad triumph and grabbed onto Jikrak's head, pulling with all his might and ripping it away from his stuck-fast body. He threw it against the wall with a wet splatter, dislodging more rubble, then he looked up at the night sky and screamed his victory to the stars.

Victor dimly remembered leaping up the jumbled stones to the top of the ruined wall of the keep and pacing over the crumbled battlements roaring and howling at the moons, brandishing Lifedrinker. His shouts were inarticulate, but they were loud and full of challenge, and it became clear to him later, when he thought of that night, that the Quinametzin in him had been challenging anything within earshot to come to try him, daring any creature, be it man or monster, to set foot in his domain.

He opened his eyes to warm sunlight and found himself still atop the wall, nestled between two fallen crenellations. Even in his disorientation, Victor had a feeling of swelling pride, left over from his gigantic alter ego, no doubt, and he grinned as he sat up. He looked at Lifedrinker, present as usual in one of his hands, and memories of his battle came rushing back. "Sorry, *chica*. I'll make sure you get more action in the next fight."

He saw that a System message was blinking in his peripheral vision, and he pulled it into view:

*****Congratulations! You have achieved level 32 Spirit Carver, gained 10 will and 10 vitality, and have 16 attribute points to allocate.*****

"Goddamn, I didn't snap out of it when I got the Energy from killing that fucker?" Victor shook his head, amazed at how long he'd stayed enraged and how much of it was a blur. It was almost like his rages from the old days, but not entirely. He remembered speaking while berserk and how furious he'd felt when that creepy asshole started to slip away. No, he'd been in control for most of it—it had just lasted a lot longer. "Why do I have sixteen points . . ."

Victor slapped himself on the head. He hadn't spent any points when he'd last leveled. He'd hardly looked at his status sheet, either. Had he looked at it at all? The last time he could remember was before he fought Rellia—he wondered if he'd subconsciously avoided it for some reason. Before he could find a reason to put it off again, he pulled up his mental and physical attributes:

Core:	**Spirit Class: Base 7**		
Energy Affinity:	**3.1, Rage 9.1, Inspiration 7.4**	**Energy:**	**2539/2539**
Strength:	**135**	**Vitality:**	**110**
Dexterity:	**40**	**Agility:**	**63**
Intelligence:	**32**	**Will:**	**253**
Points Available:	**16**		

Victor almost dumped his sixteen points into agility right then, remembering how fast Jikrak had been. He stopped, though, another thought occurring to him. Jikrak might have been fast like that because of magic. He might have even been teleporting or something. No matter Victor's agility, he wouldn't be able to move faster than that. If that were the case, he should maybe put his points into will, as he had been doing, or into intelligence. "No wonder I didn't do anything yet," he muttered.

As he wished for some good advice or a training manual of some sort, he thought of Gorz and shook his head. Gorz usually left him more frustrated than before he'd asked for help—he wanted guidance, not impartial information. Then he thought of Oynalla and smiled; if anyone might tell him what to do, the old woman was a good candidate.

"I'll be going back there now, anyway," he said, and then he heard, off in the distance, a high-pitched, scratchy voice calling out his name. "What the fuck?" He stood and looked out over the morning landscape. The shelf the old keep was built on lay before him, and at the head of the trail leading down to the canyon floor, Chandri stood. She cupped her hands to her mouth and again called his name.

"Victor!" Her voice echoed down into the canyon. Before he could answer, Victor heard a noise behind him, and he turned to see two hunters poking around in the rubble of the courtyard, turning over stones as though they might find him buried.

"Hey!" he yelled. "I'm up here!" He waved an arm at Chandri when she whirled around.

"Victor!" she shrieked in glee, charging back toward the crumbled gatehouse. Victor laughed and started clambering down from the wall, using the broken stones and loose mortar for hand and footholds. When he reached the bottom, Chandri was waiting, and the hunters had gathered as well, with Tellen at their center. Chandri smashed into him as soon as he'd put both feet on the ground and squeezed him around the waist. He hugged her back, his grin spreading from ear to ear.

"Hey, you guys act like I was missing or something! I was just taking a little snooze up there." Chandri pulled back and laughed, turning to her father with a wild grin of her own.

"I told you, Tellen!" She caught herself using his name and followed up with, "I knew he could win, Father!" The hunters didn't wait for Tellen's response but crowded forward to clap Victor on the shoulders and back. Victor's shredded ringmail vest jangled and clinked, and the hunters' faces lit up with smiles, the dark clouds behind their eyes all but gone—their death sentence had been lifted, and the gloom of their perceived curse was banished with the morning sun.

"While we listened to your battle, we feared you were dead. We thought more than one monster came to the fray because long into the night, a great beast howled and roared," Tellen said, eyeing Victor. "Was it not allied with the demon?"

"Uh, no. It definitely wasn't allied with the demon," Victor sighed, shaking his head. "The other monster was me. When I go berserk, sometimes I let myself go too far."

Chandri stepped closer and grabbed his forearm with both her hands, looking at his face. "You're no monster, Victor."

"Thanks, Chandri." Victor mustered a smile and nodded.

"We found the creature's head against the wall, Victor, and his remnants are here, mixed with the stones. I don't know how you did it, but thank you. By rights, you should examine this corpse for treasure!" Tellen said. As he backed up, pointing to the bloody mess of Jikrak's body, he continued, "I owe you my life, but more importantly, these others are safe thanks to you. I hope you'll return to the camp for a while, Victor. I'd like to find a way to reward you."

"I'll go to your camp, Tellen, of course. I want to spend some time learning from Oynalla. You don't owe me anything, though. If I didn't help my friends when I could, then what kind of asshole would I be?" Victor looked down at Chandri and winked, then moved through the small crowd to look down at Jikrak's body.

It was mostly intact, and Victor wasn't surprised, judging by how tough the bastard had been. His flesh had even rebuffed Lifedrinker, after all, though he hadn't yet charged her with Energy. It said a lot about the strength of his Titanic Rage ability that he was able to crush the creature's bones and pull his head off, he supposed. "Huh, I guess his strong flesh wasn't a match for more than five hundred strength," he said, kneeling to examine the corpse.

He heard whispered conversations among the hunters as he started to try to shift the body. It wouldn't move much, and he saw that the left arm and both feet were fully embedded in the stones of the courtyard, so he reached over and picked up the other arm, stiff now in death, and examined the fingers. "One ring," he said. He pulled off the solid black band, careful not to slice himself on the long, metallic claws protruding from the gray, knobby fingers. He tucked it into a pocket, then examined the rest of the exposed body.

"That weird-ass black jumper isn't my style, but that belt looks interesting."

"What about his finger claws?" Tellen asked.

"I don't want those fucking things. You guys can cut them off if you want," Victor said as he tugged at the belt, unbuckling the silvery, metallic strap and lifting it up to inspect. It was crafted from some sort of metallic thread and felt heavy and dense. Energy emanated from it in palpable waves. Victor was about to trickle some Energy into it to see what it might do, but he stopped, looking around at Chandri and the four hunters leaning on each other for support with weary lines around their eyes, despite their joy. They'd come out at dawn to hunt for him, and he was busy going through his loot.

"Hey, why don't we pile some rocks on top of this asshole and then go make some breakfast? I'm starving, and you all look like you haven't eaten anything good in a month. I have some delicious shit in my storage ring."

Chandri laughed at his words and said, "Yes! And I'll help you with your ink trophy!"

Tellen must have seen the disturbed look on his face because he also laughed and said, "It won't hurt much, Victor. Chandri's not gentle, but she's quick." He clapped Victor on the back and added, "Could you please cut those fingers off with your axe, though? I'd like to make trophies of those blades. Only six of my band survived this hunt, and I think it's fate that this demon had six fingers."

"Only six?" Victor glanced back toward the barricaded hall and realized Tellen had lost more hunters to their injuries than he'd thought. "All right, this skin is tough, but I should be able to get through it. Someone put a board under that hand and pull those fingers out straight."

12

A HUNTER'S FAREWELL

"No," Victor said flatly. "I'm serious, Chandri—I don't want a tattoo of that monster on my face."

"Well, what about just his claws or something? You know, to symbolize him?" Chandri asked, looking rather crestfallen. She held a needle and a little jar of ink that she said she'd "made in a special ritual." Victor studied her face, reaching up to turn it to the side to get a good look at her tattoos. They were all black, but the tiny figures of deer and boar-like animals were cleverly shaded with lots of detail. She was talented, he supposed.

"Does it have to be on my face?" Victor didn't know why, but he didn't want to be reminded of that asshole every time he looked in the mirror. "You know, he wasn't even the toughest *cabrón* I've ever fought. Like, fucking Rellia was tougher than that thing."

"Rellia?" Chandri asked.

"Ha, I guess it's cool that you don't know who she is." Victor smiled.

"I'm sorry you didn't track your earlier victories, but I could help you if you want! I have other inks we can use, too!"

"Oh, God. Let's just start with this one, and then we'll see, all right? You didn't answer me, though. Can I have it somewhere I don't have to look at it all the time?" Victor gestured vaguely at his shoulder or leg.

"Sure, this is for you, Victor. There aren't any rules." She smiled at him in a way that seemed to involve her whole body—she leaned forward, her eyes sparkled, and everything about her posture just said, "I think you're great, and

I'm glad to be here with you." Victor loved how open and genuine she was, and he couldn't help but smile back.

They were sitting to one side of the formerly barricaded, ruined hall. The front door was open wide, and a large window near the opposite side was cleared, allowing bright light and fresh air into the hall. Tellen and the surviving hunters were preparing the bodies of the fallen—he wanted to hold a vigil that evening and "send their spirits home." Victor had surmised it involved a pyre because Chandri had volunteered him to help build it when she'd finished his "hunt trophy."

"All right," he said, shrugging out of his still shredded ringmail vest. He was bummed that the garment seemed to have met its match—Jikrak's horrible claws had proved too much for it. The man-monster had torn one half of the garment, along with Victor's flesh, to ribbons, and it seemed the Energy that had once imbued the magical armor was gone. Not one link had repaired itself since the battle. Victor lifted the still heavy vest and sighed sadly, putting it into his storage ring.

The shirt he wore under the vest was also shredded and showed no recovery. "Close your eyes," he said, with a laugh, then pulled it off. He didn't bother with the buttons—the thing fell away without any effort when he pulled.

"Ancestors!" Chandri hissed when she saw his torso. He wanted to think she was exclaiming about his muscles, but he knew better—his torso, shoulder, and arms were crisscrossed with pink and white scars as if someone had used him as a practice dummy for a squadron of sword students.

"Yeah, I kind of already wear a lot of trophies from my battles, I guess." He laughed off her concern, running a hand over the freshest scars on his shoulder and side. "They don't hurt, don't worry. When I berserk, my cuts heal up pretty good. These aren't even that bad! You should have seen me before I advanced my race the last time. One of my arms didn't even work properly because my bone had healed sorta crookedly." He caught himself embellishing facts, realizing he was trying to impress her.

"I see the pink scars there, where you're rubbing. Is that where the demon cut you last night?" Chandri asked, reaching out to gently run her fingers over his shoulder. Her touch was feather-light, but little tingles of electricity ran through Victor as she traced some of the scars.

"Yeah. I caught his other arm and was holding on with both hands. He went crazy slashing into me while I squeezed," Victor said, grinning savagely.

"I'll make your hunt trophy here, on this shoulder. All right?"

"Yeah, sounds good to me, Chandri," Victor said, stretching out his legs and leaning onto his other hand so his shoulder faced her more directly. They were sitting on a pile of tanned hides, and Victor felt comfortable and relaxed. "Hey," he added, "I still have that bottle of booze your dad gave me. Let's have a drink while you work, hmm?"

"Yes! I could use it! I was so stressed and excited last night I hardly slept!"

"Excited?" Victor asked with a chuckle.

"Yes! I knew you would win, and I knew today would be a good day. I was mostly stressed because I felt so horrible for the hunters who died through the night. They were so terribly wounded, Victor. Even Tellen's best healing draughts didn't save them."

"*Dios*," Victor said, taking the bottle of cheb-cheb from his storage ring, "It sounds like you had a worse night than me. Sorry, Chandri." He pulled the cork on the bottle, breaking the wax seal with his thumbnail, and offered it to Chandri. "You first."

She took the bottle and put its mouth to her black-stained lips, and took a long pull, breathing out syrupy, eye-watering vapors into Victor's face. A little of the red-brown liquid ran down her chin, and she scrunched up her eyes at the strength of the liquor. "Great Mother! That one bites! Your turn!" She pressed the bottle into his hands and produced another bottle of alcohol. Victor raised an eyebrow while he took a swig of the cheb-cheb, and she grinned, reaching up to pour the other bottle on his shoulder.

"You need a bath, but this will do for now," she laughed, scrubbing his skin with the torn-up shirt he'd removed. Victor spluttered out some of the cheb-cheb as he matched her laughter, enjoying her ministrations more than he wanted to admit. How long had it been since he'd even kissed a girl?

He thought about it while Chandri let his shoulder dry, getting her needle ready. He hadn't kissed a girl since he last went to Marcy's house. It felt like an entirely different life. Hell, it *was* a different life! He had a sudden urge to lean forward and steal a kiss from Chandri, and he almost acted on it, but then he saw Tellen and his hunters kneeling over the corpse of one of their friends, and he sighed and took another swig. This wasn't the time.

He listened to Chandri talk about hunting and training roladii while she worked on his tattoo. While her little needle hummed with Energy, and he felt the tickle in his skin, he imagined taking her for a long ride on Thistle. He envisioned a trip like they'd just taken, but without the pressure and worry of going to rescue her father's hunting band.

Did he really like her that much, or was he just lonely? Was her situation any different from Thayla's when it came down to it? He'd told himself he wasn't getting closer to Thayla because he was going to leave. What about Chandri? Wouldn't it hurt her if he left her behind? "Damn it," he sighed, letting his frustration leak out.

"What?" Chandri asked. "I do something wrong?"

"Nah, you're fine, *chica*. I'm just annoyed at my circumstances."

"Things will look up, Victor. You're with us now, and that's not all bad, is it?" Chandri asked, her lips quirking up at the corners while she concentrated on her work.

"No, not at all. I'm happy to be with you right now." Victor determined to quit worrying so much about the future and try to enjoy what he could in the moment. He took another swig of cheb-cheb and offered the bottle to Chandri.

"No thanks! I'm already floating a little. You want to be able to make sense of this mark, don't you?"

"Yeah, I guess," Victor said, setting the bottle down and allowing his mind to drift again. He thought about many things, but he found his mind circling a particular worry that was itching at the back of his mind, and he finally forced himself to confront it. In the spring, there were a lot of people expecting him to lead some sort of conquest of a distant land. What an impossibly absurd situation!

He thought about Rellia, and he smiled at the memory. One minute they'd been trying to kill each other, and the next, she'd been telling him that her life depended on their partnership. "Fucking nuts," he said.

"Still dwelling on your crazy life?" Chandri whispered, her concentration apparently very absorbed by whatever detail she was working on.

"Yeah," he chuckled again. "I guess I have a problem with talking to myself."

"No, I do it all the time, too, especially when I'm out alone on a hunt. I talk myself through my problems sometimes or just keep myself company by narrating what I'm doing and what I'll do next. It's kind of crazy, really." She paused and sat up straight, stretching her neck by pushing on her chin with the palm of her hand.

"This hard work? Want to take a break?" Victor asked.

"No, silly! I'm almost done. Hold still," she said and reached down to dip her needle into one of her jars of ink. Victor hadn't even noticed that she'd gotten more jars out.

"Hey, this seems like you're making something a lot more complicated than your marks!"

"Not really! Just a little bigger and more colorful. Shh, now," she said, bending to the task. Victor did as she asked and grew quiet, suddenly thinking about his oldest living friend in this world—Vullu. He resolved to try to track the gruff but kind Cadwalli down when he got to Persi Gables. He wasn't sure Vullu would still be around—he'd seemed pretty depressed when he'd left the Wagon Wheel, and hadn't he said something about traveling? Still, Victor determined to look for him; it would be nice to catch up with him and tell him about his adventures.

"Done!" Chandri said. "I'd put some healing ointment on it, but your body is healing almost as fast as I move the needle!"

"Oh, yeah. One of my abilities lets me boost my vitality a bit. I was trying to outdrink you so I could get you to tell me all your secrets . . ." Victor trailed off, hoping Chandri would get the joke, and she grinned and slapped his shoulder where she'd just made the tattoo. It stung a little, but not much.

"I've got some secrets for you, but not right now," she whispered, her breath hot on his ear. She laughed and then fished around in her storage pouch and pulled out a mirror set in a handle that looked like polished bone. She held it out so Victor could see his shoulder and said, "It's a reflection, so reverse everything in your mind."

"Right," Victor said, still recovering from the way her breath had tickled his ear. He blinked a couple of times to bring himself back to reality and looked into the mirror.

There was his shoulder—tan and crisscrossed with scars, and there was Chandri's beautiful work—he saw a severed hand with six blades that looked very much like the real-life Jikrak's hand, blood pooling under the severed end. Opposite the claw were six spears adorned with turquoise and with gleaming points. Behind and above the other images was a broad, gloriously orange and yellow sun.

"It tells the story, see?" Chandri said, pointing to the claws. "You killed the monster, and with the dawn, six hunters were saved."

"It's beautiful, Chandri," Victor said. "Thank you! It means a lot to me."

"Hush! Thank you! There are six spears on your arm because that's how many hunters you saved. Tellen, my father, will come home thanks to you." When she hugged him again, Victor basked in the warmth of it, but more than that, he soaked in the feeling that he'd done something genuinely good. He'd risked himself to save some friends, and it had paid off. It felt very damn good, and he resolved, right then and there, that he'd try to re-create that feeling as many times as he could in this life.

"All right, let me get a shirt on before your dad comes over here and beats me up," Victor laughed, pushing her back a little.

Grinning, Chandri said, "How did you know about all the boys Tellen has chased from my tent?" She laughed at Victor's mock outrage, then stood and said, "I'm going to go see if he needs help with the preparations. We'll build the pyre soon, right?"

"Yeah, right. No problem," Victor replied, pulling out a brown and gray knitted sweater he'd bought in Gelica. The weather was turning chilly, and he enjoyed the cozy feel of the thick garment. Once he was sitting comfortably and saw that the others would be busy for a while yet, he pulled out the belt he'd looted from Jikrak. It was heavy—kind of like the sacks of precious metals he'd found in the dungeon, but the links seemed strong, and they gleamed differently in the light than silver did.

He trickled some Energy into it, and his mind flooded with understanding, accompanied by a System message:

*****Dragonsteel Belt of Energy Absorption. Prerequisite for use: Advanced tier Core or higher. This belt will absorb Energy attacks aimed at the wearer. It will absorb a total of 4500 points of Energy before it needs to process the absorbed Energy and reset, becoming inert for up to twelve hours.*****

"Shit!" Victor hissed. "Well, that's pretty damn cool, I guess." His Core was still at the "basic" tier, and from his understanding, he'd need to work through the entire "improved" tier before he'd be at "advanced." "Something to look forward to," he sighed, slipping the belt into his storage ring. Looking at his ring, he snapped his fingers and fished the black ring he'd taken from Jikrak out of his pocket.

When he bonded to it, trickling some Energy into the dark metal, he became aware of an immense storage space, even larger than his other dimensional containers. More than that, his mind started cataloging the thousands of items held within. At first, Victor thought he'd hit the jackpot, and he had, in a sense, but it wasn't quite what his first impression had indicated—the ring was entirely filled with items that looked suspiciously like construction materials.

The two most numerous materials in the ring, making up more than half of the total volume, were massive mounds of rectangular stone blocks and hundreds upon hundreds of hardwood beams and boards. There were other things—doorknobs, doors, plaster, roofing tiles, banisters, the list went on and on. It was mind-boggling to Victor that so much could be in that ring. He finally came upon an item that explained everything: blueprints for something called "A Great Hunter's Hermitage."

Victor looked through the blueprints briefly, confirming his suspicion that the construction materials in the ring were everything he'd need to build the "hermitage." The sketches on the blueprint made it look sort of like a squat fort with an asymmetrical shape, the right side rising three stories while the left half was a single story. The materials had interesting names like "Gray Spire Marble" and "Gith Valley Mahogany." All in all, it was an interesting find, and Victor was sure it was valuable but not something he wanted just then.

"That fucking creep was going to build this here and hunt people?" He wasn't sure he was right, but Victor remembered Jikrak saying something about not being from this world or planning to rule this world. He'd been full of himself, that was for sure, Victor thought, slipping the ring back into his pocket.

"Damn it," Victor said, feeling somewhat cheated. He'd expected Jikrak to have weapons, potions, treasure, and maybe even artifacts of great power. "Construction shit." He shook his head ruefully.

"He might have had another ring on his other hand," Chandri said, startling Victor.

"Hey! You trying to give me a heart attack?" Victor stood up and gave her a little shove, and she playfully shoved him back.

"Maybe! If you startle that easily, you must need some hunting practice!"

"Hmm, maybe." Victor shrugged. "You might be right about his other hand, though. You think we should dig it out?"

"One of the hunters broke up the stone, trying to see if he could get more claws. It's like the demon's skin and clothes became mixed with the rock—they were completely ruined. If you broke up the stone to get at his fingers, I think any rings he was wearing would break apart also."

"Oh, well." Victor shrugged. "Maybe someday I'll build a, what was it? Hermitage! Maybe I'll build a hermitage in the wilderness someday." Chandri looked at him with questions in her eyes, and he took a minute to explain what was in the ring.

"It might not be what you hoped for, but it sounds valuable, Victor. In any case, we need to get the pyre built. Are you ready?" Victor nodded, and the two of them spent several hours scouring the ruins for wood. Chandri showed Victor how the clan built their funeral pyre, which reminded him of when he and some friends made a bonfire in the wash near his friend Anthony's house. They'd partied long into the night until one of Anthony's neighbors called the cops, and they'd run, laughing and whooping, through the desert to another friend's house, where they'd all crashed on couches.

This pyre wasn't for partying, though, and when it was finished, and Tellen and his surviving hunters carried out their dead, one by one, and laid them atop the bone-dry wood, Victor and Chandri stood to the side, silently contemplating their mortality. Or, at least, that was what Victor thought about, and he figured Chandri must have had similar thoughts.

As the sun dipped behind the western hills, Tellen held a torch to the pyre, and it burst into flames. Victor had felt some Energy when Tellen lit the torch, and he felt more of it in the roaring flames that consumed the fallen hunters, and he wondered what sort of spell this was. As he thought about fire magic, he became aware of a deep, resonating hum, and then he realized some of the hunters were singing. A moment later, a higher-pitched humming joined the song, and Victor saw that Chandri and the two female hunters had also begun to sing.

He wanted to sing with them, but as the hum became words, words that he didn't recognize, even with the System Language Integration, Victor just stood still and listened, watching the fire. The song was hauntingly beautiful, and he felt Energy rising with it and more Energy from the fire, and then he saw the ghostly, ethereal forms of the hunters flowing with the smoke and sparks that flickered into the night sky before fading away.

Victor wondered if he was imagining things, but the wispy, smoke-like figures continued to float out of the flames and into the starry sky, even after he blinked his eyes rapidly. "Holy shit," he breathed, not loud enough for anyone else to hear.

He wanted to participate, to send those hunters off somehow, and inspiration hit him. He cast his Manifest Spirit spell, but rather than rage Energy, this time, he fed his pack some inspiration-attuned Energy. Suddenly, around the pyre, shimmering white-gold fragments of Victor's spirit took the shapes of his coyotes, and the bright-eyed, luminous creatures sat on their haunches, lifted their snouts to the sky, and howled.

The sound was not what regular coyotes sounded like—their voices harmonized into an ululation that brought goosebumps to Victor's skin, and the hunters took inspiration from it, lifting their own songs to match the note, and soon most of them had tears freely streaming down their cheeks.

After the song was finished and the fire had burned to coals, Tellen broke out casks of ale, and they all sat in a circle in the center of the hall and told stories about the hunters who had died. Victor didn't have any stories to share, but he listened, and he laughed and cried with his friends, and he felt like one of them, if only for a short while, and it warmed his heart. Like all the others, he drank too much and fell asleep there on the piled furs. Chandri lay down in front of him, and at some point in the night, he woke to pull her close, savoring her warmth, and he slept very soundly.

Victor, Chandri, and the hunters took nearly a week to return to the camp. Some of the hunters were wounded in ways that slowed their ability to walk, and Victor let them take turns riding on Thistle. However, someone had to keep the animal walking on a lead, or else he would outpace the others in his absent-minded perpetual hunt for the perfect piece of grass to eat.

Tellen was impressed by Thistle and grateful that Victor was happy to walk with them rather than ride ahead. They spoke a lot on their journey, and Tellen gave Victor much advice about how to hunt animals, process their hides, prepare their meat, and a million other things that Victor didn't entirely absorb. Victor had always been better at learning things by doing them, and when one of the hunters shot a bird or small animal, he volunteered to skin and dress the meat and even cook it, so long as Tellen or one of the other hunters would help him.

Victor nearly dropped the ladle he'd been using to sample his feyris stew one evening when a System message appeared in his vision:

*****Congratulations! You have learned the skill: Cooking, Basic.*****

No one else was surprised, and they laughed at his wide eyes when he started exclaiming about all the things he understood now. He knew that certain spices didn't mix well, for instance, but more than that, he knew all sorts of herbs to use with various types of cooking, even things that weren't from Earth, like ground werdwort. He understood that and so much more. For instance, he knew how to tell if certain cuts of meat were ready to eat and how it was easier to peel a jellipur if you boiled it first.

"Ha! Thayla's gonna lose it when I cook her something that actually tastes good!" Everyone laughed at that, but Chandri had a strange look in her eyes. Victor found out what was bothering her the next day when they were walking ahead of the line of hunters. She walked next to him and spoke quietly so only he could hear.

"Are you going to stay with Thayla? Will you become a father to Deyni?"

Victor was caught by surprise, and he looked down at Chandri and opened his mouth but closed it again, thinking about his words for a minute. "No, I don't think that would be fair to Thayla, Chandri. I love her, and I care about what happens to her, and she deserves to find someone who wants to live the life she wants. I've come to realize that I may find moments of peace in my life, like this, for instance, but I'm not built to stay in a life like that. I crave adventure, and part of me craves violence. I'm a Berserker, Chandri, with the blood of battle-loving titans in my veins, and I've come to accept that."

"So you and Thayla aren't lovers?" Chandri asked, and Victor wondered if she'd heard a word he said.

"No, Chandri, we're not," he laughed. She laughed too, and Victor knew she'd heard him and respected his words, but she still liked him, and that felt good.

"Victor," Tellen called from behind him. "Poyla can walk by now." He gestured to the huntress riding Thistle behind him and continued, "Why don't you and Chandri ride ahead? We're getting close to the camp. Tell them our story, so I don't have to when I get there! I'm tired and want to celebrate with a feast, not talk for hours and hours." Tellen laughed and helped Poyla down.

Victor shrugged and said, "Sounds good to me, Tellen." Then he hopped up on Thistle and reached a hand down to Chandri. "Shall we?" When she took his hand, he pulled her up, looked down at Tellen, and said, "All right, we'll hurry, but don't get too jealous when you see how fast Thistle runs!" He laughed and clicked his tongue, touching Thistle with his boots, and soon they were racing over the grasslands, the wind whistling in his ears and blue-green grass flying by in such a blur that he could imagine he was charging over an ocean.

13

WINTER CAMP

Yes!" Chandri said with a wide grin, looking around the fire at her audience—Chala, Deyni, Thayla, and Victor. "That's when we started to hear the loudest, most terrible howling, roaring, and barking you can imagine! It sounded like a mad, gigantic boyii hound!"

"Oh, Ancestors," Thayla said, under her breath, clearly having guessed the punchline.

"Ancestors, indeed! We thought all was lost! Clearly, the demon had allies! Victor was doomed! We heard the clash, heard the demon cry out, but then the roaring and howling turned to screams of challenge and wild shouts that echoed around the keep, rattling the loose stones and sending rubble down upon our heads! It went on for hours!" She paused to look at her sister and Deyni, watching their faces, making contact with their wide eyes.

"Well, what happened?" Deyni broke first.

"After the demon was gone and the fighting was over, and the mad screams and roars echoed through the ruin, I figured something out!" Chandri said.

"What?" her sister asked, red eyes staring from her black and white face paint, her voice hushed.

"I recognized something in the new monster's voice. A certain note I'd heard before! Can you guess what it was?" She winked at Thayla and waited for Chala and Deyni to answer.

"A cave howler!" Chala said.

"A . . . I don't know! A monster?" Deyni said, looking at her mother for help.

"It was a monster, all right," Thayla said, grinning at Victor. He did his best to keep his face straight, though, and turned to Chandri.

"He's as big as a cave howler, that's sure," Chandri laughed, "but it was none other than Victor! He'd finished punishing the demon that had tormented the hunters and was celebrating his victory!"

"You were barking, Victor?" Deyni asked in dismay.

"Don't believe everything she says," Victor laughed. "But sure, why shouldn't I bark?" He stood up and crouched down, hands out like claws, and approached Deyni, a low growl in his throat. She laughed, perhaps a little nervously, and cringed away, but then he lunged forward and barked, giving his best imitation of his old neighbor's pit bull. She toppled backward in giggles, and everyone else joined in, especially Chala.

Victor tickled Deyni as she squirmed away in the grass, then he stood up, still laughing, and looked around. They were camping about half a mile away from the main body of the hunter clan, about three-fourths of the way toward their winter encampment. Nearly two months had passed since he and Chandri had gone to rescue the hunters, and a lot had changed in that time. Still, a lot hadn't changed, he thought, glancing toward Thayla and Chandri.

He'd spent a lot of time with Oynalla, and the clan's Old Mother had taught him a few things, but not much, not yet. She'd insisted he needed to improve his Core, and a great deal of the time he'd spent at her tent had been in silence, cultivating inspiration and rage-attuned Energy and adding it to his Core.

He'd gotten to "Base Nine" within two weeks, but the last month, he'd struggled with that rank, trying to push into "improved" and seemingly getting nowhere. Oynalla described the different tiers like walls, saying he'd climbed up a hill to the base of the wall, but now he was scaling straight up to get to the next hill.

She'd made him practice his Spirit Walk spell almost every night, showing him tricks for traveling and finding people. She took him and Thayla with her to meet some of her distant friends; apparently, they had regular meetings on the spirit plane. Victor felt a lot more confident about himself in that realm these days, and when he arrived, his pack was there, almost as though they were waiting for him. Thinking of their spirit walks, Victor glanced at Thayla, still sitting next to the fire, hugging her daughter, who'd run back to her.

Things were good with Thayla, he decided. He'd helped her to build and set up her own tent, and she and Deyni spent even more time with Oynalla than Victor did. Recently, she'd proudly told him that her courage attunement had overcome her death-Energy in size and that Oynalla was starting to teach her more spells. Victor felt annoyed at first—Oynalla had been avoiding teaching him spells, always putting him off, sometimes with a cryptic statement like, "A warrior should find his own way with the spirit. What does an old clan mother know of it?"

He knew she was full of shit, that she had some things to teach him, but he felt that she was waiting for him to do something or prove something. He wasn't sure what, but he resolved to be patient—she guided him in her own way. That was another thing he was glad of; Oynalla had quickly admonished him to put his extra attribute points into will. She said his powerful will had saved him a dozen times and would continue to do so. He chuckled, remembering her words: "I suppose you want more strength? You're big enough, warrior! Keep building up your will—you'll know when it's enough!"

And then there was Chandri. Victor sighed, looking at the beautiful young Shadeni sitting next to Thayla and chewing on a small bone from the stew they'd made. If Oynalla's reluctance to show him spells was frustrating, then Chandri was on a whole other level. They spent a lot of time together, flirting, checking trap lines, riding, and even snuggling by the fire, but never more. Victor had tried to make a move a couple of times, leaning in for a kiss, only to be giggled at or to have her turn it into a hug, breathing maddeningly into his ear and then pulling away.

He couldn't blame her, he supposed. He'd as much as told her that he'd be gone soon and that he craved violence and adventure. Was that true? He thought about it and had to admit that it was. He'd had a fun time with the hunters but was ready to go anytime now. He'd be ready, for sure, when winter ended.

Victor figured that was what kept Chandri at arm's length—she was waiting to see when he'd leave and trying, perhaps, to keep the goodbye as painless as possible. He sighed and turned away from the fire, looking out into blackness over the endless grasslands. "Who wants a broken heart, anyway?"

Victor rested a hand on Lifedrinker and smiled. "You're always with me, aren't you, *hermosa*?"

"Talking to your axe again?" Thayla asked, quietly walking up next to him.

"You always catch me when I do it! I swear, it's like you have a sixth sense!" He laughed.

"Enjoying the stars?" Her eyes were aimed up, taking in the enormous depth of the star field.

"Well, I should be," he said, awed, as always, by the sight. The stars were so numerous and bright, and if he looked in the right areas, he was starting to recognize some of the more apparent constellations. He pointed to one such grouping of stars, four bright ones that almost made a diamond pattern, the one on the right side just a faint shade more pink than white. "What's that constellation called? The one with the pink star?"

"That's the Eye of Kvahn. At least that's what my mother told me. It's named after a powerful Yovashi lord from before the joining."

"Huh. Considering what the Yovashi did, I'm surprised people still want to remember him."

"Well, some things stick around, even if we don't want them to." Thayla shrugged. "What were you grumbling about over here? One minute you were laughing with Deyni, and the next, you were frowning into the darkness and talking to yourself again."

"Oh, nothing, really. Just wondering what Oynalla's got in store for me at the winter camp, and also thinking about the spring. You know, all that shit with Rellia." Victor was only half lying—Rellia's campaign was on the back of his mind more and more as the days grew longer and colder.

"Hmm. I guess that's allowed. I'd probably be grumbling about that, too." She nudged him in the ribs with her elbow and added, "Sure you aren't having trouble with your love life?"

"Hey!" Victor laughed, truly surprised by the question. "What do you mean?"

"Think I haven't noticed how your eyes follow Chandri everywhere she walks? How you two cling to each other but never leave the fire together?" Thayla smiled slyly, glancing over her shoulder at the fire where Chandri was in the middle of another story.

Victor took another step out into the grass and hoarsely whispered, "Hey! Seriously! Don't say shit like that! I have a hard enough time without you mixing me all up!" Was she really talking to him about his feelings for Chandri? Was this happening?

"Shh, relax, Victor. I didn't bring it up just to tease you. I know you worry about me, about leaving me, about my feelings. Sometimes I wonder if it's making your life"—she gestured again over her shoulder with her chin—"sort of difficult."

"Well . . ." he started, but she shushed him again.

"Let me get this out. You know, Oynalla tells me a lot. Sometimes we talk about you, too. She's helped me see some things. I'll always love you, Victor, but it's a warm, steady love that fills me with pride and hope. It's not a passionate, please-never-leave-me or no-one-else-can-have-you kind of love. Do you understand? Don't worry about me, okay?"

"God! I knew you loved me!" Victor laughed and pulled her into a hug. "Thank you, Thayla. I love you too, and I'll never forget about you. When I leave, I mean. You can believe I'll be back. We'll visit each other on the spirit plane, too, right?"

"Right," she said, squeezing him back.

Victor pushed her back, looked into her eyes, admiring how the stars twinkled in their depths, and said, "Do you miss Rhessa?" After a few weeks with the Shadeni, her friend had left, promising to visit Deyni but insisting that the hunter clan lifestyle wasn't a good fit for her.

"Ancestors, no!" she laughed. "She was starting to really get on my nerves, Victor. We both changed a lot over the years and not in complementary ways."

"Well, that's good, I guess. I mean that you don't miss her."

"Sure, I miss my old friend, my old life sometimes, but only when I paint the memories with nostalgia. More important to me, though, is that Deyni is starting to see me as her mother. Rhessa was good to her, Victor, and I'll always be grateful for that, but I'm glad not to have to compete for Deyni's affection. Well, I mean, I still have to compete with you . . ." She laughed, squeezed his arm, and walked off, back toward the fire, when Victor affected a stricken countenance.

He watched her, a warm feeling in his chest, as she sat down behind Deyni, pulling her into her lap as they continued to listen to another one of Chandri's hunting tales. Victor stretched; his shoulders were stiff, and he knew that if he didn't have a monstrous vitality, they'd be sore, too. He'd practiced the axe forms that Polo had taught him for nearly three hours after they'd made camp. His wagon was much faster than the rest of the Shadeni caravan, and they ended up with quite a bit of downtime each evening.

He wished he had Polo or someone with some axe-fighting skill to practice against, but the hunters almost universally preferred the spear and the bow. Some of them were competent knife fighters, and a few were skilled with a hatchet, but their styles were quite different from the way Victor and Polo Vosh fought. Tellen said he should still spar with them, that he'd improve his ability no matter what sort of weapon he faced, and Victor agreed, taking them up on it whenever they had time.

He felt that his skill was improving. He was quicker with the forms, more fluid with the parries and dodges that he'd gained when he'd reached the "advanced" tier, but Tellen said it was a long, long way through advanced with any weapon. "Ahh, well. Nothing for it but to keep practicing," he said to the night air as he turned back to the fire. When he walked over to the little group, Chandri was just finishing her story, and she looked up at Victor with a smile.

"Needed some air?"

"Yeah. I think Chala ate something that didn't sit well . . ." He had to cut himself short because Chala was instantly on her feet and screeching as she circled him, leaping onto his back and trying to choke him. "Oh," Victor said, standing up with the young woman still on his back, arms around his neck, "do you guys see a bug on my back or something?"

"Victor!" Deyni laughed, "Chala is on you!"

"Chala!" Chandri laughed. "Get off him! You're going to fall into the fire!"

The rest of the journey to the hunters' winter camp followed a basic routine. Victor and his friends traveled in his wagon, Chandri and Chala taking turns riding their roladii with a few hunters keeping pace until they reached the day's waypoint. Then they'd set up a little camp, get a fire going, and spend the afternoons and evenings sparring, cooking, telling stories, and even singing, though Victor preferred to just listen on those occasions.

On the afternoon of their twelfth day of travel, when they rounded a long rise in the grassy plains and started on the downward slope, Victor saw their destination and whistled in appreciation. He nudged Chandri, who sat on the driving bench next to him, with his elbow. "That's what I call a forest!"

"That's the Blue Deep," Chandri said.

"I can see why." Victor shaded his eyes, taking in the immense stretch of primeval forest that came to an abrupt edge along the plains a few miles south of them. The name suited it—the leaves in that sea of trees were predominantly blue, or at least he thought they would be if they didn't still have some fall foliage clinging to their branches. The trees were enormous, some with white, narrow trunks and others with darker, more standard wood colors, at least in Victor's limited experience with trees. The leaves, though, the leaves were stunning in their colors.

Victor could see quite a few of the trees were this world's equivalent to evergreens, and they were still decked out in deep blue needles, but many of the other trees were brilliant oranges and reds. From that distance and height, Victor could see the bands of late fall coloring stretching into the forest like ribbons of red-gold fire twisting around the deep blue pines. "I'm assuming those red and gold leaves are usually more blue?"

"Yes, but isn't it beautiful like this?" Chandri asked, leaning into him so she pressed against his side and rested her head against his shoulder.

"Yeah, it's something," Victor said. He glanced at Chandri and out at the hunters in the grass around them. No one was close. Even Chala was riding her roladii ahead, probably wanting to be the first to camp. "Hey, what's the deal with us?"

He'd spent most of the trip sitting by Chandri, eating with Chandri, joking with Chandri, always open, always showing that he wanted to be even closer. Still, nothing ever happened, and she never initiated anything more—Victor had given up trying to make the first move after the third or fourth rebuffed kiss. Thinking about it, he'd remembered how Thayla had been blunt and open with him and how good it felt, so he'd decided to try it with Chandri.

"Hmm? The deal with us?" She sat back and looked at him, troubled by his tone or words; Victor couldn't tell which.

"Yeah. I mean, back when we were looking for Tellen, I felt like we had something going on, and then, I don't know, you're always hanging onto me and hugging me, but whenever I try to, I don't know, take it further, you back off. So, what's the deal?"

Chandri sat back and frowned, and her eyes narrowed. Victor felt as if he was about to get screamed at, but she took a breath and said, "I suppose I don't know. Maybe I'm scared."

"Scared?"

She nodded, and her brow relaxed, her expression more open, and Victor saw moisture was starting to gather in her big magenta eyes. "I think so. You're so different from anyone I've known, Victor. My feelings are so . . . big! I'm afraid of them. I thought I could be different than Thayla. I thought I could have some fun with you and say goodbye, but . . . Grandfather's bones, Victor! I want to be with you so badly! How will I feel when you ride away on your wagon, and I'm left here with this . . . *clan*?" She said clan like she was cussing.

"Shit, Chandri. I guess you could . . ." Victor started, but she held a thin-fingered red hand to his mouth.

"Don't you dare say I could come with you! I've seen the kinds of trouble you get into. I've seen the kinds of things you fight! Even if I weren't worried about my own skin, I'd be worried that you'd get yourself killed trying to protect me." She shook her head, and now he could see that the tears weren't from sadness or joy but from frustration.

Rather than reply to her right away, Victor clamped his mouth shut and slowed his racing thoughts. She'd been right when she'd stopped him from speaking—he was going to say she could come with him, and what a boneheaded thing that would have been. She was absolutely right about the kinds of shit he got into. Instead of rambling off some half-assed solution he didn't have or hadn't thought through, he blew out a deep breath and said, "Shit's frustrating, isn't it?"

"Yes!" Chandri growled. "Shit is frustrating!" She caught him glancing at her, and a smile crept onto her lips. "You see? I would love to kiss you right now!"

For once, Victor didn't let his brain get in the way, and he leaned down and gently pressed his lips to hers. She watched him the whole way in and didn't pull back, so he figured he'd finally pegged the right moment. Her lips were soft, and he tasted salt and the hint of something sweet, but as he pressed hungrily, savoring her hot breath, she groaned and pulled away.

"You stole that!" she said, though she still wore a smile.

"I did, and it was worth it. If that's all we ever share, Chandri, I'll remember that kiss."

"Well, don't be too hasty. We'll see what happens, won't we?" Her stress and frustration seemed forgotten, and her relaxed smile was contagious. Victor leaned back and draped an arm over her shoulders, grinning like a kid who'd gotten his first kiss before getting on the bus after school. "There! See that break in the trees and those grassy mounds by the forest's edge? That's the campsite! Those mounds are buildings with sod roofs—we use them for winter dwellings and storage. Some of them have as many as five levels underground."

"That's pretty cool. So you guys just leave all that unattended for what, six months?" Victor imagined vandals and looters, broken doors and windows, and animals making dens inside.

"We don't leave much, Victor. We carry storage devices, too, you know. No, it's mostly just some emergency supplies in case we come home from a bad hunt or, as happened to Tellen's father, we're being pursued by a militia and don't have time to stock up. You know, situations like that."

"Oh, sure, sure. Militia pursuing you. Makes sense. *Dios mío.*" Victor shook his head. Sometimes he forgot that Tellen's clan hadn't always been a tribe of simple hunters, that they'd done their share of raiding in the past. As they drew nearer, Victor saw that the grassy mounds were nine long buildings, wholly covered with dirt and grass save their front walls facing inward to where a big stone well sat.

"The shelters make a circle, see? We put up some tents in the center, but we mostly use the shelters because sometimes there's a cold snap or bad snow."

"Don't you guys come south to avoid the worst weather?" Victor thought back to Rellia's map, and though he knew the overall shape of the continent, he didn't know how to place it on a globe. Were they very far north, even after traveling south like this?

"That's true. It's not that bad here most of the time—sometimes we just get rain. You'll see," Chandri said, favoring him with another smile, then hopping out of the wagon. Victor watered and fed Thistle and Starlight, giving them both a good brushing. He saw Chandri, Chala, and some of the hunters moving around between the buildings, unlocking doors, pulling back shutters, and whatever else needed doing ahead of the clan's arrival.

An hour later, Victor was sitting next to his wagon, eating some bread with hunks of dried fruit in it. One of the clan families had given him five of the dense loaves when he'd rescued Tellen and his band. He'd gotten all sorts of things like that, and he never knew who gave him what. Every morning for weeks, he'd stepped out of his wagon to another offering. Sometimes it was food, and sometimes it was art or something someone had crafted.

Victor had several beautifully beaded vests, some warm woolen shirts, more socks than he could count, and even some knitted woolen hats. Most of the clothing was dyed in the muted grays and rust reds that the clan seemed to prefer, and Victor quite liked them. He'd tried to track people down to thank them or to politely refuse something overly generous, like an exquisite, finely detailed, carved bust of a great bear-like creature—its wood was lustrous and dense, and he knew it was rare. Nobody ever admitted to giving him anything.

He was just brushing his hands off when the first pack roladii started waddling into camp, and it wasn't long after that when the whole place was abuzz with activity. Chandri and the others had done a good job getting the stale air moving out of the buildings, but it was quite a production getting everything else up and running. Victor helped wherever he could—rescuing a fallen well bucket, digging postholes for the roladii pen, and generally helping anyone to lift pretty much anything.

Long after the sun had set and glow lamps were hung from the fronts of the shelters, a great bonfire was lit near the well, and the clan began celebrating their arrival. They'd had good hunts in their other camps and were looking forward to a long and restful winter and spring. Victor stood near the shelter where Tellen and Oynalla spent their winter, leaning against the wall and sipping cheb-cheb, watching Chandri and Chala dance to the clan's wild drum and fiddle music.

He'd been told the names of the instruments, but his brain kept thinking of them as fiddles. They looked like violins, he supposed, but some were small, some were large, and they all seemed to play different notes. When three or four of the players got together, though, and played one of their rousing tunes accompanied by some of the drummers, the music stirred something in Victor, and he could see why the clan danced so much.

Thayla and Deyni joined in the dance, and soon twenty or more of the clan were gyrating in a circle around the fire. "You smile like you'd enjoy joining in, warrior," Oynalla said, forcing his smile even wider with her usual cackle.

"Looks fun, for sure." Victor nodded.

"You should have your little huntress teach you." Oynalla's cackle was particularly sharp; clearly, she was pleased with her barb.

"Hey, she's not *my huntress*," Victor chuckled.

"Good! Best you remember that. Now, are you ready for your spirit quest?" Oynalla didn't miss a beat as she completely changed the subject.

"Spirit quest? You mean to try to find another affinity?" Victor remembered her mentioning the ritual long ago, but she hadn't said anything about it in all the time he'd been "training" with her.

"More than that might come from a spirit quest, Victor, but that's one possibility. We're near a place of power here, and if we prepare properly, you could gain many insights into yourself and your potential. The spirits are strong and old around here, and they favor our clan. They'll test you, but I think they'll favor you, too."

"What do I need to do?" Victor asked, his mind racing with excitement—this was the kind of thing he'd been hoping she'd teach him.

Oynalla cackled and slapped the cup of cheb-cheb from his hand, sending it to the ground with a clatter and splash. "First, you stop drinking that—fourteen days without food or drink is the first and easiest preparation."

"Uh, fourteen days without water? I don't think so . . ."

"Foolish warrior! So quick to fill your belly that you haven't tested your body, hmm? You trust Oynalla; fourteen days will be possible for you." She paused to laugh, watching his face, then said, "You're lucky, warrior! You'll have a pure, cleansed spirit when you take up your quest. Someone with a weaker body wouldn't be able to purge so thoroughly."

Victor frowned and then nodded. He supposed if he started to die of thirst, he could just drink some water and tell Oynalla it wasn't going to happen. He gestured to the cup of spilled cheb-cheb, "You could have let me finish that. It was the good stuff!"

14

SPIRIT QUEST

Victor rolled over on his blanket and groaned. He wanted very badly to reach into his ring and pull out a seasoned bowl of rice and chopped meat. "And a whole keg of frosty ale," he muttered, clenching his fists. Truthfully, he'd stopped feeling "hungry" by the fourth day or so of his fast. He knew his body wanted the nutrients and that he'd make good use of them, but he wasn't hurting for food. No, the hard part was not drinking anything.

It was his thirteenth day, though, and Victor wouldn't give up now. Three days ago, Oynalla had instructed him to camp out on the plains, specifically there, half a day's hike from the clan's winter encampment, insisting that isolation was part of the process. More than that, she'd said that this was a place of power, a site of great battles and hunts, and she'd cautioned him not to sleep but to sit on his blanket and spend his time contemplating the world, the universe, and himself.

Oynalla had said that cultivating his Energies was a good use of his time, so Victor had spent much of his time doing so. He knew he was on the verge of the "improved" tier—he could feel the potential brimming in his Core, the Energies within pushing against their boundaries like floodwaters cracking a concrete dam.

The days had begun to bleed into each other, and in all honesty, Victor was only about eighty percent sure that he'd been alone for four days. It could have been three or five, in which case, he was done with his fast and should start the next phase of his spirit quest. He looked at the clay bowl and little clay jars filled with Oynalla's special incense and wondered if he should start burning it. "Wait . . ." his fuzzy, buzzing mind thought back to what Oynalla had said. "She'd send me a message? She'd come speak to me? I was supposed to wait for the moons . . ."

Victor sighed and flopped backward onto his blanket, his head spinning and little stars bursting in his vision. He knew that he'd probably black out if he stood up suddenly. "What the fuck am I supposed to do? I can't remember shit!" he yelled up at the pale blue sky and the steel gray clouds drifting through it. There had definitely been something about the moons and waiting for his fifth day. "Or night. It must be night if I'm supposed to wait for the moons."

His eyes started to grow heavy as his body felt the pull of the planet's gravity and the warm embrace of his blanket. Groaning again, Victor forced himself to sit up and resolved to be patient. Time seemed to move the fastest when he cultivated, so he decided to work on his Core. In an effort to make the time pass more quickly and to keep things interesting, he began to work on a new rage construct. "Let's see," he said, talking to the tall grass that swayed with the cool northern breeze. "Something from my old life or something from this world?"

Before he could answer himself, a suitable memory popped into his mind. He remembered how he'd found Gorz and the magic ring when he'd been new to Lam's squad of delvers. Victor reached up to touch Gorz and felt his bare chest. Oynalla had made him give the amulet to her for safekeeping, not wanting him to "ruin his contemplation" by speaking to the conscious artifact. His mind drifted back to the time when he'd felt as if he was figuring things out, making some progress, and then he'd foolishly isolated himself where some thugs could find him.

Victor tried to focus on those thugs, tried to remember the names he'd learned, but he couldn't. His mind kept racing forward to the time after the encounter and how he'd felt when he woke up. He thought about how angry and frustrated he'd been, partially at the guys who'd robbed and tried to kill him but mostly at himself.

He just kept screwing up—at the time, that was all he could think. Looking back, though, with the weight of the memories he'd built since then, Victor was willing to give himself a bit more grace. He'd been new to Fanwath, bullied, tortured, beaten, and forced to fight and kill over and over. Was it any wonder he hadn't made perfect decisions?

"This isn't helping," Victor chided himself. He was supposed to focus on the rage, focus on its source, and take that away from the memory, purifying it and turning it into a suitable construct for his cultivation. "All right, no self-therapy right now. Think about the rage."

Victor allowed himself to sink into the memory, allowed himself to feel that frustration and anger again, and when he had the feeling right, he zeroed in on it, examined it, tasted it, and savored it. He felt the heat start to build in his pathways, and a savage grin spread on his face as he continued to focus on the feeling, stacking it, compounding it, and slowly building the construct of pure rage that he could use over and over again to cultivate that Energy.

Victor lost himself in his hunt for rage-attuned Energy, and when he finally pushed the surging flood of scorching red Energy back into his Core, he opened his eyes to twilight. "One more night." His mind felt clearer, and he knew he needed to make it through the night and one more day before he was supposed to burn Oynalla's incense. It seemed unfathomable that he hadn't had a drop of liquid in thirteen days and had been awake for four.

Everything seemed surreal, even his thoughts, and when he looked out over the grass and saw glimmering translucent animals grazing, running, even flying in the purple twilit sky, he wasn't surprised. "Hello, spirits," he said. He watched two glimmering, long-tailed birds swoop and dive, seeming to perform an elaborate dance in the air. He realized he was smiling when his cheeks began to ache, and he closed his eyes, savoring the buzzing high he felt. "Well, how about a new inspiration construct?" he asked himself, deciding he needed to do something before he slipped into a warm, comfortable slumber.

Once again, Victor focused on his time on Fanwath, and when he thought about inspiration, his mind drifted to the time when Polo Vosh was pushing him to improve his axe skill. He remembered how Polo's movements had seemed like magic, how he'd just barely twitch his huge, furry body to avoid a tremendous, arcing cleave from Victor. He thought about how Polo had been able to make it feel as if he was getting close, make it feel as if there was a chance he might hit him. Polo was a great axe fighter and an even greater instructor, and Victor felt there was much about him to be inspired by.

As always, Victor's time building and cultivating his new inspiration construct was easier than when he worked on his rage. He gained rage Energy more quickly, thanks to his affinity, but the process was painful and exhausting, whereas focusing on his inspiration construct was almost like meditation—it felt renewing and left his mind clear and focused.

When Victor's pathways were full to bursting with inspiration Energy, he gathered it up and pulled it into his Core, and before he'd pulled half of it in, he felt the dam start to break—his Core was on the verge of advancing. Straining, sweat beading on his forehead, Victor pulled and pushed with his will, forcing the Energy into his Core.

When it happened, it wasn't the painful explosion that he'd subconsciously feared. It was more like wearing a belt two notches too small and then quickly loosening it. His Core pulsed and stretched, flaring brightly, and then the twin suns of his Energy attunements settled into their new, larger, improved orbs, and Victor knew that they had the density required to grow a hundredfold beyond what they were now. His cultivation to an advanced Core would be a long journey.

Just to confirm what he already knew, he looked at the section of his status page that described his Core and Energy.

Core:	**Spirit Class: Improved 1**		
Energy Affinity:	**3.1, Rage 9.1, Inspiration 7.4**	**Energy:**	**2839/2839**

Victor opened his eyes, pleased with himself, and saw that the sun was hanging high above his head. He'd spent the entire night and morning working through that inspiration construct. "Fucking hell," he said, grinning, though it hurt his dry lips. His tongue felt thick and swollen in his mouth, and he realized his Energy-rich body was finally starting to feel the effects of his deprivations.

Though his body might be struggling, Victor's mind was clear. Spending eighteen hours building his inspiration Energy had done wonders for his mental focus. He looked around the plain, at the swaying grass, at the colorful bugs crawling on the stems and the flying insects that buzzed or glided around, and he breathed deeply of the cool breeze. There was a hint of something colder in the air, and he knew winter was truly upon them. He supposed he was lucky Oynalla hadn't made him wait for a snowstorm to sit out in the elements.

Victor meditated and cultivated for the rest of the day. Time moved strangely now that he was truly at the end of his wakeful vigil—sometimes the sun refused to move in the sky, and sometimes he'd close his eyes to gaze upon his Core, opening them to see the sun had dipped markedly toward the horizon.

When it finally sank below the curve of the grasslands and the sisters' light fell upon him, Victor suddenly remembered, with perfect clarity, Oynalla's instructions. It was almost as if he heard her voice speaking into his ear: "On the evening of your fifth day, carefully mix the two powders I've given you. Ignite them with a touch of your Energy. When you've breathed deeply of their smoke, then you should quickly cast Spirit Walk."

Victor remembered asking her about the risk of performing a spirit walk while alone, and she'd laughed, saying the spirits in this place were strong, and few things would dare their ire by interfering. Then she'd cackled and said, "Some risk is part of the process. What good is a quest with no danger?"

"Fair enough," he muttered, his lips barely moving and his voice a hoarse whisper. He pulled the ceramic bowl closer and pulled the cork from the first little jar. The pink powder within reminded his nose of a spice he might smell in his *abuela's* kitchen. If someone asked him which spice, he'd struggle to put a finger on it, but that didn't matter, he reckoned, pouring the jar into the bowl. The second jar contained a brown powder with larger granules, and when he mixed it into the bowl, the smell that arose was something like ashes and cedar, and it tickled the back of his throat, threatening to pull forth a sneeze.

"Let's get things moving," Victor said, putting a finger into the mixture and pushing out a stream of rage-attuned Energy. He wasn't sure why he chose rage, perhaps because he was most familiar with it; perhaps he'd just randomly selected it. In any case, the hot red Energy surged through his pathway into the powder, and suddenly it was flaring with red flames, reminding Victor of a road flare his *abuelo* had sparked to life when his old truck had broken down.

Thick, colorful smoke rose from the flaring bowl, and worried that he'd miss his chance, Victor quickly leaned over it and breathed deeply. His vision instantly went dark, and he swore he saw fireworks exploding in the blackness. His mind started to slip away from the present, and Victor, clinging to his wits with a surge of will, immediately cast Spirit Walk.

As always, his surroundings changed, but things were very different this time. He stood on the spirit plane, that much was sure, but he was surrounded by a host of spirits. They'd made a circle around him, and though they didn't crowd close, Victor felt rather uneasy. Some of the spirits flared brightly with Energy, their auras overshadowing the dimmer spirits around them.

The spirits weren't all people. Some were animals—creatures like bears, antlered deer-like beasts, a huge boar, and myriad smaller things that looked like rodents or rabbits. Still, most of the spirits looked like Shadeni, with a few Ardeni and even a Cadwalli that sat nearby, smoking an ethereal pipe. Victor looked around the circle of spirits and said, "Hello."

"Warrior." Victor was surprised that it wasn't one of the Shadeni spirits that spoke to him but the massive boar, its tusks bobbing up and down as its lower jaw moved to accommodate the deep rumbling voice coming from its chest.

"I've been called that, yes. My name is Victor." For the first time, Victor realized he was holding Lifedrinker. She was limned with a red glow, and he wondered when he'd decided to channel Energy into her. He slipped her haft into the loop at his belt and carefully held his hands at his sides, empty.

"You seek a quest?" the rumbling voice of the boar asked.

"I do."

"Why would those such as we aid an outsider? A mad Berserker?" This time one of the Shadeni spoke, and Victor had to squint against the flare of his aura. The ghostly figure had long braids dressed with polished bones and teeth, and his ribbed bone vest hung down over a belt sporting two ivory-hafted hatchets.

"I'm not mad, friend," Victor said, carefully choosing the word "friend." He'd almost said, "dude," and admired his quick mental edit. "I'm a friend to the clan that hunts these lands. Tellen and Oynalla consider me family, and I'm not a stranger to the spirit plane. I seek to better myself so that I might aid my friends and continue my battles against evil." He'd have liked to take credit for that answer, but Oynalla had rehearsed with him the types of things he should say to the spirits. His words were true, though, and he didn't feel dishonest, simply grateful that he'd had a friend help him polish up his words.

"This one may be full to bursting with rage, but that's only half his story," a great bear, his fur dark but speckled with silvery hairs, lying with his chin on his paws, rumbled. He sounded similar to the boar, but the power that accompanied the rumble of his voice was undeniable—here was a creature that was strong and wise, someone to listen to and give deference. Victor wasn't alone in that understanding. The spirits near the bear turned to him and backed away a step. "Well, warrior, show us your other side; call forth your companions."

Victor knew what the bear meant, and he immediately cast Manifest Spirit, fueling the spell with inspiration-attuned Energy. Silver-white forms shimmered into existence around him, his pack forming a loose circle within the greater circle of other spirits. They sat and regarded the host with that discerning, intelligent gaze that canines sometimes affected.

"Good," the bear rumbled. "This one is strong with spirit, balanced and rich. Who among you can scoff at rage? Who among you wouldn't howl at inspiration? His spirit is thoroughly cleansed and plain to see! I can read the deeds of this warrior writ large on his soul. Can any of you deny that he's brought evil low? That he's tasted the love and gratitude of many? I will grant you a quest, warrior. Will any others?" The bear still hadn't lifted his head from his paws, lying on his stomach the entire time he spoke, but his voice rumbled and echoed over the plains, and Victor felt himself straightening with pride as the great spirit spoke about him.

"I have a quest for this warrior," another Shadeni spirit spoke up, a woman sitting with crossed legs, a long, glimmering knife in one hand.

"I will offer this warrior a quest," said the boar, digging at the ground and nodding his ponderous head.

"We have a quest for the warrior," said a small rabbit-like animal, and Victor saw that it had several more of its kind clustered close behind it.

After several moments of silence, the bear's voice rumbled again, "Good. I will offer guidance toward a new affinity, warrior. What rewards will you others offer?"

"I can tell the warrior where my family hid an artifact," said the Shadeni woman.

"I will teach the warrior how to charge as I did when I lived!" the boar growled, digging his hooves into the soil once again.

"We will teach the warrior a new way to manifest his spirit," the little rabbit creature said, its voice squeaking almost comically.

"You've heard the offers, warrior. Make a choice—which of us will you aid?"

Victor didn't hesitate; he looked at the enormous bear and said, "I will aid you, Great One."

"It is good," the bear rumbled. "Leave me to speak with this warrior now. Go back to your business, spirits of the plain." There were some grumbles and sighs, but the gathered spirits began to disperse, walking away into the grass and fading into the misty twilight, even as Victor tried to keep them focused in his view. "Are you sure you want me to uncover another spirit affinity, warrior? You'll need to work that much harder to build the strength of the ones you have."

"I'm sure, Great One, though only if you think it worthwhile. Oynalla wasn't sure I had a strong connection to another attunement." Victor watched the bear's head, wondering if he'd ever move, and then he realized he was presuming a lot by calling him a bear. The creature was ursine in shape, but long, bony tines mingled with his dark, silver-specked fur, and his canines protruded along his muzzle, longer and more curved than any bear's on Earth. The great creature must have sensed Victor's scrutiny because he finally opened his eyes, the bright red orbs boring into him.

"Oynalla is a great friend of the spirits here, but she sees little of what my gaze reveals. You have at least two more affinities rivaling what you've already uncovered. The one I guide you to will depend on how you solve my quest."

Victor started to ask what the quest was, but he held his tongue—the bear would come around to it when it was ready. Instead, he copied his coyotes and looked at the great spirit, waiting for it to speak.

"The reward I offer you is great, but the risk is commensurate. I can read on your spirit that you won't shy from danger, so I'll tell you plainly. My offspring's offspring still wander this world, warrior. One such, a great male named Bitterpaw, has become tainted by an artifact of great evil. He is beyond redemption, warrior, and I need you to find him and put him down. The artifact, a necklace of teeth that he wears like a trophy on his wrist, must be destroyed."

"Oh, this quest isn't in the spirit plane?" Victor wasn't sure why he'd thought the entire quest would be completed during his spirit walk.

"No, warrior. Will you accept my quest? It will weigh heavily upon you until you've completed it." The bear ponderously stood, and he towered over Victor on all fours. He must have weighed ten thousand pounds when he was alive, and Victor hoped his descendent wasn't that large. Victor also hoped he'd be able to find Bitterpaw without too much trouble, not wanting to be caught up in this quest for too long, but he didn't want to back down now.

"I'll accept your quest, Great Bear," he said, hoping he wasn't insulting the creature by calling it a bear.

He needn't have worried, though—the bear nodded and stepped closer, lowering his enormous head so it was just in front of Victor's. "Good, Victor. You'll find my troublesome offspring a week's journey west of the old witch's camp. If you're faster and run more like a bear, you'll find him sooner. He leaves death and destruction in his wake, and it's good that you go to face him because he'd find your friends sooner or later. Now, rest your hand upon my brow."

Victor reached his right hand up to rest on the bear's massive bony head. His fur was rough, and Victor was sure he could feel stiff spines of bone hiding among the hairs. Still, he pressed his hand down until his palm was flat on the great brow, and then a message appeared in his vision:

*****Thunderbite, the Elder Spinebear, has offered you a Quest: Hunt down the bear known as Bitterpaw, best him in combat, and destroy the**

toothed amulet that has corrupted his spirit. Reward: Thunderbite will guide you to a new spirit affinity. Warning: This Quest is a binding Energy contract—failure to work toward the goal will result in a loss of Energy affinity. Accept? Yes/No.***

"Is that what you meant when you said the quest would weigh heavily on me? I'll lose Energy affinity if I don't work toward it?"

"Yes, warrior. One should not enter into a bargain with great spirits lightly."

For a moment, Victor was tempted to touch the "no" option, leave the spirit plane, and forget about this whole business. He could return to camp, eat until he passed out, then have a relaxing winter with his friends. "Or I could stop being a chickenshit," Victor muttered and touched the "yes" option.

"I like the color of your spirit, Victor. This will not be an easy task—Bitterpaw will be a challenging opponent for you, and I would encourage you to fight him alone. It would be wise, should you bring a hunting party, to keep them away when you do battle. I predict the melee will be furious and deadly, and those lacking true strength will be cut like so much grass before the scythe."

"All right, um, Thunderbite. Will I need to come to find you when I'm finished?"

"If you walk the spirit plane from anywhere on these grasslands, we will find each other. Good luck, warrior." Thunderbite turned, then, and began to lumber away, his great shoulders and hips rolling with each ponderous step.

"See you soon," Victor said, watching the bear go, and though he never blinked or unfocused his gaze, in just a few seconds, the bear was gone, and Victor was alone on the twilit spirit plane, nothing but shimmering grasslands illuminated by bright stars in every direction. Victor reached inside himself and canceled his spirit walk, and when he woke, he found himself sprawled on his back, the sun high in the sky and shining directly into his eyes.

"Gah," Victor said, rolling feebly to his side. He felt drained and weak, his head buzzing and foggy. He closed his eyes, concentrating, and reached into his storage ring, pulling out a bowl of hot noodles, vegetables, and meat he'd bought back in Gelica. He set it on the blanket next to him, then pulled out a keg of fresh water and a tankard. Victor struggled to a sitting position, looked around the empty, sunny plains, and said, "Thanks for not letting anyone kill me, spirits."

He spent an hour eating and drinking. He remembered seeing in a VR that someone who'd been starving shouldn't overdo it with food or drink, but his body told him a different story, and though he started out slow, he ended up wolfing down more food than he could have eaten in a week in his old life. He figured admonishments like that weren't meant for Level Thirty-Two descendants of Quinametzin.

When he'd eaten and drunk his fill, Victor stood, shook out his blanket, and stowed it away. He turned toward Tellen's camp and started hiking in that direction. He felt a certain urgency to begin work on his quest, but he felt there was time to stop by the camp to let Oynalla and the others know what he was up to.

Victor felt a certain tingle in his gut, and when he thought about it, walking over the grasslands, he realized he was excited. "I'm on a fucking quest!" he said, grinning. "I need to fight an insane bear, and then his great-grandpa is going to teach me some shit!" He laughed at the craziness of it all, and then he started jogging—no sense wasting time.

15

WESTWARD

When Victor jogged into the Shadeni camp, he was greeted by the hunters on watch with friendly waves and shouts of welcome. He truly had become like family to some of the hunters over the months, especially after he and Chandri had returned, triumphant, from their hunt for Tellen. He entered the longhouse, as he'd learned the clan called the rectangular, turf-covered buildings, where Oynalla and Tellen had taken up residence and, blinking away the stinging cook smoke that hung in the air, looked around the dim interior.

Most of the smoke came from the two open hearths at the center of the building, and though they had chimneys, some smoke invariably hung in the air. Quite a few clan folk were busy in the main hall, cooking, scraping hides, stitching leather, and doing any number of other small tasks, but he didn't see Thayla or Oynalla, so he moved to the wooden steps at the far end of the long, low-ceilinged space.

Several people greeted him as he walked past their benches or work-spaces, and he smiled and returned the greeting. Victor had learned almost everyone's names, at least the ones that lived in this particular longhouse—thirty or more clan members called this building their home. He descended one level to where Oynalla, Tellen, and their immediate family members, which seemed to include Thayla and Deyni, had rooms.

The second floor was less smoky. Light being provided by glow lamps and the absence of cookfires helped that cause. Though the construction was rough, all the timbers were solid, and no dirt was present on the wooden planks of the hallway. Victor followed it until he came to Oynalla's quarters, and when he saw the beaded curtains were pulled open, he stepped into the area where the Old Mother spent most of her days—a small square room piled with furs and blankets with an Energy-driven teakettle on a low wooden table as its centerpiece.

Oynalla was sitting, facing the doorway, reading from a small red leather-bound journal, as she often did in the afternoons, steeping some very pungent smelling tea. Thayla and Deyni weren't present, so Victor was subjected to Oynalla's full attention as he stepped through the low archway, rattling some beads with his passage. "Ha!" she crowed. "I can see from your grinning, greasy face that you've had some success!"

"Greasy?" Victor asked, rubbing at his chin and mouth. He'd eaten some little sausages while jogging back to camp. Was that what she meant?

"Yes, only a successful hunt could spur such an appetite. Had you failed, you'd be depriving yourself out of guilt and self-loathing." She laughed, and Victor couldn't tell how much she was messing with him and how much she'd hit the nail on the head.

"Well," he said, trying to take some wind out of her sails, "it wasn't really a success yet. I got a quest, but now I have to complete it."

She regarded him for a moment, closing one eye and squinting at him, her crow's-feet piling atop each other. "A dangerous one, is it?"

"I'm not really sure. I have to kill a bear that's gone insane or something. I got the quest from a huge bear that said the one I have to hunt is his descendent. Why could some of the animal spirits speak to me? I mean, animals don't speak outside the spirit plane, do they?"

"Few animals gain the means to speak, even on the spirit plane, Victor. I know the bear you speak of, and he's a great, old, powerful spirit. He evolved many times during his mortal existence and has lingered around Fanwath far longer than most spirits do. Were there other creatures that spoke to you?"

"Yeah, um, a boar, a rabbit, er feyris, and some Shadeni spirits. I mean, there were like a hundred spirits crowded around when I started the spirit walk."

"Truly?" For once, Oynalla didn't chase her word with a laugh of any sort. "They must have sensed your strong Core, and, of course, the smoke I gave you helped. Yes, you can thank Oynalla that so many spirits came to witness you." This time she laughed.

"Well, I need to hunt this bear, and I should probably start soon.

Thunderbite made it so that I have to keep working toward it, or I'll lose Energy affinity. Whatever that means . . ."

"Mother's bones!" Oynalla hissed. "Fool boy! Must I teach you every little thing? You are bound to complete this quest now, or you'll make yourself a helpless, whimpering shadow of a man! Should you refuse to hunt this bear or fail, you'll slowly lose your ability to channel and absorb Energy! You'll become as you were when you first came to this world, but worse because your body and spirit now require Energy!" She looked at Victor's slack-jawed face and shook her head. "Did the bear not warn you?"

"Yeah, he said it would 'weigh heavily on me.' I mean, the System also put up a message saying this would happen; I guess I just didn't understand it fully. It doesn't matter anyway, Oynalla. I want to complete the quest. Thunderbite's going to help me uncover another affinity."

"Best you start then," the old woman said, nodding. "Keep the quest the focus of your attention, and you shouldn't suffer any loss of affinity. Can Oynalla help you with anything, warrior?"

"Where are Thayla and Deyni?" Victor looked around, indicating the empty space around Oynalla's teakettle.

"They've gone with Tellen and his daughters—a hunt for small game and a learning opportunity for the young one." Oynalla grinned and narrowed her eyes mischievously, "All your women off together on a hunt! What might they talk about?" Her cackle rang out, and Victor was glad they weren't out in the open, around other clan members.

"You're fucking nuts," Victor said before he could catch himself. Oynalla didn't seem offended, though, and she continued to laugh, though more quietly. "Anyway, I'm glad they're gone. The bear said I should go alone, that anyone who came with me would be at risk."

"At risk, hmm? It's good that you took this quest, then. If this mad bear is nearby, it threatens the clan." She regarded Victor for a long moment, her sharp, bright eyes finally resting on Lifedrinker. "Will you hunt the bear with that axe? Spinebears grow large, warrior. Perhaps a spear would be wise. What about your armor? Did not your fancy metal vest get destroyed when you rescued Tellen?"

"I figured I'd use Lifedrinker, yeah. Sure, a spear is probably better for hunting something big, but I'm good with an axe, and she's thirsty. I owe her. As far as armor goes, no, I don't have any." He rested a hand on the beaded leather vest he wore, a gift from the clan, and said, "I have other leather vests and even a leather jacket, though."

Oynalla frowned, still managing to laugh somehow, and said, "A spine-bear will scoff at leather. Help me up, warrior. I'll bring you to the clan's treasurer and tradesman. Bring your wealth—you'll need to barter."

Victor laughed and said, "My wealth? It's all in my storage rings. I guess my wagon's the most valuable thing I own, but I don't want to trade that. Let's go, Old Mother." He pulled her to her feet, thinking back to the time when she'd refused his help, saying she needed to work to remain strong. He wondered if it was a sign of her giving in to her old age or just a sign of her familiarity with him that she now let him aid her.

Oynalla clung to his arm, and they climbed up out of the lower level and then out through the longhouse into the bright afternoon sun. "Gul-dak is in yonder longhouse," Oynalla said, pointing to the building directly across the central courtyard, on the opposite side of the well.

"Gul-dak, hmm? Sounds familiar. Have I met him?" Victor asked, starting toward the building with Oynalla still gripping his elbow, her bony old fingers strong as vise grips.

"Ha! How do I know who you've met, warrior?" Oynalla shook her head, eyes on the ground in front of her feet, a chuckle bubbling up from her throat the entire time they crossed the courtyard. Victor didn't bother to answer—either he'd met the man or heard people speak about him. It didn't really matter.

They found Gul-dak on the fourth level of the longhouse, in a wide open space, though as usual, Victor had to duck to keep from cracking his skull on the long rough beams that held up the ceiling. Barrels, sacks, and crates filled the room, and Gul-dak was busy counting carefully packed bottles of wine when Oynalla spied him and called out, "Ha! Old trickster! Pretending to count the wine while you have an early drink?"

"Oynalla!" Gul-dak said, turning to face her and Victor. He had the biggest belly of any clan member Victor had seen, and he clapped his palms against it, making the fat quiver under his tight linen shirt while he laughed. He was old, though not as old as Oynalla, and his hair had gone mostly white. He wore spectacles, too, and Victor strained his brain, trying to remember if he'd seen anyone else wearing glasses in this world. It seemed to him that anyone with any levels or Energy to speak of wouldn't need them.

"I've brought you a customer, old thief. Be good to him, or I'll curse your dreams with a spell." Victor knew Oynalla was teasing the old merchant, but he was startled to see real fear in the man's eyes. He hurried forward, wringing his hands in front of himself and bowing.

"Old Mother! You wouldn't, would you?" he asked, bowing again and ducking his head.

"Oh, Ancestors! Victor, look upon a man with no sense of humor." Oynalla laughed, and as Gul-dak straightened, smiling in relief, she continued, "Also, look upon a man who spent his life counting beads instead of strengthening his Core—a man with little understanding of the workings of Energy!"

"Hello," Victor said, holding out a hand, feeling rather sorry for Gul-dak. He'd not seen that side of Oynalla before—what he'd taken for teasing seemed, in actuality, to be thinly veiled scorn. The small portly fellow reached up to take his hand, and though his hand was pudgy, his grip was firm, and he smiled genuinely at Victor.

"I've heard much about you, Victor, the demon slayer! Tellen is the son of my oldest friend, and I owe you greatly for his safe return. What can this old merchant do for you?"

"He requires armor and not something for hunting hoofed game. He needs something that might stop the claws of a great spinebear," Oynalla said before Victor could answer.

"Um, yeah, and I have goods to trade," Victor said.

"Armor, you say? Surely we have something that will work. Come over to the storage coffers," Gul-dak said, motioning Victor toward a row of rune-covered wooden and metal boxes lined up against the far wall. Some were small, about the size of a shoebox, and others were more like big wooden trunks.

"Are those all dimensional containers?" Victor asked, looking at the runes that adorned the "coffers." Some had the runes burned into the wood, and some had them etched into metal straps.

"Aye, lad," the old merchant said as he walked over to them. He gestured back toward all the barrels and crates. "All this is usually stored within a few of those coffers. I take things out to keep ready for the clan and to take inventory." He glanced nervously at Oynalla and said, "Not to steal sips of wine!"

"Ha! Old lush," Onyalla said, shaking her head. Again, Victor couldn't quite figure out if she hated the man or was just busting his chops.

"Here's where I've stored all the armor—some for the clan warriors, but most for trading when we stop by a city." He looked nervously at Oynalla and then smiled up at Victor and continued, "What sort of armor do you need, warrior?"

"Well . . ." Victor started, but Oynalla cut him off.

"Something metal. Something that can grow with him when he lets his rage run rampant. Don't hold out, Gul-dak—not if you value peaceful sleep!" Oynalla cackled, and Gul-dak flinched away. Victor swore he saw beads of sweat pop into existence on the old merchant's wrinkled red brow.

"Metal and enchanted for resizing . . ." he said softly, eyes going distant as he laid a hand on the iron-strapped wooden chest.

"Don't play your merchant games with us, Gul-dak," Oynalla said, giving Victor's elbow a squeeze. "He'll have something, Victor, don't worry."

"I'm not . . ." Victor began, but then Gul-dak exclaimed and produced a heavy metal garment, grunting with the weight as he hefted it to the top of a nearby chest.

"Enchanted scale shirt, too heavy for most of our hunters. It's been in here for a few seasons now. Couldn't get the price I wanted in Gelica, and Tellen thought it might come in handy during a raid."

"You have permission to sell it, old man?" Oynalla asked.

"Of course! If I get the right price . . ." he eyed Victor nervously.

Victor just grunted and picked up the armor. The metal looked like steel to him, and the layered scales were dense, meticulously stitched to the supple, thick leather underneath. They rippled with the lights in the storeroom as he hefted it and turned it over, looking for defects and trying to imagine what it would feel like to wear. "It's heavier than my old armor. I'm used to my arms being free, and this goes all the way to the wrists. Looks like it will hang down past my belt, too."

"It's a good piece of armor. We took it in trade for a Gethian roladii sire and two dams. The man who traded it swore the metal was ten percent amber ore. It's enchanted for self-repair and, as you asked, resizing."

"Put it on, Victor," Oynalla said.

"Well, there's the matter of the price . . ." Gul-dak said, but Victor pulled the heavy garment on over his head, grunting to get it over his shoulders. He'd made it halfway when he finally had to admit defeat.

"I'm stuck," he said, voice muffled.

"Bond with it," Oynalla said.

"Wait!" Gul-dak said, but it was too late. Victor channeled some Energy out into the armor, felt it expand, and easily pulled it on the rest of the way. When his head pulled clear of the neckhole, he looked at the message that had appeared when he bonded with the armor.

*****Amber alloy scale shirt. Artificed for durability, comfort, and self-repair. A fine armor crafted by Getchit Boyle of Fazador.*****

"Cool!" Victor said, then added, "I saw a description of the armor and the name of the guy who made it when I bonded to it."

"Ah, some Artificers add such to their creations. The System is known to do it also." Gul-dak nodded. "There's the matter of the price, though, and seeing as you've already bonded with the item, I feel somewhat disadvantaged. Oynalla, you know my profits go to the clan coffers!"

"Hush, old merchant! This clan owes Victor much. Name him a fair price."

While they bickered, Victor flexed his arms and twisted his torso. The shirt was long, hanging over his hips, and he knew he'd need to take his belt off and put it on over the armor, but other than that, it was quite comfortable. It was heavy, probably twice the weight of his old ringmail vest, but he felt it was probably better armor. He knew he'd be hot in the sun wearing it, but some discomfort might be a reasonable trade-off for receiving fewer wounds in battle. He thought back to the description and said, "It says it's enchanted for 'comfort.' What's that about?"

"That's an enchantment that allows the armor to fit you perfectly. It may have secondary effects, like making it feel lighter than it is or allowing airflow to help you keep from overheating in the sun. I really can't be sure. If I sold that shirt in Gelica, I'd expect three or four thousand beads. Can you afford that sum, Victor?" Gul-dak didn't look hopeful.

"I could, but how about a trade instead?" Victor dug around in his storage rings until he found the shortswords he'd taken from the Ilyathi bounty hunter back when he and Thayla were making their way to Gelica. "These are magical and made of an expensive metal." He laid the pair of swords on the top of the chest, and Gul-dak whistled.

"Those are fine blades, Victor." He glanced nervously at Oynalla and added, "More valuable to the clan than that heavy armor. I'll take them in trade, but you'll have credit with me. Is that fair?" He asked the last question looking at Oynalla, not Victor.

"It is good," Oynalla said, reaching up to retake Victor's elbow. "This one has a quest to begin. Enough dallying. Victor, you have enough supplies?"

"I do," he said, allowing Oynalla to tug him toward the stairs leading up from the storage room. "Thanks, Gul-dak," he called over his shoulder as they left. When he and Oynalla had made it back out into the sunlight, she took Victor's hand in hers and looked up at him, smiling into the daylight so her eyes were lost in folds of wrinkles.

"Victor, keep focused on your quest. Work ever toward your goal, and the spirit's curse won't take hold."

"Curse?"

"A turn of phrase. I mean the requirement that you keep working to solve the quest. Come now, warrior, you could discern my meaning!"

"Yeah, I get it. I'll just go fetch Thistle, and then I'll be on my way, all right? The spirit said the bear was only a few days to the west as long as I traveled 'like a bear.' I figure Thistle's even faster."

"The west? Go quickly then because Tellen took your women that way!"

"They're not my . . ." Victor started to say automatically before Oynalla's words registered. "They went west? How long ago?"

"Two mornings they've been gone now. Go, warrior!"

Victor didn't need to hear that again; he turned toward where he'd parked his wagon and ran. While he loped through the central area of the camp, he pulled off his belt, Lifedrinker and all, and then put it back on over his new armor. The belt was enchanted to resize also, and it fit easily. By the time he'd adjusted Lifedrinker's loop and felt comfortable, he was jogging up to his two vidanii, grazing near his wagon.

Victor saddled Thistle in record time, talking to him in a low soothing voice the whole while. "Ready for a run, boy?" He slipped his boot in the stirrup and pulled himself up, and then they were off, charging over the grass toward the setting sun.

He was worried about Thayla and the others, but only a little—it felt like long odds that they'd run into the rampaging bear just because they'd gone off in the same general direction. "Hey, Gorz," he said, having a sudden thought, "are there any villages or towns west of here?" When Gorz was silent, Victor slapped himself on the head—he'd forgotten to get the amulet back from Oynalla. "Oh, well. I guess I'll find out."

Victor made good time—Thistle loved to run, and carrying just Victor, big as he was, wasn't much of a struggle for the great animal. As the stars and moons came out, and he'd seen no sign of Tellen or the others, he wasn't surprised. He had no idea if they'd gone straight west or followed some game to the south into the forest or north into the plains.

While he hadn't slept, per se, Victor had been physically inactive for a long time, cultivating his Core and then taking a spirit walk, which seemed similar to sleeping as far as his body was concerned. The point was that Victor didn't feel tired, and he let Thistle have free rein, thundering over the plains long into the night. Victor felt purpose driven, and only part of it was due to his concern for his friends—the other part was a burning desire to solve his quest. Vaguely, he wondered if he'd feel so driven if he hadn't agreed to that quest contract with the bear spirit.

Morning found Victor walking ahead of Thistle, holding his lead, giving the animal a break. He'd already fed and watered him and then taken off his saddle, and Victor figured some light walking wouldn't hurt the beast. Truthfully, Thistle seemed ready to run again, and Victor wondered how great his stamina really was—he was supposedly much more evolved and rich in Energy than a roladii; did he need as much rest and sleep as Victor had been giving him? "Too bad I can't search it up on the Net, eh, boy?"

Occasionally, Victor passed thin dirt trails leading north into the plains and south into the trees of the Blue Deep, and he wondered if they were game trails or paths made by people who lived nearby. He felt the urge to explore them, but the need to progress his quest weighed more heavily—he needed to follow the edge of the forest farther west. In his mind, he still hadn't gone far enough to match a "few days of travel if he ran like a bear," at least not a bear like Thunderbite.

After walking briskly for most of the morning, Victor let Thistle wander and graze while he took a break. He sat in the grass, ate some cured meat and cheese, drank a bottle of weak wine, and stretched. Victor still didn't feel like sleeping, which he thought was rather insane, considering how long he'd been awake prior to his spirit walk. "Wait a second," he said, staring at the bright gray sky, realizing he hadn't asked Oynalla how long he'd been gone. For all he knew, he could've slept for days after his spirit walk.

"Well, no way to know for sure right now," he said to Thistle, draping his saddle blanket over the animal and getting him ready for another run. "Let's cover a bit more ground, and maybe tonight we'll camp out, all right?" Thistle turned his big head back toward him and snuffled, pushing his black velvety nose into his shoulder. "Did you want a treat? 'Cause that's how you get a treat, buddy." Victor laughed, holding a pear-like fruit on his flat open palm while the vidanii crunched it down, then snuffed as though he might find another one hidden between Victor's fingers. Victor laughed and hopped into the saddle. "Come on, boy!"

He let Thistle set the pace for the next few hours, which turned out to be a thundering gallop, and they ate up the miles, moving ever westward. Occasionally, Victor saw movement at the edge of the forest, and he wondered if he'd surprised other animals that had bolted for the cover of the trees at his approach or if monsters or people were lurking in the shadows, watching him go past. Not for the first time, he wondered what kept the trees from growing into the plains, expanding the forest year by year. He thought maybe it was doing so, but then he remembered that Tellen's clan had camped there, at the edge of the woods, for generations.

His mind was wandering down just such a train of thought when he felt Thistle's speed falter, and he jerked his eyes back into focus and saw what had startled the beast—not far ahead were lines of smoke and the low wooden structures of an encampment or village. "Good boy! Did you smell that smoke? Steady now; let's keep moving." He slowed Thistle to a trot, still moving toward the single-story wooden buildings.

Victor kept a hand on Lifedrinker, but he didn't pull her out of her loop. He figured some sentries would challenge him soon; he'd already gotten closer than anyone would get to Tellen's camp without being stopped. He was somewhat surprised when no one accosted him, and he rode past the first wooden building. It looked like a cabin to him, but no smoke came from its little stone chimney. Another similar structure was in front of him, and he had to turn Thistle to get around it, and that's when he saw the destruction and carnage.

The smoke wasn't coming from a cookfire or a chimney, he saw, but from a smoldering pyre where some bodies had been burned—not fully consumed by the flames. Whoever had built the pyre hadn't made it big or hot enough to finish the job. Victor rode past the smoldering mess, the smell of smoke and char heavy in the air, making his eyes water. He constantly scanned for movement, wondering who had killed all the people and then who had tried to clean up the mess.

Victor passed several more wooden structures made from logs, then he started to see the blood and broken doors and walls—whatever had killed the people had broken their wooden doors to pieces and sent logs rolling over the dirt paths that served as streets in the little community. More than a dozen buildings were partially destroyed and slathered with dried red blood streaks. Glancing at a log that had rolled onto the track, Victor saw four long, deep grooves, and he realized he'd found his first sign of Bitterpaw.

Nobody showed themselves to him, and Victor didn't want to linger in the ruined place. He turned Thistle to the west again and pushed him back into a trot, moving past the last building, and that's when he saw the little group of people walking ahead of him through the grassland. They appeared to panic and scattered at the sound of Thistle's hooves, but when they turned to see him riding their way, most stopped running and stood, staring while he approached.

Victor waved, trying to indicate his good intentions. None of them waved back, save one little girl with bright blonde hair. She was Ardeni, like the others, and Victor could see the soot stains on her pale blue skin and how her clothes were filthy and torn. Most of the group were young, children to Victor's eyes, though a handful were older. One older man, a burly red-bearded fellow dressed in dark leather clothing and holding a heavy axe of his own, called out, "We want no trouble."

"I'm no trouble," Victor said. "Well, not to people like you," he added.

"We've nothing to give. Our dreams lie smashed and burned behind you."

"I'm not looking to get anything from you," Victor said, slowing Thistle to a walk as he came within a few feet of the group. "Except maybe some information. What did that to your village? Was it a mad bear?"

"You know of it? A demon-possessed spinebear!" a young woman said, pulling the little yellow-haired girl close to her and backing away from Victor.

"I'm on a quest. I have to find that bear and kill it."

"Ha!" The man guffawed. "Better you turn and run, friend. Tell whoever gave you that quest that it's not worth it."

"Don't be an ass, Berom!" another man said, sitting up from where he'd squatted to rest while the group watched Victor approach. He was bald, with a tuft of black hair around his ears, and his dark eyes bored into Victor while he spoke. "The bear is in the woods south of our village. At least that's where it lumbered off after eating its fill of our kinfolk. If you truly aim to fight the thing, I'd like to come. He killed my whole family. My name's Gef. Gef ap'Horl."

"I want to help also," said a thin woman holding a bow as long as she was tall. "I'm Teil, and my husband rests in that beast's gut."

Victor thought about saying no. He almost said he didn't want them to slow him down or get hurt while he fought with the bear, but then he saw their eyes, and he knew they'd happily die if it meant they might help him avenge their loved ones. He cleared his throat and pulled Lifedrinker out to rest across his knees, then he looked into the woman's angry green eyes and said, "Well, I can use the help tracking the monster, I suppose."

16

DUTY AND MADNESS

Victor sat near the coals of the fire that Gef had used to cook a stew for the three of them. Victor had savored the roots and small game meat, seasoned in a way that he could appreciate more now that he had a bit of cooking skill himself. Gef, on the other hand, had some real talent. He saw the older hunter leaning against a tree trunk nearby, his spear propped next to him, and his eyes closed. Victor had a feeling that he'd wake at the slightest sound.

Teil had surprised Victor by scampering up into another tree, its branches heavy with blue pine needles, and then announcing that she'd be sleeping among the boughs. For his part, Victor sat, reading correspondence from Lam and Edeya. Over the last months, they'd sent him regular messages in the Far Scribe book.

Often the letters were just status updates—what they'd been up to, but more importantly, questioning what Victor was up to. He knew they were fishing for information, worried he'd get himself tied up with something that would make their rendezvous in the spring unlikely.

Today's message was more interesting, though—Edeya had sent him a bit of news.

Victor,

We miss you and Thayla and hope things continue to go well with Tellen's clan. We're settled into Lam's temporary estate in Persi Gables, and today she sent me to visit with Rellia. She wanted me to dig for information and rumors—find out how many troops Rellia had managed to raise and see that things were going according to plan.

In the past, when I'd met with Rellia in Gelica, I'd had to go through her personal guard captain, Valla. Today I was met with a different captain, though, and when I asked about Valla, he'd laughed and said she was "hunting barbarians in the grasslands."

I couldn't get him or Rellia to provide any more details, but I have a feeling Rellia sent Valla to check up on you. She knows we have the Far Scribe books, but maybe she wants her own direct line to you. Anyway, keep an eye out for her. I'm not sure you've met her, but her personality leaves much to be desired.

Yours,

Edeya

Victor grunted as he read the missive. He remembered Captain Valla and supposed he'd just deal with her when and if she ever showed up. He picked up his pen and wrote a response to Edeya.

Hey, Chica,

Thanks for reaching out. I'll keep an eye out for that lady—she reminded me of my seventh-grade English teacher, Mrs. Deppa. Maybe it had something to do with her tight collar. Anyway, things are good. I'm on a quest right now to kill a crazy bear, and I know it sounds cool, but it's pretty tragic—the thing has been going around killing people, and I have some survivors with me helping me track it down. Stay safe, and don't let Lam run you around too much!

Victor

Victor closed the book and stored it away in his ring, then he stretched out on his bedroll, propping his arms under his head while he looked for stars between the tops of the nearby trees. He fell asleep that way, trying to make up names for the different constellations he saw, and before he knew it, he woke to the sounds of someone chopping wood and the smell of something brewing on the fire.

"Tanf?" Teil asked, lifting the iron kettle from the coals.

"Tanf?" Victor echoed.

"The drink—tanf root. Do you have a cup?"

"Yeah, thanks. Sorry, I haven't had it before, but it smells familiar. I think some of the Shadeni back at the camp drink it."

"It's common enough," the woman said. She was always curt and scowled often, and Victor felt very sorry for her. He'd learned that she and her husband had been newly married, and Gef had confided in Victor that the villagers had stopped her from charging after the bear alone after it had mauled her husband and the others. She had bright coloring, like most Ardeni, with hair and eyes that reminded him of the coals in the fire—a rich, deep, rusty orange color.

"Here," Victor said, holding out a wooden mug that someone in Tellen's clan had given him. It was smooth and polished, and he knew the wood was valuable because of how heavy and dense it was. It absorbed heat nicely, and he found it perfect for drinking hot tea or broth around the fire.

Teil poured some dark brown liquid into his cup, and if Victor closed his eyes and breathed just right, he could imagine it was coffee. "Good! Thank you," he said, savoring the slightly bitter drink. It had a very different aftertaste than coffee, almost sweet with a tangy sourness.

"The tracks continue south. Even without the skill, you should be able to see it. See how those saplings are snapped and bent? The bear doesn't move around things it can smash through," Gef said, also squatting near the fire and holding out a mug to Teil.

"Yeah, but if it gets harder to spot, I'll be glad to have you along. I never learned that tracking skill."

"Not too late to try. Spend more time hunting and less time fighting, and you might pick it up." Gef took a long sip and grinned at Victor.

"What makes you think I fight a lot?" Victor asked, drinking from his mug and smiling back at the man.

"Oh, stop, you two. Let's not play word games. Drink your tanf, and let's get back on the hunt," Teil said, putting a stop to the banter before it began. Victor shrugged and stood up, throwing the remnants of his drink onto the coals and stowing his cup.

"Yeah, I'm good with that." While the other two packed their bedrolls, Victor put away Thistle's feed bag and barrel of water and then saddled him up. He'd been leading the animal since he met Gef and Teil the day before, and he figured he'd keep doing so, but he liked having the animal ready to ride in case he needed to chase something faster than his two feet could manage.

They proceeded deeper into the forest, and as they delved into the old growth, Victor began to feel grateful that they were following in the bear's path. The great animal had flattened much of the undergrowth, snapped smaller trees, and bent some of the larger ones, making progress through the thick, dense foliage easier. Still, he had to use a machete he'd bought while shopping with Thayla to push through some of the springier, heartier stuff.

After several hours of progress, they came to a fairly wide game trail, and Gef stopped them, studying the rock-strewn dirt path that ran perpendicular to their current course. "Interesting," the man said, rubbing a palm along his bald blue scalp, brushing the sweat back so it didn't run into his eyes.

"What is it?" Teil asked.

"More tracks," Gef said, then stood and gestured off to the right. "Some Shadeni went this way, and, if I'm not wrong, some forest trolls are shadowing them."

"Shadeni?" Victor asked.

"Aye," he said, leaning over and studying the tracks. "One, two, three, four, five sets. Two fairly bright, two not so much, and one barely registering—a child, I'd guess."

"I think I know who they are." Victor knelt and touched the track, wishing he had the skill Gef and most of the Shadeni clan used so freely. "How many trolls? Are they dangerous?"

"I see at least three sets of troll tracks, though they move in each others' steps, making it harder to count. You've never met a forest troll? Aye, they're dangerous, lad."

"I've got to help them, then." Victor didn't wait for them to reply. He just turned to the right and, pulling Thistle, started down the game trail.

"Hold up, Victor!" Teil called. "What about the bear?"

"We'll go for it after I've made sure my friends aren't going to become troll dinner!"

"What if it kills more? There are Ghelli villages in this part of the deep!" Teil said, rushing to grab hold of his shoulder.

"Teil." Victor whirled on her and continued, "You don't get it—those people are like my family. I'm not abandoning them. I promise we'll haul ass after that bear after we find them."

"Teil, you go with him. I'll get eyes on the bear," Gef said.

"Gef, it's mad and uncanny, and if it senses you, you're as good as dead. Stay with us," Teil said, and Victor nodded.

"Yeah, man. Let's stick together. My friends can help track it after we find them." Victor started walking again and said, "Seriously, let's go!" He said the last as if he meant it, his voice rumbling from deep in his gut, and Teil and Gef started after him. Victor nodded, pleased that they'd listened, and picked up the pace, making it hard for Gef to get around him to keep tracking. The older man broke into a trot and glided past him, though, and Victor slowed so he could stay ahead, minding the tracks.

After they'd hiked that way, moving quickly down the game trail, for nearly an hour, Victor felt an uncomfortable sensation in his gut, as if someone had reached into his innards with an icy hand and given them a squeeze. "Ungh . . ." he grunted, stumbling forward. "What the shit?" Victor pressed a hand to his stomach, and slowly the wave of discomfort seemed to fade away until he felt almost normal.

Victor turned an eye inward to his Core, trying to see if he could determine what had happened, and things looked normal to him. He shook his head and began to turn his attention back outward when a faint blue shimmer around his twin suns of Energy caught his attention. He studied it carefully and slowly exhaled a troubled breath—it looked as if a shell or cage of tiny runes had surrounded his Core. "The curse . . ." Victor called up his status sheet, looking at his Energy affinity section.

Energy Affinity:	**2.6 (3.1), Rage 8.6 (9.1), Inspiration 6.9 (7.4)**	**Energy:**	**2841/2841 (3041)**

"Shit!"

"What is it, Victor? Why curse yourself?" Teil asked, jogging lightly to come up beside him.

"I'm bound by this quest to hunt that bear, and I'm losing some Energy affinity by not focusing on it."

"We should turn then. What good will you be to your friends if you've lost your strength?"

"Look, I know you want to hunt that bear, and for a good reason. I do, too! Let's just hurry, all right? If I start to get too weak, I'll turn and get back to the quest—hopefully, that will alleviate some of this curse." Victor gazed ahead for Gef and raised his voice, "Gef, we need to move faster!" Gef turned back, looked at Teil and Victor, and then nodded. He picked up his pace, jogging ahead while he scanned the trail.

Teil gave Victor a searching look, then shrugged and hefted her bow, slipping off the trail to shadow them from the foliage. Victor had no idea how she moved so easily through the ferns, berry bushes, and other shrubs. She did, though, and he had to wonder if she had some sort of travel skill that made it possible. He was still thinking about that when he almost crashed into Gef's back. The older hunter had stopped and held a fist up, indicating they should be quiet. Victor loomed over him, Lifedrinker held ready, waiting to hear what he had to say.

Gef didn't speak but held a finger to his lips, pointing off the trail and to the right. Victor saw that Teil had also stopped, hugging the bole of a tree in the direction Gef was pointing. She pointed to her eyes, then off in the same direction, and Victor thought she either meant she saw something or she was going to go look.

His second guess proved right as she slowly, silently started to creep around the tree trunk, and, as she disappeared from sight, Gef squatted down, making himself small behind a bush. Victor followed his lead, carefully stepping on moist soil as he moved off the trail to put a wide, rough, white-barked tree trunk between him and whatever Teil had gone to investigate.

A few moments later, Teil returned to the trail, creeping noiselessly through the shadowy undergrowth. When she was squatting on the trail between Victor and Gef, she spoke, though in such a soft voice that Victor wasn't sure he'd have been able to hear it if not for his improved body and attributes. "Three trolls sharing a bloody feast not far from here."

Victor liked to think he'd gained some control over his rage, that he'd figured out how to keep himself cool and collected in high-stress situations. Still, when he heard that the trolls they were following, the trolls that had been following the people he cared about, were having a "bloody feast," his vision went red, and he turned, crashing through the undergrowth, shouldering saplings aside, and, without conscious thought, he cast Berserk.

He smashed through the last stand of shrubs between him and the little clearing where the trolls were hunched over a carcass, oblivious to the shouts and queries coming from his two companions. He'd made plenty of noise in his passage, and the trolls weren't caught unaware, though he'd moved so quickly, they didn't have much time to prepare. They stood from their shared meal, monstrous faces and fangs dripping their red delights, and lifted their clawed hands, circling Victor as he burst into the open.

Victor had one thing on his enraged mind—punish the creatures that had wronged him somehow. When his red-tinted vision met the trio, some part of his brain acknowledged their brutish, dangerous appearance. They each stood hunched with muscle and thick knobby skin, but even with their stooped posture, they matched Victor's enormous berserking physique, towering between eight and ten feet tall. One had two straight long horns, while the other two had a variety of curved spiral horns around their shaggy crowns.

Something in Victor rejoiced at seeing enemies that looked him in the eyes without fear, and he bellowed a roaring challenge, leaping forward and hacking Lifedrinker one-handed, with the speed and fury of an avalanche. The trolls were big, powerful, hearty creatures but weren't fast. Lifedrinker buried herself into the central troll's neck, carving deeply into its flesh and wedging into its spine, and Victor lifted his right foot and kicked out at the troll's gut, ripping Lifedrinker free with a shower of green-red blood.

The troll fell back, smashing through some brush, and while it thrashed, trying to right itself, the other two took the chance to leap at Victor. One charged at him as though to grab him into a bear hug, its wide maw open to reveal rows of serrated teeth. The other tried to circle Victor, swinging its claws at his back. Victor ignored the circling, clawing troll and met the charging one with a mighty grip, grabbing its rotting, uncured hide of a jerkin by the collar and then hacking Lifedrinker furiously into its side, over and over.

Victor felt the third troll scraping against his back, its claws mostly sliding off his scaled armor and serving to do little other than annoy the titan rampaging through his mind. He redoubled his efforts to hack apart the troll he held gripped by the throat. The creature struggled, fighting, kicking, gnashing its teeth, but Lifedrinker was extracting a heavy toll, tearing through its thick hide and smashing its bones, and Victor drove it back. It stumbled over a fallen branch and fell to its back, and Victor followed, driving it down with his weight, putting a knee into its groin, and then furiously hacked Lifedrinker into its collarbone, neck, face, and skull.

As the troll finally stopped moving, and Lifedrinker surged with the Energy she'd stolen from it, Victor felt a terrible, ripping pain on the back of his scalp. Even enraged, he dimly connected the discomfort with the troll that had been clawing at his back. He roared and surged up, aware of the heavy weight on his back and further angered by how it hampered his movement. He reached his free hand over his shoulder, caught hold of something, and yanked, dipping at the waist to dislodge the creature. He felt a painful scraping at the base of his skull, and then the troll flew over his shoulder to smash into the dirt.

Victor roared and leapt upon his downed foe, madly hacking Lifedrinker into its neck, over and over again, until she'd shredded through its meat and finally cut through its bones, hard as iron though they were. The creature was dead, and Victor heaved his breaths in and out, each exhalation accompanied by a savage growl. As his rage began to dim, another icy contraction hit his Core, bringing him back to his senses faster than he otherwise might have. His mind raced with what he'd done, everything a blur after Teil had announced what she'd seen. He started to turn his gaze inward toward his Core but was distracted by a shout and the sounds of crashing undergrowth.

"Don't chase, Teil!" Gef called again, and Victor saw that Teil was standing at the other edge of the clearing, an arrow nocked and pulled back, ready to fire, staring after the crashing, swaying undergrowth—the third troll, the first one Victor had hit, must have fled.

"Victor," Gef said, "are you all right? I've never seen anyone go hand-to-hand with a troll like that, let alone three. Are you mad?"

"Sort of," Victor replied, standing up and yanking Lifedrinker out of the dead monster. Moments later, he saw golden orbs of Energy begin to coalesce around the two downed trolls, and then they surged into him, refreshing his mind and body, but Victor still felt an uncomfortable pressure on his Core.

"You are mad!" Teil hissed, coming closer, her bow relaxed, but the arrow still on the string. "I was going to tell you that the trolls were eating another troll! Someone killed one of them, and those creatures aren't picky about meat. She pointed to the bloody mess where the three monsters had been hunched, and Victor saw the unmistakable carcass of a much-eaten fourth troll.

"Also," Gef added, "your friends' tracks continue down the game trail, no longer shadowed by the trolls."

"Shit, guys, I'm sorry. I . . ." Victor hunted for words, hunted for an excuse that made sense, and then he shrugged and said, "I don't have many people in my life that care about me. Those tracks, those people—they're all I've got. I lost it when I imagined some fucking trolls eating them. Let's . . . let's get back to hunting that bear." As he spoke, Victor looked at his Energy stats to see how badly the curse was hitting him.

Energy Affinity:	**1.6 (3.1), Rage 7.6 (9.1), Inspiration 5.9 (7.4)**	**Energy:**	**2141/2341 (3041)**

"Yeah, I need to focus on this quest—the curse is getting worse. You're sure the trolls weren't following my friends anymore?"

"Yes, I'm sure. Unless some of them picked up their trail further on . . ."

Victor thought about it for a moment, vacillating on what to do. Logically, he knew Tellen was an experienced hunter and that Thayla was no pushover. He wasn't sure about Chandri's fighting skills, but the young woman was skilled at tracking and wilderness craft. Was he being stupid, worrying about them so much?

He knew it would irritate Thayla to know he was interrupting an important quest to babysit her. Thinking about it, Victor realized he'd be irritated too. Why did he instantly assume they needed help? "It's not so much that I don't think they can handle themselves," he said, voicing his thoughts aloud. "I just, well, I guess I'm just worrying." He'd just finished speaking when another icy grip squeezed his Core, and he doubled over in pain.

"It's happening more quickly," he heard Gef say to Teil. "Whatever being he bargained with is not patient. Come, Victor, let's make haste back to the bear's trail."

"Yeah," Victor groaned and struggled to straighten. He felt as if someone had knocked the wind out of him, but he pushed himself to begin moving back down the game trail, keeping pace with Gef and Teil. He gathered up Thistle's lead, and, wanting to keep Lifedrinker in both hands while he jogged, he tucked the length of leather into the back of his belt. After a time, he felt as though the icy grip had subsided, and he pulled up his status screen again.

Energy Affinity:	**0.6 (3.1), Rage 6.6 (9.1), Inspiration 4.9 (7.4)**	**Energy:**	**1841/1841 (3041)**

"Fuck! Shouldn't it be getting better now that I'm back on the hunt for the bear?"

"I don't know," Gef said. "I've never had such a quest. Perhaps your patron isn't pleased with your progress?"

"Maybe the bear wreaks more havoc, and you're being punished," Teil suggested, giving Victor a rather judgmental stare.

"Well, I hope he fucking chills out because, at this rate, I'm going to have a hard fucking time fighting that thing." Victor glowered and picked up the pace, a distant alarm bell ringing in the back of his mind—this quest might be the death of him. He knew his abilities were greatly diminished already. He saw Gef and Teil exchange a pointed look, and he grunted, still jogging, "Yeah, I'm hurting, and yeah, this is going to be a hard fight, but I can still win. If you guys want to bail, though, that's fine."

He didn't fully acknowledge their responses because his ears buzzed with stress, anger, and self-judgment. Why had he been so quick to run after those tracks? Why had he leapt into battle with those trolls without listening or thinking? Was he really so hotheaded when his friends were at risk?

Did he think of them as friends? Were they more like family to him? Was it his feelings for them that made him act that way, or did it have more to do with how they felt about him? He needed to know there were people in this world that cared about him. He needed to know he wasn't alone. The thought of losing all those people in one fell swoop had brought him much closer to the madness that lurked in his rage Core.

"Victor!" Gef shouted, grabbing his shoulder. Victor stumbled to stop, realizing he was running full out, and when he looked at Gef and saw his red face and heaving chest, he realized they'd been maintaining that pace for a while. He looked around for Teil and finally caught sight of her, running up the trail, some hundred yards back. "The bear's passage through the forest is that way!" Gef pointed into the trees to the southeast.

"Shit. Sorry, Gef." He took a few steadying breaths, patting Thistle's shoulder and smoothing the rough, wiry hair on his shoulder. As Teil ran closer, he said, "Sorry, Teil. I need to get my head out of my ass."

"This way. Come," Gef said, leading the way between two trees and back into the rough passage of the great bear. Teil sighed, adjusted the bow strapped to her back, wiped the sweat from her brow, and nodded.

"If we have to hurry, so you have a chance against the bear, then I'm fine with hurrying," she said, starting along the trail, and Victor nodded, hefting Lifedrinker and following after her.

They made good progress in the bear's wake, and Victor felt some stress start to melt from his shoulders and neck when no further icy bands formed around his Core—hopefully, whatever force governed his quest and monitored his progress had decided to stop punishing him. He resolved to keep the pursuit of the bear foremost in his mind, though, and pushed thoughts of friends and family and how important they were to him out of his thoughts.

They'd lost a couple of hours tracking after the trolls, and the sun was high, past its zenith, when Gef stopped them at another trail, a much wider one, smooth and free of stones, and Victor knew it had been built by people, not animals. "The bear turned to the east, following this path. I think we've gained some ground on it!"

"Right, I'll take the lead. Just holler if the tracks leave the path," Victor said, starting down the trail at a jog. He heard Gef and Teil running behind him and kept his pace light, not wanting to exhaust them. Thistle's lead was still tucked into his belt, and the animal easily loped along, making quite a racket on the hard-packed soil. After only a few minutes, Victor started to smell woodsmoke and imagined another village.

He imagined a place where frail-looking Ghelli lived peaceful, simple lives. He imagined them working in gardens or singing songs around a central campfire. Then he imagined a great, mad-eyed bear bursting upon them, slaughtering them, laying waste to their village. "All because I didn't hurry after him like I'd promised," Victor growled through clenched teeth, and he broke into a sprint, and only Thistle could keep pace—he left his two companions in the dust as he charged toward the imagined scene of carnage.

17

BITTERPAW AND TEIL

Victor burst into a clearing with wide open skies and dozens of wooden cabin-type structures, many with smoke billowing from chimneys. He heard shouting and roars and knew the bear had made an appearance, but he didn't see any carnage, didn't see any smashed doors or homes. The shouts seemed to come from the far side of the clearing, past the little cluster of buildings, and Victor turned, leaping onto Thistle's back. Thistle felt his urgency and immediately started sprinting up the dirt path that led through the center of the settlement.

When he cleared the last pair of log homes, he saw an open meadow—a place where people had cleared the trees and planted rows of gardens—and saw the bear he'd been hunting for the first time. It was roaring and swiping, held at bay by a handful of nimble, spear-wielding people, while a larger crowd stood at a distance, some of them shooting arrows at the great beast. Victor saw spells flash in the air, felt the signature pulse of Energy gathering and releasing, and knew that these people weren't rolling over; they were fighting to defend their place in this world.

Bitterpaw wasn't like any bear on Earth, but neither was he as huge or intimidating as the great spirit, Thunderbite. He was big, bigger than a grizzly—more the size of a hippo, probably a couple of thousand pounds. His fur was dark, matted, and patchy, and Victor could see the scars of a hundred wounds on his flanks, back, and snout. The bear had the bony spines of his species, sticking up around his shoulders and down the center of his back, and as he roared and slashed, Victor saw his massive canines and sword-like claws.

Victor jumped off Thistle, hefted Lifedrinker, and charged down the slight incline through a garden with neat rows plowed into the soft dark soil and cast Inspiring Presence. He felt his Energy respond, felt the spell take effect, but noticed immediately how it felt more sluggish than usual, how the result didn't seem as significant. He didn't care. Here was the monster he was meant to fight, and he couldn't stop to contemplate or complain that he wasn't at his strongest—people needed his help!

As he drew within a few dozen bounding strides, and he was sure the people around had begun to benefit from his Inspiring Presence, Victor cast Channel Spirit, flooding Lifedrinker with rage-attuned Energy. He cast Sovereign Will, making his muscles stretch, harden, and bunch with strength.

Victor almost cast Manifest Spirit, summoning his coyotes, but he saw the villagers and how they harried the bear's flanks, and he doubted his canine companions would be much more effective. More than that, though, he was worried about his lower reserves of Energy and the considerable cost of the spell. He decided that his spirit totems would sit this one out.

Still, Victor didn't plan to hold any punches; as he charged closer, he cast Berserk, and as his body erupted with power, Victor roared a challenge that echoed over the clearing, startling the people who hadn't noticed him yet. Bitterpaw responded, as he'd hoped, turning to him and standing on his hind legs, returning the roar, jaws wide, foamy, blood-speckled saliva stringing out from his massive teeth.

Victor's rage had taken him, had flooded his body with its red hot Energy, and his Titanic Rage ability had done its job, engorging his muscles and pushing his body to surge toward the shape of one of his ancient ancestors. Still, it felt different than usual—the heat was less a furnace and more a fire, and his mind, while still seeking the furious release of combat, was cooler, and he was more himself than a titan of destruction.

Regardless, Victor roared again and leapt at the bear, Lifedrinker in his right hand held outstretched, but whistling through the air as he swung her around in a devastating arc, aiming for the bear's exposed ribs. Bitterpaw brought his massive right claw down in a swipe characteristic of his kind, smashing the heavy paw into Victor's armored forearm, and, for the first time that he could remember, his enraged form was overpowered.

Victor felt something tear in his elbow, and then the enormous paw drove his arm down, and the huge claws raked across his armored chest, sliding along his scales but catching here and there and ripping them free. Simultaneously, Victor's chop landed, and Lifedrinker bit deep between two ribs. Victor roared in pain, surprise, and fury as the bear's swipe knocked him back, and he lost his grip on the axe.

Victor flexed his arm, felt the pain and feebleness fade away as his rage slowly knit back whatever tissue had torn, and he circled the bear, watching as it roared and pawed at the axe haft jutting from its side. Even in his rage, Victor knew he couldn't grapple a beast so large, and the Quinametzin in him roared and seethed at the feebleness of his body.

With his vision red-tinted, Victor saw the corpse of an Ardeni man and saw the bronze-tipped spear by his side. He leapt toward it and snatched it up, and as the bear ripped Lifedrinker free, sending her sprawling into the dirt, he threw the spear like a bolt of lightning.

Throwing a spear isn't something that one can do without finesse, without some modicum of skill, but when you have a properly weighted spear made for throwing and a target the size of a small vehicle, success is possible. Victor was lucky that day, having picked up a decent weapon and having enough strength to launch it with the force of a ballista, sending it streaking through the air faster than the eye could follow. Bitterpaw had just dropped to all fours to charge Victor, and the spear took him in the shoulder, burying its shaft three solid feet into the massive creature's torso.

The crowd of villagers hadn't stopped their attempts to wound the bear, and when the spear impaled the monster, they redoubled their efforts, piling arrows and spear stabs into its flanks. The beast had stumbled at the impact of Victor's throw, sliding through the dark soil, digging a furrow in its passage, but it was far from dead. It roared and raged, staggering to stand on three legs, its wounded shoulder unable to hold any weight.

Bitterpaw coughed a gout of blood, screamed in fury as more spears and arrows pierced his hide, and leapt toward Victor. Or he would have if Victor had stood still. Victor had run for his dear companion, though, picking Lifedrinker up from the soil. The bear, blind in its rage and pain, lumbered toward an unlucky villager who'd been standing behind Victor's previous position. Victor charged forward, screaming his own fury as he hacked Lifedrinker into Bitterpaw's haunches.

Lifedrinker didn't bite as deeply as a spear might have, but she was sharp and hungry, and she tore long deep wounds, carving through thick hide and biting into muscle and sinew. Bitterpaw felt those quick, hacking blows as the injuries piled up, and he turned, trying to roll and swipe his massive claws at the same time.

Aware that a swipe was coming but seeing the bear's soft belly exposed, Victor stood tall, bringing Lifedrinker down with a two-handed chop that buried her deep in the bear's underside. At the same time, saber-like claws raked his forehead, face, and chest, sending him sprawling in a shower of blood.

Victor blinked away the blood that had sheeted into his eyes, its red tint adding to the already crimson haze of his rage, and he stood up. What was this beast that dared to challenge him? He felt the heat from his Core surge, felt the vestiges of his rage-attuned Energy pour like hot floodwaters into his pathways, and Victor roared, leaping to his feet. He saw the bear, rolling and grunting, coughing gouts of blood, its rage-filled eyes growing dim, and he screamed, charging it like a bull with his tormentor in his sights.

Victor smashed into Bitterpaw's side with a thunderous, wet crunch, and as they rolled through the dark, rich soil, he managed to grab hold of the spear that protruded from the bear's shoulder and with a heroic effort and his last vestiges of rage-stoked strength, he drove it deeper still, until the bear, realizing it was dead, finally heaved its last breath and ceased its struggles.

Sprawled atop his vanquished foe, Victor breathed deep, exhausted breaths, watching as thick rivulets of blood trickled off his brow to mingle with the bear's in the soil. As his rage continued to fade, he became aware of the terrible burning pains and aches in his body. His reduced Energy affinity had taken a toll, apparently reducing the regenerative effects of his rage. He groaned, stiffly lifting his head to try to take in the aftermath of his battle, his ears aware of people speaking but his brain unable to filter the various voices in a way that made sense.

Victor saw darkness begin to creep in around the edges of his vision and realized he was about to pass out. He shook his head, willing himself to hold on, then a reprieve came in the form of a flood of Energy from the carcass of the great, dead bear. He didn't see it form, likely because he was still lying atop the dead beast, but he felt it hit him with a mighty surge, physically lifting him into the air. His wounds closed, his Core sucked up the Energy, and Victor took a deep breath, allowing his euphoria to show with a loud, barbaric shout of victory.

His Quinametzin nature had faded with his rage, but still, Victor remembered the sound of his roars and challenges when he'd been enraged, and he copied one of them. His lungs were smaller, and his voice less rough and loud, but it came naturally. As the System sent him a message while he stood atop his downed foe, he repeated the shout, roaring at the skies, and when his gaze fell, he saw the crowd looking at him with awe and wonder and not a little bit of fear, and he forced himself to calm down and smile.

He glanced at the System messages before swiping them away.

*****Congratulations! You have achieved level 33 Spirit Carver, gained 10 will and 10 vitality, and have 8 attribute points to allocate.*****

*****Congratulations! You have learned the spell: Manifest Spirit, Improved.*****

*****Congratulations! You have learned the spell: Shape Spirit, Improved.*****

*****Congratulations! Your chosen Class and your mastery of your spirit have allowed you to gain a second totem. Only one totem may be active at a time.*****

"Victor! Are you all right? Your face . . ." He recognized Teil's voice and turned to the woman, taking note of her broken bow and the dirt and blood streaking her face—he hadn't been the only one rolling around during that fight.

"I'm good," he said, reaching to feel his face. It was caked with blood, sure, but he also felt tender scars on his forehead, over the bridge of his nose, and along his cheek. "Ugh," he grunted. "There go my good looks." He jumped down from the bear, and when he saw the clusters of villagers tending to their fallen defenders, he stopped grinning, realizing that many people had suffered much worse than a few scars that day.

Gef approached him and held out a hand. Victor took it, and the older man said, "I doubted you. I thought we were likely on a quest that would end with our deaths, but I didn't care. Now that this beast is dead, I can at least face my Ancestors with pride, having helped to avenge my kin. Thank you, Victor." Some people nearby had crowded forward, and many were echoing Gef's thanks, including Teil, who wore a smile for the first time in Victor's experience.

"You were a giant," she said. "I can't believe you wrestled with this thing." She gestured to the body, and Victor saw that many people had gathered around it, and he suddenly felt alarmed.

"Stand back!" he yelled. He strode forward, and as the crowd backed away, he tried to push the bear onto its side, but it wouldn't budge. He cast Sovereign Will, boosting his strength, and tried again. This time it started to turn, and he grunted, "Help me turn it!"

Gef, Teil, and a dozen others grabbed the bear's fur or shoved against its side, and they managed to roll it over. There, protruding from the bear's gut, was Lifedrinker's haft—she was more than half buried in the monster's innards. "There you are, beautiful." Victor grabbed her haft, felt her vibrate at the touch, and yanked her free, pulling a loop of slick gray intestine with her.

Victor smiled savagely when he saw the new vein of bright Heart Silver snaking through Lifedrinker's dark axe-head. "She had a big long drink from that *pendejo*."

He walked around to the front of the corpse, and people scurried to get out of his way. He was coated in blood, and so was Lifedrinker, and his mad ramblings about his axe probably didn't help people feel comfortable; they seemed eager to give him space. He examined the bear's claws, and there, buried in the thick, blood-matted fur of its right paw, Victor saw the talisman that Thunderbite had said he needed to destroy.

The necklace was difficult to cut free, and Victor had to put Lifedrinker into the loop on his belt so he could cut away the fur with a sharp knife. While he worked, he looked up at the villagers and said, "I need a hot fire, something like a forge. We need to destroy this amulet—it's what drove this bear insane."

"We have a smithy," one of the villagers said, a Shadeni woman with curly black hair wearing leather armor and wielding a long spear.

"You were one of the heroes that held the bear at bay?" Victor asked.

"Aye, but I'm no hero. I couldn't hurt the thing enough to get its attention," she said.

"Nonsense!" an older woman exclaimed. "Any who would face this beast down is a hero! Thank you, too, stranger!" she said, directing the last words to Victor.

"I'm glad I could help, and you're right: everyone who didn't run from this big bastard is a hero today. I'm sorry for the losses you've all suffered, but everyone here should be proud." Victor grunted as he finally pulled the necklace of teeth from the bear's fur, then he stood up, holding it away from everyone, keeping it at arm's length from himself, even. He doubted it would affect him with his high will and without him trying to bond with it, but still, he didn't like the looks of it.

The teeth weren't fangs like those you might collect from predators. They looked, to him, more like the teeth of people—small, mostly flat—and he could feel the sickly, cloying aura bleeding off the necklace. "Show me to the forge, please. Get the fire hot!" He followed the woman with the spear, and most of the people in the field marched behind him, though a few, probably family members, hung back, collecting the corpses of the fallen.

The woman led him to a nearby building, and he saw that there was, indeed, a workshop affixed to the side of it with an anvil, a quenching barrel, and a forge. It was a small affair, built from mud bricks, but it had actual bellows and a coal fire, and the woman used some sort of Energy ability to start the coals burning much more quickly than would have been possible otherwise. A man who introduced himself as the woman's husband pumped the bellows, and when the coals were a bright yellow-orange, and Victor could feel the heat from several feet away, he tossed the necklace into them.

The necklace sat in the coals for a moment, seemingly unharmed, but then, with a sizzling *pop* and flash of smoky gray Energy, it burst into flames. Victor felt an icy grip, one that he'd grown accustomed to and nearly forgotten, release its hold on his Core, and he breathed a deep sigh as his Core expanded and started to pull at the ambient Energy, slowly replenishing itself.

*****Congratulations! You have completed a Quest: Hunt down the bear known as Bitterpaw, best him in combat, and destroy the toothed amulet that has corrupted his spirit. Seek out Thunderbite to claim your reward.*****

"It's done," he said. "The curse is dead, and this thing won't corrupt any more people or beasts." Murmurs of approval and even a few ragged cheers rose up from the crowd of people that had gathered around the blacksmithy.

The woman who'd shown Victor the forge and helped him stoke it turned to him and said, "What's your name, hero? I've heard your companions call you Victor. Is that right?"

"That's right. Just call me Victor, not hero, all right? What's your name? What's the name of this place?" he asked, turning to the crowd with his last question.

"I'm Genna, and this village is Leaf Watch. Where do you hail from, Victor?"

"I'm from far away—another world. Recently, though, I've been living with the Shadeni on the plains. Tellen's clan. Do you know them?"

"Aye, and now we owe Tellen and his people a debt. If they've opened their homes to you, then we can do no less. Consider yourself welcome here anytime, Victor, and that goes for you as well, Teil and Gef." Victor didn't know when Teil and Gef had introduced themselves to the woman, but he supposed he'd been somewhat preoccupied.

"Thank you, Genna. I appreciate your hospitality, and I'd stick around to help further, but I have friends I'm worried about, and I want to head back."

"I can imagine it would ease your worry to see your friends again," Teil said, reaching up to take hold of Victor's shoulder, "but you should rest a night here. You need to clean yourself, and it will be dark soon in any case. If your friends saw you looking like this, they'd probably have a fright that would take years from their lives."

"I have guest accommodations," an older man said. He was Ardeni, with white hair and bright yellow eyes, and he smiled genuinely, and Victor was impressed to see he held a spear streaked with blood. "Room for two, at least."

"I'll be leaving," Gef said. "I have kin in Twilight Home and am eager to be on my way. Thank you anyway, friends."

"You sure, Gef?" Victor asked.

"Absolutely. Don't worry about me—I'm no stranger to sleeping in the woods. Thank you again, Victor. Teil, please look out for yourself, all right?"

"I will, Gef. Thank you."

"Gef, can we offer you some supplies?" Genna asked as the crowd began to disperse, people going about cleaning the mess left by the battle with the bear, helping the families of the few hunters who'd died as they tried to fend it off. While Gef spoke to Genna, Victor found himself being pulled aside by Teil and the older man.

"Would you two like to stay with me tonight? I'll give you plenty of peace, and my guest room has a tub. You could sure use it, warrior."

"Yes, I'd like that," Teil said, and she nodded to Victor. He vacillated for a moment, but then he nodded.

"All right. I could use a night to rest. I honestly haven't had a relaxing sleep in weeks." As he spoke, he saw Gef walking away toward the dirt road that had led them to the village, and he called out, "Gef! Take care, man. Thanks for your help!"

"Bye, Victor! Spend some time hunting!" He chuckled and turned, walking toward the forest's edge and the setting sun.

"He's a good man. He'll be all right," Teil said.

"My name's Norl," the older man said. "Come, I'll show you to my place." He started walking toward the southern edge of the clearing, but Victor held up a hand.

"A minute, Norl. I need to find my mount."

"Oh, the great horned beast? It wandered there, away from the battle. I saw it grazing by Shim's cabin." Norl pointed off to the right, past the building where the forge sat, smoking. Victor nodded and jogged over there and saw a narrow grassy meadow between the cabins and the trees, and there was Thistle, his lead dangling, calmly munching on the grass.

"Hey, boy," Victor said, walking toward him. The animal lifted his big black nose and snuffled, looking for a treat, and Victor obliged, handing him a rather bitter-tasting apple that he'd found growing on the edge of the forest when Gef first led him in. He'd been surprised when Gef acknowledged the fruit was called an apple—so far, every fruit Victor had eaten on Fanwath had a strange name, but he figured this fruit was similar enough to the ones on Earth that the System translated the word for him.

Leading Thistle, he walked back to Norl and Teil and followed the man toward his home. The older man spoke as they went. "I built my home bigger than I needed because my sister was supposed to come live with me out here. Her husband had died, you see, but after I made the move and built my place, I sent word for her to come, and she replied with some news: she'd remarried. Now I'm out here in the wilderness all by myself. Alone where family is concerned, I mean—I've plenty of friends here in the village. It's a great place to study plants and cultivate nature Energy, though, so I won't complain."

"Nature Energy?" Victor asked as they approached a good-sized cabin with a well-kept garden.

"Oh, yes. I'm quite good with plants and animals. I tried to calm that bear, but as you said, it was cursed—all of my attempts seemed to enrage it further." He stepped up to the door and pulled it open, motioning for Teil and Victor to precede him. "Here we are! Tie your mount there on that garden post, and I'll see to him. I'd love the chance to get to know him."

"All right, if you're sure," Victor said, unloading a barrel of water and a bag of feed for Thistle. Thinking twice, he took out his brush and took a minute to unbuckle Thistle's saddle, slipping it into his storage ring. He patted the big animal, scratching the fur on his long, muscular neck, and said, "See you soon, buddy."

Victor stooped under the lintel, walking into a warm, neat space that reminded him of the typical fishing cabin you might see in a VR. An open kitchen with a wooden butcher-block island took up the left half of the front room, while some comfortable couches and chairs, some bookcases, and a small table filled the rest. A hallway led further into the dwelling, and Norl pointed that way.

"My extra room is the one on the left down there. It's plenty big, and, as I said, there's a tub within. Go make yourselves comfortable, and I'll get some dinner started!"

"Oh, you don't have to do that, Norl," Teil said, but Victor held up his hand.

"What kind of food are we talking about, Norl? I'm hungry as a bear," he chuckled, but when he saw their faces and remembered Teil's husband, Victor's heart nearly stopped, and he slapped his palm to his forehead. "Oh, bad choice of words! I'm sorry!"

"Nothing to worry about, Victor," the man said, wrinkling his bright yellow eyes in sympathy and stroking his thin, white beard. "I've a pultii, fresh from a hunt, and need to cook it. How's that sound? Should be enough bird for even a man your size!"

"Oh! I love pultii!" Teil said, ignoring Victor's bad humor. "I haven't had one since last fall . . ." she trailed off, and her face fell, and Victor imagined she was remembering a happier time.

"Great," Victor said, clearing his throat. "Let's go see our room, Teil. You can have the bath first."

"No, Victor. You need it more," she said, following him down the hallway.

"Yeah, I'm pretty ripe," Victor said, lifting his scale-armored arm. "At least this armor is self-cleaning. I wasn't sure it would be because it has some sort of 'comfort' enchantment. I wasn't sure that was anything more than resizing."

"It's nice armor, true enough," Teil said as he opened the doorway on the left side of the hall. "I saw that bear hit you solidly a couple of times, not to mention the troll that tried to dig through your back."

Victor stepped into the room and saw it was good sized, as promised, with a separate door that probably led to the bath. Two small beds were arranged on the far wall with a nightstand between them. A woven round rug occupied the center of the floor, and a dresser with a mirror sat against the wall opposite the bed. "Not bad," he said.

"I'd hoped for a bigger bed," Teil said, pushing under his arm to get into the room.

"Uh," Victor said, not sure what she meant. "I mean, at least we don't have to share." He watched her as she walked toward the little beds, turning on the rug, then she looked over her shoulder at him and smiled.

"Victor, my husband is dead, and I need to feel like I'm not dead too. Three days ago, I tried to follow him into the spirit realm, and now I feel a weight has been removed from my soul. He's gone, probably starting his next life in a new world. Me? I want to live! I want to savor this life while I can! Can we just be together tonight and then go our separate ways?"

Victor closed the door and stepped closer to her, looking at her differently than he'd allowed himself to thus far. She was beautiful in her way. He liked how her eyes reflected the glow lamp's yellow light, catching it, deepening it, and turning it back to him like hot little embers. "I . . ." he started. He wanted to protest that his heart was taken by someone else, but was it? He thought he should say he didn't know if it was wise for her to be with him so soon after her loss. He wanted to suggest that he was the wrong guy to be with at a time like this in her life. A million protests fought for space on his tongue, but what came out was, "Yeah, Teil. That would be nice."

18

THE ROOT OF THINGS

Victor sat on the rough-spun rug in the middle of the room, looking at Teil's naked back as she breathed the steady, slow breaths of deep sleep. They'd ended up throwing the blankets on the floor because the beds were too small for the two of them to share, especially considering Victor's size. She was beautiful, that was sure, and Victor had needed the affection, the closeness that she'd provided, at least as much as she had.

As he sat there, contemplating her, Victor tried to feel any guilt and regret, and he kept coming up empty. He cared a lot about Chandri, maybe even loved her in a way, but she'd made it pretty damn clear that he was too much for her, that the idea of getting closer to him was something frightening. In a corner of his mind, he knew he was rationalizing; Chandri might come around, they might get more intimate, and now he had this hanging over him.

"Well, it's not like we're together right now," he said softly to Lifedrinker, holding her cool, silver-streaked metal to his forehead. The axe hummed slightly, vibrating the bones in his skull, and he liked how it felt, smiling as he slowly touched his molars together and pulled them apart, allowing the vibration to rattle through them. "Getting ready to talk again soon, aren't you?" he whispered.

The room was quiet, but the night sounds of the forest were loud—crickets chirped, frogs chirruped, and night birds sang their trilling, haunting melodies. He loved it. He loved the sounds that came alive in the darkness of

Fanwath, where the power of untamed nature still had that depthless, almost scary, overwhelming presence wherever people hadn't fully mastered it. He'd noticed it everywhere, from the mountains to the plains to the forest. Hell, he'd even noticed it in the mines. Nature was powerful here, and he could see why a guy like Norl would choose to study and try to master it.

Their door was secure, and though the window was open for a night breeze, and the woods outside were dark, gloomy, and full of noises, Victor's gut told him nothing dangerous was lurking there that night. He felt safe enough and wanted to make a quick spirit walk; he wanted to speak to Thunderbite. He thought about it for a few moments, deliberating on whether the risk was worth it, and then he had an idea. He reached into himself, touched his inspiration-attuned Energy, and cast Manifest Spirit.

Around the room, pearlescent white misty forms began to coalesce, and with them the characteristic yipping chatter of his coyote totems. Victor shushed them, and though she stirred and murmured softly in her sleep, Teil didn't wake.

His companions paced back and forth, silently padding on the hardwood floor and rug, and Victor stared at them, one by one, until they met his eyes, and he made clear his desires, thinking clearly about how they were to guard him and Teil and wake him if trouble came.

Amazingly, the coyotes seemed to understand his thoughts, taking up positions around the central rug where Victor sat and Teil slept and sitting on their haunches, patient and watchful as gargoyles. Victor nodded and softly said, "Thank you," and then he cast Spirit Walk. The cabin faded away, but the trees drew closer, and Victor saw no more of the night sky than he had under Norl's roof. As he stood up, though, he was pleased to see misty echoes of his coyotes, their five forms still sitting in a loose circle around him.

"Spirits, eh? I guess I can see you whether I manifest you in this realm or not." The misty forms didn't respond, and they were vague enough that Victor couldn't really look them in the eyes, so he just hoped they'd keep watching his physical body for him.

He turned around in a slow circle, awed by the endless depth of the forest in the spirit plane. The trees were solid-looking, but they had an ethereal quality that gave them a sort of shimmer, and he could see how the moon and starlight seemed to filter down through the canopy, even though Victor couldn't see the sky.

He wasn't sure where to find Thunderbite, but the bear had said he'd have no trouble reaching him if he finished his quest, so Victor just fixed the bear solidly in his mind and started walking. He passed between great boles and smaller saplings, but his going was easy, and he noted the lack of underbrush. Was it really not there? He looked farther away, between more massive trunks, and there seemed to be a lot of shadowy, glimmering undergrowth. Perhaps it simply gave way before his spirit.

Occasionally, Victor saw other spirits flitting away between trunks or even up into the high mist-veiled branches. Were they people? Animals? He didn't know, and it didn't seem to matter—they were intent on avoiding him.

After a time, he came to a clearing, and at its center was a hollow that sloped down away from the forest floor. Victor walked toward the hollow, trudging down the shallow grade, stepping around boulders wreathed in mist. As the sides of the hollow stretched up over his head, he came to a wide sunken area before a deep black pit of a cave.

He could feel Thunderbite within, and Victor felt very reluctant to step into the bear's home uninvited, so he called out, "Thunderbite! It's Victor! I finished your quest." No response came from the dark depths, and he cleared his throat to call out again, but a deep rumble issued forth.

"No more yelling, warrior. I come." Ponderous steps echoed up out of the darkness, accompanied by the scrape of claws on stone. After a dozen steps or so, two bright yellow lanterns appeared in the gloom, then they blinked, and a gray-furred muzzle and brow appeared around them.

After another step, the massive bone-spur mane of the elder spinebear came into view, and the monstrous animal padded the rest of the way out of the cave, looming over Victor like a mastiff standing over a toddler. "You've done well, Victor," the bear rumbled, and Victor stood a little taller for the praise.

"Thank you, I . . ."

"You've done well, but it could have gone better. The spirits of the forest tested you, didn't they? Set a distraction in your path to see if you'd stray from your task. You did well enough, but their test revealed much about you." The huge bear sat back on his haunches then ponderously lay down in front of Victor, resting his enormous head on his paws, still able to look Victor in the eyes.

"Test? The spirits were messing with me?" Victor could feel the spirit bear's breath, strange as that was in this realm, wafting over him with each pump of his bellows-like lungs.

"You want me to unravel a mystery of your spirit, do you not? I saw enough to help you with that. I can point you to another affinity, though you might rather I didn't." The bear spoke slowly, and Victor felt his heart race with excitement, then felt a cold knife of worry press into his heart at the final words.

"Why would I rather you didn't?"

"It's not an easy affinity, warrior. It will weigh on you as much or more than your rage does. It's not a breath of effortless air like your inspiration affinity. You'll have to fight this affinity; you'll have to face it down and make it your own. Your cultivation will be fraught, and you'll curse me a hundred times before you feel you've gained something worthwhile from it. I can offer you a different prize if that's more to your liking."

Victor didn't speak right away; instead, he thought about Thunderbite's words. He thought about how the bear had said he'd been tested. He ran it over in his mind—an affinity that would weigh on him like his rage did. "What sort of other prize?"

"So that is your choice?"

"No! Can't I know more before I choose?"

"Something to help you fight or something to make you stronger. I'd have to think on it a moment," the bear rumbled, finishing his statement with a yawn. Victor felt as if he was in a trap, that if he chose a new reward, he'd be disappointed. Was the bear testing him again? Did it matter? Victor wasn't the type to back down from a challenge, despite his nerves, so he straightened his back, rested one hand on top of Lifedrinker's head, and nodded.

"It doesn't matter. I want my original prize, despite your warnings."

"As I knew you would," Thunderbite said, blinking his huge lantern-like eyes.

"You knew?"

"Yes, even in your ignorance, you follow this affinity like a hound on a chain. You fight against it, snapping and lashing out wherever you can, but it's there, leading you along. It's good that you're going to have your eyes opened to it because you should learn to take control of the chain and be the one leading the way."

"Well? What's the affinity?"

"Be patient. I'll need to guide you to this slowly, else your spirit will rebel, and you might lose this opportunity. Sit." Thunderbite blew a tremendous snort of air out of his nose, blasting the twigs and loose grass away from the ground in front of him, and Victor complied, sitting down at the bear's paws, marveling at the size of his claws, each easily the length of Victor's forearms.

"Shall I manipulate your Core, or would you like to try? I can guide you." Thunderbite's lips hardly moved while he spoke, but they did quiver up and down, and Victor, close as he was, noticed the enormous, yellow teeth in the elder's mouth.

"I'd like to try," Victor replied.

"Good. Turn your mind inward, look at your Core, but first, place one of your paws upon my long foreclaw. I'll go with you and gaze upon your Energy as well."

"All right," Victor said, reaching out and resting his palm along the hard black claw. It felt like touching a live wire at first, the surging Energy within so potent that Victor feared for the safety of his flesh. It faded, though, and soon it was like holding a buzzing, bucking, morphing thing—something so full of potential that it was hard to wrap his mind around its actual shape.

"Yes, I see it," Thunderbite rumbled, but this time his voice came from within Victor's skull, and he realized the bear had somehow merged his consciousness with his own. "Quite a job you've done, warrior. Your two affinities rage and pulse like twin suns—a strong configuration. We'll build upon this."

"Okay," Victor said, turning his own gaze inward, trying to ignore the nuclear reactor he'd rested his hand upon.

"You should take some potential from each of your other affinities to craft your third. Gather yourself a strand from each, pull them apart and into an empty area nearby, and start to ball them together. Wrap them tightly, Victor!"

"Like this?" Victor asked, tugging a thread of Energy from his rage-attuned orb and another from his inspiration-attuned orb. He pulled the two threads out and began to weave them together, much as he had done when he'd tried to create some courage-attuned Energy.

"Close, but stop that weave. We won't make courage today, warrior. Simply ball the Energies together, and press with your will. Crush them tight!" The bear's voice was louder than ever, echoing in Victor's skull, and he winced, trying to comply.

He folded the Energies together, pressing, squeezing, driving them into a ball with all the terrible pressure he could muster with his prodigious will. "Good, see how they grow muddy? See the corruption in their attunements? You've broken the affinities—crushing them together without any sort of weave."

"And that's good?" Victor asked through clenched teeth.

"Yes!" the bear roared. "Keep pressing. Drive them together. Pull more!"

Victor complied, pulling Energy from both of his attunements, smashing them together into a ball until it was neither the white-gold of inspiration nor the throbbing crimson of rage. The third orb of Energy at his Core grew, and with each herculean, crushing press of Victor's will, it grew denser and darker, a swirling, gray ball of Energy, not pure, but not attuned—something in between.

"Stop!" the bear roared. And Victor felt his grasp on the threads of attuned Energy slip away—the bear had pulled them loose. "You've taken a third of your Energy from your Core. You won't want more than that in your new affinity."

"How do I tell what the affinity is? This new orb feels . . . it feels wrong or something, like I can't use it. I can't even pull any Energy out of it."

"Patience, warrior. Did you not say you wanted to learn?"

"Yes, sorry," Victor said, forcing himself to take a deep breath while he studied his Core. His red and white-gold orbs still pulsed brightly, smaller than before, but not terribly. The third orb, the one he'd built, sat offset between the others, forming a sort of triangle if you drew imaginary lines between them all. It hung there, smoky and gray, and he realized it was sort of like a blank slate. It wasn't pure Energy that could be used to craft spells; no, it was spirit Energy, part of Victor and waiting for an imprint—an attunement.

"Now, warrior, I'm going to guide you to your affinity. You must grasp it when you see it. Grab the emotions and feelings as you do when you cultivate your other attunements. Do you understand me?"

"I think so."

"Good. Let us examine you, warrior. When you were hunting the bear, my diseased kin, you left his trail to hunt after your loved ones—why was that?"

"I couldn't let them get killed by trolls!"

"Why?"

"Because I care about them!"

"You do; that is right and good. Why do you care about them so? What do they make you feel?"

"Friendship?" Victor knew that answer wasn't right, or at least not complete. He tried again, "Companionship. They make me feel like I belong somewhere. Like I have a home."

"Now we grow closer to the point. Victor, why did you chase after your friends?"

"Because I don't want to be alone." Victor knew he was right before he spoke. He'd drawn the conclusion before the bear asked the question.

"You don't want to be alone, or you fear being alone?" Thunderbite pressed.

"I fear it." Victor shuddered at the unraveling of his motivations. He hadn't chased after his friends for love or out of bravery—he'd done it out of fear. The idea that he could be alone in this world without anyone to care about him or return to was terrifying. He already felt that he'd lost his entire family and all of his friends on Earth—if he lost Thayla, Deyni, Chandri, Tellen, and even Chala all in one fell swoop? He'd be gutted. Would he even be able to go on?

"Good, Victor. Grab that feeling. Tell me something more, Victor. When you mated with that she-bear, that woman that helped you slay my kin, how did you feel after?"

"Uh, good?" He knew that wasn't what the bear was getting at. "I felt good, but I felt worried. I feared how it might affect my relationship with Chandri. Shit, I even worried about how Thayla would react if she found out." Was he really that fearful?

"Victor, are you a coward?"

"No!"

"No, indeed. Warrior that you are, how many battles have you fought?" Thunderbite's voice rumbled, but it was low and gentle, coaxing him to see something.

"I don't know. A lot. Many. I don't think I could count them all."

"You speak truly. Have you ever fled?"

"Well, I ran from a horde of giant rats but ended up fighting them all. I don't think so?"

"Did you want to fight all those times, Victor?"

"No! Fuck no! I was forced to fight many times. Shit, man, I can't think of a time when I went looking for a fight for the fun of it. Even when I fought for sport, you know, not to the death, but in wrestling, I was nervous, stressed, and only really happy after the match was over. I only did it because I was good at it, and the coach and my friends would lose their shit if I quit." Victor hadn't ever told anyone that. Was the bear performing some sort of magic on him to make him honest?

"I ask again, Victor—are you a coward?"

"No! Goddamn it!" Victor felt some heat enter his words, and he saw his red orb of rage-attuned Energy start to bleed off into his pathways.

"Victor, you speak the truth. I would say you are a courageous man. You are brave. Can a bear, or a person, have courage if he has no fear?"

"What?"

"You constantly battle with your fear. You fear being alone. You fear your friends being harmed. You fear the consequences of fighting, not fighting, killing, not killing. But, warrior, you never fear for your person, your physical life. You face your fear over and over again, and that makes you brave. Still, you're much closer to your fear than your bravery. Do you feel it? Look into your mind, at your memories, and find your fear—it's your strongest affinity."

Victor reeled at the bear's words. Was he really full of fear? Was he ruled by fear? He couldn't lie about his motivation for rushing after his friends' tracks in the forest—he feared being alone, but wasn't that normal?

He looked back at his life before Fanwath, at his strained relationship with his family. He'd lost his connection to his mother's family after her death. His cousins on his father's side were distant. Yeah, it hurt, and he hated it, and things had been scary as hell when his *abuelo* died. Who would really care about him when his *abuela* followed him? She was the only person in the world—in any world—left alive that loved him unconditionally. That shit was scary.

Why did he hate fighting if he was so good at it? He wasn't afraid of getting hurt, that was sure. Had the bear hit the nail on the head when it talked about consequences? He hated the pressure of people, including himself, expecting him to win. That feeling before the match or fight that he had to perform, that people were watching and counting on him. He feared failure. Did it really rule him so? Had he failed to finish Rellia out of fear? When he'd imagined Yrella and his rage had faded, and he'd let Rellia live, was he doing what he thought was right, or was he being a chicken?

"I'm not a fucking chickenshit!" he growled. The bear didn't respond, and he kept thinking. Yes, he often acted based on a deep-rooted fear, a dread of what could be. He didn't let those feelings force him into acting like a coward, though. He lived with them, and he overcame them. "Sure, I have fear. It's a big part of me and why I do things, but I don't let it win. I don't let it freeze me up, and I never act like a coward."

"Agreed, but when the fear does overcome you, you must acknowledge it. Face it, gather it, use it. When you fled the path of Bitterpaw to chase after your friends, you didn't act out of courage. Come, face it. Gather it. *Use* it!"

Victor forced his mind back and remembered how he'd felt when he'd imagined a gang of trolls ambushing the people he cared about. He forced himself to relive how he'd felt when Teil had said the trolls were having a feast. He'd panicked. He'd charged into a battle with no thought because of the hopeless well of despair that yawned at the core of his being when he'd imagined life with no one that knew or cared about him.

Victor gasped as he felt that despair, that terrible fear, and grabbed ahold of the feeling. He choked out a sob and yanked it close, and then, acting on instinct, he drove that feeling into the ball of shifting gray Energy at his Core.

He felt a cold, dark hunger come to life in the center of his being, and he watched as the gray orb bloomed with a terrible new life—dark and angry, swirling with hunger, it took on a purple-black aspect, pulsing in counterpoint to the furious crimson and bright white-gold of his other affinities.

Victor looked at his status to see what he'd done.

Energy Affinity:	**3.1, Fear 9.4, Rage 9.1, Inspiration 7.4**	**Energy:**	**3041/3041**

"You've done it, warrior. I hope this new affinity will not bring you more pain than you bargained for. At the very least, you've learned much about yourself on this journey."

"What? That I'm a coward? Filled with fear?" Victor couldn't believe his affinity for fear was higher than rage. He closed his spirit body's eyes and shook his head. This couldn't be real—he'd come looking for a new boost, a way to better himself, and all he'd done was expose that he'd been acting out of fear for most of his life.

"Come, we just spoke of this. You're smarter than that, Victor. A bear with no fear cannot be brave, simply bold. To show bravery, you must overcome fear, and you do so all the time."

"But it's . . . it's so high! I'm closer to fear than rage? It doesn't even make sense! Why did I find my rage affinity first?"

"Your rage is a response to your fear, Victor. It's how you fight through it. That doesn't mean it's not there, underlying your actions, your motivations, your feelings, and your words. Now you know it, warrior—turn it to your advantage. Face your fears when they come bubbling up; show your enemies what you deal with all the time. Make them cower!" The great bear snuffed and lifted his head, looking into the distance. "Go now. Our bargain is done. I wish you luck, Victor Sandoval."

"You know me so well?"

"I do," the bear said, twitching his paw and extricating his long, powerful claw from Victor's hand. "I do," he said more softly, huffing a warm breath at

Victor. "Know that if all else is gone, if all else gets broken into dust, you've made a friend here, a friend who admires your bravery."

The bear lifted one paw and, more quickly than Victor thought possible, tapped it against his chest. The twilit spirit plane faded away, and Victor found himself sitting in Norl's guest room, Teil still sleeping peacefully in a nest of blankets, and his coyotes looking at him with expectant eyes.

"Thanks," he whispered, dismissing his spirit totems, and they faded away, dispersing into a pale mist that wafted into nothing.

Victor sighed heavily and lay back, stretching his back and legs out so the blood could flow into his cramped muscles. He must have been on his spirit walk for a few hours at least, judging by how he felt.

He held a hand up in front of his eyes and flexed his long, thick fingers into a fist, releasing it again as he thought about what he'd done. In a way, he wished he'd taken the bear's offer and accepted another reward—he could have been happy with rage and inspiration. He could have lived his life with those two affinities, but now he had this dark ball of fear at his Core.

"God," he whispered, "if I thought cultivating rage sucked, wait till I start analyzing how I was fucking scared all the time." He lay there for a long time, thinking about things and wondering if he should be upset or happy, annoyed that he couldn't really decide. Was it true? Had he been scared all of his life? He supposed there had to be some truth in it, especially as he looked at his Core and saw the ominous ball of purple-black Energy—there was no doubt his affinity with it was strong.

"Doesn't mean I have to let it rule me. Now I know about it, I can use it. I can face my fears and not let them control me." Victor startled himself when he realized he was holding Lifedrinker against his chest and directing his whispers to her. Holding her, he realized that when she'd given herself to him and shared everything she had to save him, he'd been afraid.

Victor had been afraid that she was doing something he didn't deserve, that she was making a sacrifice that he'd squander. He'd worried that her faith in him was misplaced and that he'd fail to restore her. He really did seem to have fear at the root of many of his thoughts and actions.

Victor focused on those memories, on how he'd felt, and he found the seeds of his despair and grabbed them, pulling them out of the memories, and, just as he had with his rage, he made a construct of fear that he could study, focus on, and use to cultivate his new affinity.

"Take that shit, *pendejo*!" he hissed through the discomfort of the memory. "Already facing this bullshit down." Pride blossomed in his chest, and he knew, then and there, that he'd made the right decision—if he hadn't learned this about himself, it still would have been there. At least now he could improve himself and use it.

"What are you doing?" Teil's voice was sleepy, and Victor realized what a sight he must be, lying on his back, wearing just his pants, with his axe on his chest, talking to himself.

"Eh, just cultivating."

"Put that axe down and come closer; it's cold out there," she said, lifting her blanket as an invitation. Victor thought about it, about his gut reaction to do what she asked, to put off facing his reality for a while, and then he sat up and pulled his shirt out of his storage ring.

"Actually, Teil, I'm gonna get an early start. I miss my friends, and I want to spend some time with them before I take off for what will probably be a long time. You okay?"

"Mmhmm. I'm okay, Victor," she said, opening her eyes and pulling her blanket back tight under her chin. She smiled, though it didn't seem to be reflected in her eyes. "I'm sad, and I'll need a lot of time to get over things, but you helped. You helped me a lot, Victor. Thank you."

"I hope . . . I hope things are better for you, Teil. Take care, all right?"

"You too, hero. You too."

19

CORRUPTION

Victor tried to saddle Thistle without bothering anyone, but Norl came out of his front door, sipping a steaming mug, and said, "Leaving before dawn, hmm? The beds that bad?"

"No, your place is great, Norl. I'm just eager to be on my way back to Tellen's camp. I'm worried about my friends, and I miss them." Victor grunted as he cinched the buckles tight on his saddle.

"Understandable, young man. What about your friend? She staying a while?" Norl glanced toward his home as though he could see Teil sleeping in the guest room through the walls.

"Yeah, she was soundly sleeping, but she knows I'm leaving, don't worry." Victor buckled the bridle around Thistle's ears and down under his neck. "I mean, I'm not dipping out on her if you're worried about that."

"No, no. I was wondering, though—she lost her loved ones? Her village was destroyed? Do you think she'd want to stay with us for a while?" He took another sip from his mug and sighed loudly in pleasure, smacking his lips after he swallowed.

"Maybe. It won't offend her if you ask; I'm sure of that." Victor stepped into his stirrup, hoisting himself onto Thistle's back. "Well, that's it for me, Norl. I'm off. Thanks for everything, and I'm sorry if I woke you."

"Oh, you didn't. I don't sleep much these days. Victor, by the way, you'll find a path on the north edge of the village that leads directly to the plains." Norl gestured toward Victor's left with his mug. "Wasn't sure you knew that."

"Well, I didn't! Thank you, Norl; I was going to backtrack the way I came."

"Thank you, warrior. Thank you. That bear woulda done us just as it had your lady friend's village. We owe you a debt; you're welcome in my home anytime."

Victor looked into the older man's eyes and gave him a nod, then he clicked his tongue and started Thistle moving through the village. When he got to the path and saw that it was wide and clear of obstructions, he pushed the vidanii into a canter and made quick progress through the woods toward the plains. He had a lot to think about and allowed his mind to wander while Thistle did most of the work.

He thought about his time on the spirit plane with Thunderbite and everything he'd learned about himself. He was feeling a lot better about his new affinity now that he'd already managed to build a fear construct and do some cultivating. He reasoned that if he'd improved himself by dealing with the memories that caused him to feel anger, he'd only continue to do so by facing his fears.

It was unpleasant and difficult stuff for Victor to admit to being scared, to look at a time in his life when he'd describe his feelings by saying, "I was pissed off," only to really analyze it and say, "I lashed out because I was afraid of someone leaving me again."

Several times while riding between the tall, beautifully colorful trees, he turned his vision inward and looked at his Core, admiring the three orbs of attuned Energy and how they balanced each other in appearance. He felt the dark, shadowy purple orb of his fear affinity was a good counterpoint to his inspiration Energy while his rage smoldered, ready to add raw power to either one. "I wonder if I can find a weave to mix that fear with my rage." He figured he'd ask Gorz and Oynalla for ideas when he got back.

Victor looked up as the sky began to grow light and admired the height of the trees. True, he'd hardly seen any sort of forest, living in southern Arizona, but he felt these trees were truly immense. They soared many times higher than telephone poles, some of their trunks wider than his *tío's* pickup truck.

"Heck, that one's bigger than my *abuela's* house!" he said to Thistle, patting the vidanii's rough red shoulder. The tree was a good fifty yards from the trail, but its enormous black-barked trunk was easy to see with the wide clearing around it. Victor figured its canopy made it hard for smaller trees to grow very close to it.

"Let's check it out," he said to Thistle and steered him off the trail toward the clearing and the forest giant. Thistle's steps were loud and the only noise in the area, the birds and animals either holding still or having fled. His big hooves pressed into the mulch of fallen leaves, and when he stepped into the clearing around the tree, Thistle balked. Even when he'd been hunting the "demon" that terrorized Tellen's hunting party, Thistle hadn't acted spooked—this was new. "You all right, boy?"

The vidanii snorted, steam pluming from his nose, and stamped a front foot, but he wouldn't move closer to the tree. "All right," Victor said, sliding out of the saddle. He stood next to Thistle, one hand on his neck, the other on Lifedrinker's head, and studied the great tree.

It was almost like looking at a tall building, standing this close. Victor couldn't see around the trunk to either side, so vast it was. The bark was gnarled and dark, all blacks and grays, and the first branches didn't start for nearly a hundred feet. Looking up at those branches, though, Victor marveled at the amount of wood suspended in the air over his head—hundreds, no, thousands, or tens of thousands of tree-sized boughs hung from the great trunk, their long, silver-blue needles blocking out the sky.

"Wait here," he said to Thistle, and still resting a hand on Lifedrinker, he approached the colossal trunk. He wasn't sure why he wanted to, but Victor's palm almost itched with the desire to rest it on that rough bark. He didn't have any sense in his gut about why Thistle was spooked—he felt that he'd know it if he had some fear tickling the back of his neck. There was nothing, though; all Victor felt was curiosity and a desire to feel the enormous life of that tree beneath his hand.

As he drew near, within a few feet, Victor began to experience the tree's aura—thick, vibrant, a life so strong it could snuff out lesser plants before they took their first sips of the rich air or soil. He outstretched his arm and slowly, like a man reaching out to pet a crocodile, placed his palm against the dark mossy bark.

Victor's vision went dim, and then his mind was filled with a series of vivid images. He saw a sapling growing out of rich dark soil; its trunk was supple and silvery, and it grew toward a bright blue sky. He saw it grow over a hundred, then a thousand years, ever larger, stretching above the nearby forest canopy until it stood like a skyscraper among smaller buildings. All the while, its trunk shone silver-white, and its silver-tipped, blue needles hung like a massive, beautiful umbrella over the expansive clearing.

People, Ghelli with their shimmering dragonfly wings and their cousins the Naghelli, visited the tree day and night, performing their strange rituals. Then something happened, the sky shifted, the stars moved, and the forest was pulled away from its world and smashed into a new one—the System had come and merged the planets. The tree continued to thrive, but then something came, something it wasn't familiar with, a dark slithering presence that presented itself in supplication, touching the great tree's bark.

Rather than pay its respects and leave, though, this new creature began to worm its way into the tree, pressing into a hairline crack, widening it, and slowly corrupting the tree's flesh as it sank into its heart. The silvery bark began to crack and harden, turning gray and black.

The Ghelli and Naghelli stopped their visits, and the plants and smaller trees began to shrink away from their great cousin, avoiding the soil tainted by its roots. As a final image, Victor saw himself approaching, reaching out to touch the tree. Then his vision returned to normal, and he saw a System message.

*****The Silverbark Monarch has offered you a Quest: Descend to the great tree's roots and cut out the corruption that has plagued it for nearly two centuries. Reward: A rare natural treasure. Accept? Yes/No.*****

Victor paused to consider things, reigning in his impulse to touch the "yes" response. "Why do I want to say yes?" he asked the forest, looking over his shoulder at Thistle, still lingering at the edge of the clearing. "Because I'm an adventurer?" Victor studied his motivations, making sure he wasn't acting out of some kind of hidden fear, as if he was trying to prove something to some bogeyman that lived in his memories, but he didn't think that was the case.

The truth was, while he used to dread fighting, even harbor fears about it and the expectations people had for him, he'd been forced to fight so much that he was starting to enjoy it, especially when no one was watching, no friends were on the line—it was just Victor and the tree, and it felt right.

"A rare natural treasure, huh?" He supposed he didn't mind getting magical rewards, either. He accepted the quest and stepped back as the rough bark near him loudly cracked as it split, opening a jagged hole in the enormous trunk. Victor lifted Lifedrinker from his belt and peered into the new-formed hollow in the tree to see a narrow tunnel leading down, through loose soil and dark wood into the depths beneath the tree. Victor cast Globe of Inspiration and, in its white-gold glow, he stepped into the opening.

The tunnel the tree had made was narrow, and Victor had to stoop to keep from banging his head on the low ceiling, but as he descended, it began to grow wider, and the walls were made up more and more of hard, dark soil. Victor began to notice that he was constantly curving to the right, and he realized he was descending into the ground beneath the tree in a spiral. Thick roots, some the size of his arms, some so wide he could take two steps to walk over them, crossed the tunnel, always near the floor or the ceiling, leaving room for him to pass through.

It smelled of damp, rich earth, and Victor didn't feel any hint of the "corruption" he was supposed to find. He felt his nerves begin to settle as he grew used to the gently sloping tunnel, lit with his bright, powerful light. That changed when he came upon the first skeleton—ragged, rotten clothing clung to the white brittle bones, and its bony fingers still held a rusted axe.

Victor knelt to examine the body, concluding that the person had died a long time ago. He saw that it had bones resembling a human with many sharp teeth. "Probably an Ardeni or Shadeni. So I'm not the first one you've offered this quest to, hmm?" he asked a nearby root.

Victor cast Sovereign Will, enhancing his agility, then he cast Inspiring Presence. If he was seeing dead questors, then danger was probably near, and he wanted to be ready. He wanted to conserve his rage, so he channeled some fear-attuned Energy into Lifedrinker, wondering if the smoky, black-purple Energy that infused her would be as effective as his other affinities.

Finally, before he stepped farther into the tunnel, Victor cast Manifest Spirit, summoning his coyotes with rage Energy. His red, angry companions sprang forth, growling and yipping, and Victor sent them forward, pacing in front of him, sniffing and scanning the shadows for trouble.

The tunnel was brightly lit with his orb, his glowing hounds, and his Inspiring Presence, and Victor held Lifedrinker ready, scanning left to right, waiting for his coyotes to alert him to anything. They did so several times as they passed by more bones, more dead adventurers, and then the air shifted, and Victor smelled the corruption for the first time. It reminded him of battle, of spilled guts and hot, coppery blood. It reminded him of rotting things and shit, and he felt his rage start to slip out of his Core into his pathways.

"Not yet," he hissed and, for the first time realized that it had happened because he was scared. "Goddamn it, I don't need to self-analyze right now!" He pushed his rage back into his Core and lifted Lifedrinker, dark and steaming with purple fumes. "Ready to share my fear with something, *chica*?" Then his coyotes erupted in howls and yelps, snapping barks and growls, and Victor charged forward, his bright orb following close behind.

He burst into a great open space, a deep oblong cavern bordered by enormous roots and hard-packed soil. His coyotes surrounded a dark shape that clung to a massive knot of roots near the chamber's center. It hissed and coiled, writhing around the roots like a multi-headed serpent made of shadow and rot. Long, looping tendrils shot forth, swiping at his companions, and they danced back, yipping and snapping.

Victor couldn't get a good idea of what exactly he was looking at, so wrapped in shadows was it. He pushed his orb of inspiration-attuned Energy in front of himself, sending it streaking toward the dark corruption, and as it drew near, it shrank down from a ball of bright light to a glimmering mote, then to nothing, snuffed out by the shadows. Victor felt irrationally angry at the destruction of his orb, and he immediately cast Dauntless Radiance, centering the stationary spell near the cavern's ceiling where the thick knot of roots emerged.

A brilliant crack of red-gold light erupted at the top of the cavern and shone down upon the writhing mass of shadowy tendrils, and like mist before the morning sun, they evaporated. Victor recoiled at what was left in their wake—pale, twisting tubes of flesh, balled up at their center around the huge roots, pulsing as they drank from the tree. They fanned out from their central knot into dozens of long, wriggling, worm-like tendrils with sucking, sphincter-like mouths ringed with rows of triangular hooked teeth.

They lashed out at Victor's coyotes, keeping them at bay, and as he watched, one of them made contact. It hooked its sucker mouth onto the coyote's haunch, lifted it from the ground, and thrashed it back and forth as it sucked the red Energy out of it. A heartbeat later, the yelping coyote dispersed in a cloud of red mist. Seeing his companion destroyed like that ignited something in Victor, and he launched forward, eyes tracking the many writhing tubes, calculating a truly inspired swing of Lifedrinker as he leapt into the fray.

Five or six of the enormous worms squirmed toward him as he approached, and Victor grinned, dodging among their uncoordinated attacks, and cleaving not one but three in half with a whistling, snapping cut. Thick gouts of green and yellow fluid sprayed from the cut tentacle things, sluicing over the cavern floor and onto Victor, and it sizzled where it hit his armor.

Suddenly a thought pierced his mind; words formed in his perception without the need for sound, and he knew the tree was speaking to him, "Do not sever the roots!" Though he didn't hear the words, they reverberated in his consciousness, and he understood that he needed to avoid cutting through or drenching that massive central root with acid.

Close as he now was, Victor could see that the things really were worms, and they might act together, but they weren't part of the same organism. Inspiration struck him, and, dodging their swinging, wriggling advances, he put Lifedrinker away in her loop and cast Berserk. His vision went red, but he kept firmly in his mind the need to rip and smash those worms, and he waded into them, his enormous hands seizing them near the root and yanking them, one by one, out of the tree's flesh.

Victor roared and screamed as the worms sank their teeth into his hands and legs, even his neck. Some of them bit into him with both of their tooth-ringed ends, pulling at his blood and Energy. The vast majority fruitlessly bit into his armor, hanging from it while he went around the massive taproot, pulling the worms free, flinging many of them with tremendous force against the hard-packed wall of the cavern. Soon, a pile of dazed, partially smashed worms throbbed and wriggled there, the least harmed ones inching over the ground, back toward Victor.

He roared again; this time, his coyotes caught Victor's meaning, wrangling the loose worms, dragging them back toward the pile, and delivering bites that bled away the worms' vitality in the process. In his rage, enhanced by the horrible itching and sucking bites, Victor began to lose sight of what he was doing. He stumbled away from the roots and the remaining worms and began to roar, breathing heavily and choking on the gouts of blood and spittle in his throat.

Why was he so tired? What was this horrible itch? He began to yank the worms out of himself, and as he saw them, his rage was stoked to new heights—he veritably steamed with it. Victor lifted his arms up and out, looked at the cavern ceiling, and screamed with such horrible ferocity that it would have deafened a bystander. He arched his back, and with all his being, he screamed again and flooded his pathways with the last of his rage. The worms clinging to his flesh burst apart, shredded by the violence of his fury.

Bereft of rage but cleared of the parasites, Victor looked around the cavern, gasping with effort. The ground near him was drenched with green and yellow ichor, littered with the shredded flesh of the worms. His coyotes were corralling a pile of worms near one of the cavern walls, biting and tearing at them as they tried to separate from the ball.

The plucky canines seemed only mildly bothered by the acidic ichor released with each of their bites, and Victor felt they could contain that squirming mass near the wall. Finally, at the center of the cavern, a dozen or so fat, long worms still clung to the enormous taproot of the tree.

Victor pulled Lifedrinker off his belt again and strode toward the root. As he got near, he cast Project Spirit, and a wave of black and purple Energy surged out of him, drenching the worms in fear made manifest.

In the past, when he'd cast Project Spirit and directed sickly, twisted inspiration at his foes, he'd struck doubt into their hearts. This was something far more visceral—Victor knew at a fundamental level that he'd just inundated those worms with terror incarnate, and some primal instinct in their parasitic brains caused them to panic.

Every single long, thick tube of toothy flesh released the enormous root and began to flap spastically along the cavern floor away from Victor. He laughed and charged after them, cleaving them into chunks of ruined, acidic flesh with Lifedrinker. She arced through the air and flesh alike, not slowing as she sheared through them. The acidic blood seemed to bother her not at all, and Victor saw her silvery veins pulse and throb with the Energy she pulled away from each severed worm. "Fuck yes! Run, fuckers!" Victor laughed, hacking them to bits as they retreated.

When the last of the fleeing worms was shredded, Victor turned back to the pile his coyotes had been working on and saw that he was down to just two beleaguered companions. Most of the worms were dead, shredded, and torn, but a few still struggled to work their way back to the root, and Victor charged forward, helping his coyotes to finish them off. When the last one lay twitching at his feet, Victor stood and, lungs heaving for breath, howled his victory, laughing as his two coyotes joined in.

The air was foul, and his eyes stung from the vapors of the acid in the soil, so Victor started walking back toward the tunnel that led away from the cavern. That's when he saw the thousands of golden motes of Energy beginning to form along the cavern floor, and he braced himself for the impact.

A few heartbeats later, Victor saw the motes stream together and then surge toward him, and he was transfixed by the effect. His aches and itchy scabs faded away, and his Core instantly recharged. Victor howled again, and his two companions, stubbornly clinging to this plane of existence, joined in again, their high, yelping voices mingling with his deeper, madder sound.

*****Congratulations! You have completed a Quest: Descend to the great tree's roots and cut out the corruption that has plagued it for nearly two centuries. Approach the Silverbark Monarch's taproot to claim your reward.*****

As Victor swiped away the message, he noticed that the air was already more clear—he didn't smell the corruption so heavily anymore, and his eyes weren't burning. Looking around, he saw hundreds of tiny roots probing out of the hard-packed soil, wrapping around the bits of torn worm flesh and dragging it under.

He turned to the massive knot of roots at the cavern's center, pleased to see it wasn't as dark as before. The ragged holes where the worms had been burrowing were already healed over, and the flesh of the root was lighter; Victor thought he saw a shimmer of golden Energy pulse through it, but it might have been a trick of the light—his Dauntless Radiance still shone down upon the center of the cavern. Walking toward it, Victor saw the ground shift, and then a distinctly blue root wriggled out of the soil and coiled upon itself to form a kind of basin.

Again, a soundless voice filled his mind, this time not shouting, but clear, almost soothing, "The sap of my heart, hero. For you or your companion—only one may drink." As he watched, the coiled blue root bowl filled with a shimmering, silvery liquid. Even from a few feet away, Victor could feel the Energy within that sap, and his body yearned for it like a man seeing pizza after a ten-day fast.

"Me or my companion?" At first, Victor thought the tree had meant his coyotes, but as he looked around, he realized they were gone. Then it clicked—it meant Lifedrinker. "Oh, of course. You're definitely up, *chica.* Don't even doubt it," he said, lifting the axe free of his belt. He knelt over the coiled root and very gently dipped her blade into the sap. She throbbed and vibrated in his hand, and then he saw the thick fluid slowly start to drain, and he knew she was drinking it.

Lifedrinker had already regained two of her long, silvery veins, but now they thickened, grew branches, and spread out through the dark metal. Victor felt his cheeks start to ache and realized he was smiling broadly, his eyes filling with tears as he watched Lifedrinker not only restored but pushed further. Her axe-head pulsed with silvery light, and when it faded, he saw the sap was gone, but she was radiant, her Heart Silver edge and veins glowing from within, only slowly fading back to their usual luster.

Victor stood and hefted Lifedrinker, and she felt different somehow. When he moved her, it almost felt as if she was moving with him, like the difference between lifting an unconscious person and helping someone to stand. "Are you there, beautiful?" he asked, wondering if he should touch his head to her metal again.

He felt the axe vibrate so rapidly in his hand that it was practically humming. He lifted her, looking into the bright silvery veins, and then he heard her voice, undeniably feminine, rich, like crystal, chiming over placid waters, "I'm here, Victor." With those simple words, a flood of emotion surged into him through Lifedrinker's living handle—love, pride, satisfaction. She'd known she could count on him to restore her, and she was exceedingly proud of him and herself for being right.

"That's it. That's it," he said, lifting her to rest on his shoulder. Victor, still beaming ear to ear, turned and began his journey out of the tree, wondering at his luck. Had he stumbled upon something rare and impossibly fortuitous, or was this world just filled with opportunity, ripe for the taking for an enterprising adventurer?

20

A DANGEROUS AFFINITY

When Victor rode into the Shadeni winter camp, he was greeted by the watching hunters, and before he could get Thistle brushed down and fed, Thayla, Deyni, and Chandri found him, smothering him with hugs and questions. "What happened to your face?" Thayla asked, touching the long, still-pink scars from the bear's claws.

"I . . ." he began, but then Chandri interrupted.

"Lifedrinker looks different!" she said, reaching out to touch the silver-streaked axe-head.

"Victor, can you teach me to ride Starlight now that you're back?" Deyni asked at the same time, reaching to grab hold of his hand, wrapping her little fist around two of his fingers.

"I . . ." he began again, but then Tellen rounded the corner of the lodge near which Victor's wagon was staked.

"Victor, welcome back! Ahh! A new battle scar, I see!" He strode forward to clap Victor on the shoulder, and Victor could only look at the little crowd and laugh.

"It's great to be back and see your faces! I missed you guys!" He laughed again, pulling Thayla, Chandri, and even little Deyni into a hug, squishing them together against his chest. "Yeah," he said over the tops of their heads to Tellen, "the bear got me pretty good."

"Oof," Thayla said, trying to push him away, "I can't breathe!"

"Yes, you can, Mommy," Deyni laughed, squeezing Victor around one leg.

"All right, all right," Victor said, letting go of them all, though he really had savored their closeness. "Let me finish with Thistle, then I'll meet you guys in the longhouse. I'll tell you everything!"

They agreed and started back around the side of the longhouse, but Chandri lingered behind. "The scars don't look bad—I'm sure some hunters would love to copy them if they could get away with it! You really fought a mad spinebear? Oynalla told us that much . . ."

"Yeah," Victor said, still brushing Thistle. "I did, and I wasn't really smart about it. Luck was on my side, though, and I learned a lot about myself in the process. Well, the old bear spirit helped me with that part."

"Old bear spirit?"

"You're really going to make me tell this story twice?" Victor laughed, leading Thistle further out, near Starlight, so he could graze some of the late fall grass. It wasn't as blue-green as it had been when Victor first came to the plains, but it wasn't dried and yellow, just shorter and paler. Tellen had told him that the plains grass never really went dormant unless it had a thick blanket of snow on top.

"Well, I feel like I won't be heard among all the others shouting questions at you." She followed him out onto the grass, lingering close.

"How about you? I heard you all went on a hunt. Did Deyni get anything?"

"She learned to track! We brought home a dozen feyris."

"Damn! So fast?" Victor almost automatically reached down to take her hand as they walked back toward the longhouse, and that's when he felt the first nagging bite of guilt in the pit of his stomach. He paused and took a deep breath, thinking about his words, and then said, "Hey, Chandri, we haven't spoken about this, really, in a while, but we're good, right?"

"We're good?"

"I mean, what we have. We're, well, happy? I mean, yeah, we're into each other, but we both know nothing much is going to happen right now. Maybe someday, though, right?"

"Well . . ." her face had grown severe, and Victor could see he'd caught her off guard.

"I'm sorry to be so blunt, but I'm a guy who needs some clarity, okay?"

"Well, I never put it in so many words, but I guess you're right. Is that fine with you? Are you mad?"

"No! Shit, no, Chandri. How could I be mad? Everyone knows I'm leaving, so why would you want me to, you know"—he gestured around the camp to the various longhouses in view—"scare off all the competition? I mean, if I was with you officially, you'd never have another guy come near you!" He laughed at her outraged face. "I'm teasing, I'm teasing!" He kept laughing as she chased him to the longhouse.

Victor knew, in his heart, that he'd taken a chickenshit way out of dealing with his feelings for Chandri. He'd gotten her to confirm that they weren't anything yet, that they might be someday, and then he'd turned it into a joke. Still, she was happy and laughing, and what else really mattered?

That night, they sat in the main hall of the longhouse, and Victor told his tale to more than two dozen of the clan members, including Oynalla, who came up to join them by the fire. The storytelling had become a kind of celebratory feast. The hunters cracked open several casks of cheb-cheb and passed around platters of smoked meats and roasted root vegetables glazed with tallow and heavily seasoned.

Victor had never really considered himself an outgoing person, but he found himself enjoying all the attention and told the tale with little embellishment—none was really needed. He described his fasting, the spirit realm, the great bear, and his quest. Then he told the tale of how he rode out on Thistle, searching for the bear, found the ruined village, met Teil and Gef, and encountered the strange tracks of his friends being chased by trolls.

"But we never went into the forest!" Deyni interrupted.

"I know, munchkin," Victor said. "The spirits were testing me!" Then he went on to explain his encounter with the trolls and how the curse started to affect him. Oynalla watched him the whole while he spoke, never interrupting, not even to erupt into one of her trademark cackles. When Victor finished describing how he'd killed the bear and destroyed the necklace of teeth, Oynalla still didn't comment, and her silence was beginning to unnerve him.

Victor paused to sit back down and take a bite of meat, chasing it with a long pull of liquor, and Oynalla finally cleared her throat. Everyone paused their side conversations and laughter to look her way, and she said, "Aren't you going to tell us about your reward, warrior?"

"Well, I suppose," Victor said, though his stomach had knotted up at the mention. "I mean, I had to do another spirit walk, and the bear, well, he helped me to improve my Core, finding another affinity. I can tell you more later, Oynalla. I think it's boring stuff to most everyone else."

"No, it isn't!" Chandri said, and ten people echoed her sentiment.

"What affinities do you have, Victor?" one of Tellen's hunters asked, demonstrating that his Core and abilities weren't as common knowledge as it often felt to Victor. Oynalla, for the first time, cackled, and Victor could see she'd been wanting to ambush him with this.

"All right," he said, straightening his back and taking a deep breath. "I'll be honest, my first instinct is to avoid talking about this, to play things off like nothing much happened, but that's one of the things I'm learning about myself—I often react out of fear. I think I . . ."

"No, you don't, Victor!" Thayla interjected. "You're the bravest man I know!"

"True!" Tellen said, and Chandri banged her mug on the table in agreement. All of Tellen's hunting band were present, and they, too, took up their mugs in objection, crashing them against the long table.

"Wait, wait!" Victor said, holding up his hands. "Let me explain!" He paused, waiting for people to be quiet, and then he looked into Oynalla's shrewd eyes and said, "I didn't say I wasn't brave, but it's true—the bear helped me see it—I do often act out of fear. Listen!" Again he had to wait, and then he picked one of the older women who often gave Victor baked goods to sample and asked, "Letha, can I ask you a question?"

"Aye, warrior, go ahead!" She spoke forcefully, though she slurred her words, and Victor knew she was a bit drunk.

"If there are two hunters, and one is terribly afraid of wolves, while the other isn't, but they both go out, track down and kill a wolf, which one was braver?"

"Why . . ." she paused to think, and several people started to mutter their own answers, but she cleared her throat and said, "The one who was afraid!"

"Isn't she wise, everyone?" Victor asked, laughing. "Well, that's what the bear helped me to see; I wasn't as wise as Letha, so I thought when he said I had a lot of fear, he was calling me a coward. He helped me to see that when I overcome my fears, I'm brave. Anyway, to shorten the story, he helped me to find my third affinity. Fear."

The table erupted in chatter, people arguing about what bravery was, others exclaiming about what Victor said, wondering what it meant to have a fear affinity, and others still sat quietly, contemplating their own thoughts or Victor's words. Chandri was one of those, and though her eyes were fixed on Victor's, she didn't seem to notice when he smiled at her. The conversations continued, and Victor realized he was done with the storytelling part of the night. He leaned forward on the table, resting on an elbow, and began to eat in earnest.

"Deyni," Thayla said from beside him, "it's time you went to bed. Say goodnight to Victor."

"Wait, Mommy! Victor, what about Lifedrinker? You didn't tell us that part of the story!"

"Oh? You want to hear about a giant tree and the evil creature sucking its life away, corrupting its roots?" Victor asked, leaning past Thayla to lock eyes with the little girl.

"Yes!"

"Well, then, you better go to bed because that's a story for tomorrow. How about a ride on Starlight, too?"

"Promise?" Deyni asked, looking at her mom. "Promise you'll save the story? Don't tell anyone else first, Victor!"

Victor mimed locking his lips shut, then he held out his arms, and the little girl rushed forward to hug him. "See you in the morning, runt." Thayla gave his neck a gentle squeeze then she led Deyni down toward their sleeping quarters.

"You're good with the girl, warrior," Oynalla said from across the table.

"He is, isn't he?" Chandri asked, apparently having recovered from whatever deep thought she'd been struck with.

"It's easy to speak to the young when your heart is young, girl. Victor is young in his soul, and a good soul it is. I'm glad you weren't ruined by your new affinity, warrior. There are many horror stories about spirit casters with fear affinities." Oynalla favored him with a genuine smile, and he nodded.

"Yeah, I can see how it could go in a very different direction."

"What do you mean?" Chandri asked, looking from Victor to Oynalla.

"I mean, being afraid but not conquering that fear can make a person really shitty. If you had that affinity and a shitty persona? You could do a lot of damage."

"So eloquent, warrior—always speaking of scat like it had a million uses. Girl, Victor is saying that someone ruled by fear but able to share it, someone willing to do so could destroy a community. It's happened many times in the past to clans, towns, and even cities, sometimes before anyone realized what the cause was."

Chandri nodded and reached across the table to take Victor's hand. "Good thing you aren't ruled by it, then."

Victor looked at Chandri, at her open face and the pride in her eyes, and he felt hot shame in his chest. He looked down and cleared his throat. "You're embarrassing me with all that," he said, playing it off with a laugh. Chandri laughed along, but Oynalla tsked with her tongue and stood up.

"Off to bed for me. Victor, you should walk the perimeter. Take Chandri with you. I'll see you in the morning, and we'll review what you've learned." Victor stood and nodded to the old woman, understanding all too well what she wanted him to do. He knew he had to, also, and that was what really chafed—why did it matter? What Chandri didn't know wouldn't hurt her, right? He shook his head as the answer came to him—it wouldn't hurt her, but it would hurt him. He needed to face his fears, even one as annoying as this one.

Chandri nodded and stood, though her face betrayed some hesitation, some doubt. She nodded quickly and reached out for Victor's hand. "Come, I doubt anything will be stirring out on the plains, but it's good to have a look around." Victor accepted her outstretched hand, and they walked out of the longhouse in the cold night air, woodsmoke heavy in the air from all the longhouses.

It was quiet out, and Victor could hear the roladii shuffling together in the low shelter the clan had built for them. It was attached to their nighttime pen and only a hundred yards or so from Tellen's longhouse. Chandri gestured in that direction and said, "Let's start with a look at the roladii."

Victor didn't say anything but walked with her, still holding her warm, small fingers in his. He struggled with what to say, how to broach the subject of his guilt. His instinct was to rip the Band-Aid off and face his fear head-on, but he recognized that he wasn't dealing with a monster here; he was dealing with Chandri, and anything he said would have some repercussions with regard to his relationship with her. More than that, he worried that he'd hurt her. Was it worth hurting her to make himself stronger? To face down a fear?

"Hey, I should tell you . . ."

"Wait, Victor. I need to say something before I lose the courage," Chandri said, squeezing his fingers, still walking, still not looking into his face.

"All right . . ." he started, but again, she interrupted.

"You see, when you were talking in there, when you spoke about how you had to face your fears to be brave, I started to feel guilty. I know you, Victor. I know you fear hurting the people you care about. You care about me, right? And here I am, holding your hand, acting like I want something from you, but knowing in my heart that I'll never go anywhere with you. I can't, Victor." She paused when Victor started to object and reached up to gently place her fingers over his mouth. "No, shush, I have a lot to say, okay?"

As Victor nodded, she continued, stopping to look up at him, "You're destined for great, big things, Victor, and I'm not the kind of person that seeks that out. I love my clan. I love the hunt. I loathe the idea of cities and crowds, but more than that, Victor, I'm not cut out for facing down spinebears or going to wars! I have a Pearl Class Core and can barely manage to imbue a fire arrow before I struggle for lack of Energy."

"I didn't realize that . . ."

"Let's agree to love each other, as much as we can, the way we are, but never to hold each other back. I want a family and a husband that will hunt with me. You have a lot of living to do and great adventures to seek out, and I don't want you to feel like you owe me anything. Can you agree to that? I hope I haven't hurt you, Victor."

Victor was flabbergasted. He'd been about to confess an indiscretion he'd built up in his mind, and here was the object of his guilt telling him that she wanted to just let things cool off. He felt so lucky and relieved, but his guilt was still chewing at him. It was like he couldn't let himself off the hook so easily, but as he opened his mouth to push forward with his confession, he saw the kindness, the sweet concern in Chandri's eyes, and he knew it wasn't worth mentioning. Why should he hurt her to assuage his guilt? The braver thing was to swallow it and let her have this clean, happy break.

"No, you're not hurting me, Chandri. How could I be mad to have someone love me and care enough to want what's best for me? Of course, I want you to be happy, too, so don't even think about it. I mean, life is long in this world, and who knows what might happen in fifty or a hundred years, right? I'm glad to have you in my life as things are, though."

Chandri grabbed him around the waist and pulled him into a hug, and Victor laughed, relieved to have things settled. He kissed the top of her head and gently rubbed her back while she squeezed him. "You're a good man, Victor. Don't let your doubts or fears ever tell you otherwise."

"Well, you're pretty damn good, yourself, Chandri." After they'd hugged for a while, Victor and Chandri walked the camp's perimeter, checking in with the hunters on watch, making sure all the roladii were sheltered, and even spending a few minutes with Thistle and Starlight. The two vidanii enjoyed the cold weather more than the roladii and didn't seem at all bothered to be out in the wind, eating grass by moonlight. Victor knew they'd sleep sometime around midnight if left to their own devices, having witnessed their behavior many times over the past months.

When they returned to the longhouse, it was much quieter, and nearly everyone had turned in for the night. Chandri hugged Victor again, heading off to Tellen's quarters, and he snuck into Oynalla's section to throw a bedroll down between her room and Thayla's. Victor knew they'd wake him up early, as he was effectively sleeping in their living space, but he didn't mind; he only needed a few hours of sleep each night and wanted to spend time with Oynalla as early as he could—he figured she'd have a lot to say about his new affinity and how he'd dealt with Chandri.

He slept well that night, happy to be among friends and in a comfortable place. His belly was full, and his conscience felt clean. Though he replayed his conversation with Chandri over in his mind, he didn't feel bothered by how things had gone, and he drifted into an easy sleep, unplagued by nightmares or any dreams he could remember. He woke to the smell of Oynalla's pungent tea and a murmured conversation between Thayla and Deyni.

"Good morning, warrior," Oynalla said, never one to be fooled by feigned sleep. "Thayla, take your daughter out and practice summoning your orb. I want Deyni to try to feel the difference between your spirit Energy and the air-attuned Energy on the winter wind."

"Can we ride Starlight later, Victor?" Deyni asked as Thayla stood up.

"If he's not busy," Thayla said, trying to rescue him.

"I'll be very upset if we can't, Deyni. I've been looking forward to it all night!" Victor said. "Will you give her a good scratch for me while you're out there?"

"Yes!"

"Come on, then," Thayla said, shaking her head ruefully. "See you later, Victor."

"Yep. See you." Victor watched them leave, then turned to the Old Mother and shrugged. "All right, let's have it."

"Have it?"

"Sure. I imagine you're about to chew me out about something. My affinity, my . . . behavior regarding Chandri."

"Oh, hush, warrior. You did fine last night. Chandri rescued you, but you chose your words correctly."

"Really?"

"Yes, forgive me for spying, but I'm a nosy old woman, and my little friend made it too easy."

"Your little friend?"

"Yes, I made a new friend since we returned to camp. Tsst, tsst," she said, clicking her tongue and holding her hand toward a pile of furs near the wall. A moment later, a whiskered snout poked out from under a shaggy hide, and a long, white-furred, ferret-type animal slinked out and coiled itself around

Oynalla's wrist. She lifted the creature and hugged it to her bosom, smiling in a genuine and vulnerable way Victor rarely saw from her.

"You spied on me with him?" Victor asked, raising his eyebrows.

"Of course. How else do you think I know so much about what goes on around here? Oh sure, I spy with my spirit, and I have auguries, but little friends like this are the most useful for finding out what's bothering the clan."

"I've never heard of a spy being so open about their nosiness," Victor laughed, shaking his head.

"I have good intentions, though. Like making sure a certain warrior doesn't harbor any fears or regrets, poisoning his spirit and embracing the darker natures of his affinities."

"Right."

"Now, come here, warrior. Put your hands in mine, and let's have a look at your Core. Let's see what that great old bear has done to you." She held hands out, palms up, and their smooth red flesh belied her age. Victor scooted closer and gently took them, careful not to squeeze too hard with his calloused, rough fingers. "Good, now look at your Core and let my Energy in; let it trickle through your pathways. You can trust me, warrior."

"I know," Victor said, following her instructions. He turned his gaze inward, studying the three orbs of his affinities, and when he felt Oynalla's warm, thin stream of Energy begin to explore his pathways through his hands, he didn't resist it. Instead, he reached out with his will and pulled on it, guiding her deep into his Core, and she inhaled deeply through her nose.

"Such heat," she breathed. "I could lose myself in the blaze of your rage, but . . . aha, there it is! Oh, Victor, you're lucky! The fear is balanced by your inspiration, though it's so strong! Never cultivate it more than your other affinities, Victor. Keep it in balance like you've done. Use it only against those you despise, those you wish to see harmed—no matter how much you might be tempted to sway an argument or drive home a point."

"Yeah, I appreciate the warning, but I don't think I would use my fear affinity like that."

"Good, because that's how it always begins. Spirit affinities are beguiling, and without control, they can start to influence the caster's mind. You've done well to improve your will so much and gained great control of your rage. Rage is a tricky one because it's not always negative, do you see? Fear, though, fear is a hard one to master, a dangerous affinity, and you must remain vigilant—never let it control you. Tell me, how have you used your fear affinity?"

"I've only used it once—when I was fighting the corruption beneath a great tree, I projected it to make some monstrous worm-things let go of the tree's roots and run away."

"Can you imagine the effect of such a working on a crowd of people? What if you were more subtle, only sending out a light, wispy wave, restraining that flood of mighty Energy at your Core? Do you see how it could ruin a population over time?"

"Yeah, I guess so. Oynalla, I'm not going to do something like that."

"Good, warrior. Be wary upon your next class refinement, please. Don't let your new affinity define you too much."

"I will. I promise!" he added as he saw that concern in her eyes.

"Good, then let's talk about some new uses for your combination of affinities."

Victor leaned forward, "All right! That's what I was hoping for . . ."

"Victor?" Thayla poked her head back into the room, interrupting his sentence.

"Has his visitor arrived?" Oynalla asked, surprising Victor.

"Visitor?"

"Aye, I saw a woman, an Ardeni with green features, speaking to you outside the longhouse." She saw the confusion on Victor's and Thayla's faces and added, "In a dream I had last week."

"Oh," Thayla said, her eyes squinting in surprise as she looked from Victor to Oynalla. "Yes, that's what I was about to say. She came riding a great cat! I've never seen a mount like it! Victor, she says she works for Rellia and wants to speak with you."

"Oh, jeez," Victor said, standing up with a sigh as his knees popped. "I'm sorry, Oynalla. Can we speak more about this later?"

"Perhaps. I think you'll be rather busy soon, but Oynalla will be here when you're ready." She laughed softly at first but then more of her usual cackle. "We can always speak more on the spirit plane, warrior. Go now; she's not a patient one."

21

A SUDDEN FAREWELL

When Victor saw Captain Valla leaning against her mount a few dozen steps away from the backside of the longhouse, he had to stop and do a double take. "Thayla, you weren't fucking around—she really has a saddle on that tiger!"

"Tiger?"

"That big fucking cat!"

"I don't know what it's called, but yes, she rode into camp on it." Thayla shrugged and tugged his arm, eager to get closer to the captain; she'd been annoyed that Valla wouldn't relay any of her news until Victor was present to hear what she had to say.

The animal wasn't like any tiger from Earth, but it certainly had a resemblance, down to the stripes, though they were yellow on dark blue-gray fur. More than that, it was huge. Victor had never seen a tiger up close. In fact, if pressed, he doubted he could say with certainty that they weren't extinct—he'd only ever seen them in VRs. Still, he knew they didn't get that big; he figured this thing was two-thirds as tall as Thistle and probably quite a lot longer. "Especially with that *pinche* tail," he hissed between his teeth as they walked up.

"Victor," Captain Valla said, standing up from where she'd been leaning against the cat. She was, as always, dressed smartly in her uniform pants and high-collared, perfectly pressed white shirt, and he wondered just how the hell she kept so clean after being on the road for, presumably, weeks.

"Hi, Captain Valla. What brings you out this way?"

"I bear messages. From Lady Rellia. Also, Polo Vosh stopped me as I was leaving Persi Gables. He sent a package for you." She stood perfectly straight, her hands clasped behind her back. As he and Thayla got closer, he noticed that Valla was quite tall, easily a head taller than Thayla, and in his experience, that was unusual—Shadeni were usually taller than Ardeni. He supposed part of it was her shiny military boots. Still, she was rather imposing, especially with a twenty-five-hundred-pound cat behind her.

"Really? Polo knew you were heading my way?"

"Yes." She stood stock still after uttering the clipped response, and Victor only figured out after an awkward silence that she wasn't going to say more.

"Well, let's have the messages first, huh?" he said, stepping closer, and then her big cat lifted its head and glared at him, a low rumble starting in its chest.

"Shush, Uvu!" she said, turning to thwap him on his big black nose. He chuffed and turned away, laying his head back down on his front paws with an annoyed yawn. Victor caught a glimpse of his long canines and didn't fancy the idea of tangling with the creature. "I have two messages and accompanying materials. Are you fine with this lady hearing Rellia's words?"

"You mean Thayla? Yes, Valla, you can speak in front of her."

"Very well. Ahem." She cleared her throat and looked into the sky over Victor's shoulder as though to concentrate. "Victor. I hope Valla finds you well. Things progress well here in Persi Gables. I've raised a full regiment of five companies, each comprised of two hundred soldiers. Hostility abounds in my family because I've kept my promises to you. House ap'Yensha no longer traffics in contracts for indentured servants, and I've sold off our share of the Greatbone Mine. I'd be dead by now if not for the enormous investment I've put into our expedition. If I were killed before it could bear fruit, our family's debts would take a hundred years to clear. I've sent a Far Scribe book with Valla so that we might better keep each other updated until spring. Yours, Rellia."

Again, Victor stared at Valla for a moment before he realized she was done speaking. "That it?"

"Yes. There is a second message, though it's written." She produced a scroll and held it out for Victor. He stepped forward to take it, frowning toward the big cat's front end, ready to react in case it decided it wanted to taste him more than it wanted to obey Valla. Once it was in hand, he backed up a step and looked back at Valla, locking onto her light green eyes.

"Why did one message come verbally and one written? This shit's strange."

"The lady grew tired of my presence," Valla said with a shrug.

"Huh?"

"What does that mean?" Thayla added.

"She wanted an excuse to send me. Any messenger could have brought you scrolls for a price. She thinks I don't know her mind, but I do." Again Valla shrugged.

"Oh, right, so she said only you could deliver me the first message or some shit?"

"Correct. She said she didn't want to 'put our expedition details, including troop numbers, in writing.'"

"I guess the stuff about her family wanting her dead was kind of sensitive . . ." Victor said as he dug his thumbnail under the purple wax seal on the scroll.

Victor,

Since the day after our fight when I spoke to Lam and learned about your origins, I've been fascinated by the story. It shouldn't surprise you, then, to learn that I sent some of our house investigators ahead of me to Persi Gables with the simple instruction to discover what they could about the circumstances of your summoning. Just a day before I gave this message to Valla and sent her on her way, one of those investigators came to me bearing fruit.

It seems there is a cabal of sorts operating out of Persi Gables—a group of sorcerers who gain power by summoning strong Energy users from other worlds. What they do with those they choose to keep, I do not know, but it is well understood that their castoffs, for lack of a better word, are often sold into slavery of one form or another.

Victor, my investigator retraced the various transfers of your old contract and learned from a man named Yund the name of the cabal agent that first sold you. A little more digging revealed that you were summoned using biological material from a particularly gifted student from Fainhallow Academy. Strange, don't you think? More than this, though, he learned the location of this group of sorcerers, or at least the site where they perform their summoning rituals.

I've given Valla a map and a list of names should you want to investigate your origin further. I would caution you, though, Victor: these people are quite powerful—summoning people through rips in the fabric of reality isn't something done by novices. More than that, they were expecting success, even had you been more powerful at the time. Overpowering a person's will, assuming they have any sort of developed Core, is no mean feat.

In anticipation of our next meeting,

Rellia ap'Yensha

"Shit," Victor said after reading the letter. Thayla had been trying to read over his shoulder, but the disparity in their heights made it difficult, and she reached for the scroll. Victor handed it to her but turned to speak to Valla, "Why would she give me this?"

"An excellent question. I find the distraction from our campaign rather troublesome." Valla still stood, straight as an arrow, hands behind her back.

"Right." Victor sighed, rubbing his hand through his hair, looking out over the plains to the west, the sun still bright and low behind him. It was beautiful, really, the long azure blades of grass rippling in waves as the crisp morning breeze passed over them. The deep shadows of the forest to his left drew his eye, and he searched among the blue, green, and fiery branches as though he might find an answer to his unspoken question: should he go try to find some answers about his summoning? Should he put a stop to these assholes?

"She did this as a show of good faith, Victor," Thayla said, rolling the scroll up.

"Yeah, something like that, I guess," he said, digging his thumbs into the meat at the base of his neck.

"She's trying to show you that you're not just a means to an end to her. I mean, that's what this letter indicates, but how much of it is calculated, I don't know." She held the scroll out to him, and Victor took it, slipping it into his ring.

"Logical," Valla said, nodding curtly to Thayla.

"Anything else?" Victor asked.

"Yes," Valla replied, producing a large polished wooden box. She grunted as she removed it from whatever dimensional container she'd had it in and lurched toward the ground, setting it with a thud on the grass before Victor. "Your package from Polo Vosh."

The box was nearly a perfect square, though it was a bit taller than it was wide. Victor squatted in front of it, looking for a clasp or hinges, but saw that the top was meant simply to lift off. He did so, revealing an interior padded with pillowed, burgundy silk and a dark gray helmet nestled within. It reminded him of an ancient Viking helmet. It seemed to glower at him from within the case, brooding and heavy. "Huh," he said, reaching in to lift it out, and he was startled by its weight. "*Madre*, this thing's fucking heavy," he hissed, straining as he pulled it forth.

"Yes, I noticed the weight." Valla's face didn't betray any emotion.

The dark gray helmet was rounded at the top, with a thicker band around the crown. It had heavy cheek guards and a glowering eye and nose guard that would cover about half of the wearer's face. The eye holes were wide enough to allow good visibility, but they were angled in such a way that the helmet just looked angry. "It seems pissed off," Victor said, chuckling.

Grunting, he lifted it to his head and was surprised that it wasn't too small. As it settled onto his head, though, and he had to strain to hold his neck straight, he knew it was too heavy and unwieldy to be of any use in a fight.

"Bond with it," Thayla suggested.

"Right." Victor trickled some Energy into the metal, and suddenly it conformed to the shape of his skull, the soft leather padding cupping his bones snugly and the visor holes lining up perfectly with his eyes. More than that, Victor felt its weight grow more comfortable, spreading down over his shoulders and arms and even down his back to his legs. It was as though it had somehow distributed its mass over his entire body.

*****Kethian Juggernaut Helm. Artificed for: Damage Resistance, Weight Distribution. Crafted from Imperial Keth Bedrock Magma. Crafted by: Tek'vah, slave to Keth.*****

"What the hell?" Victor looked from Thayla to Valla, both of whom gave him quizzical expressions. He told them about the message he'd received upon bonding with the helmet, and their confused looks only deepened.

"I've never heard of the Keth Empire," Thayla finally said with a shrug.

"Perhaps Polo Vosh received this item from another world. Or the System." Valla, too, shrugged.

"Well, it looks like good head protection," Thayla finally said, standing on her tiptoes to reach up and rap her knuckles against it. "Good choice from Polo. Too bad he didn't get to you earlier—you might not have lost your pretty face to that bear's claws."

"Hey, now!" Victor laughed, giving Thayla a shrug.

"Your scars do not make you ugly," Valla said, and Victor quickly glanced at her, but her face was stoic.

"Um, thanks."

"I was teasing him, Valla."

"Regardless. Victor, I'm instructed to make camp near you. Rellia wants me to report regularly via the Far Scribe book she sent. Will you be remaining here much longer?"

"Uh. Let me get back to you on that, Valla. I need to talk to Thayla and some others. You could give me the book. I promise to keep in touch, and that way, you can get back to your life. I doubt you want to follow me all over the place."

"I have my duty. It matters not whether I perform it here or elsewhere." Again, Victor looked at her face for any sign of emotion. Though her words often indicated some displeasure, her expression was neutral, and her posture hadn't altered at all.

"Well, do you want to come in with us?" Thayla offered.

"Thank you, but I'll attend to Uvu." She gestured to the enormous cat.

"Right," Victor said with a nod. "Thayla, let's go talk to Oynalla, hmm? Do you know where Tellen is?"

"Yes. I'll get him and meet you within," she said as they started walking away. "You're thinking of leaving early, aren't you?"

"Thayla, this is huge. I mean, I've come to terms with not being able to get home, but I'd sure love to get some answers. More than that, I'd like to fucking let these *pinche* motherfuckers know how much I *appreciate* what they've done for me!" Victor's voice had grown heavy with anger as some of his rage affinity leaked into his pathways. He'd been thinking about returning to Persi Gables to punish Yund—how stupid! Yund was an asshole, sure, but the real culprits, the origin of Victor's suffering, had begun with the ones who'd summoned him.

Victor wanted answers, and he wanted some justice. Maybe he could never go home, but he might be able to help some other poor slob from experiencing what he'd gone through. They were back to the front of the longhouse when Thayla turned to him and grabbed his shoulders, looking at his eyes, set back behind the thick metal openings of his new helmet.

"Victor, I understand. I just. . . well, I just was hoping we still had a couple of months together. I'm afraid I'll never see you again." Her voice had grown small, and Victor realized he wasn't the only one who needed people in this world to care about. He wasn't the only one who needed connections.

"Thayla, I'm not going to let that happen. It might take some time, years even, but I'll get back to you. You and Deyni are important to me. Hell, this whole clan has treated me like family. You know you're just as important to me as I am to you, right?"

"Okay. Well, hug me for real, then. Hug me so I'll remember it," she said, reaching up under his arms to pull him close. Victor hugged her back, chuckling at her sudden sentimentality.

"I'm not going just yet, you know."

"Yes, well, after the whole clan knows you're leaving, I doubt I'll get another minute alone with you." She squeezed him for another solid minute and then extricated herself, and Victor saw that her eyes were moist. His throat felt suddenly thick, and the fact that he was leaving really hit home. She'd known before he did. "I'll get Tellen."

"Right." He nodded, then went into the longhouse, making his way down to Oynalla's room. The old woman was sitting in front of her teakettle, sipping her cup, and when she saw Victor, her smile was broad and knowing.

"So, my visions told me true? You're leaving to chase down a thread from your past?"

"You knew?"

"It wasn't as clear as some of my auguries, but it was clear enough. Sit down, then." She pointed to the furs across from her, and Victor grunted, lowering himself. "Remove that monstrous hunk of metal from your head, warrior! I promise I won't hit you with anything heavy," she said, brightening the mood with a cackle.

"Oh, right," Victor chuckled, lifting the helmet off his head. He grunted as it suddenly assumed all of its weight in his hands, and he almost dropped it, lurching forward toward the teakettle. "*Pinche* . . ." he hissed under his breath, slipping the helmet into his storage ring.

"Good; now, before the others arrive, let's talk about what you're to work on," Oynalla said, offering him a cup of tea.

"Okay." Victor took the tea and sipped; it was hot, bitter, and precisely what he'd been expecting. He grimaced and waited for Oynalla's next words.

"You must continue to build up your Core. Never let your fear affinity outgrow your others!" She glared at him until he nodded. "I've drawn you a weave to practice—your trapped spirit and I spoke for a while and came up with a clever way to combine your fear with your rage."

"Gorz?"

"Yes. Did you forget I had him?"

"Well, for a while, yeah. I'm not the best friend a trapped spirit could have, I guess." Victor sighed, growing weary of listing his faults to people.

"Nonsense. He's just a fragment of a spirit. He hardly knows time's passage when he's not being spoken to." Oynalla scoffed and slurped at her tea.

"Oh, well, that makes me feel better. I mean, he told me something similar, but I always feel like he's downplaying things, you know?"

Oynalla just grunted and reached into the folds of her leather beaded coat and pulled out his amulet, tossing it to him. He caught Gorz and slipped him back over his neck, tucking him down inside his armored shirt.

"Victor! It's good to be back with you!"

"You too, Gorz. I'll catch you up on what you missed when we get on the road."

"The pattern we made for you will be difficult to form, but you must practice it each night before cultivating. Once you've mastered it, I believe many doors will open for you," Oynalla said, picking up where she'd left off.

"All right, um, will it be another new attuned Energy? Like my courage weave?"

"Exactly. And once you've created it, you should use it with your existing spell patterns to see what new abilities you can uncover." She sat back and stared at the beaded curtain behind Victor, and he turned to see what she was looking at. A moment later, they flew into the air as Deyni burst into the room.

"Victor! Is it true?" she wailed, tears streaming down her cheeks.

"Oh, gosh. Deyni, I . . ." Victor started, but she interrupted him.

"You promised, Victor! You were going to teach me to ride Starlight!"

Stunned by her outburst, Victor didn't reply immediately, but then Thayla rushed into the room and scooped up her daughter. "I'm sorry, Victor. She heard me talking to Tellen. She's so sneaky!"

"Listen," Victor said, standing up with a grunt. He reached for Deyni and was relieved when the little girl didn't resist him. He pulled her away from Thayla, held her against his chest, and softly said, "Deyni, I'm sorry. I didn't plan things to happen this way, but I have some plans to make things up to you. Will you hear me out?"

She pulled away to look at his face, her eyes red and filled with tears, and nodded. Victor said, "I plan to move quickly, and I think I'm just going to take Thistle. Will you adopt Starlight from me? She needs a good home—someone who will take care of her and brush her, and . . ."

"Yes!" Deyni cried before he could say more.

"I know I promised to teach you to ride, but you know who taught me, right?"

"Chandri!"

"Would it be okay if she taught you?"

"Victor, you don't have to . . ." Thayla started, but he held up a hand.

"I'm not going to want to pull a wagon everywhere I'm going, Thayla. I only need Thistle. Will you guys take Starlight for me? I might come back for her someday . . ."

"Yes. Of course, we will," Thayla said, her eyes starting to tear up.

"Oh jeez, you two! I can't spend the whole day crying. Let's cheer up, okay? I'm not leaving forever. Even Oynalla will agree with that, right, Old Mother?"

"I can't see that far ahead, warrior," she replied with a cackle.

"See? She can't deny it!" Victor laughed, and then Tellen came into the room, followed by Chandri and Chala, and Victor held Deyni close while he told everyone about his plans to leave. They took it with more stoic reactions than Deyni's, but he saw the troubled look in Chandri's eyes, and he knew he'd need to speak to her again before he left. Tellen tried to talk him into a feast before he left, but he knew that it would only prolong the painful goodbyes and insisted that he wanted to get on the road as soon as possible.

"Will you sell Thayla some roladii to pull that wagon when you guys head to your summer camp?"

"She won't need to buy them . . ."

"I have plenty of funds, Tellen," Thayla said, reaching out to rest a hand on his shoulder. He opened his mouth to argue but changed his mind when he looked at Thayla's face. He shrugged and nodded. Victor hadn't seen that familiarity between them before, and he suddenly wondered at all he'd missed while busy with his quests and spending time with Chandri. Thinking of Chandri, he looked at her face, saw the lack of any sort of smile or amusement, and reached out for her hand.

"Chandri, will you come with Deyni and me to see Starlight? I think we should talk about what it means to be a good mother to a vidanii." He winked at her, and she forced a smile, taking his hand.

"Yes," Oynalla said, "Go do that. The rest of us will follow soon—I can tell this warrior doesn't want to linger around, feeling sorrow at long goodbyes. Chala, run; tell the clan mothers to gather their families outside to shout their goodbyes."

"I will," Chala said, but then she charged forward and grabbed Victor in a hug. "I'll miss you, too, Victor," she said as he squeezed her back, one arm still holding Deyni.

"Thanks for everything, Chala. You're going to be a fierce warrior one day. The clan's lucky to have you." When she pulled away, Victor had a white and black smear of face paint on his armor, and she laughed, rubbing at it with her palm. Then she turned and hurried out of the room, the beads rattling in her wake. Victor reached down, took Chandri's hand again, and walked outside. When they got to Victor's wagon, where the two vidanii were staked, still grazing happily, Victor set Deyni down.

"Hey, can you go over to Starlight and give her a brushing? I want Chandri to see that you know how to do it perfectly."

"I will," Deyni said, eyes wide and serious, and Victor handed her the brush.

"Good huntress," Chandri called after her as she hurried over to the huge animal. "She can't even reach its back. I hope you didn't create trouble giving such an animal to a child . . ."

"She'll be fine. I know you'll teach her well. Just don't let her go out alone until she's bigger, all right?"

"So now I'm in charge of this beast and the girl? You're certainly leaving with a lot of demands." She scowled at him, but he knew she wasn't serious. Victor reached down to take her hands and looked into her big magenta eyes.

"It's better like this, don't you think?"

"What?"

"Me leaving kind of suddenly. I mean, who wants to have a long slow buildup to a goodbye? This way, we can rip the bandage off. Er, is that a thing in this world? The phrase, I mean? 'Rip the bandage off?'"

"Yes. I know what you mean, and no, I don't think it's better. Oh, Ancestors! I thought this would be easier after how we left things last night, but I'm sorry to see you go, Victor. I hope it's not forever." She squeezed his hands, looked up at his face, and added, "Kiss me, then. At least one more time. Friends can kiss, can't they?"

"Certain kinds of friends, sure," Victor said, leaning down and gently pressing his lips to hers. As the heat grew between them, and his heart started to beat faster, they kissed hungrily for several seconds, and then Victor grew aware of people approaching, and he pulled away, embarrassed but grinning. "You're the best kisser I've ever known," he said. "Too bad you're just my friend."

"Well, who knows. Look me up in fifty or a hundred years," she said, throwing his words from the previous night back at him. Then she squeezed his hand one more time and walked away toward the group of people gathering, including Tellen and Thayla. Victor smiled and nodded at them, then walked over to Deyni.

"Hey, huntress. How's she doing?"

"She's good, Victor. She asked me to ride her soon," Deyni said, still diligently brushing the parts of the vidanii she could reach. Victor lifted the little girl up so she could brush Starlight's back and shoulders and said, "Thistle's favorite spot is around his ears and horns. Does Starlight like that?"

"She does! She loves it!"

"Oh, good! Listen, Deyni; this is your vidanii now. You have to be responsible about feeding her and caring for her, and when Chandri says you're ready, you can learn to ride her. Don't try to rush things, though. Let Chandri help you, and remember that it's her decision when you get to ride alone, okay? Do you promise?"

"I promise, Victor," Deyni said, and her voice was solemn. Victor smiled and put her down.

"Come over to Thistle now, and watch me get him saddled up." With that, Victor began his preparations to leave. Many clan members came over, clapped him on the back, or shook his hand, giving him their well-wishes, and it took him several times longer than usual to get Thistle's tack on, but he enjoyed it. It was good to know so many people cared about him and would miss him.

Realizing how much he'd miss the clan, not just his close friends, Victor's heart began to grow heavy, and he almost talked himself into putting off his departure, but then he saw a shape lope around the longhouse out into the grass, pacing back and forth. He waved to Valla and knew it was best that he get going. He walked over to Tellen and shook his hand. He hugged Oynalla, Thayla, Chandri, and Deyni one more time. Then, he pulled himself into Thistle's saddle, waved to the assembled crowd, and thundered away, racing past Valla, wondering if her cat was as fast as his mighty vidanii.

22

NIGHT CONVERSATIONS

"Your cat isn't going to try to eat my vidanii, is he?" Victor asked Captain Valla when they stopped for their first camp. She'd surprised him the day before, suggesting they keep riding for a day, insisting she needed little rest and neither did Uvu, her mount. Thistle had seemed fine, so Victor had shrugged and agreed, and though they had stopped several times to feed and water the animals, this was the first time they'd stopped to sleep. Thistle was huffing and more tired than Victor had ever seen him, but he seemed good—as you might imagine a horse would be after a hard day of travel.

"Uvu knows better," Valla said, producing a large haunch of raw meat and tossing it off into the grass for the big cat. It was the fourth time she'd fed him that day.

"He eats a lot of meat," Victor observed.

"Yes," Valla said, not one to elaborate or drive a conversation. She began pulling out parts to a large canvas tent, and Victor contemplated asking her if she needed a hand, but a streak of stubbornness in him wanted her to ask him for help or at least communicate what she was doing. He sighed and began walking in a spiral pattern out from their campsite, looking for stones to use for the fire pit.

After he'd gathered ten good-sized rocks, he walked back to the camp and set them up in a ring and saw that Valla had already erected a tall rectangular tent with the flaps pinned open and a rather luxurious interior exposed—rich carpeting, a polished wooden table with two ornate, cushioned wooden chairs, and a spacious, fluffy bed complete with insect netting. "Goddamn—makes me miss my wagon," Victor said as he set up the fire, producing logs from his storage ring.

He did miss his wagon and, not for the first time, cursed his guilty conscience and his impulsive decision to leave it with Thayla and Deyni. He'd felt that he had to make the gesture for Deyni's sake—he'd had no idea how much her not wanting him to leave would affect him. If he were being honest, saying goodbye to the little girl had been harder than leaving Thayla or Chandri. "Shit, it was harder than both combined," he said, finishing his thoughts aloud.

"Are you addressing me?" Valla asked, sitting in one of her cushioned chairs, legs crossed, sipping something from a silver cup.

"Uh, nah, just muttering to myself. Don't sweat it."

"Will you want to spar before supper?" The question caught Victor off guard, and he glanced at Valla in surprise.

"Spar?"

"Lady Rellia suggested I could learn a thing or two from you and that I might be a suitable partner for you to hone your skills against."

"Oh, well, yeah. I can always use the practice. Sorry, I didn't think of you as a fighter. I guess I should have, considering you're a captain."

"Yes." Valla stood, tossed the remainder of her drink into the grass, then produced a surprisingly heavy-looking, deep blue, almost black broadsword. The sword was about as long as her legs, and she rested the point in the grass so the pommel jutted up past her waist. She leaned against it and stared at Victor, clearly waiting for him to finish fiddling with the fire.

"Quite a sword," he said, straightening up. "You sure you want to spar with sharp weapons? I have some weighted wooden weapons I bought back in Gelica."

"I'll be fine. Will you?" she asked, her face betraying no judgment, no amusement.

"Yeah, I'll be fine. Mind if I ask what tier you're in?"

"I'm newly fifth tier."

"Ah. No shit?"

"I speak truly."

"No wonder Rellia had you hanging around. So, um, you know Captain Lam?"

"Yes, we served together for a time." Again, she didn't elaborate, and Victor was tired of fishing for details from the obstinate woman. He lifted

Lifedrinker from his belt and started walking out into the plains, on the opposite side of the camp from their mounts. He cast Globe of Inspiration, not because it was too dark to see, but because if he was going to practice, he wanted to maximize his benefit.

"Effective," Valla said, following behind him, basking in the white-gold glow of the orb.

"Yeah, I'll keep it going while we practice—should be helpful." After he spoke, Victor cast Inspiring Presence, knowing full well the spell wouldn't affect Valla if he faced off with her. "Too bad. I can't share all my benefits, can I?"

"I don't have any spells that will be beneficial for you; I'm sorry," Valla said, perhaps misinterpreting Victor's constant chatter with himself.

"You're good," he said, using Sovereign Will to boost his agility, then he squared off with Valla, raised his axe, and nodded. She lifted her big, dark sword and, holding it sideways so the blade rested on the palm of her left hand, performed a low bow at the waist.

"Oh, am I supposed to bow? You're only my second sparring partner outside the pits, and Polo Vosh didn't do any bowing."

"It's customary from the school I attended. Not necessary." She paused for a moment as though struggling with a decision, and finally she said, "Are you ready?"

"Yeah," Victor said, and there began a truly humiliating ass-kicking. Valla was fast—not as fast as Rellia when she used her shadow magic, but faster than Victor. More than that, she was good with her sword, like Polo Vosh levels of good. Victor had learned a lot when he gained the advanced rank with his axe, but Valla seemed to have a maneuver and a reaction for every one of his attacks. Worse, she repeatedly slipped her long, wickedly heavy blade past his guard attempts.

Sometimes she'd stab her sword forward in a thrust, faster than he could swing his axe to parry it, and sometimes she'd cleave it with such weight and force that Victor found himself knocked out of his stance, open for her quick remise—a term meaning follow-up attack that she taught him after she'd struck him with it several times.

Perhaps compounding his humiliation, she pulled every hit she scored, tapping his armor or shallowly nicking his legs. Twice she deftly rang the flat of her blade on his heavy helm. Victor, for his part, threw everything he had at her, and as he felt his anger building, he pushed it down—he knew he'd learn more if he didn't go berserk and overpower her with brute force.

Accepting that he couldn't beat her without his rage, Victor contemplated using his fear affinity or projecting twisted inspiration at her. He held back, though, wanting to learn as much true fighting skill as possible.

After a long while, when he was drenched in sweat and she was starting to breathe heavily, Victor noted the look of consternation on her face, and finally she backed off, stabbed her sword into the grass, and stared at him. "Why do you toy with me? Why let me think I can beat you?" Her usually cool, calm voice was angry, and the emotion in it caught Victor by surprise.

"What?"

"I missed your match with Rellia, but I heard tales of your fury, of your insane strength. Why do you hold it all back?"

"I mean, I'm trying to learn to fight better. I don't want to go berserk and whip your ass. I don't like thinking I have to unleash my rage or . . . darker abilities to win a fight. I want . . . I should be able to win based on skill."

She frowned, narrowed her eyes, and nodded. "I, too, haven't used all of my abilities. I suppose this is more fruitful for now. Even against your lackluster martial skills, I feel my forms improving. Perhaps it is your orb."

"Can I ask? What's your sword skill up to?"

"Epic, but Blue Razor pushes me closer to legendary when I have it in hand."

"Blue Razor? Your sword? Is it awake, er, conscious?"

"No, but it's a masterwork artifact, enchanted beyond what the smiths in Tharcray can ken." It seemed Victor had found the key to getting the woman to talk—ask her about fighting or her sword.

"Where'd you get it?"

"A dungeon near the World Spine. I was with Rellia and two of her friends."

"Oh, so you don't just work for her?"

"No, I've known Rellia for twenty-two years."

Victor couldn't stop his mouth from dropping open. When he'd first seen Captain Valla, she'd looked like a teenager to him. "Fuck, man, I'll never get used to this world. I didn't realize you . . . oh, never mind. I'm going to end up eating my boot at this rate."

To his surprise, she smirked and nodded. "Good. Shall we continue?"

Victor motioned with his hand as if to say "after you," lifting his axe, and this time, when he nodded his head, he bent at the waist—not comfortable with a full bow, but willing to try a bit to show he respected Valla. Her smirk turned into a half-smile, and she bowed. Then they were at it again, and Victor learned many lessons over the next two hours.

They traveled that way for the next ten days, riding for a full day and night, then camping the following evening until dawn. Uvu was fast and sturdy, but Victor knew Thistle could outpace him, which made him feel a little better when he considered the giant cat was also a formidable fighter. Each evening that they made camp, and also at noon on the days when they were riding through, he and Valla would spar, and he'd use his inspiration Energy to try to speed up what they learned from each other.

By the evening of the tenth night, Victor was getting a lot better at predicting Valla's movements and countering her. He'd taken what the System gave him with regard to forms and styles, attacks and counters, and he'd begun to make them his own, adding his own flair and combining them into maneuvers that not every System-taught fighter would be able to predict or deal with.

That night, while they sat near the fire, Victor on a blanket in front of his low one-man tent and Valla sitting in one of her comfortable chairs, she surprised him by saying, "You improve quickly. I think you'll move through the advanced ranking much faster than I did."

"Really?"

"I can tell," she nodded, sipping wine from her silver cup, and continued. "You're a born fighter. It's no shame that Rellia lost to you."

"Well, thanks for working with me. I know I'm learning a lot more than you are."

"I'm glad to do it." She stopped, and Victor thought she was returning to her old reticent self, but then she said, "I was only seven when Rellia took me in."

"Oh?" Victor drank from his mug of honeyed mead to mask his surprise. This was the first time Valla had ever volunteered any personal information.

"Yes. She's more a mother than a friend, sister, or, well, an employer. At least to me. I think she sees me differently, but I owe her, quite literally, everything." She took another long drink from her cup, and Victor tried to think of something to say—Valla had caught him completely by surprise.

"Uh, well, I'm sorry if I've said some unflattering shit about her. I mean, we did have a rocky start to our relationship . . ."

"I'm not trying to sell you on Rellia. I don't know why I said all that." She blushed furiously, the pale blue of her cheeks darkening toward purple, and she turned to the side, downing the rest of her wine in a huge gulp.

"Chill, Valla. It's because we've spent more than a week traveling together and it's nice to chat by the fire. Nothing weird about it. Didn't you bullshit with other soldiers while you were in the Legion?"

"No." She shook her head and clamped her mouth shut, pressing her lips into a tight line, and, just as Victor was about to try to coax her to say more, she added, "I was promoted young. The other officers resented me, even though I bested most of them on the practice field, even though I never lost an engagement with my troops. No, I didn't 'bullshit' with others." She sighed heavily, looked at the inky black sky and the sea of glittering stars, and said, "What will you do in Persi Gables? We're only a few days away."

"I'm going to figure out who the fuck summoned me and give them a piece of my mind," Victor said without thinking, allowing his mouth to give voice to his impulse.

"You'll want the details and map to the location that Rellia's investigator found, then." She turned away from the stars and stared at Victor, meeting his eyes over the fire. "I'll come with you. I'd like to help, and Rellia will be angry if I lose you somehow."

"Yeah, that's cool. It's likely to get ugly. You sure you're up for that?"

"You're speaking to a captain of the Imperial Legion. Do you think I've not seen 'ugly?'"

"Nah. You're right. Well, thanks; I won't turn down the company. Speaking of the Legion, you said Lam served with you for a while? You weren't friends, I take it? What was she like?"

"Captain Lam is the opposite of me. Gregarious, clever, plotting, successful. She never caused me trouble, but we didn't share more than a few sentences with each other in the seven years I served." Valla sighed again, then produced a dark blue wine bottle and refilled her cup.

"Yeah, Lam's an alpha," Victor said, laughing and shaking his head. "I think she'd come out on top of pretty much any situation." As he rubbed his eyes, still shaking his head ruefully, he saw the moons near the middle of the sky, and he said, "Hey, do you mind watching me while I do a spirit walk? I want to try to talk to Thayla or Oynalla."

"Spirit walk?" Valla leaned forward with interest.

"Oh, yeah. I have a spirit Core—you know that, right?" She nodded, and he continued. "Well, a spell I know lets me walk around on the spirit plane. I can meet with other Spirit Casters that way."

"But you want me to watch you?" She looked puzzled.

"My body. My spirit will be free, but my body is going to sit here like a lump. I'm trusting you to keep me from getting eaten by a monster. Well, and to not kill me and take my stuff. That okay?"

Valla stood swiftly, and suddenly her huge, dark broadsword was in her hands, glimmering strangely in the starlight. She whipped it through the air, turning it so the point was down, then knelt before it, facing Victor, "I swear! No harm will come to you while I watch over your person."

"Oh," Victor said, halfway to his feet already, alarmed by Valla's sudden, armed movements. He finished standing and nodded to her, keeping his expression solemn. "Thank you, Valla. I accept your oath."

His words must have been near enough to what she'd wanted to hear because she stood up and lifted Blue Razor up to her shoulder, and began walking around the camp's perimeter. She whistled a complicated series of notes, and Victor heard Uvu grumble and yawn in the darkness. Then the huge cat's padding steps faded into the distance.

"Uvu will watch as well," she said.

"Badass. Pretty damn cool mount," Victor said.

"He's much more than a mount," Valla said, and Victor could only grunt in agreement.

"Well, here goes. I don't think I'll be gone long." Victor sat down again, and feeling very secure knowing Valla was keeping watch, he closed his eyes and cast Spirit Walk.

He stood up and looked around the vast, open grassland—no fire, no tents, no Valla. Rather than the dead of night, lit only by the stars and moons, he stood in the perpetual twilight of the spirit plane. Smiling, he concentrated on Thayla and Oynalla, and, Lifedrinker warm in his hands, he began walking.

He strode confidently, his feelings and connection to the two other Spirit Casters strong in his mind, and he wasn't surprised when, in just a few minutes, he found himself striding down a lightly treed, grassy slope. He heard the babble of a brook in the distance, and he picked up his pace, jogging toward the sound. He burst out of the tree line into the little clearing that Oynalla had shown him in the past—the place where her mother had taught her about the spirit plane.

Thayla and Oynalla sat together in the clearing, and the young-seeming Old Mother looked up at Victor and smiled as he approached. "Here's our visitor, daughter."

Thayla stood and rushed over to him, hugging him tight, and Victor was exceedingly pleased to feel her warmth—he'd feared that their connection in the spirit plane wouldn't be as solid or visceral as in the physical world. "Why'd you wait so long to visit?" she asked, pulling back and looking into his eyes.

"Well, to be honest, that captain, Valla? She's been wearing me out every damn day, and we've been riding for two days at a time between camps."

"What?" Thayla's mouth fell open. "What do you mean she's been wearing you out?"

"She's a fucking good fighter! We've been sparring every day, and I'm tired as hell most of the time." Victor saw Thayla's face relax, and it only then clicked that she'd been thinking something very different. "Oh, come on," he laughed.

"And what of my work, warrior? Have you been studying your pattern?"

"Well, yeah, but I haven't built it yet. I've got it mostly memorized, though. I draw it a couple of times each night." Victor knew she wasn't going to be happy with that and looked away, unwilling to meet her eyes.

"Oh? What do you think, daughter? Has he been diligent enough with my instruction? Does his Core feel stronger to you?"

"Well, Old Mother," Thayla said, reaching out to rest her faintly glimmering fingers on Victor's shoulder. "It's only been a bit more than a week. I don't feel much difference, though . . ." she trailed off, smirking sideways at Victor.

"Oh, God, really? If you guys are going to bully me like this, I won't make these visits very often!"

"Now he threatens us with his absence? What love is this? Are we not family, warrior?"

"Yeah. Yes! All right, I admit, I could be working harder on my Core and the pattern." Victor sighed and stepped past Thayla to sit by Oynalla. Thayla, still holding his shoulder, followed and sat down next to him.

"This is a good time to show me what you know of the pattern, don't you think?" Oynalla asked, her youthful face breaking into a beaming smile and a trilling little laugh escaping her lips.

"Well . . ." Victor tried to think of a way out of this but shrugged and said, "Okay." He closed his eyes, and reaching into his Core, he teased a thread of fear-attuned Energy into his pathway. Then, with a slight strain of will, he pulled out a thread of rage-attuned Energy. He manipulated the two threads, twisting, folding, and bending them into the pattern that Oynalla had given him. He truly had been practicing with it, and he'd drawn it from memory several times.

While he was weaving the Energies, he briefly contemplated why he hadn't tried to build the pattern in his pathway yet. He almost lost his concentration when a subconscious needle of doubt entered his mind—was he afraid of this new pattern? Maybe he didn't want to see what kind of new terrible Energy he was going to make. He ground his teeth and kept working, forcing his mind to focus on the task. He'd gotten to the last few twists in the pattern when Oynalla suddenly stood and took his face in her hands.

"Stop, warrior! Stop!" she shrieked, and Victor lost his concentration, letting go of the threads. He looked at her in confusion. "Oh, good, good. That was a mistake! Your amulet and I were foolish, indeed! I thought we were leading you to a weave of justice, but you nearly created shame. You don't need more dark Energies in your heart, Victor."

Thayla reached out a hand to take one of his, and he saw the concern in her eyes, and then he said, "Well, shit. I mean, yeah, I'm not super excited about casting spells with shame-attuned Energy."

"I see the mistake we made, though, Victor. Rage and fear—two dark, powerful affinities—we should have thought more broadly and remembered your prodigious will. After watching how quickly you built that weave, I think you can make one from three Energies. Give me a day or two to work with the pattern; I'll add in a third twist of inspiration." Oynalla reached out a slender hand to join Thayla's gripping his hand, grabbing onto a couple of his fingers.

"Okay," he said, and when he saw the concern still lingering in their eyes, he added, "Guys, relax! I'm not going to go out and try to finish the weave. I'm already stressed about the fear affinity."

"Good." Oynalla nodded and squinted as though she were trying to see into his mind, but she squeezed his fingers again and then sat back. "Daughter, your aura fades. This has been a long spirit walk for you."

"Yes, but I'm so glad I got to see you, Victor! Come to us more often, okay?"

"I'll try, but we're getting close to Persi Gables, and I don't know what kind of shit's about to go down. Don't get mad at me if I'm not here for a few days."

"No, come tomorrow, warrior. After that, you can take your time, but I want to get the new pattern into your hands," Oynalla said with finality.

"Oh, all right, *Young* Mother," Victor laughed.

"See how he grows so full of himself?" Oynalla asked Thayla, shaking her head in dismay.

"He's always been full of himself, Old Mother," she replied, reaching out to flick Victor's ear.

"All right, all right," Victor laughed, standing up. "I'll see you ladies tomorrow. I need to get back before some giant cat eats me or something."

He waved, but before he could end his spell, Thayla jumped up and squeezed him again, and that reminded him to think of more people than himself. "Hey," he said into the top of her head, wishing he could smell her physical hair instead of the clean, neutral scent of the spirit plane, "hug Deyni for me and tell Chandri and everyone I said hello, okay?"

"I will," Thayla said, squeezing him once more. Then Victor ended his spell and opened his eyes. He almost fell backward when he saw Valla squatting in front of him, peering with narrowed eyes at his face.

"You're back?" she asked.

"Yeah. Everything all right?" He looked around, wondering why she'd been peering into his face like that, but he didn't see anything alarming.

"Everything is fine. I felt you building up Energy," she said as if that explained everything.

"Oh, right. Well, all's good."

"You contacted them? Your hunter friends?" Valla moved back to her chair and sat down, crossing her legs and regarding him, almost like a queen staring down at a kneeling subject. Now that he'd learned a bit about her past, Victor didn't think that haughty expression was intentional—she was socially awkward.

"Yeah, I did." He scooted back toward his tent and looked at the moons; they hadn't moved much while he was gone. "Your cat good to keep watch?" Victor knew the answer—Uvu had allowed them to sleep soundly at each of their camps so far, but he figured he shouldn't take it for granted.

"Yes, he's very alert. More than either of us could be. Were your friends doing well, Victor?" Valla asked, and he saw that she was pouring herself another cup of wine. It appeared she wasn't ready to call it a night.

Victor shrugged and dug another honey mead out of his ring. He'd found that, of all the strange alcohols he'd sampled on Fanwath, he enjoyed it the most. "My friends are doing well; thanks for asking, Valla. How's Rellia? You've been sending her messages in the book, right?"

"Rellia is doing well, though she fears the schemes of her family on a constant basis. I wish she hadn't sent me away, but I knew I was driving her mad with my vigilance. She's surrounded by those loyal to me and her, though, so I'm not very worried. I wish I could walk to her the way you just did."

"Do you mind me asking what your affinity is?"

"I have two, three if you count pure Energy: air and iron."

"Iron? I've heard of air affinities but not iron." Victor took a swig of his ale.

"It's a more focused form of an earth affinity. I don't think it's very common, but it's nothing too unusual."

"So it's technically an elemental affinity?"

"Correct."

"That's pretty cool. Can you weave the two of them for additional effects?"

"Yes, in theory, I could weave a meta-element from them, but my will, well, I've not been able to do it yet. I'm working on it, though."

"I can tell you focused a lot of your attribute points on agility, huh?"

"Yes, I was raised to perform well in combat." She smirked. She looked as if she had more to say but shook her head slightly and took another sip of wine. Victor decided not to push it and sat back, leaning on his elbows and studying the stars while he swirled the thick, spiced mead around in his cup.

"It's a nice night," he said, "a good night to talk with friends." He looked at Captain Valla, and she met his gaze, and though it was awkward, and she quickly turned away, she smiled and nodded.

23

PERSI GABLES

On their twelfth day of travel, Victor began to smell, on the wind from the east, the scent of Lake Beliss. He knew from his previous time in Persi Gables that the lake was more like an inland sea, maybe comparable to one of the great lakes in North America. It had a distinctive smell, and though they were too far away to catch the fishy odors of the docks district, there was a tang to the air that felt different in his nose.

"We were lucky," Valla said from her saddle, riding a dozen feet to Victor's left.

"Oh?"

"Yes. We could have been caught out in a storm. I've worried about the skies, gray and threatening, but nothing falls." She gestured to the steel gray, perpetual cloud cover they'd ridden under for the last two days.

"Is it cold enough? It doesn't feel that cold to me. Or do you mean rain?" Victor had been quite comfortable, in fact, enjoying the lack of sun and the sweat that came with it.

"When the winds stir up and the storms roll in, the temperature drops quickly. As I said, we've had a lucky journey. We'll pick up the Northern Highway soon and can follow that into the city."

"Is that an official name? The Northern Highway?" Victor asked, easing Thistle closer to Valla and Uvu with a nudge of a knee.

"Yes. The Empire shared the cost of its creation with the city-state. It runs north from Persi Gables to Gelica and south toward the sea."

"Right. Edeya was telling me about that—Persi Gables isn't part of the Empire?"

"No. Ridonne tolerates the city's independence because the city council pays a tax to the Empire. They say it's a mutual defense pact—the Legion even has barracks in the city." Valla scanned the low rise off to the north and said, "We should ride up that hill. It's the only chance you'll get of a full vista of the city—soon we'll be in the woods that surround the walls."

"Cool," Victor said and clicked his tongue, urging Thistle to the right and up the slope. The climb was deceptively long, and the hill seemed gentle enough, but when Victor looked back to see Valla following him, he was surprised by how much elevation they'd gained. By the time he came up to the top of the rise, he could see the ground falling away before him toward a sparse, deciduous forest with mostly bare branches, just a few brightly colored leaves clinging here and there.

Over the tops of the trees, he saw the distant walls of Persi Gables. They were high and washed white, though many buildings within stood taller. It didn't look as big as Gelica, but it was far larger than Victor ever imagined medieval cities to be. "We're not really in a medieval world, though, are we?" he asked Thistle, scratching his neck.

"Persi Gables differs from Gelica in that they don't allow construction outside the walls. If you want to live outside to hunt or farm, you need to travel ten miles to the north or south, where villages are permitted."

"Why?" Victor frowned at the cluster of civilization, wondering what their reasons might be—defense, perhaps?

"Their agreement with the Empire. Persi Gables is sovereign over the land within her walls and 'the ten miles of uninhabited lands outside.'"

"Huh," Victor frowned and rubbed at his chin, staring out past the distant city to the blue-gray horizon of water—Lake Beliss. "Well, do we go into the city or straight to the location on your map? I'm not sure I want to bring Thistle when we confront the, well, you know, the guys doing the summoning."

"You should secure lodging. Do you want to stay at Lady Rellia's estate? Lam's?"

"Nah, I'll get a hotel, er, an inn. I don't really want to announce my presence yet. I know you've been checking in with Rellia, and I've been messaging Lam, but if you don't mind, let's keep my exact location in the city between us. Is that weird? I'm not trying to be sneaky; I just kinda don't want to deal with them trying to meet with me and involve me in all sorts of campaign business. We've still got months until spring."

"My orders were to stay near you and to make sure you survived to report to Persi Gables in the spring. I can do that without divulging your exact location." Valla had become more and more verbose during their journey, either growing more comfortable with Victor or with herself. Victor figured it was probably a mixture of the two.

"Cool. Well, since you're making that sacrifice, I'll pay for your room."

"I have sufficient funds for lodging," she snorted, and Victor thought he almost heard a chuckle bubbling beneath the words.

"Hey! I'm just trying to be polite."

"Acknowledged."

"Well, I take it that's the North Road?" Victor pointed to a wide, flat ribbon of brown heading out of the woods and then north through the plains.

"The Northern Highway. Yes, that's it."

"Not much traffic," he said, scanning the road for as far as he could see, only spotting a couple of figures far to the north that might have been people or animals.

"The weather is threatening, and it's barely past dawn. I'm sure some countryfolk are on their way with goods to sell, but we've beaten the crowds."

"Ah, the benefits of riding all night like lunatics!" Victor chuckled and clicked his tongue. Ever ready to move, Thistle started toward the road, walking down the grassy, miles-long slope. Valla followed him, a rumble coming from Uvu's chest. Victor couldn't tell if it was a growl or a purr. The cat hadn't ever shown any aggression to Thistle, but he still worried it might try to pounce on his trusty steed from some sort of instinct.

"Hey," he shouted over his shoulder. "Last stretch of open plains, and it's downhill! Let's race!" With that, he stood slightly in his stirrups, leaning forward, clicking his tongue, and twitching his reins. Thistle didn't require much in the way of direction—he seemed to know what Victor wanted most of the time, and their desires coincided nicely at that moment. The big vidanii bucked once and then broke into a mad charge down the slope, kicking up clods of moist soil and grass as he veritably flew over the ground.

Victor howled and whooped, and as they thundered over the flat section of plains before the road, he turned to see that he'd left Valla and Uvu in the dust, easily a quarter mile behind him. "Fuck yes, Thistle! Let's go, boy!" There was a culvert and berm before the road, and Thistle sailed over it, leaping a good twenty feet. He landed on the hard-packed dirt of the road, sliding on his hooves, and then he was charging again into the sparse, manicured woods outside the city. His hooves were even louder, even more like thunder, on the road.

They'd only charged into the woods for a few hundred yards before Victor saw a large wagon ahead of him and several people and roladii, so he slowed, pulling on the reins until Thistle stopped, and then he pivoted and waited for Valla. To his surprise, after a few minutes, she came crashing out of the forest to the right, leaping over the underbrush near the side of the road.

"Whoa! Trying to take a shortcut?" he laughed, and Valla, face flushed with the thrill of the ride, laughed with him, the first real laugh he'd heard out of her in days.

"I think Uvu wanted to try to circle you; I couldn't force him back to the road!" She reached up and gave the big cat's ear a tweak, and he opened his mouth, exposing six-inch canines as he yawned and chuffed.

"Ha, on the hunt, I guess." Victor turned Thistle back toward the city and began to ride at a relaxed trot toward the group of travelers ahead. He soon saw that the wagon was loaded with farm goods, and the roladii were also burdened with sacks of vegetables, piles of fur, and packaged meats. "On your way to market?" he called as he edged around the group, and one dark-haired Ardeni woman called back from beside her roladii.

"Aye, early to market, early to the tavern!" She laughed, and many of the others around her joined in.

"Well, I hope you get good prices!" Victor waved and hurried around them onto the open stretch of road leading through the woods. He could just make out a faint glimmer of white in the distance, and he knew it was the city gate. He heard Valla speaking loudly to the farmers, but he couldn't make out her words. A moment later, she caught up to him.

"They think it's going to storm tonight. Snow."

"Oh? Looks like we made it just in time." Victor thumped Thistle's shoulder and said, "Good idea, only sleeping every other night, Valla."

Passage through the gate was painless at that hour. The guards on watch had the gates wide open, and when Victor and Valla rode up, there wasn't anyone ahead of them. Victor had a sudden feeling of déjà vu when he saw the gate—its high portcullis, its steel doors, some twenty feet high, flung wide, and most of all, the guards with their polearms and green and black livery. This was the gate where he'd first entered the city, the gate through which his abductors had brought him to sell.

"I recognize this," he said.

"Well, weren't you in the city for quite a while?"

"Yeah, but not the gates. This is where I was brought through, in my first few minutes in this world."

"It makes sense," Valla said, and perhaps because of the guards standing nearby, she seemed to have fallen back into her old habit of not elaborating.

"Why?" Victor asked, rolling his hand as if to say "keep going."

"Oh, the map indicates the summoning circle is east and north of here. Not far from the walls."

"Oy! Are you two coming through or what?" the guard on the left asked, a large Vodkin with sleek black fur.

Victor glanced left and right, then behind him, pointedly staring up and down the empty road, then said, "Is there some kind of hurry?" He still wore his armor, and when he frowned down at the guard from Thistle's back, the man backed up a step.

"No big hurry, I s'pose."

"Let's go find some rooms," Victor said to Valla, and the two of them started forward.

"Oy! 'Old up, there, friends," the guard said as they road under the portcullis. "What's your business in town?"

"Shopping," Victor said.

"Visiting family," Valla said.

"Some of both." Victor nodded to Valla.

"You got means for lodging?" the guard on the other side asked. He was much shorter, though just as stocky as the Vodkin—a Cadwalli with long black goat horns that made wearing the uniform conical helmet of the city watch impossible.

"Do you jest?" Valla asked, raising an arched eyebrow. As always, she was impeccably dressed in her standard uniform—striped, close-fitting pants and high-collared, magically pressed white shirt. More than that, she rode on a saddle and mount that probably cost more than the average person's home. She patted Uvu's shoulder and continued to stare. The guard glanced from Valla to Victor, then shrugged.

"Enjoy your stay."

Victor followed Valla through the city's narrow streets and markets that were just waking up—merchants were busily setting up stalls and pulling their carts into place. Uvu cleared the way for them several times by roaring in spite of Valla's admonishments. Roladii and other lesser beasts were quick to trot out of his way, oftentimes upending carts and sending goods rolling.

Merchants cursed and complained, but they didn't make eye contact with Victor or Valla, and the two of them made quick progress.

"Where we going, by the way? You have a place in mind?" Victor asked after they'd made their sixth or seventh turn and crossed yet another market square.

"An inn run by an old Legion quartermaster. He's a good man and discreet."

"Cool," Victor said, looking around, wondering how many of the streets they rode down he'd been led through in chains on his way to one pit fight or another. He wondered if he should go see Yund, walk into the Wagon Wheel, and kick his ass. "Maybe fucking Ponda, too." Victor chuckled; he didn't know why, but he really didn't hold a grudge against Ponda. He felt the big Vodkin had been as fair as he could be while still working for Yund.

"Still," he said to Thistle, "Yund doesn't run a very nice setup. There are people sitting in cages in their underwear right now, wondering if they'll live through the night."

"What?" Valla asked, turning to him.

"Hey, I know I can't right all the wrongs in this city by myself, but there's one place I'd like to visit before we head out to investigate the summoning circle."

"All right."

"Like, let's stable these guys, then I want to go. Today."

"Understood." Valla didn't argue or ask him if he was sure; hell, she didn't even look at him. She just agreed, and Victor found that kind of refreshing. She might have her own motives for doing things, but she wasn't constantly second-guessing him.

"You're a good traveling companion, Valla."

"You're a good sparring student," she said, and Victor laughed.

"Is that how it is? All right, Valla, all right." She still hadn't turned to look at him, so he couldn't tell if she was smiling, but he imagined she was.

A short while later, they arrived at the inn. It was a tall, narrow building sandwiched between a forge and a stable building. High red stone walls rose up to a peaked cedar, or whatever wood in that world looked like cedar, gabled roof. The sign above the open double doors read "The Soldier's Rest."

A Shadeni boy rushed out of the stable toward Victor, and an older stoop-backed Ardeni walked carefully toward Valla. As the boy approached, he heard the other stablehand say to Valla, "I have advanced Animal Handling. Your terashii is in good hands."

"Sir, I'll take care of that vidanii!" the boy said, standing to Victor's side.

"Oh?" Victor asked, hopping down and lifting Lifedrinker from her loop in the saddle. "You can't even reach his back. How will you brush him properly?"

"I have a stool in the stable, sir! I'll be good to him!" He spoke earnestly, reaching out to rest a hand on Thistle's haunch, and Victor didn't detect any sort of flinch or alarm from the animal. He shrugged.

"All right, how much?"

"It's complimentary for people staying at the inn." The boy gestured toward the tall stone building. Victor nodded but reached into his ring and took out a few Energy beads, holding them out for the boy.

"Make sure he eats well and gets plenty of space in there." He gestured with his head toward the stable. The boy nodded and took the proffered beads.

"Many thanks, good sir!"

"Be good, Thistle," he said to the vidanii, moving around to scratch his nose. Thistle huffed and pressed his big damp nose into Victor's shoulder, making him laugh. He produced a blue, crisp, apple-sized fruit that he'd stored away back in Gelica, and Thistle munched it noisily. "He likes treats," he said to the boy, and the kid nodded, bowing his head as Victor handed him the reins.

He saw that Valla was waiting up the short flight of stone steps by the inn's doors. He gave Thistle one more pat then climbed them two at a time, and together they walked in. The common room was quiet at that hour, though a few patrons sat around one of the long wooden tables eating breakfast. It was a bright room, especially with the doors flung wide the way they were. High plaster ceilings with wooden beams drew the eye to the far wall where an ornate banistered stairway led up to the guest rooms.

"Captain Valla?" a deep, scratchy voice asked. Victor followed the sound to his left, where a white-mustached Ardeni man polished a gleaming wooden bartop. He wore an apron, but Victor could see he was very fit—a man who'd not seen a lazy day in his life. The top of his head was devoid of hair, but his amber eyes were bright and shrewd.

"Sergeant Hine." Valla strode forward and stretched a hand over the bar, and the man enthusiastically took it.

"Wonderful to have you in! You won't be staying at the ap'Yensha estate?"

"No. This is Victor. He and I will be staying here a while, and we'd like that kept discreet."

"Not a problem, not a problem," Hine said, reaching a hand out toward Victor.

"Good to meet you, Sergeant," Victor said, striding forward and crushing the man's hand in a firm grip. Hine squeezed back without a complaint, favoring him with a large smile.

"That's a warrior if I saw one. Legion?"

"No. He's on a different path," Valla answered for him. "Still, he's a good fighter and a good ally to have."

"Very good, very good. Excellent. One room or two, Captain?"

"Two, but neighboring."

"Excellent. I'll show you up myself. Shall I put it on the ap'Yensha account?"

"Yes," Valla said before Victor could respond.

"Good, good. Follow me up," Hine said, and he walked around the end of the bar toward the stairway. Victor and Valla followed, and he led them to the third floor, down a narrow hallway with impeccably clean white plaster walls and polished hardwood floors. "Four rooms on this floor. I'll give you two the front corner suites. The rear suites are vacant, so you shouldn't be bothered."

"Very good. Thank you, Sergeant," Valla said, standing before the two closed doors at the end of the hall.

"Do you want me to show you in?" For the first time, he seemed a little unsure, awkward even, and Victor could see why—it felt as if Valla was dismissing the man.

"We're good, Sergeant," Victor said, stepping in. "I think we're both pretty road weary, so we kind of just want to get unpacked and unwind a bit. We've got a lot of business to handle in town."

"Oh, yes, of course. Well, here are your keys." He held out two identical-looking keys, labeled 31 and 32.

"We'll speak soon, Sergeant. Thank you," Valla said, taking the keys. She stared at him until he nodded and turned, but to her credit, she did smile pleasantly at him the entire time.

"Uh, well, it seems like he's friendly with you. I thought you didn't have any friends in the Legion."

"I don't. I met him after I served. He's a good friend to the ap'Yensha clan." She held out the key labeled 32, and Victor noted it was for the door to his right. "Let's meet out here in half an hour, and then we can take care of your first objective."

"Good with me." Victor took the key, a brass, many-toothed design, and pushed it into the lock above his door handle. Twisting it produced a satisfying thunk as the bolt slid open, and then he opened the door and went in. He wanted to tell Valla that she'd probably offended the innkeeper when she'd sent him away so abruptly. He didn't really get it—she'd seemed friendly and affable when she'd first spoken to the guy, but then she'd just awkwardly shifted gears as if she had a checklist she was moving through.

"Well, not my problem," he said, pulling Lifedrinker out of his belt loop. "I mean, I want to give her advice, but it's not like we're that close, you know?" The axe vibrated in his hand, and he chuckled, looking around the room. A spacious bed sat near the front window, and the curtains were pulled wide, giving a view down the street via which they'd approached the inn. Many more people were out already, and it seemed like a totally different place than the one he'd been paraded through as part of Yund's pit-fighting chain gang.

"I suppose we didn't see this part of the city. Well, and we were always out at night," he said, still talking to the axe. "I don't think I'll feel any better if I kill that dude, but I wouldn't mind putting him outta business." He moved through the room, stepping over the lovely embroidered pale green rug into the bathroom, where he saw that there was not only a brass tub but also a stone-tiled shower in the corner. "Oh, fuck yes! I haven't had a shower in a while, beautiful," he said, laying the axe on the counter.

He took off his helm, setting it on the counter next to the axe, then his armor, grunting as he pulled it over his head. Then he stripped down to his birthday suit and turned on the shower tap. It sputtered for a moment, but then hot, steaming water started to jet out of the brass showerhead, and Victor almost laughed in his anticipation. "God, yes! This is going to feel good."

He stepped into the hot water, groaning in pleasure as it rolled over his scalp, down his shoulders and back. He laughed as he rubbed his fingers through his hair, but as his laughter died down, he heard a scraping sound, like someone dragging metal over tile, and he quickly rubbed the water out of his eyes. A figure stood in his doorway, cloaked in black, and in its shadow-clad hands was Lifedrinker. To his horror, Lifedrinker blinked out of existence, clearly stowed in a dimensional container.

"You motherfucker!" Victor roared, his rage suddenly off the charts. He exploded out of the shower, and the shadowy figure turned and took a step, trying to run, but not before Victor, naked, wet, roaring, and speeding like a freight train, smashed into its back. He felt the lithe bones of the figure bend and collapse as he hit it, and the two crashed and rolled onto the floor, accompanied by the cracks of more bones and wood as Victor drove them into the bed's footboard, smashing through it, ripping the feather-filled mattress in the process.

The thief, as Victor's rage-fueled mind had come to think of the figure, screamed in agony, and the sound, filled with despair, pain, and the weak wheeze of terrible wounds, calmed Victor enough for him to pull back and flip him over. He reached down and jerked his shadowy hood away from his head, revealing a young Ardeni man's face, bloodied and bruised from its impact with the bed. "Get her out. Right fucking now!"

"Her?" the man gasped.

"The fucking axe!"

He held the man by his throat, squeezing just enough not to kill him. He saw him fumbling with his left arm, grimacing and sobbing, unable to straighten the broken limb. Giving up, the thief used his other arm, holding it toward his chest, and then Lifedrinker appeared, falling through his broken fingers to clatter onto the floor. Victor thrust the man away, sending him smashing back to the ruins of the bed, then he picked up Lifedrinker and held her to his head.

"I'm sorry, beautiful. I'm sorry. I'm sorry," he said, his rage replaced by worry. Was the axe okay? Had her spirit suffered? He knew dimensional containers were horrible places for conscious beings.

"My pain was brief, my faith rewarded," the axe sang, crystal clear, chiming in his mind, and nothing but love and pride coming through with the words—no anger, no suffering.

"Oh, thank God," Victor said, hugging the axe to his chest. He looked down at the thief, little more than a child, really. His cloak looked to be made of shadows, shifting and kind of misty on his shoulders. "You're fucking lucky," he said. The thief didn't respond, and Victor prodded him with his toe, but he didn't move. "Fuck," he said, bending to jostle his shoulder.

Suddenly the door burst open, splinters flying from the frame. "Victor!" Valla said, striding into the room to take in the scene, her wicked blue sword before her. She looked at Victor standing naked, holding his axe, and the crumpled form of the thief amidst the ruin of the bed. "I heard the crash and acted with haste," she said, glancing away from him.

"He was stealing my shit when I was in the shower. I might have overreacted, but he put Lifedrinker into a dimensional container, and I lost it. Jesus, I hope I didn't kill him," Victor added, frowning down at the kid.

"I'll see to him. You could, perhaps, clothe yourself." Valla said, stepping forward, eyes trained on the thief, and Victor nodded, turning back to the bathroom. He was pulling on his pants when Valla called, "He'll live. He bears the mark of Clan ap'Dreysha—a den of thieves and assassins if ever there was one. They're at direct odds with Lady Rellia."

"Ap'Dreysha?" Victor asked, but before Valla could respond, pounding feet could be heard in the hallway, and then Sergeant Hine and two burly city watchmen were crowding into the room. From the bathroom, he saw the guards and heard them questioning Valla, and he sighed and buttoned his pants. "So much for a relaxing shower."

24

YUND

"We'll take 'im, m'lady," Victor heard one of the guards say to Valla, but she looked at him with a frown and shook her head.

"No. I'll be bringing him to Lady ap'Yensha."

"No, ma'am, I'm sorry, but he's coming with us," the other guard said. Victor stepped out of the bathroom, now clad in his armored shirt and holding Lifedrinker, and stepped up next to Valla.

"No, men. We'll take him from here. If you feel that's a problem, have a magistrate collect him from the ap'Yensha estate." Valla stared at the two guardsmen, brow furrowed, eyes brooking no argument.

The two guards looked at each other, clearly conflicted, and Victor noted their better-than-average fitting uniforms, shiny mail, and polished boots. These guys either took their job more seriously than most or got paid better than most. Both were Ardeni and young. They looked fit, and their hands rested on their weapons comfortably.

"What clan are you two from?" Victor asked on impulse.

"Yes. What are your names, guardsmen?" Valla asked, her sword still naked in her hands.

Sergeant Hine backed away from the two guards and held up his hands. "Now, now, guards. I appreciate you coming to investigate, but I think Lady ap'Yensha will be within her rights to look into this matter. As she said, seek a magistrate's order if you'd like to pursue things."

"Right," the taller guard said; he had perfectly coiffed red hair, curly and glistening—a sign that Victor had come to understand meant he'd advanced his race a time or two. "We'll be on our way." He tugged at his friend's elbow, a dark-haired fellow with bright yellow eyes, and the two of them made a hasty exit.

"They didn't want to give us their clan name," Victor said.

"Correct. I wish I had the staff here to follow them," Valla said. She glanced at Sergeant Hine. "Do you have someone to spare?"

"Not anyone that wouldn't make a fool of themselves. I'm sorry."

"Did you fetch those guardsmen?" Valla pressed.

"No! They came into the common room—said they'd heard a clash while standing out front."

"That's bullshit," Victor said.

"Aye," Valla grunted as she knelt to inspect the "thief" again. He was breathing, but some of his bones were clearly bent in the wrong places. "Ancestors! Do me a favor and never tackle me, Victor."

"I'll get this room sorted. Just give me an hour, please?" Hine said, glancing at Victor as he surveyed the damage.

"Yeah, I've got somewhere to go anyway." He turned to Valla, "You gonna take this guy to Rellia? I'd like to know what was going on. Was he targeting my axe, or was he just lucky?"

"Rellia has people that will get the information from him." She glanced at Victor and then at Hine, "Don't worry. I'm talking about an imperial licensed Mind Caster."

"Mind Caster?"

"Aye," Hine grunted, "someone with a mind affinity. Damn rare, and damn illegal if you don't register with the Empire."

"Fuck that," Victor grunted on instinct. He didn't like the idea of the Empire or anyone requiring someone to register so they could keep tabs on their magic.

"What do you mean?" Valla asked, producing a small amber vial and holding it to the thief's lips.

"I mean, I don't like the idea of some imperial agency in charge of my magic. I'm not a Mind Caster or whatever, but I wouldn't do it."

"You don't understand how dangerous they are. They can make suggestions that, if you heard them, you'd struggle to resist. I could spend the afternoon telling you the horror stories I've heard."

"I've seen it," Hine said quietly.

"Oh?" Victor looked at the man while the thief gasped, and his bones began to click and crack back into the correct positions.

"Aye. We was on duty out near the World Breakers. Me and the rest of the Red Slayer Company. Captain came round and told us to head to a village up in the foothills; I still remember its name—Misty Hollow. When we got there, me and four other hard men and women, we found a man sitting by the village well, just weeping into his hands. In a circle, all round him were the people of the village. Every one of them was slumped over like they'd been sitting on their knees, and their throats were cut. Only one of them held a knife, though, and that's when shit went weird." He glanced at Valla and nervously added, "Pardon my language, Captain."

"What?" Victor asked as Valla shrugged and shook her head. Not only was the story interesting, but the man was only the second or third native he'd heard say the word "shit." The sergeant looked down at the thief, and Valla took the hint, flipped him over on his stomach, to his protestations, and tied his hands behind his back. Then the sergeant continued.

"The weeping man took his hands away from his face and looked at us. He said, 'Stand still,' and we did. Not one of us took another step. Then he said, to my mate Yorfil, 'Pick up the knife.' Ancestors be damned if he didn't step forward and pick up the knife. Then the weeping man said, tears still falling from his cheeks, 'Why don't you cut your throat?'"

"What the fuck?" Victor asked.

"Aye. The others of us, we stood like dummies, unable to move while Yorfil lifted that knife to his throat. I thought he was a goner, and I strained with everything I had to move, but I couldn't do it! Luckily, I wasn't the strongest among us, and Batha, the hardest, meanest legionnaire you ever saw, suddenly broke into a charge and drove her spear right through the weepin' man's eye. Yorfil dropped the knife, and all was well. At least for us."

"That's not the worst, though," Valla added. "It's the subtle suggestions that can cause real havoc. The wrong word in a mayor's ear, a seductive whisper to an attractive man or woman, the hint that a price should be changed on an expensive item—an unregistered Mind Caster can do a lot of damage."

"Damn, Valla, sounds like you've got more than a few good stories to tell," Victor said, surprised the woman had said so much.

"On that note," Valla said, grabbing hold of the thief's shoulder, "up you go, lad. Come with me; time to tell your tale." The boy grunted and mumbled something about things not being fair, but Valla hauled him up, then turned to Victor. "You don't need me for this thing you've got to do?"

"No, I'll be all right. See you here in a few hours. Hey, remember what I said about not wanting people to know where I am."

"That bird's flown free, I'm afraid. Still, I'll let people know you don't want to be bothered."

"I'll be sure no one comes knocking, Victor. I don't know how this one got in here. Maybe he hid in here after the maids finished last." He looked at the thief and said, "Well? At least tell us that much! How'd you get in here, boy?"

The young thief winced as Valla squeezed his arm, then he said, "My cloak. I slipped past all three of you, and the lock was no trouble. I came in while you all stood chatting at the landing."

"Old uncle's bones!" Hine said. "I thought those locks were good!"

"Not for someone with the right talent," the kid said; this time, he sounded almost cocky.

"Don't get too smug," Valla said. "You've got an unpleasant few hours ahead of you." She turned to Victor as she strode for the door, the thief in tow. "Later, then."

"Later," he said, then she was gone. Victor turned to Hine and added, "Sorry about the room. I wasn't aiming for the bed."

"I'm embarrassed that this happened to you in my inn. Is there anything I can do to help you with your business?"

Victor thought about it for a minute as he put Lifedrinker into her loop on his belt, then said, "I could use directions. I'm not sure how to get to a place called the Wagon Wheel from here. It's a, uh, pit fighting place."

"Aye, I've heard of it. I know the way. Would you like me to write out the directions?"

"Nah," Victor said over his shoulder as he collected his helmet from the bathroom counter. "Just tell me—I won't forget." He grinned as he patted his chest where Gorz hung, long neglected. "I have a memory trick."

Not long after that, Victor was wending his way through the streets of Persi Gables, glad to have most of his belongings tucked away in his storage rings. People pressed close in the narrower alley-like roads, and though he was big and people hurried out of his way, he still was bumped into constantly. Victor didn't know much about pickpocketing, but he'd heard of it and figured this was the perfect place for such an activity.

Gorz spoke up from time to time to tell him where to turn, and Victor mentally resolved to talk to the amulet that night—he wanted to show him the new pattern Oynalla had made for him before he made an effort to study and use it. Thinking of Oynalla, Victor smiled—two nights ago, he'd met with her and Thayla again, and they'd given him an update on Deyni. The little girl was already riding around on Starlight, with Chandri leading the animal.

Apparently, she'd gained her Animal Handling skill almost immediately. The clan was excited because they saw great promise in her ability—they hoped she'd advance the skill much further than most hunter folk usually did. Oynalla had groused that the girl should be focusing on her spirit cultivation, but Thayla had retorted, "She can do both!" Victor laughed at the memory as he rounded a corner in the tight, debris-strewn alley, and a familiar sight opened up before his eyes, bringing him back to the present.

"God, it's so fucking small," he said, looking at the front of the warehouse with the big, dried-out, warped wagon wheel nailed above the doors. In his memories, the warehouse had loomed large, big as any gym back in Tucson, but that wasn't the case. Looking through the open doors, he saw a few fighters sparring on the sawdust, and to him, it looked like a hovel—nothing close to the practice facilities back at Rellia's estate. A burly Shadeni stood near the doors, arms crossed, glaring at the people practicing, and Victor knew he was Yund's employee, not one he recognized, but the guard was clearly keeping the fighters from leaving.

"How to do this," Victor muttered as he started striding forward through the alley, kicking an old crate out of his way with his steel-toed boot. It clattered and skidded over the debris-strewn cobbles, and the guard lazily turned toward him. His eyes bulged open, and he straightened up when he saw Victor stomping his way. For lack of a better, more thoughtful plan, Victor had decided to go with muscle and intimidation.

Before he was close enough to talk, he cast Manifest Spirit, and, on an impulsive whim, he fueled it with fear-attuned Energy. His spectral pack of coyotes shimmered into existence, and they were dark, like purple-black shadows. They followed along at his heels, yipping, growling, and looking around with menacing violet, smoky eyes.

"Hold up," the Shadeni said, putting his hand on a knobby wooden cudgel he wore at his belt.

"Ah-ah," Victor replied, resting his hand on Lifedrinker. The man was tall, probably over six feet, and had long, twisted black horns, so Victor knew he wasn't a baseline Shadeni. Still, whatever aura he could project was swallowed by his, and Victor could see the fear in his eyes as they darted around, taking in his weird, yipping companions. Victor dug deep for his most stern voice, allowing some rage to flood his pathways, and said, "I'm not here to kill everyone, but I can if you guys want to push me."

"What do you want?" the guard asked, his hand falling away from his cudgel.

"Is Yund here? Ponda?"

"Yes, in his office, but he doesn't want . . ." Victor brushed past the man, and with a mental nudge, one of his coyotes sat down in the doorway, staring at him, a low growl in its chest, and black smoky fur standing up on its back in a ridge.

"Don't move around, or that hound will rip out your throat." Victor didn't know if the coyote could really take the man, but he didn't think the guard did either. He stood there, mouth open, and watched as Victor and his other four companions stalked onto the practice floor.

Victor glared around at the eight or so fighters, all dressed in rags of cloth or scraps of leather. Not one of them looked as if they'd seen a good meal in the last week, and they were universally filthy. "Be calm!" Victor called out, and he cast Inspiring Presence.

The dingy straw and sand-covered hall grew brighter, and the fighters stood up a little straighter, nodding at Victor, and he saw something light up in their eyes, something bright, and it took him a minute to understand—he was seeing hope born. "Wait here." He looked at them each and settled on an older man, a lean Ardeni with violet hair and eyes, and he added, "If Ponda comes around, come and knock on the door. I'm going to talk to Yund."

"Aye," the man said, not missing a beat, staring at Victor with that gleam in his eyes. Victor nodded and, not wanting to pin everything on a stranger, willed one of his coyotes to sit in the center of the practice hall, alert for any other of Yund's thugs that might wander in. Then he walked up to Yund's office door and yanked it open, ripping the bolt through the wooden doorframe.

"What in the hells?" Yund yowled, standing up from behind his desk and reaching for a twin-bladed axe that hung on the wall next to his chair. He was the same old guy Victor used to know, but he seemed puny, which really threw Victor for a loop. Sure, he expected the Wagon Wheel to appear different. He knew places you experience in one phase of your life could seem smaller or emptier, minus the people and feelings you had while there.

Yund, though, he'd been a giant in Victor's mind, a terrifying menace that could swat him like a fly. Someone with immense power and wealth that held Victor's life in the palm of his hand. Here he was, though, not so tall, quite fat, slow, with jiggling jowls and cheap clothes. Even his axe looked like something Victor would leave lying on the battlefield. "Hey, Yund, you old asshole."

"Wha . . ."

Victor stepped through the doorway, ducking to avoid hitting his head on the lintel, and his three yipping, growling shadows slinked in around him, taking up various dark corners of the room. Yund began to sweat, and his words died in his throat as his eyes bulged and his hands began to tremble. "Sit down," Victor said, and Yund practically collapsed into his chair.

"Do I know you, sir? Is this about the money I owe Tharjis?" Yund looked from Victor to Lifedrinker, then let his eyes dart around at the shadowy hounds emanating their dark aura, and Victor actually saw him gulp. That gave him pause, and as he took in a deep breath, he realized he was channeling a lot of rage-attuned Energy into his pathways, more than he'd intended.

Looming there, over Yund's desk, Victor saw a red flickering light reflected on the shiny brass shield hanging behind Yund, and he knew he was starting to glow with a red aura. Not only that, but he had, at some point, lifted Lifedrinker free from his belt, and the fact that she was in his hands, humming for action, almost drove him into a frenzy. It was with a monumental effort of will that he reeled in his rage and slowly forced in and out another long, slow breath.

"You don't recognize me, asshole?" Victor asked, leaning closer.

"No, um, is it you that I owe?" Yund stammered, his jowls shaking with the way his head darted left and right, searching for answers in the corners of the room.

"How I've changed, eh? So much that you can't see it in my eyes. Isn't my skin enough? Sure, I've seen some sun, but I'm still the only tan-colored motherfucker in this city with no wings. Come on, asshole. Look into my eyes." Victor leaned in close, and that's when the light ignited in Yund's panicked face.

"V . . .V . . . Victor? Ancestors, boy! You can't blame me for what that noble did! My hands were tied . . ."

"No, *pendejo*, *my* fucking hands were tied!" Victor growled, and suddenly all his rage was back, and he smashed Yund's desk with Lifedrinker, utterly reducing it to kindling with the rage-fueled swing. He pushed through the ruined furnishing and grabbed Yund's leather collar, lifting the man from his feet and pressing him against the rear wall of the office, crumpling the cheap shield hanging there. "God, I want to fucking squeeze your head off," he hissed, pushing his face an inch from Yund's.

"Wa . . . wait, Victor!" Yund wheezed.

"Where are your fucking contracts?" Victor growled, and he knew he was glowing again. He knew his hand was hot where it pressed into Yund's chest, and Lifedrinker buzzed in his other hand, begging him to let go, to berserk and lay waste to the entire place.

"In my ring . . ."

"Right, if you want to live . . ." Just then, a bang on the door sounded while his coyote howled from the practice floor. "Sit down!" He pushed Yund into his chair and gestured to his coyotes. "They're watching you." Then he gripped Lifedrinker and, with a kick that finished off the door, sending it flying off its hinges, strode back onto the practice floor.

Ponda, the door guy, and two other thugs were standing in the center of the hall, cudgels and even shields equipped. The two coyotes Victor had left on watch were stalking them, walking in slow circles around the four henchmen, and when Victor exploded from the office, they broke off and came to stand on either side of him. Victor stared at Ponda, and it only took a moment for the light of recognition to shine in the big Vodkin's eyes.

Victor grinned, staring at Ponda. At one time, he'd almost thought of the Vodkin in friendly terms—he'd seemed sort of cool the way he spoke with the fighters and talked shit about Yund behind his back. He'd seemed a giant to Victor back then, and he was a huge man, close to Victor's size, though that would be a different story if Victor lost himself to rage, and he felt damn close. "You fucking stupid, Ponda? The game's over. Time to go find a new job."

"Victor? Little runt with an anger problem? Why'd you come back, kid? Yund ain't worth your time, especially if you got free."

"You're right about that much, Ponda. He's not worth my time, but they are," Victor gestured with his axe at the fighters standing around.

"Come on, Victor! There're hundreds, thousands of people like them in the city. How about Gelica? Or a dozen other cities I could name. You think killing Yund and taking a handful of fighters will make a difference?"

"It'll make a difference to them," Victor growled, pointing at a woman sitting against the wall, head in her hands. He stepped forward, desperately wanting to project his fear Energy, wanting to see the panic in their eyes, wanting to hear their screams as he ran behind them and cut them down with merciless cleaves. His fear Core pulsed and throbbed, begging him to release it, and then Oynalla's words came to him, bouncing around in his skull, warning him to hold back from overusing that attunement. He stopped and sucked in a deep breath, and said, "Fuck off, Ponda. I don't want to wake up at night thinking about how I cut you to pieces."

"C'mon, Victor, I know you, kid. Sure, you've put on some muscle, but it hasn't been that long. I'm Tier Three, and these whoresons aren't far behind. Just take off, huh? I'll tell Yund we beat you up and sent you packing." He glanced at his wide-eyed companions, and they seemed to take heart in his words. In fact, they appeared bolstered, and Victor wondered if Ponda was using some kind of ability.

Victor decided it was time to put an end to the talking; he reached into his Core and reversed the pressure of his will on his rage-attuned Core. He cast Berserk as the heat of his Energy flooded him, and he screamed his titanic fury at the sky. His body doubled in mass, maybe more, and tremendous corded muscles shot up around his shoulders, neck, and arms. His legs became like tree trunks, and his terrible shriek grew in volume until the people standing around clapped their hands to their ears and backed away, wide-eyed, as Victor lifted Lifedrinker, one-handed, into the air.

"I said fucking leave, Ponda!" he roared, his voice like a monster's, hoarse, deep, grinding. It rolled out of his throat like an avalanche. So effective were his words and actions that Ponda and his three cronies turned and, without a second glance, bolted from the warehouse. Victor's instinct was to give chase, to cut them down, and his coyotes looked at him, whining, prancing toward the door and back again, shaking with the urge to run after the fleeing enemies.

"Hold," he rumbled, and Victor realized he was still himself. He'd pushed his rage out, cast Berserk, but he wasn't truly angry; the fury of his scream had come from a deeper part of himself, and his waking mind didn't resonate with it—not that day. He turned—a giant limned in red, glowing Energy, eyes bloody with harnessed murder—and growled at the people standing around, "Don't flee. I'm getting your contracts."

Victor turned and, still berserk, stomped toward the office. He didn't fit in the doorway, so he smashed a shoulder into the wall next to the door, widening it. Stooped over, he advanced on Yund and growled, his breath coming out like a bellows, "Ring."

Yund fumbled with his hand, trying to slide the ring from his left pointer finger, but it was tight, and didn't want to come off. Victor reached out and snatched the man's hand, tiny, like a child's, and a part of Victor's mind wanted to bite it off—who was this puny man to stand in his presence? He clamped down on that thought, though, and with his thumb and the meat of his pointer finger, he grabbed Yund's ring and pulled. It slid off easily, though Yund screamed, and Victor realized he'd pulled off a long strip of the man's skin.

He shook the ring, so the bloody skin fell off, then he grunted, "Unbond." Yund's face, red by nature, had faded to a wan pink, and his eyes widened further still at the command.

"Victor, all my contracts, much of my wealth is in that . . ."

"Unbond," Victor growled again and, already stooping over, leaned closer, so his huge blood-red eyes were staring into Yund's. The man gingerly reached out with his non-bloodied hand and touched the ring. He held his finger there for a brief moment, and then he pulled it away, a crestfallen, ruined look on his face.

Victor felt his rage cooling and knew he'd lose his Berserk any moment, so he took Yund by the neck and dragged him out of the office. He threw him, tumbling through the sand and filthy hay, to slide up to a group of three fighters lingering closer to the exit than Victor had last seen them. "Hold," he grunted, then he put his hands on his knees and breathed, allowing his anger to fade and his rage-attuned Energy to seep back into his Core.

Yund groaned and writhed, clearly further injured by his long slide over the rough floor, but the three fighters pounced on him. One slid his practice sword under Yund's chin and braced his knees against his back, forcing the much larger man to gasp and struggle for breath. Victor, back to his usual self, cleared his throat and said, "Someone come here. I'll give you the key to the cells, and I want everyone out here. Tell them I'm giving you all your contracts and a share of Yund's wealth."

25

RECONNAISSANCE

While he waited for Yund's fighters to assemble, he took a look in the man's storage ring. His mind reeled at the clutter, and he cussed while he tried to make sense of the contents. At first, he was stymied by the piles of hundreds of clothing items, but he mentally nudged those all into a corner of the space, away from the other contents. Then he had to sift through dozens of personal items from beard oil to toothpicks, from novels about lusty women to letters Yund had written to people and never delivered.

Notably missing from the jumble was any sort of real wealth. Victor didn't find more than a handful of Energy beads, nor did he find any valuable weapons or armor. If he were given the ring, not knowing who it had belonged to, Victor would have guessed it was from a man very down on his luck. After much digging, he finally came up with two contract binders. One was very thick, and one relatively thin, and when he flipped through them, he realized why—the thick binder held the contracts of Yund's deceased fighters, and the thin one held the contracts of his current stable.

"Drag him over here, please," Victor said to the group of fighters holding Yund in place. As they complied, tugging and pulling him to the tune of yelps and curses, a thin line of sickly, filthy, barely clothed individuals started to trickle into the practice hall from the holding pens. When Yund was pulled prostrate in front of Victor, he said, "Yund, where's your money?"

"I'd have told you, Victor," he gasped, clearly in pain from bruised and bent limbs. "I'm broke! I've made a few bad deals and wagers, and I owe a lot of money to some bad people!"

Victor snorted. "Bad people, Yund? Talk about the pot insulting the kettle." Victor ignored Yund's protestations and looked out over the crowd of gathered fighters, his eyes darting to the female faces, hoping to see his old cagemate, Belsa. He didn't see her, though, and he spoke up, loud enough for them all to hear over their muttering and conversations, "Any of you know Belsa?"

Silence met his words as they all turned to stare at him, some with fear in their eyes, others with hope. Victor let his gaze travel from face to face, and finally a tall scarred Shadeni with one long black horn and the stump of another raised his hand and said, "I knew her."

"Knew?"

"Aye, sir. She died some time ago in a five-man melee."

"Goddamn it," Victor growled, grinding his teeth together. He hardly remembered the girl, but he remembered being kind of an asshole to her. She was really the only other person left at the Wagon Wheel that he'd hoped to see. Suddenly, despite his victory and Yund cowering at his feet, the whole thing just felt kind of pointless, kind of empty.

Again, he glanced at Yund, searching for the anger he'd need to smash the man into a pulp, but he couldn't find it. All he felt was empty sadness, a hollow ache, and he wondered if he'd made a mistake coming there. If he'd never come back, he could have at least imagined Belsa might have won her way free. He might have imagined that Yund had met justice at the hands of his own fighters. Now he was responsible for the scummy asshole, and nothing about squashing him like a bug felt good to him.

He closed his eyes, listening to the muttering crowd, some of them asking their neighbors what was wrong with him, others suggesting they make a run for it. Victor tried to tune them out and focused on his memories of the last week or so in his cell at the Wagon Wheel. He tried to remember Belsa's face, and though he strained, he kept picturing women from Tellen's clan—Chandri, Chala, and so many others. In a gut-wrenching moment, Deyni's face flashed into his mind, and he growled, opening his eyes and lifting a foot as though he might stomp the life out of Yund.

The pit boss cowered and writhed and looked so pathetic that Victor's smoldering rage faded away, and he put his foot down. Belsa was gone, and killing this asshole wouldn't bring her back. He sighed, shaking his head, and intending to have one of them hand out the contracts, asked, "Who can read?"

Several people raised their hands, but a thin man with the wings of a Ghelli strode forward and said, "Victor?" Sudden recognition washed over Victor's face, and flashes of memories ran through his mind—a shared drink after a pit night, encouraging words, a man standing tall against a stronger opponent, and a whispered confession about terrible crimes and the lengths a man would go to for justice.

"Sarl!" he said and stepped forward to clap the smaller man into an embrace. He didn't know why he hugged him—maybe it had something to do with not finding Belsa alive, maybe it was just relief that at least one person who'd been friendly to him was still at the Wagon Wheel, one person could stand witness to his return.

"We thought you were dead," Sarl said, laughing and pushing Victor back with strong, wiry arms.

"Almost, man, almost. A few times!" Victor said, wincing sheepishly at memories of hectic battles. "Anyway, I turned things around a bit, and now I'm here to help you all out." Victor held up the binder of contracts.

"Ahh! I see. Well, you can't just kill Yund and give us our contracts—the magistrates would put a price on our heads."

Victor stepped back and grunted, looking at Yund. "I wasn't going to kill him, I don't think. I was going to take your contracts, though. I don't give a fuck about the laws regarding slavery here, but I don't want you all to suffer for my actions. Well, what can I do?"

The crowd erupted in snarls and outbursts. Words like "Kill him!" or "Cut off his fingers!" or "Just let us run for it!" rose up out of the noise, but Sarl held up a hand and whistled shrilly.

"Quiet!" Victor added to the whistle, and everyone settled down.

"Victor, if you really want to help, we need someone else to buy the contracts—someone better than Yund."

"Oh, shit. Yeah, I could do that." He nodded.

"It's a lot of money for some of us, Victor," Sarl said, shaking his head.

"Yeah, I got it, Sarl. How do we make this legal?"

"You and Yund have to sign off on the sale with the correct payment going to him in front of witnesses."

"All right, everyone, sit down and get comfortable. We'll do this right." Victor pointed at two men standing close to Yund's ruined office. "Bring us one of the mess hall tables and get some pens or something from Yund's office."

After that, Victor spent the next hour working through each contract with Yund. He told the big pit boss to sit at the table across from him, and then it was just a matter of Sarl writing the sale notations at the bottom of each contract and Victor and Yund signing. After each contract was finished, Victor stacked it to his left and placed the correct number of Energy beads in front of Yund.

Some sales were absurdly cheap—one was only three beads. Others were "expensive," ranging from a hundred to one that was just over five hundred beads—Sarl's. All told, Victor spent over a thousand beads paying off the fighters' contracts. Each time they completed a sale, Victor had two of the fighters sign as witnesses, and at the end, he gave Yund back his ring and let him keep the beads. He didn't like it, but he didn't like the idea of murdering or robbing the guy and having some overzealous magistrate take it out on him or Yund's former slaves.

"Yund, I'll keep these guys from killing you for exactly five minutes. If I were you, I'd get running," Victor said when the contracts were all settled.

Yund blanched and looked around at the thirty-three pairs of hate-filled eyes, snatched up his ring, and ran for the door. Some of the fighters started to give chase, but Victor bellowed after them to stop. His smoky, purple-black coyotes were still lurking in the corners of the room, and Victor willed two of them to pursue Yund until he'd cleared the alley. With that done, he turned to the gathered fighters and stood on the table.

"First, you should know that I'm about to sign over your contracts to you. You'll all be free." A ragged cheer greeted his words, but just as he'd suspected, some of the faces didn't look so happy—they looked lost, doubtful, or even afraid. "Second, I want you to know that I have work for any of you that have no place to go." Another more heartfelt cheer broke out.

"I have powerful allies, and we're putting together an army. In the spring, we'll launch a campaign to claim lands in the Untamed Marches. Any of you can join and receive food, equipment, and a salary, or you can leave, go your own way, and accomplish your own goals." With that, Victor sat down and began signing off all the contracts. As he finished each one, he handed it to Sarl, and the Ghelli gave it to the correct fighter.

When he was finished, Victor set down Yund's magical quill and looked around the room. The crowd was thinner than before, but he still counted twenty-four fighters standing around. He looked at Sarl and said, "What about you? What will you do?"

"I'll stay and serve in your new army, Victor."

Victor smiled and reached out a hand. Sarl took it in his strong grip, and the two of them grinned at each other while they shook. "I'm putting you in charge of these fighters, then. Give me a minute," Victor said, then took out his Far Scribe book and began to write a note to Lam.

Captain Lam,

I'm sending you a group of twenty-five fighters I liberated from my old fighting stable. They're all free men who've chosen to join our cause. Their leader is a former nobleman named Sarl, and I'd like him to remain in command of these soldiers in our campaign force. Please enlist, equip, and house these fighters, placing them, as a unit, in our ranks where you deem most appropriate.

Victor

He snapped the book closed and then turned to Sarl, "Okay, Captain Lam knows to expect you. I'm not sure where her estate is in the city—I just got here myself. If you ask around, though, I'm sure you'll find it."

"Just like that, Victor? Your fortunes truly have changed. Thank you, my friend." He turned to the ragged, filthy fighters and said, "Keep your contracts to hand! I'm sure we'll be challenged walking through the city like this."

"Yeah," Victor said, "hold on." He dug into his dimensional ring and pulled out a hundred more Energy beads. He handed them to Sarl and said, "If you guys want to stop and get cleaned up and maybe buy some clean shirts and pants, that would be fine."

"You heard the man! Line up!" Sarl yelled, and Victor smiled, watching him get the rough group into an orderly line, barking orders. Sarl's background as a disgraced nobleman suited him well as a sergeant.

Victor left the Wagon Wheel feeling much better than he had earlier. Sarl's presence and advice about legally handling the contracts had changed the sour twist in Victor's gut into a glow of warmth in his chest.

When he retraced his steps out of the alley, leaving Sarl to manage the group of fighters, he carried Lifedrinker in his hands, partially expecting trouble from Yund or Ponda, but he worked his way back to the busier streets of Persi Gables without incident. "Well, gorgeous," he said to Lifedrinker as he put her back in her loop, "that's what happens when you lead a dirty life—you don't feel too excited about running for help when someone fucks your shit up."

When he got back to Sergeant Hine's inn, it was late afternoon, and Captain Valla was sitting in the common room waiting for him. "Victor!" she called, her voice cutting through the noise of conversations, clinking dishes, and a man strumming a stringed instrument in the corner. Victor smiled at her and made his way through the light crowd to the corner table where she sat and pulled out the chair, sitting down with a grunt.

"How's it going?" he asked, scooting back the chair so he could stretch out his legs, his feet crossed at the ankles near Valla's chair.

"Well. Lady Rellia will update our book when she's found answers from the thief. And you? Was your old business settled?" As she spoke, Valla waved down a server, and the apron-clad Ardeni nodded to her, indicating he'd come over when he could.

"Yeah, pretty well settled, I'd say. My old demon was sort of pathetic, really. I ended up letting him live, and with a fatter stack of beads than he deserved. I doubt I really changed much about what's going on in this city, but at least I helped out a few people, including one old friend."

Valla held up her cup, presumably filled with liquor, and said, "To small victories, then." She took a sip and held the cup out to Victor, and he grinned, taking it. When he looked into the cup, he saw the telltale red of the wine Valla seemed to enjoy, and he took a drink. It wasn't bad, and he smiled at her, then downed the rest of the cup's contents.

"Hey!" Valla laughed.

"What? Don't tell me that was your first cup. I need to catch up somehow, don't I?"

"A mark well scored." She laughed again. "Well? Do you want to hunt out the lair of those responsible for your arrival in this world, or would you like to rest?"

"Wow! Really tempting my impulsive side, aren't you? C'mon, Valla—I would think a captain from the Legion would know that the best time to fuck with your enemies is early in the morning. I learned that playing VR sims."

"Yes. You're right, Victor, and you were right about the amount of wine I've had to drink. I'm a touch annoyed from my visit with Rellia, and I feel like lashing out at something."

"Oh?" Victor knew something was up because Valla rarely called Rellia by her first name. "What happened?"

"Well, it started when I wouldn't tell her where we're staying. I told her I'd promised to keep people from bothering you, which further irritated her, and she said she'd just find the answer from the thief and that I was being stupid . . ." Valla smiled as the server dropped off another cup and a pitcher of wine.

After he walked away, she continued, "Anyway, you don't want to know all of it. It's stupid."

"Eh, I guess I'm being kind of selfish, expecting you to keep secrets like that. If it's causing you trouble, tell Rellia whatever you want. I'm not promising to stick around the city after we've dealt with a couple more things, though—like the summoner assholes you mentioned earlier."

"It's fine, Victor. Our issues go further back than my dealings with you." She paused and filled their cups from the pitcher. "Let's forget about Rellia, hmm? Shall we have a few drinks and then retire early? We can rise before dawn and visit the location of the summoner's hall."

"Sounds fucking perfect," Victor said and picked up his cup.

When Victor woke very early in the morning, he was glad for his enormous vitality and improved body. He must have drunk a gallon or two of wine the night before, yet he felt excellent. He was a little annoyed at himself for spending the evening drinking instead of cultivating or working on his new Energy weave pattern, but he was only human and figured it was good to let off some steam now and then.

He pulled out the little pocketwatch he'd purchased so long ago when he was scratching out an existence deep beneath the earth and saw that it was just two hours past midnight. Nodding to himself, he stood up, used the bathroom, then got dressed. Fully armored and with his axe loose on his belt, he left his room and gently tapped on Valla's door. Three heartbeats later, the handle silently turned, and the door opened an inch to reveal Valla's seafoam green eye. "Ready?" she asked, in a voice so low Victor wasn't sure she'd spoken.

"Yeah," he whispered. She pulled the door open, stepped out, and silently latched it. Then she moved past Victor and led the way out of the inn, ghosting down the hallway, and Victor noted she wore black pants and a dark military cape over a mail shirt. It was the first time she'd worn something other than her military pants and perfectly starched white shirt, and it felt weird to Victor, like when your favorite cartoon character doesn't wear their usual outfit.

The streets were quiet and cold, and their breath plumed forth as they strode through the dark cloudy night toward the gates. "Do you think I need to cover up my armor?" Victor asked, gesturing to his scaled shirt and his helmet.

"No, they're not shiny. That dull gray metal looks dark enough in this light—clouds hide the moons."

"Right," Victor said, and they continued. On their shadowy trek through the city, they encountered few people. Valla told Victor that there was a loosely enforced curfew after midnight. The few guards who challenged them, though, were quickly satisfied when Valla announced herself and said she was on official Clan ap'Yensha business. Victor just followed her silently, allowing her to clear their passage. Occasionally he saw figures in the shadows that seemed to slip away before they came near, and Valla suggested that they were probably up to no good themselves.

The gates were open, but the portcullis was down, and Valla had to threaten the gate captain on duty with Rellia's wrath before he finally agreed to let them out the sally port built into the portcullis. "Why are they so fussy about people leaving at night?" Victor asked as they walked away from the city.

"We could be criminals running from a robbery or murder, for all they know. People have always been warier during the dark, wee hours—it stems from our past before we knew how to work Energy or build fires to banish the monsters that lurk in the shadows."

"Yeah, I guess."

"Can you run?" Valla asked, giving him a sidelong look.

"What kinda question is that? I look like I can't run?"

"Well, you're so large. When I picture you running in my mind, it looks more like you falling forward. Show me, then!" she said and started jogging. Victor chuckled and sprang after her, easily matching her pace and surprisingly nimbly. He used Sovereign Will to boost his agility, making his feet more graceful as he followed her steps and tried to avoid making noise. They only ran down the road for a few minutes before they turned up a well-rutted path into the trees. Valla looked at him over her shoulder and said, "The map says the structure's about three miles into these woods."

Victor nodded and followed after her, glad he had worn a belt to keep his scale shirt from flopping and bouncing as he ran. He lifted Lifedrinker from her loop, though, and as he liked to do, he carried her crossways in front of himself. The forest was dark, and the shadows clingy, and Victor began to have trouble seeing where to place his feet, so he cast Inspiring Presence. He didn't want to give them away by creating a light, but the spell was almost as good. Everything grew clearer, and he knew exactly where to step. He grinned broadly as Valla looked back at him with an appreciative nod.

After just a few minutes of jogging, Valla held up her hand and slipped off the trail into the soft, damp mulch between the trees. The ground was coated with frosty layers of fallen leaves and needles, and it was a trivial matter, inspired as they were, to slip between the trees noiselessly. They were no longer jogging, but the two moved quickly, parallel to the trail but twenty yards away from it. With Victor's inspiration, the shadows weren't so heavy, and they could see the gap in the trees where the trail ran, making it easy to navigate in the correct direction.

They traveled that way another ten minutes before Valla held up her hand again and crouched behind a thick trunk, motioning for Victor to join her. "Did you see the light?" she asked when he crouched down next to her.

"No, I was watching you," he grunted in amusement at himself and added, "I mean to see where to go."

"Right. There's a dim light ahead. I think from a window."

Victor nodded and slowly stood up, gradually moving his head around the trunk to take a look. As his eye cleared the obstruction, he saw a yellow rectangle ahead about twenty or thirty paces through the woods. He watched it for a moment, then a shadow shifting to his right alerted him to the presence of a darker shadow among the trees by the trail. He knelt, and, barely allowing air to flow past his lips, he whispered, "A watcher by the trail. Close to where the window is."

Valla nodded and seemed to consider something for a minute, then held out a hand in which a bundle of dark, smoky fabric appeared. "The thief's cloak," she whispered, handing it to Victor.

"Why me?" he breathed.

"This is your quest. Take it," she whispered. He shrugged and took the bundle. He could see the long ties near where the shoulders were, so it wasn't a complicated equation to figure out how to put it on. He swung it over his shoulders, hooked the ties together in a bow, and pulled the hood up. Victor looked to Valla for approval, and she mouthed, "Bond."

Victor nodded and ran a trickle of Energy into the cloak.

*****Cloak of Shadow Imp Hair. This cloak has been crafted from the hairs of a Yohathian Shadow Imp. The imp's natural ability to blend with shadows has been preserved by a master Artificer and will aid the wearer in doing the same.*****

"Cool," he hissed, and Valla nodded, giving him the thumbs-up. Cloaked in shadow, Victor slipped around the tree, Lifedrinker held in one hand, head down, back by his side, obscured by the cloak's magic. He glided through the forest, tree to tree, aiming for a point to the left and behind where he'd seen the lurking watcher. When he was sure he'd passed the point where he'd seen the movement, Victor slipped up behind a tree and watched the shadows, waiting for the figure to move again.

He barely breathed as he leaned into the trunk, just a dark spot against the frosty, knobby bark, and he watched, patient as a glacier. The minutes ticked by, and Victor began to worry that Valla would become impatient, but then his watching was rewarded—a shadow just a few feet away from him shifted, and he saw a pale hand lift a water skin from a belt. Now knowing where to look, Victor saw a Ghelli man sipping from the skin. Victor slipped around the trunk, and before the watcher could cry out, he snaked an arm around his shadowy neck and held Lifedrinker's gleaming blade up in front of his hood.

"Don't make a fucking sound," Victor hissed, squeezing his massive arm around the watcher's skinny neck. The watcher rapidly tapped on his arm, grunting snot through his nose as he struggled to breathe. Victor loosened up slightly and hissed again, "Stay quiet, or I'll pop off your head." He swiveled so he could see the yellow rectangle, and from this angle, he could see that it was a window in a large barn-like building. Victor, still holding the watcher's neck tightly, walked backward, pulling him along, putting some more trees between them and the building.

When he'd moved past a dozen or more trees, Victor slightly loosened his arm and hissed, "Whisper answers to my questions, and you might not die tonight."

"Yes," the watcher wheezed, sucking air through his nose.

"How many more are out here? How many in the building?"

"No more outside. I don't know who's within—maybe no one," the Ghelli answered, coughing loudly.

"Quiet! I said, whisper, you dumbass," Victor squeezed his arm tight again, silencing the man's coughs. The man rapidly tapped his hands on Victor's arm, and Victor let him go so he could breathe.

"Sorry," the man wheezed, then took deep breaths.

"Who are you?"

"I'm—" Suddenly Victor felt a gathering surge of Energy from the man, and then he said, "Let me go!" His voice was resonant and strong, and Victor felt his arm start to relax, but then he realized what was happening, and he asserted his will, forcing his arm to flex tight, and this time he didn't fuck around—he squeezed until the man began to flop and flail, and then went limp.

"Did you kill him?" Valla's whisper came from behind a nearby tree.

"Nah, but he's out for a second. Help me bind him up. I think he's one of those Mind Casters you and Hine were telling me about."

Valla immediately slipped forward and jammed a rolled-up wad of cloth into the watcher's mouth, then she tied a gag around it. "Flip him over," she said, and Victor obliged. Valla bound his hands with a length of rope that constricted and tied itself, then she did the same to his feet. "Take him for questioning or investigate further?" she whispered.

"I want to see what's in that barn. It seems . . . familiar."

"I'll watch him," Valla said, but then the watcher inhaled sharply through his nose and started to writhe. Valla pulled a glass vial from her dimensional container and flicked the cork out with her thumb, holding the vial under the watcher's nose as green vapors began to float out. He got one whiff of the vapors, then the thrashing stopped, and he slumped down, unconscious. Valla looked at Victor and nodded.

Victor nodded back and, still cloaked in shadows, slipped through the trees toward the barn. When he came to the last clump of trees before the clearing where the building sat, he studied it for a moment, making sure there weren't any watchers around it. When he was satisfied, he slipped forward toward the little window set in the center of the left of the two double doors. He reached the side of the building, slid along the rough planks, and then, ever so carefully, he peered through the dusty glass with one eye.

Suddenly he was transported back to when he'd first arrived in this world. He was weak, small, and unable to move as a powerful mage pointed at him and told him to be silent. Victor blinked furiously, banishing the memory, and took in the room he saw through the glass—the wooden interior of the building. Planks lined the floor, painted with an elaborate spell pattern. Posts were arranged in a circle around the pattern and carved with thousands of runes, each carefully inlaid with some rich, gleaming metal. A dais stood before the spell pattern, and at its center was a lectern holding a thick tome.

"Fucking hell," Victor said, still reeling from the memory. He started to reach for the door latch when flickering orange light reflected off the glass, he felt immense heat at his back, and a massive concussion blew him through the door to sprawl on the floor in a scatter of embers, fiery splinters, and glass. His cloak was crackling and smoking as it burned, so Victor flailed, ripping the garment off his neck and flinging it away. He rolled to his side, reaching out to grab Lifedrinker from where she'd fallen, then a tall, gray-robed figure stepped into the smoking ruin of the doorway.

"Curiosity is often met with disaster!" the figure boomed, holding out hands that were gathering another ball of seething, hungry fire.

26

FIRE

Victor rolled over his shoulder, trying to get his feet under himself before the mage could throw his second ball of fire. He was already boosting his agility, and his Inspiring Presence hadn't faded, so he moved like an acrobat, rolling and leaping to his feet as the fireball exploded into the floorboards, splashing over them in a concussive spray of sparks and embers. Victor jumped at the gray-cloaked mage, Lifedrinker over his head, bringing her down in a wicked chop.

Before the axe could hit home, though, the mage said, in a deep, resonating voice, "Stop," and for a split second, Victor . . . stopped. He froze his leg muscles mid-stride, and he jerked his axe to a halt, quivering a few inches from the mage's head. Victor growled, exerted his will, and jerked Lifedrinker back into motion, but it was too late to finish his attack—in a blur of gray shadows, the mage rushed past him, but not before he smashed a vial of acrid, caustic-smelling green fluid into Victor's armored chest.

"Gah," Victor said as the concoction filled his face with fumes, rapidly eating through his metal armor. He turned to track the mage while he tried to get off the defensive. He cast Manifest Spirit, summoning his coyotes with rage-attuned Energy. As their wispy red forms shimmered into existence and began to solidify, Victor saw the mage on the far side of the barn-like structure, his fingers bent in a strange symbol and chanting rapidly. "Kill him!" Victor barked to his pack, too frazzled to focus his intentions without the words.

Just as his pack sprang into motion, Victor felt heat and sudden sharp pain in his chest, and he realized the potion had eaten through his armor and was starting on his flesh. "Fuck!" he spat, fury starting to come unbidden into his mind, and he roared, ripping at his armor, trying to get it off without smearing more of the acidic solution on his hands and arms.

As more and more of the acid made contact with his flesh, he grew frantic in his actions. Before he knew it, he'd dropped Lifedrinker at his feet and was spastically yanking at the hauberk, pulling it over his head, only to get it caught on his bulky helmet.

"God-fucking-damn it!" he roared, ripping his helmet off and yanking the chain shirt over his head. Just as he flung it aside, red-faced and furious, his coyotes leapt at his enemy, and the mage finished his spell. A tremendous ripping, concussive explosion erupted around Victor, and the wooden floorboards he stood on burst into a million stinging, smoldering splinters, and a pit of roiling flames opened up beneath his feet.

Victor fell toward the flames, but he didn't try to save himself—he saw Lifedrinker tumbling in front of him, and he snatched hold of her warm, vibrating haft and flung her away over the edge of the newly formed pit. Booming laughter echoed above him as he tumbled, and then searing pain became his existence, and Victor screamed in agony, giving way to his instinctual desire to unleash his rage.

As his clothing ignited and his flesh began to char, Victor's hereditary memories and instincts took over. His body flared with red-Energy, overshadowing the flames in the magical pit, and his body stretched and grew. He screamed again, and this time his voice rattled and echoed off the planks of the building above him, shattering the little window in the door. So mad was he with pain and fury that he instinctively cast Sovereign Will to boost his strength, and with blackened, cracked flesh, he leapt out of the pit like a smoldering demon of vengeance.

The gray-robed mage was doubtless surprised to see him emerge from his intended immolation, but he was quick and reacted with a spray of fiery magma darts that tore into Victor's chest and stomach as he landed, cracking and shattering more floorboards. Victor was unrecognizable as a man, so horrific was the twisted, leering madness that had overcome him. His flesh was charred, covered in soot, cracked, bleeding, and raw, but it was the madness in his glare and his savage snarl that finally put doubt into the eyes of the mage.

"What are you?"

Victor had no semblance of thought other than mad rage at the idea that this little man had the nerve to use his pitiful magic on him. Victor saw his coyotes writhing and yelping in pain as smoldering lances held them to the floor. Who was this man to put his pack to the torch? Victor stared at the mage and bellowed. This time, there was no hint of pain in his voice, only raw, terrible fury. He didn't think or contemplate the consequences; he simply unleashed his fear-attuned Core, sending forth a roiling wave of dark Energy with Project Spirit.

The wizard, already starting to cast another complex spell, suddenly blanched, and his eyes darted around, trying to take in the horrors Victor had summoned from his mind. He turned and with shaky hands began to cast a different spell. Victor screamed again, leapt the ten feet to the mage's back, and fell on him like an avalanche of charred flesh.

"You dare challenge the Quinametzin?" he roared into the pinned mage's ear. The mage's face was red from the strain of breathing as Victor pressed his massive knee into his spine. "Worm!" he roared, grabbed the mage by the neck, and rolled, flinging his arm out and hurling him through the air to smash into one of the rune-carved posts. A shattering sound and wet crunches accompanied the impact, and suddenly the fires blazing in the hall faded to embers.

Victor sat among the floorboards he'd shattered when he'd landed, eyes glowering and brooding, wondering what else he could kill. Where were the little man's friends? Why did his body sting all over? He reached for the worst of his pains, feeling the hard, hot stone shards sticking out of his chest. Grunting, he began to pluck them out, each about four inches in length. His fury cooled as pain took its place, and no further challengers showed themselves.

Very slowly, Victor returned to himself, and when he blearily looked up from his pain-shrowded stupor, he saw that Valla stood in the shattered doorway of the structure, looking at Victor through narrowed eyes, her blue sword held ready. After a moment, her eyes sparked with recognition, and she darted forward. "Victor?"

"Ungh," he said. He held out a hand to her, and when he saw it, blackened, cracked, raw, he could only think that it was a mistake. Whose hand was that?

"Ancestors! What happened to you? I heard the most horrible sounds! I tried to get in, Victor, I really did, but flames encircled the building!"

"Why . . ." Victor started, but then he coughed and winced, and tears filled his eyes at the terrible pain. When the fit passed, he tried again, "Why didn't I get any Energy? I killed him . . ." He looked toward where he vaguely remembered his Quinametzin alter ego throwing the mage.

"Drink this," Valla said, tilting a small glimmering red vial toward his lips.

"Ungh," Victor managed again as he opened his mouth. The liquid was cold, tasted like copper, and seemed to soak through the flesh of his mouth like water into a sponge. Suddenly his mind cleared as much of his pain vanished. As his rationality began to return, he cast Sovereign Will again, this time boosting his vitality. He could feel the potion, cold as ice, scouring through his pathways, stimulating his flesh's naturally high healing rate, and he watched as the horribly burned and cracked flesh on his forearms and hands started to mend.

"Your chest needs stronger healing than my potion, Victor. Ancestors! How did you keep fighting through that?"

"I heal when berserk. I must have been worse . . ." Victor winced and coughed as he struggled to his feet, blood flecking the saliva that spattered on the smoking floorboards. Valla tried to help him, but he shrugged her off and hobbled toward the still-smoldering pit of fire the mage had created. He saw Lifedrinker lying next to a nearby wall and stooped to pick her up. She seemed fine—any burns she might have suffered were already healed by the powerful self-repairing nature of the living wood haft.

"There's not a body here," Valla said, and Victor looked up from Lifedrinker. He hadn't realized he'd spaced out. He tried to slip the axe into the loop on his belt, but it was gone. He looked down at himself and saw that his belt was still there but badly charred. His boots were black with soot, and most of his pants were simply gone, only shredded, charred rags hanging down from his belt. His torso was completely bare, black with soot, and red with swollen scars. A dozen puckered round wounds covered his abdomen, and Victor winced as he gingerly touched them.

"*Chingado*! That guy fucking messed me up."

"You should see your hair," Valla said, motioning at her head and wincing.

"Oh, fuck no!" Victor said, feeling his scalp gingerly. Scars and smooth flesh met his fingers. Spitting out more bloody saliva, he walked over to where Valla stood, and he saw the gray robe and shattered pieces of glass or crystal, but no body. "He fucking got out? I smashed him against that pole hard enough to kill anyone!"

"He was powerful, Victor. He might have had a relic or something that preserved him," Valla said, kneeling to collect the shattered object and folding it within the robe's fabric. "I'll have Rellia's people examine this." She looked up at Victor and winced again. "You need to recover before we go further into this."

"What do you mean he might have had a relic to preserve him?" Victor felt his rage Core begin to stir—the idea that he'd been mangled by that guy, that he'd beaten him and smashed him like a cockroach and he'd still survived was enough to nearly trigger his bloodline, almost enough to make him berserk.

"I've heard of such things. Rellia has an uncle who's rumored to have one—a powerful artificed device that will spirit him away to a place of safety if he's near death. You can imagine what powerful, wealthy people would pay for such a thing."

"So I can't kill this fucker?"

"No! I'm not saying that," Valla said, turning to look him in his bloodshot eyes. "Those things are rare! If you made him use it, he'll have lost a great treasure today. There are also ways to lock down an opponent, so they can't flee so easily, even with magic. I have a skill that might work, and you might gain something as you level or explore new uses for your Energy."

"Ungh." This time, Victor grunted on purpose. He didn't have anything to say; he felt like death warmed over, and he wanted to get someplace where he could lie down and let the world fade away for a while.

"Can you make it back to town?" Valla asked. "I'll handle the prisoner." Victor suddenly remembered the watcher they'd captured. "I tied him to a tree."

"Yeah. Go get him, and I'll put a shirt on." Valla nodded and hurried out the door. Victor pulled a soft linen shirt and a pair of comfortable pants out of his ring and slipped them on, then he stepped outside, still holding his axe. He was feeling better—his vitality was slowly mending the deeper wounds he'd suffered, but he knew he looked like hell, and his body wasn't moving easily—the scars he'd suffered from the horrible burns were making his joints stiff, and his hands felt sort of numb.

He knew more of him would feel numb if he explored his skin with his fingertips, and he dreaded seeing himself in the mirror. He supposed he was lucky to be alive—he'd suffered plenty of terrible wounds but never had his whole body torched before. "Goddamn it. That guy was good—not just that his spells were strong; he was fucking fast with them. You could tell he'd fought a lot of battles."

"Well, it sounds like he had an elemental affinity and was clearly high-tier. Considering the people we're looking for, he might not even be from this world. I know you've fought a lot," Valla said, leading the way with the blindfolded, bound watcher trailing behind, still gagged. Victor followed along as she kept speaking. "But there are people who've been dueling for centuries. Longer in some of the older worlds. I suppose it's lucky you're as strong as you are. If you made him use a relic to survive, he'll be furious, so that's a win."

"God, he fucked me up, though," Victor grumbled, rubbing at the rough flesh of his forearm with his free hand.

"I can ask Rellia to pay for a racial enhancement treasure. That will help with the scarring," Valla said, looking back at him over her shoulder.

"No, I'm not running to Rellia just cause I got messed up. I'm the one who wanted to avoid her and Lam, right? I got myself into this; I'll get out of it. How much would a fruit or something cost?"

"Well, if you're still in the base tier, we can get some pretty cheap advancement fruits—a few hundred beads each."

"Nah, I'm at improved," Victor grunted.

"Well, more like a thousand or two, then. I can help you out if you need . . ."

"No, I've got it. Maybe you can do some shopping for me, though? I need to lie down—I haven't felt this bad since . . . God, I can't remember. I've never felt this bad." Victor wasn't exaggerating; he limped with each step, half his body was numb, and the other half was burning. He kept catching himself panicking, his heart racing, as fragmented memories of the hell he'd experienced in the firepit flickered through his mind.

"I will do so. We should speak strategy when you feel better. If there had been another mage present . . ."

"Yeah, I get it."

When they made it back to the main road, the sun was coming up, and there were already farmers waiting to get into town when they reached the gate. Valla drew her sword and, holding it in one hand and the rope to her prisoner in the other, she hollered for people to clear the way. Victor, dazed and foggy, was happy to let her handle things as she threatened her way through the gate.

He heard her mention "Lady Rellia" and imperial business, and then they were through, and she flagged down one of the dozen coaches parked nearby, still waiting for their first business of the day. Victor groaned and gingerly climbed into the coach, and he dozed off briefly on their way back to the inn.

His mind wandered to pretty much anything other than the fight he'd just had. Victor didn't want to think of the fire, of the mage's laughs. He didn't want to remember the pain. He found himself imagining Deyni riding around on Starlight's back, laughing as the vidanii pranced around, and he smiled, his lips stiff and unresponsive.

"We're here, Victor. Can you manage, or do you need a hand? I'd like to take this one to Rellia's interrogator." Victor opened his eyes in time to see Valla point at her prisoner with a thumb.

"Yeah, I can manage. Here," he said, then Victor dug around in his ring and pulled out one of his large bags of beads. "There are around five thousand beads in here. Please get me something to advance my race, um, some new armor . . . fuck! My helmet!"

"I got it, Victor," Valla said, producing his helmet and handing it to him.

"Shit, thank you, Valla," Victor said, pleased that he hadn't lost Polo Vosh's gift.

"Oh, I imagine we might meet that dickhead again, so maybe something to help me resist fire. Is there such a thing?"

"Yes. I'll do my best, Victor. Just to be clear, you don't want me to mention your injuries to Rellia?"

"That's right. Thank you, Valla," Victor said as he started to clamber out of the coach. When he stepped into the bright morning light and saw all the people walking by in front of Hine's inn, he suddenly wished he had a good hat or a cloak he could pull down over his face. He figured he could get out another shirt or one of the jackets Tellen's people had gifted him but decided it would be lame to wrap something around his head just because he'd gotten messed up in battle.

"Take care, Victor. I'll be back soon. I'm sorry I wasn't with you when . . ."

"Not your fault. I'm glad you didn't get the same treatment I did," Victor said, gesturing toward his face. "See you soon." He turned and walked up the steps to the inn, then through the open doors. He started toward the stairs on the far side of the common room and had almost made it, thinking he might be able to avoid explaining his injuries to anyone, but then Hine's voice boomed out.

"Victor? Is that you, lad?"

"Uh, yeah," Victor said, turning to see the sergeant drop his rag on the bar and hurriedly walk around the end so he could approach Victor.

"Ancestor's balls, man. You look like you had a rough go of it!"

"Yeah, met a mage that wasn't playing around. Um . . ." he glanced up and down at himself from his feet, then out at his outstretched hand—the one not holding Lifedrinker. "Lots of fire and shit."

"Anything I can do?" Hine asked, wincing as he looked at Victor's face.

"Yeah, make sure no one bugs me. Except for Valla, that is. Don't stop Valla." He looked at Hine's face and the sadness and pity in his eyes and said, "I'll be all right, Hine. I'm good at healing, and, you know, racial advancements tend to help clear up scarring."

Hine glanced around the common room, eyes lingering on the few patrons sitting at the tables, but none seemed to be listening. He said in a low tone, "You can afford it?"

"Yeah, I've made some money recently. I mean, I'm going to run out at this rate, but I'm good for now."

"Good for you, lad, good for you. Not many of us make it past the first few ranks. Those of us willing to fight and risk our lives, I mean. Well, I suppose if you're born into one of the wealthy clans, it's a different story, but plenty of people in this city would kill for a rank or two, if you know what I mean. Seems you've got your hands full with the trouble already on your plate—might be best not to go inviting more. You get what I'm saying?" He winked and nodded toward the streets and, Victor guessed, the people out there.

"Yeah, I get it—quit running my mouth about things I can get that other people can't." He nodded and winked, and Hine winced, making Victor wonder what the action had looked like with his scars. "I'm hurting, man. Going to my room. Later." Victor turned to the stairs and started climbing.

"I'll make sure you're not bothered," Hine said, following behind him. "Don't mind the new guard in the hallway—he's there to be sure no more surprises await my guests in their rooms!"

"Good," Victor replied, steadily climbing away from the older man. When he reached the landing, he saw that there was, indeed, a new guard posted at the top of the stairs. He sat on a stool and scrutinized Victor through faintly glowing brass and crystal glasses. Victor nodded to him, and the bulky Shadeni nodded back, his palms resting on the two short swords he wore at his belt.

"No activity the last few hours," the man said.

"Good," Victor said, chuckling at his repetition, then shuffled down the hall to his doorway.

Victor entered his room, and as he closed the door and turned toward his bed, he vacillated between going into the bathroom, studying himself in the mirror, or just climbing into bed. He shook his head and started toward the bed, but then he stopped himself. Why was he avoiding looking at himself? "Am I afraid?"

He looked within himself and realized that he was terrified. He'd never really thought of himself as vain, but he'd sure never had anyone tell him he was ugly. Would he be able to cope if Valla couldn't find what he needed or if he advanced his race and it wasn't enough? Maybe he wouldn't be able to heal those scars until he'd made it all the way to advanced race—he didn't think he had the treasure to buy ten ranks.

"Quit being chickenshit," he said and stalked toward the bathroom. He started to undress with stiff, sore limbs, piling his things on the counter. He had a momentary flashback to when the thief had taken advantage of him doing just that, and he quickly jerked around, looking intently into the shadowy corners of his room. He didn't see anything, but he closed the bathroom door anyway.

Undressed, he moved to stand in front of the big mirror that hung above the sink, and he looked at the destruction the mage's magical fire had wrought on his body. "Jesus," he hissed. He was still covered in soot, and he was rather happy for it—the parts of his body that weren't blackened by char looked like melted wax. Thick scars covered most of him, including his face. His head was bereft of hair and discolored pink flesh mixed with the scars that had formed over his dead, burned skin.

The puckered puncture wounds in his chest and stomach were mostly healed, thanks to his colossal vitality, but they still hurt when he poked at them. Briefly, he wondered if some of the mage's magical molten shards had broken off inside his torso. "Fuck me," he hissed again, then shaking his head and feeling like weeping, he took a deep breath and walked over to the shower. "Might as well get clean," he said, for some reason finding the sound of his voice comforting.

As he stood under the shower, Victor let out a long, shuddering sob and confronted the fact that he missed his *abuela*, missed his mom. "God, I miss you, Mom. Why'd you fucking die?" he said, for the first time in many years, voicing the source of much of his anger.

He knew his anger at his mom was irrational, but he knew it was there all the same. Facing it like that, when he was down at his lowest for a long while, Victor wondered if he was changing—if something in his mind had turned a corner and now he was willing to look at his irrational anger and the fears he held so deeply, so closely, that he had trouble voicing them even to himself. He stood there, shuddering with emotion for many minutes, letting the water of the shower wash over him, and when he dried off and crawled into his bed, he slept almost instantly.

Victor's body, his mind, and his spirit were exhausted, and he didn't stir, hardly moved other than his chest's slow rise and fall as he faded into a deep, dreamless sleep. When he cracked his eyes open, he saw sunlight coming through his window, and he couldn't have guessed if he'd only slept a few minutes or for a week. He stretched, instantly annoyed at how stiff his joints were and how his skin felt thick and taut over his bones.

"Awake?" Valla asked, startling him. He jerked his head toward the sound and saw her standing near a small wooden chair, perhaps having just stood when she saw him move.

"Yeah, uh, how long?"

"You slept a day. I had some luck, Victor." She approached his bed, and Victor, never really self-conscious before, quickly pulled his sheets up to his chin. For some reason, he felt embarrassed by his scars—as if they were his fault. Valla smiled as though to reassure him, and he felt further embarrassed that he'd suddenly earned her pity.

"Luck?" he asked, trying to bury the bullshit emotions that were making him feel crazy.

"Yes. I told Rellia I was seeking to buy some racial enhancement treasures." She paused and looked Victor in the eye. "I did not mention your troubles." He nodded, and she continued, "Rellia told me that house ap'Torux was having money troubles—they'd been auctioning some of their art and a few relics recently. I approached their estate and let them know what I wished to purchase, and they sold me two treasures they'd been saving for one of the family scions—a young man who'd recently proved to be something of a disappointment to the matriarch."

Valla produced an ornate little box that looked as if it was made from ivory and set it on the bed next to Victor. Then a dark, smoky jar appeared in her hand. It glittered like crystal in the light, but the contents seemed to swallow any light that penetrated the container. "The box has a cake made by a master Artisan from a distant world—according to the ap'Torux treasurer I spoke to, he was a Tier Seven craftsman and made this cake to help unlock bloodline secrets and advance racial ranks for the person that eats it."

"Uh, cool," Victor said, picking up the box, surprised by its heft.

"Don't open it yet! Light and air will reduce the cake's potency."

"Oh, okay." Victor left the box on his chest and let his hands fall back to the mattress. "And the other thing?"

"This is smoke from the lungs of a firedrake—a close relative to dragons."

"What does it do?"

"It's rumored that if you inhale it, wounds caused by fire will mend. The treasurer even told me that sometimes people develop resistance to flames from it."

"So dragons are a thing?" Victor asked. He wanted to be excited, wanted to take the jar and inhale its contents right away, but he didn't want to make himself vulnerable to a hope that sounded very much like horseshit to him.

"Yes, they're one of the elder races—present on their world and many others long before the System came along. They aren't on Fanwath, though, at least not anywhere where people have found them. This smoke would be very hard to acquire, Victor—drakes don't live on this world, either."

"Really? This sounds like a fairy tale to me, but fuck, I guess I've seen plenty of weirder shit since I've been here. You think this smoke will help me?"

"Yes!"

"Well, was the money I gave you enough?"

Valla's face took on a funny expression, and Victor couldn't figure out why at first, but then he realized she was debating whether to tell him the truth or not. "Well . . ."

"Come on, Valla."

"You owe me three thousand beads, and I've yet to buy you new armor."

"Fuck. Just a sec." Victor looked into his storage ring at the various stashes of beads he'd gathered from adventuring, selling loot, and Thayla's gambling. His impression was that he was down to his last ten thousand or so. He took out a bag that held roughly another five thousand and handed it to Valla.

"Some extra for the armor. Money well spent, Valla. Which one do you think I should use first?" He gestured to the box and bottle and raised a smooth, hairless eyebrow.

27

VISIONS

"I don't know, Victor," Valla replied, looking at the two treasures. "I'm sure the cake will help your body to heal—part of the process of improving your racial rank is the rebuilding and refining of your tissues. The biggest changes occur at new tiers, of course, but each rank will help. I think that cake is good for more than one, but the treasurer for ap'Torux wouldn't guarantee it." Valla paused and picked up the stoppered crystal bottle, staring into its weird, swirling gray contents.

"As for the bottle, the treasurer had a firsthand account that the smoke had been used by a royal family from . . . agh, I can't remember the name of the world. In any case, they used the smoke to make themselves more resistant to heat and to cure burns they suffered while trying to tame their drakes. Apparently, they used them as mounts."

"And the drakes are related to dragons?" Victor asked, reaching for the bottle. Valla nodded as she handed it to him. "Well, how do I take it? Just pop the cork and inhale?"

"The treasurer's notes indicated the smoke would dissipate quickly. You need to inhale as much as you can and hold it for as long as possible. The accounts made it sound like it would be painful—not just because, you know, it's smoke, but because it would burn your lungs before it worked its healing magic."

"You fucking serious?" The idea of suffering more burns—on purpose—seemed madness to Victor as he lay there in bed, covered with scars.

"Yes," Valla said, nodding curtly.

"I like that you don't sugarcoat things, Valla. Well, I'm going to cheat then," Victor said, and then he concentrated and cast Dauntless Radiance, bathing his bed in the red-gold glow of courage. He suddenly felt very much more capable, more sure, and he saw Valla's shoulders pull back and her spine straighten. She looked at him with new confidence and nodded.

"This shouldn't be a problem, Victor. You've done worse—had worse done to you."

"That's the spirit," Victor said, then he blew out all his air, emptying his prodigious lungs. When his breath trailed off to a soft wheeze, he lifted the crystal bottle to his chin and twisted the cork, breaking the wax seal. As he pulled the cork away, the gray smoke started immediately to drift out, and Victor began inhaling, siphoning the gray, magical smoke out of the bottle. His lungs were far more capacious than the bottle, and he soon drained the smoke away, pulling it deeper and packing air on top of it.

At first, Victor thought the treasurer had been mistaken because he didn't feel the urge to cough, and he didn't feel any discomfort. As he held his breath, though, he felt a warmness in his chest, then it rapidly ramped up to heat, then white-hot agony that spread through his lungs. He held his breath as long as possible, but when the pain was so blinding that he thought he was about to lose consciousness, he coughed it out.

Victor hacked and coughed, his eyes bulging and watering from the convulsions, but no smoke emerged from his lips. Worse, the burning hadn't subsided at all; in fact, it was spreading outward from his lungs, into his shoulders and stomach, and then into his limbs. Even his head felt as if it was burning. When the coughing stopped, Victor inhaled a massive lungful of air and then began to scream, vibrating in his bed as his body burned from the inside out. It felt as though someone had laced his bone marrow with thermite.

Vaguely, he was aware that Valla had run to the door, presumably to tell the guard to stand down—Victor couldn't concentrate on what was happening around him, but he imagined his screams were terrifying. He gripped his sheets, ripping them to shreds in his convulsions of agony. At some point, the pain became too much for his conscious mind, and Victor seemed to drift outside himself.

He watched his body writhe and thrash, and though he knew it was a trick of his mind, that he was probably seeing things through his own eyes, it seemed to him that he was floating above his body and that black smoke was erupting from his pores, making a cloud that obscured what he saw. After an eternity of agony, Victor felt the pain begin to fade where it first started, in his lungs.

He focused on that relief, sank his consciousness into that small, pain free part of his body, and it slowly spread. By the time it was just his arms and legs still alight with agony, Victor was calmed and lay back on his wet, ripped sheets. Valla had come back to his bedside and looked at him with concern, but Victor could also see relief in her eyes.

"It's working," she said.

"The pain is fading," Victor croaked, his voice a hoarse whisper.

"Your scars are largely gone, Victor."

*****Congratulations! You have gained a new feat: Flame Touched.*****

*****Flame Touched: By inhaling the final breath of a Firedrake, you've absorbed a part of its spirit. Your body is reborn in flame—while intense fire and heat can harm you, lesser flames will wash over your flesh with little effect, and you will heal more easily from such injuries.*****

"Oh, cool," Victor said, reading the message that appeared as the last burning pains faded away from his fingers and toes. He saw Valla's raised eyebrow and told her about his new boon.

"Even better than the ap'Torux treasurer thought," Valla said, leaning closer, peering at his shoulder. "What colors! Whoever created this tattoo was talented," she said.

"Oh shit, it's back? I thought my scarring would wreck it." Victor turned and saw his tattoo, the bladed claw surrounded by spears, and oddly, it looked bolder—more real than before. Maybe it was his relief at not seeing his arm covered with horrible scars playing tricks on him, but he thought the tattoo looked better than ever. After seeing his arm and shoulder, still crisscrossed with scars from blades and claws but with smooth, unblemished skin in between, he glanced down at the rest of himself.

"Did all the fire scars go away?" he asked, reaching up to feel at his head—it was still smooth and hairless, but he didn't feel the lumpy, thick scarring he'd had before.

"It seems so, Victor! You've still got plenty of others, though," Valla laughed, glancing over his body. Victor suddenly became very aware of his near-naked state—when he'd gotten into bed, he'd been in nothing but his underwear. He chuckled and folded his arms behind his head; Valla had already seen plenty, anyway.

"I owe you, Valla. That was a lucky find, and, well, you could have taken my money and bought something cheaper. I'm glad I can trust you."

"Ha. If I didn't trust your good intentions, I'd be offended. I'm a captain of the Imperial Legion. I'm a Tier Five Sword Dancer. You wouldn't besmirch my honor, would you?"

"No, hell no, Valla! I meant that as a compliment—sorry, but I trust easily, and I get burned a lot. It just feels good to know I've got another person who won't screw me over." She nodded and gave him a half smile, and Victor continued, "I gotta say, though, that treasurer guy wasn't right about everything—that was the worst fucking pain I've ever felt, and I've had some bad shit happen to me. Also, that wasn't just 'smoke from a drake's lungs;' it was the last breath of the drake and apparently held part of its spirit."

"Well, now you have a record of it. You could probably sell that information to some of the more wealthy houses."

"Same goes for you."

"I'll share it with Lady Rellia, but I won't try to profit from the knowledge; it's too hard to know what house might be aligned against ap'Yensha in the future."

Victor gave her another appraising look; at some point, she'd changed clothes to her usual uniform, and her hair and skin were perfectly coiffed and clean. She stood as if she was at attention, her hands clasped behind her back, and her pale green eyes looked lovely in the light from his Dauntless Radiance spell. Victor laughed inwardly. Was he falling for yet another pretty face? To bring himself back to reality, he said, "Rellia's lucky to have you. Your loyalty is admirable."

She nodded, smiling at the praise, then said, "How do you feel? Will you be able to eat the cake now?"

"Yeah, I think so. I feel all right, just a little wrung out. It's crazy, but when I think about the pain I just went through, it doesn't seem real—like my mind is already putting fog around it. I suppose I'll wake up sweating with nightmares about it, but right now, I feel okay."

"Good. Racial advancements often bring on sleep . . ."

"Yeah!" Victor interrupted, "I passed out for like ten days the last time."

"Ten days? That's a long one. I hope the cake won't put you out for that long, but if you do sleep, I'll purchase your armor and then put some pressure on Rellia's questioner—I assume you'd like to know more about the mage that burned you when you wake up."

"Yes! Hey, if I'm going to be out of it, I should ask: do you know anything about the guard Hine put in the hallway? Can we trust him?"

"Yes." Valla nodded firmly. "He's one of Hine's men from the Legion. He'll not betray you."

"All right, let's do this," Victor said, looking for the box that held the cake.

Valla held it out to him and said, "I picked it up when you began to thrash."

"Thanks," Victor said, taking it. For such a small box, it was quite heavy. He saw that the top lid was sealed with gold foil, so he summoned a sharp knife from his ring and dug the tip into the gold, running it along the seam between the lid and the bottom half. When he was done, he put the knife away and gently lifted the lid. The scent of cinnamon and sugar hit his nostrils and his mouth filled with saliva. "*Dios*! That smells good!"

He saw Valla move out of the corner of his eye, and Victor glanced at her. She'd taken a step back and gripped her hands in tight fists. "You all right?"

"Hurry and eat it, Victor! It smells too good!"

"Right," Victor said. He knew what she meant—every bone in his body was screaming at him to eat that cake. He picked it up, dense like an over-moist poundcake, and took a bite. The flavors that overwhelmed his taste-buds were too many to comprehend. His nose told him there was cinnamon, honey, and some other cloying scent for which he didn't know the name. The cake, while dense, dissolved in his mouth and seemed to flood his blood vessels with a warmth that spread from his mouth into his entire body.

"Ungh," he managed, stuffing the rest of the cake into his mouth. Then, as the potent alchemical and magical mixture flooded his pathways and the heat rose into his brain, he felt himself falling back into his bed. Instead of hitting the pillow, though, he fell through it and sank to the center of the world. He felt as if he were descending at a million miles per hour, and the world's depths shot by in a blur—caverns, magma, strange creatures in their multitudes, different layers of rocks and soil, then he was sinking through space, Fanwath rapidly shrinking and disappearing as he fell.

Planets and stars shot by in a haze, and as Victor began to lose his grip on reality and a long ululating scream rose from his throat, he closed his eyes. An instant later, he felt his feet standing on solid ground, and he opened them to see he was standing on damp grass in a clearing surrounded by a dense, hot jungle. A rocky slope rose before him, and a path littered with white, humanoid bones led up the hill to a dark cave mouth.

Victor, no, Tenecoalt, gripped his macuahuitl in a sweaty grip. He looked down at himself and saw his bone breastplate carved from the thousand-toothed lizard, his wyrm-hide pants, and his feathered boots. He was ready! He was Tenecoalt! He was Quinametzin, and anything that threatened his lands must be crushed! He lifted his throat to the sun and howled again, his ululation echoing off the rocks and trees, sending birds in the hundreds squawking and flapping into the orange-tinted sky.

He lifted his macuahuitl and leapt up the slope to the cave. When he stepped into the stinking, evil darkness, Tenecoalt urged his ancestor's spirits to brighten the shadows. Suddenly shapes took form in his yellow-limned magical sight—boulders, bones, skins, horns, and there, in the back, hunched over its latest meal, a small man from the southern jungle, was the feathered bear. It grunted and crunched a bone, dark marrow dripping over the mutilated corpse.

The feathered bear was big, heavier than a Quinametzin, but Tenecoalt didn't care—his ancestors would strengthen him. He roared his challenge, and when the monster turned to regard him, baleful red eyes glaring down its long, tooth-lined snout, it barked a coughing growl in response, and then the fight was on.

The monster charged out of the cave, long spear-like claws ripping over the stones in a clatter, horrible teeth gnashing in a fury, and feathered mane and tails streaming behind it. It smashed into Tenecoalt, and the two rolled in a furious melee down the rocky slope leaving a trail of blood and feathers to glisten in the fading orange sunlight. Tenecoalt gripped the bear's mane, holding onto it while he employed his jagged macuahuitl to horrible effect, smashing the heavy stone-wood weapon into the monster's snout, limbs, and neck.

They rolled in a frenzy, and when the feathered bear crunched its enormous fangs into Tenecoalt's shoulder, breaking flesh and bone and piercing organs, it only further agitated the giant warrior. His eyes turned red, and the fury of his ancestors entered him, filling him with their strength and pride. Tenecoalt drove a thick, hard-nailed thumb into the bear's eye, and with the power of a true titan, he pulled its enormous skull away from his shoulder, its teeth popping free with wet, bloody suction.

Tenecoalt stood, holding the great bear at arm's length while it thrashed in agony, and then he finished the battle with a series of terrible, hacking blows of his macuahuitl. The first few strikes pulverized the feathered fur and flesh of the bear's chest. The next shattered bones, and the final strike resounded into the bear's heart, bursting it with the terrible concussion.

Tenecoalt threw the bear to the stony ground and punched his mighty fist into its shattered chest, pulling forth part of its torn, steaming heart. He bit into the bloody meat, and as he felt the bear's strength flooding into him, he lifted his head and roared with new vigor and potency. He gave thanks to his ancestors, and he gave thanks to his enemies because each of them had made him stronger with their deaths.

When Victor woke, it was dark in his room, and though he was snug under a heavy blanket, he could feel the chill in the air. He glanced around the shadowy periphery, saw moonlight coming through the window, and found that he was alone. He felt tired, though good, and the vision he'd had of his ancestor, if that's what Tenecoalt was, loomed vividly in his mind. Like his other bloodline vision, he knew it was different from a dream or a fantasy—it felt like a memory that had been hidden but was now unlocked.

When Victor thought back to the way Tenecoalt had torn the heart from the bear and eaten, he didn't feel any revulsion—it was as if he understood Tenecoalt's motivations, and that understanding extended to his beliefs and the undeniable effects of the practice on his strength. Tenecoalt had grown powerful, eating the hearts of his strongest enemies. "Fucking weird," Victor said, his voice rumbling into the dark room.

He held up his hand in the dim light, flexing his powerful fingers and noting how the muscles on his forearm bunched with the gesture. He looked down at his feet, saw that he still fit on the bed, and sighed a breath of relief—he hadn't turned into a giant. He saw something glimmering from the corner of his eye and glanced at his shoulder. There, glinting in the darkness, was the tattoo Chandri had given him. The sun was gleaming with faint yellow light, and the spears seemed to reflect the light on their silvery tips. "Even fucking weirder . . ."

With a grunt, he stood up and stepped onto the cold wooden floorboards. He felt terrific, if he were being honest. All his aches and pains were gone, and the sore, stiff spots where thick scars had formed over deep wounds were dim memories. He padded into the bathroom, and when he turned on the Energy lamp, he had to squint against the glare until his eyes adjusted. As he blinked away the spots in his vision, he looked into the mirror and was happy to see that not a whole lot had changed.

The first thing that brought a smile to his face was the quarter inch of dense black hair that covered his scalp. He saw he still had four thin white scars that crossed half his face where the bear had clawed him, though they were much subtler than before. His other scars were similarly faded, even the thick ones where he'd been impaled or nearly eviscerated. Victor reached down to the sink to splash some water on his face, and that's when he realized he'd grown again. The sink was definitely more of a reach than before, though only slightly.

Victor saw Gorz on the counter where he'd thrown off most of his ruined clothes, and he picked the amulet up, slipping it around his neck. "Gorz?"

"Victor? I was growing worried about you."

"I got hurt pretty badly, but I'm good now. You doing okay?"

"I am, thank you."

"Hey, can you measure me? Based on the dimension of this room? You can do that, right?"

"You are two point one six meters tall, Victor."

"That's . . ." Victor concentrated and did the math far more quickly than he would have done back on Earth. "Around seven-one? *Chingado*!" He patted the amulet and said, "Thanks, buddy. By the way, we're in a city again. I'll buy some books before I leave again, all right?"

"Yes! Some maps, too, please! Could you not find an Artificer and ask for a slate—something I could interface with? I'm sure it can be crafted because Reevus had one."

"Yeah, I'll look into it, Gorz. I know you told me that before, and I dropped the ball. I'm going to make it a priority." Victor dug around in his ring and found his watch. "Four in the morning. Not bad." Just then, he remembered to look at his status sheet to see what exactly the cake had done.

Name:	**Victor Sandoval**
Race:	**Human (Quinametzin Bloodline): Improved 4**
Class:	**Spirit Carver: Epic**
Level:	**33**

"Not bad! Three ranks from that cake." More than that, though, he felt that he understood his bloodline more, and as the minutes ticked by, putting him further and further from his vision, he began to worry about the implications. "Do I really want to try eating my enemies' hearts?" Truthfully, he figured it wouldn't be much of a stretch from his usual behavior if he were berserk.

Victor didn't know how long he'd slept, but he could smell himself standing there, so he took a shower before getting dressed. When he went into the main room again, the light from the bathroom spilling out behind him, he saw a package on the chair where Valla had been sitting before. He walked over and realized it was a neatly folded, faintly glimmering chainmail shirt.

When he picked it up and turned toward the bathroom light, he saw that the chain links shimmered between green and brass. He walked back into the bathroom and pulled it over his head, but got stuck there, the opening too narrow to go over his shoulders. Holding a finger to the shirt, he trickled forth some Energy, and a message appeared in his vision as the shirt expanded to the point where he could pull it on.

*****Shimmersteel Chainmail Shirt. Smelted and crafted by the great mage Artisan Zefin-dak—a fine armored shirt benefiting from the peerless self-repairing properties of shimmersteel. This shirt will resist sharp attacks, repair itself rapidly, and stretch or shrink to fit a wide range of people.*****

"Zefin-dak, huh?" Victor smoothed the chainmail out, noticing that it only covered the tops of his arms like his old ringmail armor. He didn't mind much—he sort of liked having his arms free, especially when he wore his armor almost all the time. He picked up his belt, happy to see that it had repaired itself from the scorching it had suffered, and put it on over the chainmail, then he looked in the mirror. "Damn, that's pretty."

The shimmersteel one moment looked yellow-green, but if he moved, it shimmered toward a more brassy color. "I guess that's why it's called shimmersteel." He liked the cut of it, and the comfort was undeniable—he resolved to compliment Valla on her choice when he next saw her.

Victor returned to the bedroom and turned on the Energy lamp, scanning the room. He knew he'd had Lifedrinker with him when he lay in the bed, but he didn't see her right away. A slight twinge of worry ignited in his chest, but then he saw her handle sticking up next to the nightstand.

"Valla must have moved you when I was going bonkers, huh?" he said as he picked the axe up. He took a few minutes to cut some strips of leather from a piece of hide in his ring, then he twisted them into a braided loop that he attached to his belt. He slipped Lifedrinker into the loop and nodded in satisfaction. He figured that would work until he replaced the metal ring he'd lost in the barn fire.

When he checked his watch, he saw it was almost five thirty, so he stepped out into the hallway. He saw a different guard sitting on his stool by the stairway and waved. The guard, peering through the same strange goggles, waved back. Victor shrugged and tapped gently on Valla's door. Rapid footsteps signaled her approach, then Valla opened the door, her sword held back and to her side, blade down. "Victor?"

"Yeah," he said, smiling.

"You're looking a lot better!" She pulled the door wide, and Victor saw that she'd been awake—her fireplace was lit, her lamps were on, and stacks of paper covered the little table in her room.

"How long was I out?"

"Only three days."

"Well, I feel pretty damn great. Thanks for the armor, by the way!" He held his arms up to display the scaled shirt he wore.

"You're welcome. I have some beads for you—the shirt was only five hundred." She motioned for him to come through the doorway, which he did, though he had to duck, then she shut the door. "You didn't change much, though your scars are further faded, and you seem more . . . robust."

"Robust?"

"Yes. Your aura is stronger. People will feel you enter a room. Well, that already happened, but it's . . . more profound now. Did anything else happen? The cake was supposed to uncover bloodline traits . . ."

"Yeah, I had another vision. Did I ever tell you about my bloodline vision? It's kinda crazy shit. I'll, um, I'll go over it with you, but first, have you learned anything from the wizard we captured?"

"Yes, Victor. As you would say, there's a lot of shit for us to go over." Valla smiled wryly and gestured to the table, indicating that he should take a seat.

28

IN THE HARSH LIGHT

Victor sat at Valla's table, watching as the woman carefully piled her documents and books into neat stacks and then took a seat across from him. "A lot to go over, huh?"

"Yes," she said, nodding, "Rellia's questioner had quite a time with the watcher we captured. Trayzil's mental attacks didn't work at first—the mage had a will that was nearly a match for him. Of course, that didn't matter much after the proper soporifics were applied. An alchemist able to concoct tailor-made mixtures makes such work endlessly more palatable—no fingers were removed or eyes poked out with hot irons . . ."

"What the fuck, Valla? I mean, I know the guy wasn't going to a spa, but . . . why bring that stuff up if your guy didn't even use it?"

"Oh, I'm sorry, Victor. When I think of questioning people, I'm often reminded of my time in the Legion, and it heartens me to know Lady Rellia doesn't generally have to go to the lengths some of the field captains would to get answers."

"Okay," Victor said, cracking his neck. "What did you find out?" he prompted after Valla sat quietly for a minute.

"Right. Well, we learned that the Pyromancer is not from Fanwath. He's an off-world powerhouse that was hired by a wealthy, influential man by the name of ap'Gravin. He's well known and almost universally loathed and feared in equal parts. He's seen as sort of the emperor regent for the western cities, though he'd never claim such a title—not if he wanted to keep his head."

"So that's my enemy?"

"No, not exactly," Valla said, holding up a finger.

"But the asshole that burned me works for him?"

"No; he did work for him, yes, but no longer. Yes, he was contracted, for other work, at great expense by ap'Gravin, but that work was done months and months ago. The Pyromancer, Boaegh, apparently took a liking to Persi Gables and has chosen to linger here on his own accord, though it seems he's taken up work with a lesser noble. This name might interest you: Lord ap'Horrin."

"Are you fucking serious? That's the asshole that broke my Core and sent me to the mines!" Victor's knuckles cracked as he involuntarily clenched his fists.

"Yes, I knew that from Rellia's research into your origins."

"So, how does a little creep like that afford a mage like, what was it? Boge?"

"Exactly the right question! His name is Boaegh, but you were close enough," Valla said, waving a hand as she continued. "The mage we questioned claimed that Boaegh is working out of ap'Horrin's estate but insisted that he calls no man master."

"So it's just a coincidence that the dick who almost killed me is working with the other dick who almost killed me? What about the guys who summoned me?"

Valla looked at him quizzically for a minute, opened her mouth a few times, but shook her head and said, "We think Boaegh is largely responsible for the summonings that took place in that barn. We think he's still doing it, but he originally did it as part of his contract with ap'Gravin. There are still many questions left to answer regarding that series of events."

"So, what's the move? You mind pointing me toward that dude's estate? I think it's long past time I gave him a visit."

"Victor," Valla started, and Victor could see she was struggling with her choice of words. Finally, she started again. "Victor, did you learn nothing from our encounter a few days ago?"

"I . . ." Victor was stumped. She had a damn good point. When he'd rushed off into the woods, hoping to confront the cabal of wizards that had summoned him, he'd expected to waltz in, maybe go berserk, and beat the shit out of them all. He'd had a vague plan in his mind to smash first and figure out the answers afterward.

He'd gotten some answers, but he'd also lost the main bad guy because he hadn't done any research—hadn't had any kind of clue that he might be able to escape the way he did. "Plus, I almost died," he finished aloud, and Valla continued to stare at him.

"Yeah, I learned something. So, I need to do what? Spy on the estate for a while?"

"I've put that process in motion for you," Valla said with a smile. "I have many connections here in Persi Gables, and I've sent some people for intelligence gathering. People far more capable of going unseen than you, Victor," she said, holding out a hand placatingly as Victor took a deep breath, forestalling his objections.

"So, how long?" Victor asked, getting to the point of his concerns.

"Not long. A day or three. My people have already been working on getting agents in place for two days."

"Hmm, and me?"

"I think you should stay in the inn. As far as Boaegh knows, you're disfigured, near death, or dead." Valla drummed her fingers on the table, watching Victor's face, then she said, "Is there some cultivating you can do? Do you need me to buy you any ingredients? I'm not sure how spirit Cores work."

"Well," Victor sighed and then nodded. "I've been putting something off for a while, and I think I need to go work on it. Give me until noon or so, then come check on me—I might have a list of things I need you to buy." He stood up, his chair scraping noisily over the wooden floor, and then he pushed it back under the table.

"I will do so. In your room?"

"Yeah. Thanks, Valla," Victor said, turning to let himself out of her room. He felt a little guilty, roping her into his problems the way he had, but it seemed as if she was sort of enjoying it. "Not to mention, she works for Rellia—I'm sure she's getting a bonus for staying so close to me." He stepped into his room and locked the door behind himself.

He pushed his little table away toward the wall, clearing more space on the floor at the foot of his bed, then he sat down, summoning the weave pattern out of his ring that Oynalla had made him copy while spirit walking. It was a complicated pattern—a twist of all three of his affinities, and the whorls, loops, and knots they made were hard to make sense of at first glance.

Luckily, while Victor hadn't tried the pattern yet, he'd spent quite a few hours studying the design and committing parts of it to memory while they'd traveled. "All right, let's do this right," he said, then he took out a fresh sheet of parchment and three differently colored inks that he could use with his magical quill. He was determined to learn the weave perfectly, by hand, before he tried to build it in his pathways.

Hours ticked by while he worked. He drew the different lines one at a time at first—red ink for rage, black ink for fear, and blue ink for inspiration. When he'd made the entire weave five times, he started to complete sections of it from memory without looking at his original or copies for hints.

This activity really drove home to him how much he'd changed since coming to Fanwath. He knew he was different, of course; many of the changes were impossible not to see—his height, his muscle mass, the way his face and voice had matured beyond his years, thanks to his Quinametzin bloodline, no doubt. Still, he felt like the same old Victor inside, in his heart. When he got the complicated Energy weave almost entirely right on his first try, he knew it had to do with his mental attributes.

It had taken him longer to learn to multiply by fives than it had for him to memorize this thing that looked like something da Vinci might sketch while high on mushrooms. He pulled his watch out of his ring and looked at the time—he still had an hour before noon. "Well, time to stop stalling, I guess."

Victor set the pattern in front of himself on the floor and performed a few stretches, working the kinks out of his back and neck. Then he assumed the lotus position and turned his mind inward, looking at his Core and the three swirling, pulsating orbs of Energy within. He felt as if his dark, purple-black orb of fear was in constant battle with the white-gold of his inspiration, and yet they both seemed to shrink away from the baleful, pulsing red of his rage. "None of you guys is the boss, but if I had to pick one, I suppose it would be inspiration."

With that thought in mind, he decided to build the foundation of his weave with inspiration, twisting the other two Energies around it. He wanted to ensure that the Energy he finished with had the right tone and connotation. He thought of it like rage—it could either be the full-throated, partially beneficial rage that he cast on himself, or it could be twisted to only create a mad lust for violence. He knew that this new Energy he was about to form in his pathways could have more than one tone, and he wanted it to have a positive base.

That done, Victor held the convoluted pattern of inspiration-attuned Energy firmly in place in his large, central pathway, and he pulled forth a thread of fear. It tried to surge and work its way loose from his grip so that it could push into the pathway and wrap tightly around the inspiration thread, but Victor clamped down with his will, grinning at his mastery over the writhing, lashing Energy. With the delicate touch of a watchmaker, Victor carefully wound the thread here and there, on the pattern, purposefully leaving large swathes of inspiration Energy free from the touch of the fear.

When he'd worked through all the parts of the main pattern and still had a long dangling strand of fear-attuned Energy waiting for his direction, Victor clamped it in place and pulled forth his third strand, a burning, scorching, baleful ribbon of rage. He froze his other two threads in place, smashing them into submission with his will so that he could concentrate on the rage. He worked it in and around the other two threads, keeping a light touch where it came to the inspiration Energy, but a heavier, balancing double-weave around parts of the fear-infused section of the tapestry.

He knew, from his conversations with Oynalla, that she had an idea of what kind of Energy he might be weaving. She'd hoped he'd find justice with only fear and rage but had seen the mistake in that—justice was an Energy with many facets, and a large part of it was positive. Her initial plan had lacked the crucial component of inspiration. With a base of inspiration, pulling forth the positive aspects of fear and rage, Victor thought—and felt—that something was going right.

He could feel how the rage was being focused into a righteous fury, and he could sense how the fear was being twisted into guilt and a dread of repercussions. The overall tone of the pattern, though, was one of virtue, of wrongs made right. When he finished up his weaving of the rage thread and twisted it off with the remainder of the fear strand, he looped them both back to the thick, heavy trunk of inspiration that he'd woven at the start.

The entire construct pulsed in his pathways, the three colors of Energy melding together into a dark, smoky black, and then the shadows fell from it, and nothing but a solid, blazing white fire remained, bright and harsh. Victor could feel its righteous desire to burn the guilty, and he surprised himself by flinching back from his own Energy. He gritted his teeth, though, and while he had the power primed in his pathways, he chose a spell to cast: Globe of Insight.

He formed the spell pattern in his pathway, instantly pushing the weave of justice-attuned Energy into it. Suddenly his room was bathed with a sourceless white, glaring light, and not a single shadow could survive its presence—every crack in the plaster, every gap in the floorboards, every mite, every mote of dust—all were exposed in its glare. Deep in his soul, Victor knew that if someone he deemed guilty, someone he felt deserved to feel the weight of justice, were in that room, they'd feel that glare in a most uncomfortable way.

*****Congratulations! You've learned the spell: Harsh Light of Justice, Improved.*****

*****Harsh Light of Justice, Improved: You create an area around your person illuminated by the light of justice-attuned Energy. This light will reflect the morality of the caster, damning or blessing those within the light based on that perception. Those deemed unworthy will suffer a constant leeching effect on their Energy and find their movements slow and cumbersome. Those receiving a blessing will instead find themselves invigorated, encouraged, and driven to deliver swift judgment to their enemies. Energy cost variable based on the intended area of effect: minimum 150. Cooldown: minimal.*****

As Victor read the System message, a slow grin spread on his face, and he stood up to whoop and punch his fist into his hand. He was getting ready to go find Valla, excited to share his news, when golden motes of Energy gathered in his room and streamed into him. "Fuck yes!" he howled, feeling the surge of power and well-being that always accompanied such things. He didn't gain a level, but he felt he might be getting close—it was similar to the sensation he got when his Core was getting ready to bump up a rank, almost like a sense of fullness.

"Awesome! Gorz, why do you think I just learned a spell at the improved rank?"

"You did, Victor? Congratulations! It could be that you managed to make the pattern in a way that automatically elevated the spell. You began at a point far beyond basic because of that."

"Hell, yes! I knew that weave was feeling good," Victor said, and then spent a few minutes describing what he'd done. Gorz, unable to truly show emotion, did his best to act impressed.

When the euphoria of his success began to pass and he could concentrate again, Victor contemplated something he'd been avoiding—he'd never cast Berserk with fear-attuned Energy to find out what it did. He only forced himself to think about it now because he was tempted to try it with his justice-attuned weave of Energy. When he'd made his courage weave, he'd been excited to test it, to see what kind of spell it would make, and he'd come away with a potent spell—Heroic Heart.

Still, he was hesitant. Berserk was no joke of a spell, and, yeah, it might be harmless to test with ostensibly benign Energies like inspiration or courage, but fear was negative and dangerous. What if it affected him in a way similar to rage? He might hurt someone. Even justice gave him pause—twisted into that pattern of righteousness were threads of fury and guilt. What if he went mad, delivering "justice" to anyone he thought wasn't perfect?

He was still struggling with the decision when a knock sounded at his door, and he sighed with relief, welcoming the distraction. He found Valla standing in the hallway, and she raised an eyebrow and said, "You found a new spell? The Energy is thick in the air. It has a different feel."

"Yes, I've been working on weaving some of my attunements into a new affinity." Victor shrugged, and Valla opened her eyes wider.

"Perhaps you can give me some pointers. I've yet to create a meta-element with my affinities."

"Well, you know it requires an effort of will, and . . . yeah, I can't teach that."

"Still. I'd be curious to see your weaves." Valla started to move forward, and Victor realized he was blocking the door. He backed up and motioned her through.

"There," he said, pointing, "on the floor. The weave I just made." He leaned a shoulder against the doorframe, watching her and trying to think of his next move. Valla stepped over to his pattern and picked up the page, densely packed with three different colors of ink.

"This is . . . complex." She shook her head and turned the page sideways and then upside down. "How long did you work on this?"

"Remember that last time I went for a spirit walk?" She nodded, and he continued, "I met with Oynalla, and we made that pattern together—she'd already had a good chunk of it done. I started studying it after that, an hour here and there."

"Truly? And you could form this in your pathway? All these bends and curls? These twists of different Energy?"

"Yeah, I'm telling you—it's all about the will."

"May I ask your will attribute's level?" she asked, very uncharacteristically. He could tell she was feeling frustrated, maybe even angry.

"Well, between you and me, it's up to two eighty-seven."

"Nearly three hundred?" She stared at him with open shock. "I'm sorry I asked," she huffed and slapped his spell weave down on the table, yanking a chair back to sit down and glowering toward a blank spot on the wall a bit left of Victor's shoulder.

"Hey," Victor said, moving over to the table and pulling out a chair. He sat down in front of her and said, "Don't kill the messenger, all right? I lucked out, I guess—my classes up to now have had automatic will gains, and I've also had free points to distribute, and I've dumped a lot into the stat. On another note, you can kick my ass with a sword, and you're faster than I am!"

That got a small smile out of her, and she sighed, "I'm just frustrated. Rellia paid an Elementalist at the academy a lot of money for a weave of air and iron. He divulged a 'secret' to her; I'll never be able to weave the two because they cancel each other out. Iron is a type of earth affinity, and apparently it's anathema to air. I have to either gain another affinity, somehow, that I can use to mix with the other two, or I'll be limited to what I can do with these two affinities separately."

"One, that mage might be full of shit, and two, there's gotta be a way to gain new affinities, right?"

"Oh, there are ways. Impossibly expensive treasures can be found at exclusive auctions. Awards from the System can be found on the older worlds or in high-tier dungeons that might offer a solution." She paused and looked at Victor, narrowing her eyes. "Alternatively, I could be born with an absurdly powerful Core that seems able to split into new affinities at a whim."

She laughed and shook her head when she saw him open his mouth, then close it again, struggling with how to respond. "I know, I know. Nothing you do is easy. Anyway, it's a problem for another day, I suppose." She sighed heavily and visibly forced a smile. "Did you think of a shopping list for me?"

"No. I have another problem that I need your help with."

"Another one?"

"Hey!" Victor laughed. "Okay, I deserve that. This one's a good problem, though. I need to try out a couple of new spells that might be very dangerous for the people around me. Can we go somewhere . . . safe for that?"

"Well, I'd hoped we could avoid people seeing you out and about. Let me get a cloak from Hine—something to hide your face and . . . coloring. We can go to Rellia's estate." She held up a hand and added, "Just her grounds—we won't go inside. She has a lovely grove of plum trees that should be perfect; no one's working them this time of year."

"Plums? I'm so happy to hear another word I recognize! They must be a lot like the ones on my world, or the System wouldn't have used my word. I mean, that's how it worked with pork, I think."

"Sure." Valla shrugged. Then she stood up, and the two of them walked down to the common room, where Valla asked Hine to call them a coach and pestered him for a cloak. The sergeant ended up giving Victor an old Legion rain cloak. It was dark brown leather and oiled very heavily. It covered most of Victor's torso, being large enough to fit over a legionnaire's pack, and he could pull the hood far enough forward to obscure his face in shadow.

Thus concealed, he and Valla stepped outside to get into the coach, and twenty minutes later, they were riding onto the smooth cobbled stones of the noble district of Persi Gables. Large manors lined the boulevard with high stone walls and extensive gardens. The enormous estates within the city walls really drove home to Victor just how large the city-state was. "Quite a lot different from the other districts," Victor said, looking around at the clean sidewalks, the smooth cobbles, and the light foot traffic.

"Oh, yes. The difference between old consolidated power and wealth and the rest of the people in the world. When there're ten or even a hundred natural treasures discovered every year, who do you think gets them? The upstart adventurers or one of the houses filled with old monsters?"

"You talking about things like I used a few days ago? The smoke and the cake?"

"Well, the smoke was a natural treasure, yes. The cake was crafted, but I'm sure the ingredients included rare natural resources. I was talking more about things found in this world, though. Even if someone from a lower family found a hunk of amber ore or an advancement fruit, do you think they'd use it, making them a stronger force for their family, or do you think they'd sell it, using the money to feed and house their family for years?"

"I guess it depends," Victor shrugged.

"Yes. I suppose so." Valla didn't smile or frown, and Victor thought maybe she thought he didn't get what she was talking about.

"I know what you mean, okay? It's like that on Earth, too. I mean my homeworld. Families born with money tend to keep it and make more of it. Some of us feel like we're doing okay because they like us to think that. We can watch vids and VR, get plenty to eat, and even get to earn an education that's supposed to help us better our station. I guess it does for some people, but for most of us, we just keep walking in the same rut."

Valla nodded, and Victor frowned and said, "Life's not fair, I guess. I don't know what I would have made of myself back on my homeworld, but I didn't have an easy shake at things here, either. I've been caged, chained, beaten, burned, lost, chopped up, fucking thrown into pits and deep bottomless trenches. I've had ghouls bite the shit out of me, wrestled with deep hulks, and I've been betrayed, robbed, and lied to more times than I can count. I know I have a strong Core, but I didn't come into this world any tougher than that little kid out there." Victor pointed to a boy holding a string that trailed a colorful, long-tailed kite.

"So, your argument for all the people who don't get a fair shot at things is to . . . what? Try harder?" Valla snorted.

"Heh." Victor couldn't help laughing at her simplification of his outburst. "Maybe. No. Fuck, I don't know. Pretty much the only thing I do know is that I don't know how to fix things, but I *want* to. Hell, I'm just a dumb Berserker, anyway, right?" He winked at her, and she barked a short laugh as the coach came to a halt.

"We're at the lady's grove, ma'am," the coachman called back, and Victor popped the door open for Valla, then followed her outside.

The air was brisk, and the trees that stretched out in neat rows away from the street were bare and leafless. Thick layers of leaves covered the ground, and Victor's breath plumed forth while he rubbed his hands together briskly. He looked into the grove, saw that it encompassed nearly an acre, and nodded. "This'll do. You'll wait with the coach? If something terrible happens, have him take off."

"You think something terrible might happen?"

"Well, I didn't make you bring me out here for nothing. I'm about to employ some rather scary affinities in my most powerful spell. Here's hoping I'm just being paranoid." Victor shrugged and started trudging through the damp, thick leaves, hooded like an executioner, his long bearded axe clutched in one hand, resting on his shoulder.

29

SPELLS AND CONSEQUENCES

Victor stood in the middle of the grove and slowly turned around in a circle. He could see a wall with a gate at one edge of the tree rows, and he figured that led into Rellia's estate. A steep slope and a higher wall with wrought iron spikes along the top bordered another edge, and streets meeting in a corner formed the rest of the boundary.

As he finished his circle, his eyes came to rest on the little black coach, its pair of roladii, and the coachman sitting on the bench. Valla stood to the side, wrapped in her cloak, breath pluming out as she peered back into the gloomy orchard toward Victor. She was only about a hundred feet from him, and he suddenly wished the grove was more extensive. Traffic on the streets was very light, and when Victor considered it was only noon, he tried to think of what day of the week it was. Shaking his head, he realized he had no idea.

"Maybe it's like Sunday or something. Do they go to church in this world?" The absurdity of his lack of knowledge suddenly hit him, and he chuckled. Had he really been so busy that he didn't know about a thing like that? He remembered the pocket realm where Belikot and the Naghelli lived—there had been a kind of Ghelli church there. Did they meet on Sundays, though? Victor had no idea. "Do they even have cemeteries here?" he wondered aloud as he considered the way Shadeni and Ardeni seemed to worship their ancestors.

Stamping his feet and rubbing his hands together, he chastised himself for letting his mind wander so—was he stalling? "All right, which one first?"

he asked Lifedrinker, tilting the handle on his shoulder, so her cool metal rested against his cheek. Her haft was warm where his fingers rested against it, and Victor felt immeasurably comforted knowing she was with him. He'd sort of hoped she'd have something to say, but her silence was enough of a statement—this was something he could handle.

"Fair enough, *mi cielo*," he said, slipping her into the loop at his belt. His use of the endearment surprised him—it was something his mom used to call him, and he hadn't thought of it in many years. It felt good to say it, though, and he took a deep, cleansing breath of the cold air, staring up at the gray sky for a minute, allowing his thoughts to drift back in time. When had she last called him that? He couldn't remember, but he could picture her standing in the kitchen, next to their little table, watching him try to do some kind of artwork. He couldn't for the life of him remember what it had been.

Victor rubbed his hands briskly, trying to get his head back into the moment, then he closed his eyes and started building his weave for justice-attuned Energy. He felt less apprehensive about that Energy, knowing he'd weighed the inspiration against the fear and rage, knowing it was an Energy that was all about balance. When he finished the pattern, he focused his will against his Core, holding the Energy within, and cast Berserk, feeding the spell with the weave of justice-attuned Energy.

As the spell hungrily devoured his prepared Energy, Victor released his hold on his Core and allowed the pattern to pull from his three affinities as needed to complete its creation. He felt a profound calm come over him, his sensations faded to dull background noise, and even his vision changed. At first, he didn't notice it because his eyes were aimed at the sky, at the dark gray clouds and the barren grayish-brown branches, but when he started to feel the disconnect from his other senses, he lowered his gaze and saw that the entire world was washed in grays, whites, and blacks. There was no color.

He felt dispassionate as he looked around. Though something else had changed—he didn't feel confused or lost. He didn't feel love or hate. His affections for Chandri, Thayla, Deyni, and even Lifedrinker were dull, distant things. He wanted to be alarmed but couldn't find the requisite emotions within himself—alarm was out of reach. He looked at his colorless pale hands, flexed his fingers, and felt the strength within. He was capable, and there was work to be done.

"Yes," he growled, narrowing his eyes and looking around. He had work to do. There were those out there who required justice, and it was his job, his duty, to find them. His mind drifted to the most pressing, most recent offender, and he pictured the gray-robed mage: the Pyromancer, Boaegh. Suddenly, in the sea of gray, colorless, emotionless existence, Victor felt a heat, a pull, and he whirled toward the street that ran perpendicular to the one where Valla stood with the coach.

Before he knew what he was doing, Victor began stalking toward that street. He could feel the pull of injustice. He could feel the heat of his quarry and knew it was his duty to bring him to heel. Something built up in his chest, no, not his chest, his Core, and as the strange pressure mounted and began to grow uncomfortable, Victor released it, and though he was still fifty paces from the street, his next footfall was on cobblestones. He nodded and kept marching toward the pull of the fugitive, the target of his justice.

As he continued down the road, Victor was dimly aware of the people he passed and how they looked at him and hurried out of his path. They were of no consequence, however; only his quarry mattered. He could feel the pressure building in his Core, and as it rose to a crescendo, roiling and bubbling, begging for release, he held onto it. This was his power—he was not at its mercy.

He could feel his target as he came to a narrow street that ran along the city wall and could feel the pull of it, no longer directly in front of him. The wall was in his way. He looked left and right and saw guard stations and stairs leading to battlements but no nearby gates. Victor faced the heat of his prey, stepped toward it, and released the surging, pressing Energy at his Core. His next footfall was upon grass and twigs, the wall no longer obscuring his path.

Victor dispassionately looked over his shoulder to see the city wall rising high behind him, its cold shadow falling over the cleared fields separating Persi Gables from the surrounding woods. He nodded and turned, facing the heat of his quarry, and began striding toward the forest, the roiling pressure starting to build in his gut once again.

Something stirred in the corner of his mind, and Victor allowed himself to see what it was—a thought! Should he be hunting this prey just now? Should he be delivering justice, or was it the wrong time for such action? As those thoughts infiltrated his single-minded pursuit, they were like cracks in a dam, holding back a flood of other ideas. What about Valla? Wasn't he supposed to wait for her intelligence gatherers? What if the mage was ready for him? Shouldn't he develop a plan?

Even as the dam began to burst, Victor's gut began to roil with pent-up Energy, and he released it. One second he was stepping down onto stiff, frigid grass, and the next he was striding among the shadows of thick, dense woods. His quarry was there, ever closer with each of his steps, the heat and wrongness of it drawing him. He was meant to extinguish that baleful presence!

"Stop." Victor looked around, wondering from whence the word had come. He took another step, and the voice came again; this time, he realized the voice was his. "Stop," Victor said again, and his body obeyed. Though his leg muscles screamed for release, urged him to keep moving toward the target of his justice, he held still.

With several deep breaths, Victor reasserted his will and saw the colors start to bleed back into his surroundings. He felt the chill in the air again, and he allowed his emotions to surge back into existence, starting with relief—he'd almost lost himself to the hunt, but he'd managed to gain control before he did anything stupid.

Before he could think of his next move, he saw that System messages were waiting for his attention, and he looked at them:

*****Congratulations! You have learned the spell: The Inevitable Huntsman, Improved.*****

*****The Inevitable Huntsman, Improved. Prerequisite: affinity for or ability to manifest justice-attuned Energy. When the form of the Inevitable Huntsman is assumed, the caster will gain a singular, dispassionate focus on a target. As mastery of this spell progresses, the Huntsman will gain the ability to bypass barriers and distance, drawing ever nearer to the quarry. Energy Cost: Minimum 500, scalable. Cooldown: Long.*****

Victor looked around and saw that he was deep in the woods, only vaguely aware of the direction that led back to Persi Gables. "Well, that was pretty fucking wild."

"Wait here," Valla said to the coachman and started walking along the street toward the corner. She'd felt Victor's aura surge, seen how shadows had seemed to coalesce around him, bursting forth and leaving behind a strange, smoky gray steam that seemed to limn his figure, clinging to him like a shifting gray cloak. She'd watched him start to walk toward the other street and figured it was in his best interest, her best interest, and Rellia's best interest that she follow.

Valla kept pace with Victor, and he'd only taken a few steps when golden motes of Energy coalesced in the grove around him and surged into him. He didn't slow his steps or even seem to notice the influx of Energy, but it was a good clue that he'd created a new spell.

She had no trouble keeping up with him at first, but then the smoky gray cloak surged, and with a burst of white-gray, steaming Energy, Victor was gone. She followed the trail of steam with her eyes and found him, now striding down the center of the cobbled road, some fifty paces further ahead. "Did he teleport or move quickly?" she breathed as she jogged to the corner and followed after him.

Victor seemed oblivious to the people around him. Roladii warbled and pulled at their reins to get out of his way, and people scurried left and right as he strode steadily down the road. Valla kept to the sidewalk a dozen paces behind him, having to stutter step into a short jog now and then so she didn't lose ground. His gait seemed unhurried, but it was steady, and his legs were long, and nothing seemed to give him pause.

She was happy to see his axe still hooked to his belt—he didn't seem to be doing anything violent or destructive, and she hoped this strange march through town had a purpose in his mind. She contemplated calling out to him, asking him what he was doing, offering her help. She decided to just watch for now and followed him past two more turns until the city wall loomed ahead of them.

Valla wondered if this had been his goal. Was he going to follow the wall to one of the gates? Where was he going? For the first time, Victor slowed his pace as he came to the wall road, and he peered left, then right, then back at the wall. Valla opened her mouth, and before she could stop herself, she called out, "Victor, what are you doing?"

In answer, he took a step toward the wall, and then the gray, shifting, smoky aura burst into white steam again, and he was gone. The white trail dissipated quickly, but Valla saw it lead directly into the stone of the massive wall. She rushed forward to look around—he was gone. "Ancestors' bones!" she hissed and turned to sprint toward the nearest gate, some two miles distant.

Before he could do anything he might regret, Victor sat down on a frost-rimed log and took stock of himself. He was down nearly two thousand Energy, and when he looked at his Core, he saw that all of his Energies were depleted, but his inspiration-attuned orb was almost dark. He supposed it made sense—his weave of justice-attuned Energy called for nearly two parts of inspiration for each of his other attunements.

He had a vague recollection of his time under the influence of the new spell. He could remember a blurry passage through town, moving ever closer to his target. Suddenly, his heart raced as he jerked his head in the direction where he'd last felt the heat of the "quarry" for his spell. He'd still been quite a ways from Boaegh, though, and he was pretty sure miles of dense woods still separated them. Sighing, he looked around again.

The woods were thick, and he hadn't been following any sort of trail. He sat amongst tall trees of all types. Though the undergrowth in the woods around Persi Gables wasn't as heavy as in a wilder forest, there were still quite a few bushes, shrubs, and trees big and small, and visibility was limited, especially in the overcast, gray winter light. "At least I've got a little more space out here," he muttered, still determined to try out his fear-attuned Energy with his Berserk spell.

He stood and looked at the ground and the nearby underbrush, and when he saw the broken branches of a leafless sapling, he felt reasonably confident he knew what direction he'd come from. With that in mind, he turned and started hiking perpendicularly to his earlier passage; he wanted more distance between himself and others before he tried his fear affinity with Berserk.

He knew Valla was probably freaking out, probably circling the city looking for him, but she was smart, and she'd figure out to wait for him at the inn eventually. He felt that it was better this way, better that he be truly alone when he tried out this spell. While he hiked, letting his Energy accumulate, he contemplated the Inevitable Huntsman.

He could see how it would be useful, tracking down someone. He didn't remember having much of a thought process when he'd chosen his "quarry," though. It seemed he might be at the mercy of whatever his subconscious deemed was his most pressing potential target. He wished it would work for tracking down anyone—friend or neutral party included. Still, it was good to be able to hunt an enemy when needed. The spell was costly, though, and he felt as though a big part was the teleportation aspect. If he used it whenever it was ready, he'd be drained pretty rapidly.

"Wonder what happens when I catch up to them, too," Victor muttered as he stopped to stretch, his Energy much recovered. Once more, he looked around the woods, listening carefully to the sounds of distant trees popping and creaking, birds squawking and rustling in the brush here and there. Nothing seemed to be coming toward him, and he didn't think there were any people nearby.

Victor dreaded using his fear affinity with his most powerful spell. He kept thinking back to when he'd been new at casting Berserk and how his rage would take him over. What if he became engrossed in his fear? What if it left him catatonic or caused him to do terrible things? He wished he had someone powerful there to help him, to watch over him. "Someone like Oynalla." As he thought of the Old Mother, Victor pictured meeting with her on the spirit plane, and that brought to mind his coyotes, who often accompanied him in that realm.

Suddenly a spark of an idea flared in his mind, and Victor concentrated on his Core, building his pattern for courage-attuned Energy. What better way to balance his fear than with some brave companions? With his other Energies locked down, Victor cast Manifest Spirit and fed the courage-attuned Energy into the spell. As always, his five companions began to shimmer into existence, like mist rising from the forest floor.

This time, rather than red, purplish-black, or brilliant gold, the coyotes shone with a deep red-gold luminescence that filled Victor's heart to bursting with pride and admiration. "*Qué guapo*!" Victor hissed, squatting down and holding out his hands as one of the golden canines, a big male, walked toward him, neck arched, nose down, tail wagging, as if he was proud of himself. Victor ran his hands along the coyote's neck and back, marveling at how the fur felt real and charged with Energy.

"Okay, watch over me. Don't let me do anything terrible, *mis compañeros*."

With his pack surrounding him, Victor reached into his Core and pressed hard against his rage Energy, holding it firm, then cast Berserk, and when the spell pattern flared to life, he fed it with fear-attuned Energy. Victor screamed. He felt black, caustic Energy pour through his pathways into his body, and he felt it ripping him apart. He arched his back, lifted his face to the gray sky, and screamed, and it sounded like a thousand people being put to the torch. His voice rose and rang out among the trees, building on itself, echoing off itself, and sending the animals nearby fleeing in abject terror.

Victor held out his arms, glanced from left to right at them, saw his flesh turn black, saw it peeling from his body in shadowy wisps, saw it hug his white bones, and saw his limbs lengthen, his fingers extend into claws. As the horror of what he witnessed registered in his mind, he screamed again, but this time it sounded more like a roar, more like a howl. He looked down at his legs and saw the same thing happening—his flesh becoming purple-black smoke that sheathed his bones in thick shadow.

His back arched and jerked again, and this time Victor fell forward, but he caught himself on his hands. He felt his legs lengthen and twist, felt his bones reshaping themselves to better run on all fours, and as the pain of his transformation faded and the terror of his presence sank in, Victor had one thought in mind—find something to kill, find something to share the terror of his existence. His vision had grown dim—everything was gray, but nothing was obscured by shadow. More importantly, he could see living things like orange torches amid the bleak environment.

He dove through a thicket of leafless berry bushes, shattering the hard, thorny branches with his presence, exploding like a massive shadow-clad, skeletal hound into the woods, grunting and roaring and occasionally howling. His shrieks echoed through the woods, and he could hear things fleeing, which only sent him into more of a frenzy. He was the stuff of nightmares, and there were beings nearby that needed to experience the true horror he could deliver.

The first creature he encountered was a giant forest animal, deerlike in shape, with enormous red antlers and dark blue fur. When he burst into the clearing where it munched at the blue needles of a tree, the creature's eyes rolled back, exposing the whites, and honked a frenzied, warbling panic sound, turning to flee. It crashed through trees and brush, much the way Victor had done.

Something ignited in Victor's chest as he saw the flaming outline of his quarry leap away between the gray trees. He gave chase, and as the waves of fear and terror rolled off his intended victim, he howled and panted, reveling in the thrill of the rich Energy source, absorbing it and feeding his Core, perpetuating his nightmare visage. He knew he could catch the animal, pluck its hamstrings with his claws, and pick it apart bit by bit, ever increasing the horror it felt until its heart inevitably stopped beating.

"I will!" Victor roared, sounding like a hellhound shrieking. He leapt, claws raised, and when he reached the apex of his arcing flight, something caught his attention—in the gray world of his existence, a sea of flames flickered a short way beyond the trees. His quarry forgotten, he landed on all fours and started stalking toward the mass of Energy. If he could get to that sea of bright Energy and turn himself loose amid it, he could harvest terror and fear until he burst, until he became something truly awesome, something that could terrorize the world!

He prowled through the trees, his shadowy throat rumbling, saliva dripping from his fang-filled, skeletal snout. Victor knew the flames, the spirits, were behind a barrier. He needed to find a way through, so he circled, scanning the pale gray existence for more spots of color, closer than what he'd seen. He was still eager for fear, eager for terror, but he was hunting now, stalking, and he ceased his screaming roars.

His silence paid off—a bright spirit wandered in his direction, wending between trees, cautiously stepping through thorny brambles. Smaller but much brighter than the deer-creature, Victor saw his opportunity to gain strength, to slake his thirst for terror. "Yes," he hissed, "you'll feed me enough to reach the others." Anyone who bore witness to his words wouldn't have heard them, though, only a low, rumbling growl that would have sent cold shivers down their spines.

"Victor!" the flaming spirit called, hands cupped to its face. Victor recognized the word at some level, but it seemed meaningless. He was close now, lurking between two tree trunks behind a perennial shrub covered with white winter blooms. The torch-like being was so close he could feel the heat of it. Only one thing mattered—sharing his terror and feeding off what he created.

Victor exploded through the shrub in a shower of torn leaves and white petals. As he descended through the air toward his quarry, a flickering bright line of metal crashed into his side, shearing away his shadowy flesh and notching his bony torso. It didn't hurt, but the force of the blow thwarted his perfect leap, and he rolled to the side with a thunderous howling shriek.

"Ancestors!" the blazing spirit said, holding its bright metal before it as it backpedaled from Victor. He stood, his hunger rumbling from his throat, and lifted his head to shriek about it, to tell the world that he hungered for fear, for terror. His terrible cry rose above the forest, bounced off the trees, and people near and distant twisted their fingers, warding against evil, seeking warmth and the company of others.

The bright spirit in front of him started to radiate dark wispy bands of fear, and Victor howled again, drawing them in. "Yes!" he cried, though no word was coherent in the sound he made. He crept toward his quarry and saw how it backed away, seeking something to stand against so he couldn't circle it. It held its bright metal before it as its back came against a thick tree. "Victor!" the spirit cried, though it wasn't speaking to him, it was screaming into the woods. Seeking salvation? Was there something more coming to challenge him?

"No," he growled, laughing. The sound that emerged from his throat was like the ripping of flesh and cries of children. He inched forward, haunches high, snout low, forelimbs outstretched, testing the spirit, waiting to see if it would break—crumble to its fear. It lashed out with its bright metal, and Victor pulled his taloned hand back, narrowly escaping the touch.

Again, the spirit cried, "Victor!" He heard the word echo through the woods around them. This time, however, the spirit's call didn't fall on deaf ears. Five brilliant loping spirits bound into the clearing, leaping over brambles and tearing through the brush. They streaked forward, little red-gold comets that hurt Victor's eyes, and they stood in a semicircle in front of his prey.

The new spirits made troubled yipping sounds, some growled and snapped at Victor, and he saw the tendrils of fear start to fade away from the spirit he'd been hunting. It stood straighter against the tree, and its bright steel stopped wavering and shaking as it held it toward Victor. This enraged Victor—what were these bright little spirits to stand before him? Why was their brightness anathema to his fear? They felt familiar. They felt hated! Victor felt the terrible force of his fear rise up in his throat, felt his hunger assert its will, and he screamed with everything he had.

The five smaller, bright spirits shrank back from his cry, shifting their little forms out of the central cone of his scream, leaving his prey to suffer the brunt. Victor could see them trying, struggling to move in front of the spirit, but his power was greater—together, they were a lantern against his dark typhoon, and separate, they were simply candles. Still, the spirit lunged through their ranks and tried to strike him with its bright cold steel.

In response, Victor pounced; faster than thought, he clasped its frail arm in his massive clawed hand and yanked, smashing the spirit to the ground and sending the bright metal bouncing away from it. Sobs erupted from the spirit's bright flaming face, and the purple-black smoke of terror began to radiate from it in earnest. The bright golden spirits started to growl and lunge, snapping at Victor's dark flesh, grabbing hold and pulling, but he muscled through their attempts.

He felt his prey gathering Energy, felt it attack him somehow, but he shrugged it off. He reached out with his other talon, grabbed the hand that had tried to damage his shadowy flesh, and pinned it to the ground. Then he held his snarling, shifting, fanged face close to the spirit's head, putting his shadow-wreathed eye close, a mere inch away, wanting to see through the bright aura, wanting to see the terror in the flesh.

Beyond the shadows that wreathed him, behind the brightness of the spirit's aura and the wisps of fear and terror that bled from it, he caught a glimpse of color—a distinct shade of green. Victor jerked back from the spirit like it had burned him. As he released his prey, he felt the smaller spirits leaping upon him, growling and thrashing as they burrowed into his dark, shadowy flesh, sinking into his body, driving some of the fear from his pathways, the dark Energy melting before their golden essence.

Victor shook his head and blinked his eyes, aware that the shadows had begun to fall away from his frame. Suddenly cognizant of who he was and what he'd done, he looked at Valla struggling to inch away from him, pushing with her feet as she slid through the dead, cold leaves. Victor cried out in dismay and loped away through the trees as if he'd been burned, as if he'd caught fire and the only water in the world was far away—far from the spirit he'd almost killed, almost *harvested.*

As the shame and anger woke up within him, they continued pushing away the fear, terror, and hunger for more. They banished his desire to share those torturous feelings. His pace slowed, and he became fully aware of himself, and as that sense of self resurfaced, as he remembered he was Victor, he lashed out with fury and drove the fear-attuned Energy from his pathways, yanking it back into his Core. He felt the shadows cloaking his body solidify back into flesh, felt the terrible grinding snaps of bones taking their usual shape, and then he was lying flat on his face.

Panic and guilt spurred him to action, despite the horror of feeling his bones move the way they had. He sat up and saw that he was still clothed and still had Lifedrinker at his belt. "How the fuck?" he hissed. "Was it real?" Almost as if it wanted to answer him, Victor saw the blinking notifications of more System messages. Standing up, he read through them as he started retracing his obvious passage through the forest:

*****Congratulations! You have learned the spell: Aspect of Terror, Basic.*****

*****Aspect of Terror, Basic. Prerequisite: Fear or related affinity. You change your appearance to represent something terrifying. While you wear this illusion, you will passively harvest and cultivate fear-attuned Energy emanating from those who perceive you and cannot resist your will. Energy Cost: Minimum 100, scalable. Cooldown: Long.*****

*****Congratulations! You have achieved level 34 Spirit Carver, gained 10 will and 10 vitality, and have 8 attribute points to allocate.*****

"What the fuck," Victor said, feeling much worse than he ever had for gaining a level. He could only remember snatches of what he'd done while wearing his terror aspect, and none of it felt good. He started to run, jogging through the forest, smashing through brambles and shrubs, dodging around trees. He called out, "Valla!" when he started to get back to the area where he'd encountered her.

He saw the tree where he'd cornered her, saw her sword lying in the damp, dead leaves, and he hurried over to pick it up. The hilt was wet and smeared with mud, and the blade was heavy—far heavier than he'd imagined. He heard movement off to his left, branches breaking and the stomp of a running step, and he hurried after it. The noises got louder as he gained ground, and he shouted again, "Valla! Wait!"

Two dozen more steps, and he broke through the tree line. The cleared fields between the city walls and the forest were before him, and he saw Valla, thirty yards distant, stumble-running toward the road that led out of the city. He ran after her and called again, "Valla!"

She kept running but slowed to look over her shoulder, her eyes wide and her cheek smeared with dirt, and she screamed, "Get away from me!"

"Valla, wait," Victor tried again, more softly, as he gained on her. "Your sword . . ." he said when she refused to turn. That seemed to get her attention, and she whirled on him. They were still in the field, still halfway between the trees and the wall, still fifty yards from the road. No one was around other than a distant crowd outside the city gate.

"Break it! Throw it away! Stay away from me!" she hissed, and Victor could see she wasn't herself, wasn't anything like the Valla he'd come to know. Her hands trembled, her voice was shaky and shrill, and she had a crazed look behind her eyes. He opened his mouth to reply but, as usual, struggled for the right thing to say.

30

LIFTING SPIRITS

Victor opened his mouth and tried to think of the perfect thing to say but came up short. Instead, he tossed Valla's sword into the grass next to her, strode forward, and grabbed her shoulders. She tried to flinch away, and as his hands grabbed her, she scowled and jerked back, but Victor held on and cast Inspiring Presence, shouting, "Valla! Get ahold of yourself!"

As Victor's warm, positive Energy surged through his pathways and out, he saw it wash over her, saw her eyes, previously unfocused and crazed, narrow and for the first time really look at his face. She stopped jerking and took in a deep, shuddering breath. Victor felt a surge of relief wash over him, perhaps an effect of his spell, but he knew it was warranted—it was working. Valla had grown calm and reached a hand up to wipe at her eyes shakily.

"What, on my Ancestors' bones, was that?" she asked, looking past Victor's shoulder toward the woods. "Why did I think it was you?"

Victor thought about the question, thought about the easiest way to make things right, but he knew better than that—that was a fearful response, and he wasn't going to give into fear anymore. "Because it was me. I fucked up and cast a spell I wasn't ready for."

Valla looked at him quizzically and, with the light of inspiration behind her eyes, said, "Well, I'm glad you figured it out. Did you see those hounds? They saved me, I think."

"Those were my spirit totems. Yeah, I'm glad I summoned them before I cast the other spell. They represent the best part of me, Valla. At least those did—I called them with courage-attuned Energy." Victor looked around the cold field and saw a farmer had stopped his wagon on the dirt road leading to the gates and was staring at them. The man raised a hand and waved, and Victor waved back, wondering if he was just making sure they were all right.

"Courage . . ." she sighed, shaking her head. "I could use some of that right now. Victor, I'd never felt such terror. I'm ashamed!" she hissed, pulling out of his grip and looking around the field until her eyes fell on her sword. "I don't deserve that sword. I left it and ran!"

"Hey, chill with that stuff, Valla. That was a powerful spell—it got into your mind and made you see things that weren't real. You weren't yourself. That was one hundred percent my fault. If it makes you feel better, I lost control of myself, too! It was fucking awful. I feel absolutely wrecked about what I did to you!"

"This spell—you don't have to cast it?" Valla asked, wiping at her nose where it had started to run. Victor thought it was more due to the chilly air than her crying. She seemed to have gotten a grip on herself. Before he answered, Victor bent down to pick up her sword and held the hilt out toward her.

"Fuck no; I don't. I'll never cast that again if anyone I care about is within ten miles of me. No, fuck that, a hundred miles. Maybe if I'm in an enemy castle and there's no other way out, maybe I'd try it then, but it'll be a last resort. I need to talk to Oynalla about it, about what went wrong. She might have some ideas for me."

Valla took her sword, to Victor's relief, and whipped it through the air, sending the leaves and bits of mud flying off it to spatter in the frosty grass. She drew the blade over her sleeve, further cleaning it, and then it disappeared, presumably stored in her dimensional container. "I'll hold you to that, Victor. I don't want to encounter that side of you ever again." She paused and looked into his eyes, her seafoam green irises clear and focused once again. "Also, thank you."

"Thank you? For what?"

"For this." She touched her chest, right below her throat. "Your inspiration spell. It helped me to see things the way they were, helped me to push that horror out of my mind."

"The least I could do! Again, I'm sorry, Valla. C'mon, let's get to the inn and have a hot meal, hmm? Something to put this chilly, creepy experience out of our minds."

"Yes." She nodded and turned to start walking, and Victor smiled when she slowed, waiting for him to keep pace with her.

"What do you say we stop by a bookshop on the way? I've wanted to buy some for a while." Victor reached up to his chest to feel Gorz's outline.

"What kinds of books?"

"All kinds, but I'd love to get my hands on some history books or an atlas."

"Ahh! I know a good place—I've seen it off Gaul-dak Square a few times and thought about stopping in. Never had the time," she said with a shrug. They finally crossed the field and came to the berm leading up to the road. Victor hopped over the loose soil and stones to the flat graveled surface and held his hand out for Valla. She smirked and hopped up next to him, giving his hand a slap.

"Right," Victor laughed, having momentarily forgotten how this woman could move when she held a sword in her hand—something like a cross between an Olympic gymnast and a ballerina.

"The thought was nice, I guess," Valla laughed. They walked through the gates, Victor once again hooded with Hine's big cloak. He let Valla do the talking, and soon they were working their way through busy streets that smelled like animals, sweat, and food. Victor's stomach started to growl, and he fantasized about some hot *albóndigas* soup, wishing his *abuela* was waiting for him back at the inn with a pot simmering on the stove.

"I hope Hine has some good soup in the kitchen; this is perfect weather for it."

"I agree! It feels like we might be in for some snow tonight. Feel that breeze? Look to the north—see those dark gray clouds?"

"Yeah. Aren't there, like, people with weather magic or something?"

"Yes, I'm sure if we were at Rellia's estate, she'd have told us exactly what to expect from the weather. We could probably ask around the town and get some concrete information—Weather Witches are common enough."

"Can they control the weather?"

"Not usually, and only in small areas when they can. The one that works for Rellia is good at predicting the weather and can keep the worst of storms from affecting the grounds of her estate."

"That's pretty cool, though." Victor nodded as they walked along. They continued through the city for a good ten or fifteen minutes, then they entered a market square dominated by a large bronze statue at its center.

It depicted a warrior with a giant curved sword riding atop a mount that reminded Victor of a velociraptor. "Who's that?"

"Gaul-dak. He was a hero in the early days of Fanwath—killed a lot of Yovashi. Now he lives in Tharcray when he's not off-world."

"Not here? You'd think he'd want to see his statue!"

"Oh, I'm sure there are statues and streets named after him in Tharcray, too. There's the bookstore," Valla said, pointing to a corner shop with window displays of stacked books. A wooden pyrographed sign above the door read "The Sisters' Books." Next to the lettering were painted depictions of the two sister moons of Fanwath.

"Seems like the third moon doesn't get much attention," Victor said.

"Well, the sisters are in the sky more when it's dark. Easier to notice them, right? Also, don't worry; there are cults dedicated to Dohl."

"Dohl? That's the name of the third moon? Do the sisters have names?"

"Yes," Valla said, reaching to open the shop's door, "Thivia and Galia."

Victor grunted, acknowledging the information while he surveyed the inside of the little shop. Thousands of books lined the walls and stood in stacks all over the wooden floor, and he was instantly doused in the smell of them—musty with a hint of dust, but this shop had something more. He could smell the scent of oiled leather and spice, and all together, he found he quite liked it. A young woman, a Ghelli with tiny wings and bright red hair, sat on a stool near the front counter. She looked up at their approach and smiled, though she didn't say anything.

"Miss," Valla said, striding forward. "Could you direct us to texts on the history of Fanwath, its cities, and its wars?"

"Oh, sure," she said, yawning and putting her book down on the counter. "Let's see." She walked around a stack of dusty texts toward the wall to Victor's right. The young woman looked over the bookcases as she walked, and when she stood in the middle, she gestured vaguely toward six or eight shelves and said, "These should cover that request."

"Thanks." Victor squeezed past Valla so he could walk between some stacks toward the wall. His axe haft brushed against a narrow column of texts, and it tottered and would have collapsed had Valla not quickly put out a hand to balance it.

"Please be careful!" the young shopkeeper said, scowling at Victor. He was still hooded and cloaked, and she added, "We don't normally get Vodkin in here. I'll have to tell Mr. Vollun to widen the aisles!"

Victor laughed and pulled his hood down. "I'm not a Vodkin, but yeah, I'll try to be careful. Hey, while I'm looking at these books, can you find me a few volumes with maps in them? I'm mostly looking for maps of the Empire and the surrounding areas, but I'll take anything."

"Oh." The girl seemed flustered at mistakenly calling Victor a Vodkin, and her pale skin blushed a brilliant shade of red. "I'll see what I can find," she squeaked and hurried behind the counter.

"Silly girl," Valla said from near Victor's left elbow, and he looked down at her to see amusement in her eyes.

"I'm glad you're feeling better," he said.

"Yes, I am. The horror of that experience is fading quickly. I think that's a good sign—you were right that my behavior was caused by the magic you wielded, not by a failing in my character."

"Exactly!" Victor clapped his hands together for emphasis. "If that was a reflection of anyone's character, it was mine." He glanced at her, saw a puzzled look in her eyes, and added, "I'll explain it some time, but trust me: spirit Cores can be a real bitch to deal with."

"*Veeja's Treatises*," Valla said, pointing, "Those are very good. Rellia made me study them. You're in luck; I see the whole series on wars and the Empire." Victor followed her finger and saw two rows of books with similar bindings and a stylized, gold-leaf "Veeja" printed over numerals one through eight and one through six.

"Cool," Victor said, reaching up to pull them down. He carried them to the counter, four at a time, and Valla helped. By the time they'd set all the books down, the young Ghelli had returned with a huge leather-bound book. It was easily two feet square, and the cover was embossed with a stitched map depicting mountains, rivers, and lakes. Colorful stars represented cities and towns, and Victor didn't have to guess the contents of its pages.

"This atlas is rather in demand at the moment, but we have a few copies. It's the latest edition of *Gorndilia's Wide Surveys*.

"Nice," Victor said, nodding. "I'll take that and these Veeja books."

The girl's eyes bulged. "All of them?"

"Yep," Victor said, and before he could reach into his dimensional container, Valla put a hand on the counter holding an official-looking signet ring.

"House ap'Yensha will pay for them," she said and looked at Victor. "They're part of the lady's spring campaign expenses."

"Oh! I'm so sorry! I didn't realize you were representing the ap'Yensha clan. Of course . . . Will you be taking them with you, or shall I have them delivered to the estate?"

"We'll take them," Victor said.

"Excellent. Give me a moment to write up a bill of sale, and then we can have you sign it, Lady . . ." she trailed off, looking at Valla hopefully.

"Valla ap'Yensha, and please address me as Captain, not Lady."

"I'm so sorry! One minute, please," the woman said, and then she lifted a black slate and quill. She carefully traced the names of the books onto the slate, and Victor saw the lettering appear in the stone as if etched. When she was done, she placed the slate before Valla, who touched her finger to it. A pulse of crackling electrical Energy shot over the slate's surface, and the woman took it back and nodded with a pleased smile.

"Take your books, Victor," Valla said, gesturing.

"Thanks," he said and touched each book, sending them all into his storage ring.

"Please pass my regards on to the Lady ap'Yensha! Thank you for your patronage, Captain Valla," the young woman called as they wended back through the stacks of books to the door. Once they were outside, Victor chuckled and looked at Valla.

"Are you going to get in trouble for that?"

"For what?"

"For spending that money and saying you're an ap'Yensha!"

"No, Victor. I told you Rellia was like a mother to me, didn't I?"

"Yeah, the key word being 'like,'" he chuckled.

"Well, she adopted me, so I suppose, legally, I'm her daughter."

"What the fuck?" Victor hadn't been able to edit his outburst; it came out so quickly.

"What?" Valla looked a little surprised by Victor's explosive tone, but he saw a bit of a smirk tilting the corner of her mouth.

"Oh, I don't know. Never mind—maybe I'm just stupid; I should have put two and two together," Victor laughed, shaking his head as they resumed their walk through town. "How much were those books, anyway?"

"Less than three thousand beads."

"Shit! Rellia's going to be pissed!"

"No, she's not!" Valla laughed and took hold of Victor's shoulder, giving it a comradely squeeze. "It's a good investment! How can she expect you to lead her expedition if you haven't learned about important wars or even the lay of the land? I'll be happy to explain this purchase to her."

"If you say so." Victor grinned at the idea of Rellia receiving that bill. They made their way back to the inn, and Victor went up to his room while Valla got them some food. She still wanted him to try to keep a low profile while they waited to make their next move against Lord ap'Horrin, Boaegh, and his band of summoners.

Victor was thrilled when Valla showed up carrying a small cask with one of Hine's kitchen staff in tow, holding a pot of steaming soup and two bowls. He gave the young man a couple of beads and then locked the door, and the two of them spent the evening eating vegetable and pultii soup—a game bird that tasted very much like turkey—and drinking a sweet, honeyed mead. By the time the cask was empty and their bellies were stuffed, Valla claimed to be feeling much better, and the two of them agreed to turn in early.

After Victor saw Valla to her room, he closed his door, threw the bolt, and pulled one of his chairs over to it, jamming it up under the handle. He prowled around his room, jabbing Lifedrinker into the shadows, making sure some invisible lurker wasn't hanging around. That done, he made sure the windows were latched and went into the bathroom, again locking the door.

Nodding to himself in satisfaction, he cast Manifest Spirit using inspiration-attuned Energy, and when his white-gold coyotes were curled up around him, he cast Spirit Walk. Victor stood up on the spirit plane and immediately started marching toward the east, his mind set on Oynalla, hoping she was out that night—she seemed to have an uncanny knack for knowing when Victor would come looking for her, so he was hopeful.

He felt lonely striding through the twilit plains, the brilliant, limitless star field stretching out over his head. Victor had grown accustomed to having his companion coyotes walk with him, but they couldn't do that while they watched his body, and he felt that was the more important job for them at the moment. Idly, he wondered what it would be like to have a place of his own, some place where he could feel secure while he cast spells like Spirit Walk. "Maybe one of these days, I'll build that hermitage or whatever it's called."

Victor's journey was quick and uneventful—it seemed the more he gained power and control over his spirit-self, the more other spirits seemed to give him space; he wasn't sure if it was a show of respect or fear, and again, he was bothered by the loneliness of it, but he knew it was for the best—it might be fun to glimpse animal spirits here and there or notice the passing of another spirit walker, but it was safer for all involved if he didn't have to deal with any challenges.

Suddenly, Victor found himself striding down a familiar slope. He could hear the babbling of Oynalla's brook up ahead, and he knew he'd been lucky yet again—Oynalla was waiting for him. He broke into a trot, flying down the hill, through the tall birch-like trees, and into her clearing. When Victor caught sight of Oynalla, he was happy to see that she was waiting with Thayla for his arrival.

"Old Mother," he said, hurrying forward to sit next to Thayla before the young-old Oynalla, and she looked up at him with concern in her eyes.

"I felt your struggle earlier." She glanced at Thayla as if weighing what words to use in front of her, but then she scowled and added, "Did I not warn you about that affinity?"

Thayla reached a slightly luminescent hand out to take hold of his and smiled at him while Oynalla continued, "I can see that your spirit is still bright. You won your first battle with your fear, though it might not feel like it, warrior."

"I won? I don't think so, Oynalla! I totally lost control of myself! I almost killed a friend . . ." he glanced at Thayla, suddenly very thankful that she and Deyni were so far away from him.

"Did you kill your friend? Did you destroy her mind with terror?"

"No, I had cast Manifest . . ."

"No! That's right, Victor. If you had lost that battle, there would be great tragedy behind your eyes, and your soul would be many shades darker. Whatever you did to banish the fear away and not run amok, savaging innocents, be glad for it. Be proud of yourself, Victor—you've done well to gird yourself against the darker Energies of your spirit. Your soul is strong, your heart is true, and you have powerful Energies and allies to aid you."

"The weave worked," Victor said, suddenly remembering his success with justice-attuned Energy.

"You created justice?" Oynalla cackled, though it never sounded quite right coming from her younger form—more a sharp laugh than a true cackle.

"Yes! I learned some new spells, obviously one I won't ever use again."

"What?" Thayla asked.

"Why?" Oynalla echoed.

"Um, were you guys asleep just now? Didn't I tell you I almost killed my friend?"

"Victor, do you conquer fear by hiding from it?" Oynalla chuckled and gave Thayla a knowing look.

"You were right," Thayla said, grinning and shaking her head.

"What?" Victor asked, starting to feel pissed off.

"Oynalla said you'd swear off using your fear Energy after what she felt earlier. I was dumb enough to make a bet with her!"

"Well, you guys didn't fucking go through that, did you? It's not a joke, all right?"

"You didn't answer my question, warrior," Oynalla said, tsking her tongue.

"What? Oh, well, no, I guess I can't conquer fear by being afraid of it, but I'm trying to protect innocent people, don't you see that? You're the one that told me to be cautious!"

"True, and cautious you must be, but you've felt its bite now. Next time you'll have the upper hand. Keep strengthening your will, and keep building your Core stronger and stronger. When next you let the fear-beast ride your skin, you tell it who the lord is!"

"If you say so . . ." Victor said, but Oynalla held up a hand and continued speaking.

"Tell me, warrior, why do you never manifest your other totem?"

"Huh?" Victor's mind raced as he tried to make sense of the Old Mother's words. Did she mean using a different Energy to summon his coyotes? He'd tried most of them by now; he supposed he'd yet to try his new Justice weave. Would that allow the coyotes to hunt his enemies? "I . . ." he started, but then he remembered—when he'd killed Bitterpaw, gained a level in Spirit Carver, and improved his Manifest Spirit and Shape Spirit spells, he'd gained access to another totem. "Fuck me, have I been damaged in the brain from all the hits I've taken?"

"Ha!" Oynalla cackled, and this time it sounded right. Thayla giggled and squeezed his hand.

"So, warrior? You had a hard day; why not see if another totem might help you sleep more easily?" Oynalla grinned at him slyly, her magenta eyes twinkling in the starlight. Victor couldn't help smiling in response, his mood already considerably lifted simply from being able to spend time with the two women.

"Right now? Can I cast Shape Spirit here?"

"What better place?" Oynalla nodded enthusiastically.

"Will you two be able to come with me?"

"We'll follow behind—don't think about us, lest we influence your choices."

"Right," Victor said, standing up and looking around. The little clearing was idyllic, as usual. The grass was soft, the trees tall and peacefully swaying in the ever-present breeze. Between the wind whispering through the leaves and the brook babbling in the background, Victor knew he could very easily sleep there. "Not that I need to sleep right now," he muttered, then he cleared his mind and cast Shape Spirit.

The last time he'd cast it, he'd stepped from the ordinary world into the spirit plane, but this time he was already there. Nothing really changed except for a tugging at his Core, a feeling that he should walk along the ridgeline above, so he started up the hill. When he came up out of Oynalla's hollow, he turned left and followed the feeling at his center.

As he walked, the grass grew long, and the forest to his left seemed to fade away to more grasslands. The warmth in his Core swelled, and Victor felt it tugging to the right, and he turned just in time to see a luminescent, nearly spectral mustang charging over the grass. As it raced past him, it lifted its head in a mighty, trumpeting neigh, and Victor felt his heart stir with emotion. "What a beauty you are!" he called after the horse. It was fast and agile, as it demonstrated, standing on its hind legs, lifting its forehooves in the air, and whinnying as it looked at Victor.

"What fun it would be to charge through town or over the grasslands on your back, eh, *hermoso*? I don't know, though, sir—I have a good mount, and I'm not sure you're the right fit for me right now. I'll find you if I change my mind!" Victor called as the stallion neighed again and charged off over the grasslands, its hooves reverberating like thunder. Victor smiled, watching it fade away; he didn't worry that he'd made a mistake, for he knew his soul would pull him back to the horse if he decided it was the right totem for him.

A thought lurked in the back of his mind, though—he had fighting to do and dangerous enemies to meet. He kept remembering his coyotes staked out by the Pyromancer's flaming spears. They were brave companions and great at harrying an enemy that Victor could put pressure on, but they were limited when it came to fighting a strong opponent on their own. Shouldn't he be looking for a totem that wasn't so easily brushed aside?

An image came to his mind—on his first totem quest, he'd come across a mighty old bear, and something had made him turn away from it. Maybe he'd feel differently this time. "Maybe I need to look at that old *oso* again, eh?" As the words left his lips, Victor felt another tug at his Core, and he turned to his left, walking down an incline he hadn't noticed before. A thick, twilit forest loomed ahead of him, and Victor grinned as he followed the tugging sensation into the woods.

31

PORTENTS AND PROPHECIES

Victor watched the enormous dark-furred bear, once again fishing the sparkling waters of the twilit stream. The bear was a mighty creature with long shaggy fur and a massive set of shoulders that rose in a hump of muscle over its huge head. It grumbled and huffed as it fished through the water, and though it resembled grizzly bears Victor had seen in VR, it stood taller, with longer limbs than any bear he'd ever seen depicted. It seemed primal, ancient, something from a time long before humanity had dominated the lands of Earth.

"Well, shit, maybe you aren't from Earth," Victor said, though he felt as if the bear was—weren't coyotes and mustangs from Earth? It felt to him that his spirit totems were rooted in his experiences and the experiences of his ancestors. Maybe it had something to do with his bloodline or even his DNA.

He started down the wooded slope to the stream, walking tall with his head high, staring at the bear, waiting for it to look his way. As he cleared the wood line and stepped along the water bank, the great bear lifted its head from the water, a glistening, massive fish in its maw. Luminescent blood dripped from where huge teeth pierced the fish's scales as the great creature stared at Victor. The bear had bright, deep-set brown eyes, and though Victor was still twenty paces from it, across a ribbon of flowing water, he could see the intelligence therein.

The bear closed its jaws, bisecting the fish and letting the two halves drop to the rocky shore at its feet. Before Victor could guess its next move, the mountain of fur and muscle bounded into the stream, splashing through the crystal waters in an explosion of frothing spray. Victor stood stock still, staring at the enormous creature as it rushed through the water and up the stony shore to stand before him.

The bear towered over him, hunching its boulder-like shoulders to lower its head and stare into Victor's eyes. It huffed damp, hot, copper-scented breath into his face, but the only sound that emerged from its sedan-sized chest was a low rumble that sounded more like a welcome than a warning. Victor grinned and reached up a hand to scratch at the bear's shaggy, wet jaw. He had nothing to fear here, for wasn't this totem a part of him, a fragment of his spirit?

When he'd found his coyotes, Victor had awoken shortly after from his spirit walk, the purpose of his Shape Spirit spell having been met. This time, things were different; Victor had cast the spell while already on the spirit plane, and though he'd made his decision, welcoming the bear into his heart, he still stood there with his new totem. "Get your fish, big *oso*! I don't have work for you right now."

The bear huffed another hot, fishy breath into his face and then turned and bounded through the water, snatching up another fish on its way back to its meal. A snap of a twig alerted Victor to movement behind him, and he turned, smiling, and said, "There you are, Old Mother."

"Getting too clever for your britches," the young, beautiful version of Oynalla said, grinning as she made her way down the slope to the creek.

"To be fair, his britches are pretty big," Thayla said, following behind the old Spirit Caster. She glanced past Victor to the bear and said, "Couldn't you find a bigger totem?"

"He and I have some pretty bad assholes to deal with. I thought he was a better choice right now than a mustang."

"Mustang?"

"The horse that ran up to me on the grassland." Victor gestured up the hill toward the vast plains where he'd been walking earlier.

"Oh, we didn't see that, warrior," Oynalla replied. "We tried to follow you, but it's hard to keep pace with a spirit walker until they stop for a while."

"Horse?" Thayla said, still trying to make sense of Victor's words.

"Uh, it's a kind of animal from my world that people use for mounts. Maybe I'll get another chance to pick him someday, and then I can show you."

"Your mastery of the spirit begins to extend into areas I've only heard of in old stories. I wouldn't be surprised if you earn another totem," Oynalla said, nodding. "Well, warrior? Thayla's time grows short—she'll need to leave the spirit plane soon. I still have a word or two for you, so say your goodbyes to her."

Something about her words or her delivery sounded ominous to Victor, so he let the smile fall away from his face and took her words seriously. "Come here," he said, walking toward Thayla and reaching out to hug her. As she folded into his embrace, he said, to the top of her head, "I'm so glad I can still hug you in this realm. I needed this." He kissed her soft, luminescent black hair, and she squeezed him tightly in her arms.

"I know things aren't easy for you, Victor," she said, pulling back so she could look into his face. "Don't let Old Mother fool you—she was distraught when she felt your struggles. She tried to play it off, but I could feel it and got worried, too. I'm glad you're okay, and you need to remember that we're here for you, all right?"

"I know, Thayla. It means everything to me. Please give Deyni a hug and tell her I miss her."

"I will. Take care, Victor," Thayla said, squeezing the backs of his arms and looking him in the eyes, her magenta irises shimmering in the strange light of the spirit plane. He opened his mouth to say something else, but then she simply faded away, and Victor knew she'd ended her spirit walk.

"Well, warrior? Come sit with Oynalla by the river a moment."

Victor looked toward her voice and saw that the young-looking Old Mother had taken a seat on a flat stone, and she pointed to the rock across from her. He walked over and grunted as he ponderously lowered his bulk to the little stone. "You know, some people aren't as close to the ground as you are."

"Hush! Young as you are! Complaining about sitting with an old woman!"

"You're not . . ."

"Hush, now! I have important things to say. When I felt your struggles earlier, I cast my strongest divination, trying to see what I could of you and your path. Victor, your future was obscured from me, but I felt you have dire challenges ahead." She paused, and Victor thought about her words; they didn't really bother him. What else was new? He'd had one "dire" struggle after another since those assholes yanked him out of his *abuela's* living room.

"Yeah?" he said, and from Oynalla's facial expression, she'd been expecting something more. "Look, Oynalla, what can I say? I'm doing my best to prepare for trouble. I've made some boneheaded mistakes in the past, but my friend and I are trying to be smart now. She's seeking information, and I'm not planning to do anything stupid. If there are struggles ahead, I'll face 'em as they come."

"Oh, Victor! I know you've had a hard road, and I debated even telling you about this, but I felt I should help you to prepare, if not physically, at least mentally. You have to be ready for more setbacks, for further losses. You have to focus on the strength here," she held a flat hand to his stomach, and Victor knew she was talking about his Core, "and never give in to your darker aspects.

"Keep working to master your fear; keep working to master your rage. Use your Energy for good. Remember that things go on past the life you're living on Fanwath. Look around you—spirits are real, and you want yours to be bright and strong. Never let it grow twisted with hatred or fear. Never let your light, your light in here"—this time she held her hand over his heart—"grow dim. Do you promise me?"

Victor reached up and put his rough, heavy hand over Oynalla's slender, delicate red fingers, and he said, "I promise, Oynalla. I won't let you down. When I think about my life here on Fanwath and all the things I've done, nothing brings me more joy than when I've managed to do something that felt right. I don't cherish my memories of fighting, of killing; I cherish my time with Deyni, with Chandri. Nothing feels so good as to stand up for people who can't help themselves. That's who I am." Victor squeezed her hand and thumped it against his chest. "In here."

"Good, warrior. Good. I'll listen to the spirits, and I'll come when you're here looking for me." She pulled his big hand up to her face and kissed the backs of his knuckles, and then she was gone, slipping through his fingers like mist. Victor found himself holding his hands out as if to grasp at the remnants of her spirit, and then his eyes started to fill with moisture, and he furiously scrubbed at them with the backs of his hand.

"Why did that feel like she was saying goodbye? Like, really saying goodbye?" he asked the spirit plane. No answer came to him from the babbling brook or the luminescent sky, and he sighed heavily, reached inside himself, and ended his spirit walk.

Victor opened his eyes to his dim bathroom and faintly glowing silvery coyote companions. "Thank you," he said as they stood up from where they'd been lying around him, some yipping and licking at his face. Victor laughed and continued, "I'm safe and home now. You guys can get some rest." Then he canceled his Manifest Spirit spell.

Victor still felt a little hollow pit at the center of his stomach from Oynalla's words as he opened the door and looked to the window to try to gauge how long he'd been gone—the sky outside was still dark, and rather than look at his watch to see the exact time, he decided to crawl into bed. Victor was tired and knew that if he saw the time, and if it were early morning, he might decide to stay awake. He kicked off his boots, shrugged out of his clothes, and collapsed onto the comforter, unable to summon the effort to pull it over himself.

He woke to the sound of steady knocking at his door. When he looked around, eyes bleary, he saw bright light through his window and could smell the unmistakable aroma of bacon, or at least lard, cooking. The knocks at his door were steady and insistent, but he lay there on his back, blinking his eyes and stretching for a minute or two, trying to think about his dreams but failing to bring them into his conscious mind.

The knocks kept coming, and as he woke up, he found it harder and harder to ignore them, so he grunted, lurched out of bed, and made his way over to the door. "Who is it?" He knew it would be Valla, but he felt like making her announce herself.

"It's Valla!" She sounded a little strained, and Victor suddenly felt guilty for not hurrying more. He unlocked the door, and as soon as the bolt slid free, it swung wide, and Valla stood there, green eyebrows brooding and lips pressed into a thin line. She looked Victor up and down and said, "Well? Please put on some pants and move so I can come in."

"Right," Victor said, glancing at himself—he wore a pair of knit holbyis wool underwear, and, in his opinion, they were modest enough. Still, he walked over to the bathroom, splashed water on his face, and got dressed. When he returned to the larger space, Valla had taken a seat at the table and arrayed some documents on the wood in front of her.

"I have some information on ap'Horrin's estate." She tapped the papers in front of her and smiled. "You don't normally sleep so much! It's nearly noon, and I was starting to think something might be wrong." For the first time, Victor realized she hadn't been so much annoyed by his slow response to her knocking as she had been worried.

"Ah, shit. Sorry if you were worried. I, well, I didn't go right to sleep last night. I think I fell asleep right before dawn." He walked over and pulled out a chair, sitting to her left so he could look at the pages she'd lain out.

"Oh! I should have let you sleep. My apologies."

"Nah, stop it. I'm fine—don't usually need much sleep, but I think last night took a lot outta me; I went on a spirit walk."

"Victor! Who watched your body?" She scooted out her chair, and he could see that she was warring with how to respond to him; was she guilty, angry, annoyed? He didn't think she could decide.

"Relax! I had my spirit coyotes watch over me. You know, the ones that protected you in the forest. Besides, you were shit-faced."

"What?"

"I mean drunk. You were drunk and needed your sleep. You had a rough day, too, right?" He could see turning the conversation to her was making her uncomfortable; she straightened, looked down at the table, and then cleared her throat, pulling one of the papers in front of Victor.

"I have a map of ap'Horrin's estate. More importantly, one of my agents managed to observe Pyromancer Boaegh's movements yesterday. She followed him to a secured, guarded door, and her investigations revealed that it was a place ap'Horrin calls his 'oubliette.'"

"Oh, fuck," Victor said, remembering the agent of ap'Horrin's that he killed in Gelica. "I've heard that word before—I think it's where ap'Horrin keeps his pet Yovashi. It's where he broke my Core."

"Well, Rasha, my agent, did some research at the city records hall. There are some indications that the oubliette was built atop a much older structure that existed on ap'Horrin's grounds when his ancestors built their estate." Valla pushed a charcoal sketch depicting a cross-section map of a many-leveled structure, presumably all beneath the ground. It was rough and had many vague sections and hallways that seemed to lead nowhere.

"Not very detailed."

"It's more than a hundred years old. Before ap'Horrin built the estate, the city planner insisted on a survey of the ruins. This is the map he made. Rasha couldn't find anything else."

"So Boaegh spends his time in there?"

"Boaegh, yes, and Lord ap'Horrin. Rumors on the estate indicate that he's been down there for more than a week."

Victor grunted and looked at the map, wondering if he could recognize the room where the Yovashi had reached into his stomach to fiddle with his Core. Nothing on the sketch was detailed enough to jog his memory, though, and he looked back into Valla's eyes, "No idea what they're up to?"

"No, but at least it's proof that the Pyromancer is still around."

"As of yesterday?"

"Correct. Rasha left her partner to observe the oubliette's entrance. They're connected via artificed communication devices—no further comings or goings have occurred."

"So . . . is it time already? Should I go in there? My gut says I should go in there." Victor stood up and cracked his knuckles loudly.

"Victor, it's the middle of the day. The entrance to the oubliette is secluded from the rest of the estate, but you should still use caution—an assault after sundown is likely to result in you having to kill fewer of ap'Horrin's people. You do want to avoid unnecessary bloodshed, don't you?" Valla scooted her chair back and crossed one long, uniformed leg over the other, cooly observing Victor as he paced back and forth.

"Yeah, I guess so. I can remember his fucking lackeys dragging me down there, guarding me, and joking about how I was fucked while I lay on that stone slab, waiting for the Yovashi to come and pull my guts out. I feel like going there and wrecking everything and everyone, but I know that's not rational. I'm sure not all of his men are evil." Victor was furiously grinding his right hand's knuckles into his left palm while he paced and spoke his thoughts aloud. "Yeah, I think it's best if I wait. Won't do any good to slaughter a bunch of minions."

"Good, because when we get into the oubliette, we should only encounter his most loyal men and agents that belong to Boaegh. It will make things easier."

"We?" Victor shook his head. "Nah, Valla. You've done enough. Let me handle this one."

"There's no chance of that, Victor! You almost died the last time you encountered Boaegh, and there might well be more of his kind in there. At the very least, I need to know what befalls you so I can report to Rellia. If you die, she'll need to flee."

Victor stared at her for a long minute, his mind furiously chasing the implications of her words. It was true—if he died and Rellia couldn't prop him up as the figurehead of her conquest into the Untamed Marches, her enemies would kill her. "She'd do that? Run for it?"

"I think so. I've begged her to empty the family's vault and buy passage off-world. She refuses, of course, but I might be able to get her to take just enough to get away. She won't want to see me killed, and if I refuse to flee without her . . ."

"They'd kill you too?" Victor sat down, suddenly feeling a bit deflated.

Valla laughed, a short barking sound, and said, "Of course! My loyalty to Rellia is well known in the family, and most think of me as illegitimate, in any case. Without her protection, there are plenty who resent me enough to see me dead."

"I'm surprised Rellia doesn't have you trying to steer me away from this confrontation. I mean, you could have told me Boaegh was in Persi Gables, then somewhere else, and kept me chasing ghosts until spring."

"You're quite right, and I proposed such a plan back before she sent me to help you." Valla grinned at Victor's outraged look. "Rellia wouldn't have it, though. She says we need to earn your trust, that she's 'built too many bridges that require a strong foundation' with you." Valla paused and nodded. "Sometimes I forget how wise she is." She stared at Victor, where he sat, brooding, and added, "Rellia would banish me for a year if she knew I was about to share this. Promise me you won't repeat it?"

"Sure," Victor said automatically. Then he looked at her, saw the doubt in her eyes, and said, more seriously, "Yeah, Valla, I'm not going to betray you."

Valla nodded and continued, "Rellia has seen much, been through more than most people could bear. Victor, she claims there's something about you that's magnetic, a kind of gravity. Her words were something like, 'He's a falling star that's smashed into Fanwath, and we can either ride the shockwave with him or be buried in the wreckage he leaves behind.'"

"Seriously?" In Victor's mind, he was still a teenager from Earth. A kid trying to figure out the world, still trying to find a girl and a purpose. He knew objectively that wasn't the case, that he'd changed a great deal, but he still had that feeling inside. He couldn't take himself that seriously; how could someone like Rellia?

"She keeps counsel with powerful oracles. Doesn't that sound like a prophecy? She wouldn't say as much to me, but she said she felt there are things about you—portents, that cannot be ignored. You might not be aware of it, but your spirit weighs heavily on Fanwath. In any case, you made me promise not to report your activities to Rellia, remember? She doesn't know about the oubliette. She doesn't know about the Pyromancer. If she did, she'd probably put a lot more pressure on me to stop you or at least allow her to send more of her agents to help."

Victor sat there and thought about her words, his brow creasing in an ever-deepening frown. He'd come to accept the idea that he would be helping Rellia with a conquest of some unknown, distant lands. He'd come to grips with the notion that his spirit craved adventure and conflict, but he didn't like the idea that so much weight was being put on his actions by so many people. What had he done to deserve such attention? It felt as if he was losing the little bit of autonomy he'd struggled to grasp over the last few months.

Finally, unable to think of any profound statement or action, he shrugged and said, "Thanks for keeping your word to me, but you should know: I think Rellia is full of shit. I think she's trying to build me up into something much greater than I am simply because I beat her in the arena. She can't stand the idea that she lost to someone who isn't some kind of 'meteor smashing into the world,' or whatever."

"I must admit to having similar thoughts . . ." Valla started to say.

"Good! Then let's drop this dumbass subject and go get some food. I want to kick ap'Horrin's ass on a full stomach tonight."

Valla snorted and scooped up her papers. "Hine's still serving breakfast, and I saw a platter of glazed pastries."

"I suppose I should stay out of sight still. No sense ruining any surprise advantage I might have. Do you mind getting me some food?"

"No, I don't mind." Valla nodded curtly and turned to leave, but as she opened the door, she turned back to Victor and said, "I don't think Rellia's completely deluded. There's something about you, Victor." She looked as if she wanted to say more, but she shook her head and stepped out, quietly closing the door behind herself.

Victor walked over to his bed and picked up Lifedrinker from where she leaned against the headboard. He held the axe for a minute, admiring the silvery streaks, like lightning striking out from the edge into the black metal. He knew he'd picked her up because he wanted comfort; he wanted to grab onto something solid that always felt good to him after the unsettling visit he'd had with Oynalla and then this further discussion about bullshit prophesies and portents. He pressed the cold metal to his forehead and said, "It is all bullshit, isn't it, lovely?"

Lifedrinker didn't answer him, not with words, but she vibrated softly against his head, and he swore he heard a delicate soprano humming. He closed his eyes and followed the sound and his mind's eye saw a beautiful vale surrounded by tall hills. He saw a river cutting through the blue-green grass; at its head, a misty waterfall fell into a gleaming pool. The cliffside behind the waterfall was streaked with silvery ore, and Victor knew it was Heart Silver. "Is this where you're from, beautiful?"

The sound of his door opening startled him, and Victor opened his eyes, whirling to see Valla holding the door open for one of Hine's kitchen staff.

The man ducked his head apologetically when he saw Victor standing there with his axe and hastily set his tray on the table. Valla thanked him, and he left. Then she looked at Victor and said, "What are you doing? You look like you just fell out of bed and can't figure out where you woke up."

"I, uh, how long were you gone?"

"Not long. Maybe fifteen minutes."

"Fucking crazy. I was just listening to my axe, and it felt like less than a minute."

"Listening to your axe?"

"Yeah, she was singing to me, and I saw where she came from, I think." Victor laughed at himself and gently slipped Lifedrinker into the loop on his belt. "I know I sound crazy, don't worry."

"No, you don't. I've seen crazy, and you aren't it." Valla pulled out a chair and sat down, "Come. I got enough food here for three or four people. Let's break our fast, and you can tell me what Lifedrinker's home is like."

"You're all right, you know that, Valla? You might be a little tight-laced, but you know the right thing to say most of the time." Victor walked over to sit down. The tray was laden with thick-cut bacon, a bowl of scrambled eggs, two enormous sweet rolls dripping with glazed sugar that Victor could smell the second they came through the door, and a pitcher of fresh-squeezed juice.

"Tight-laced?"

"Yeah, like, you know, prim and proper. Shit, when we first met, I couldn't get you to say more than three words at a time."

"I . . ." she started, and Victor saw her pale blue skin start to deepen toward purple on her cheeks, and he reached out to gently jostle her shoulder.

"Relax, Valla; I'm just busting your balls."

"My balls?" Her voice rose an octave, and Victor laughed.

"See? This is called bullshitting, Valla. Isn't it better than all that serious business? Now, c'mon, let's see who can eat their pastry the fastest!"

32

BLOOD WILL FLOW

Victor smashed Lifedrinker into his target, the guard standing to the right of the oubliette door. The poor man had seemed bored, yawning and chatting with his partner as Victor crept over the grass in his blind spot. Lifedrinker's razor edge sank into the crook of his neck, cleaving arteries and a collarbone and resting six inches into his chest. The guard only managed a wet, coughing grunt before he slumped, and Victor's arms strained, holding him up with his grip on the axe haft.

At the same time, Valla streaked over the grass using some sort of Energy-based charge, grabbed the guard on the left, threw him to the ground, and jerked a wicked single-edged dagger through the flesh at his throat, letting the blood flood out over the front of him and onto the grass.

Their assault was brutal, savage even, and Victor and Valla had long argued about the need for lethal force to gain entry to ap'Horrin's sanctum, but the risk of leaving guards still breathing seemed to outweigh the benefits. Victor had clinched things when he'd said, "We aren't going in there to make friends. These are bad people, and lots of blood is going to flow. I won't kid myself."

Ap'Horrin was a minor noble, though wealthy, and Victor knew there might be repercussions for their actions that night. He'd tried to talk Valla out of accompanying him, but she wouldn't be dissuaded. She'd shown Victor a black ring that she wore on her thumb and said, "No scrying will reveal my actions. Worry not about my reputation."

Victor had contemplated Valla's ring, apparently quite a rare artifact, and then he'd shown her his talisman for shielding scryings and asked if it would protect him in the same way. Valla had shrugged and said, "Maybe." Victor knew it worked to stop people actively watching him, but he didn't know if it would hide his actions that night at ap'Horrin's estate. He'd ultimately decided he didn't give a damn.

As the two guards watered the grass with their blood, Victor stood up and tried the handle on the strange round metal door. It was dark gray, covered in bronze carved vines, and the handle was recessed, requiring Valla and Victor to cooperate to reach into the three holes that depressed the separate levers. "I bet this was a door meant to be opened by Yovashi," Valla said, sliding two slender hands into the left and center holes. Victor barely managed to squeeze his left hand into the other one, but neither of them could get their levers to move.

"Locked," he said.

"Try your ring," she said, and Victor nodded, lifting his right hand and tapping one of his oldest treasures on the metal door—his Ring of the Guest. He was so surprised that it worked that he almost laughed. The door shuddered and loudly clicked, then it popped ajar. He and Valla pulled it open the rest of the way, revealing the entry chamber to ap'Horrin's oubliette.

While Valla scouted inside, Victor grabbed the two dead guards and dragged them into the antechamber. The room was roughly oval, with sloping hallways leading downward to the left and right. An orange glow lamp hung in the center of the stone room, and wooden benches along the far wall were the only other furnishings.

He held the two guards by the collars of their chainmail shirts and easily hoisted them up to the bench, leaning their two heads against each other. A twinge of guilt started to creep into his mind, but Victor shook his head—he had dirty work to do, and these people worked for a man who had tried to kill him on multiple occasions. "What's the old saying?" he asked as he finished propping them up against each other. "Sleep with pigs, and you get dirty? Something like that."

"It seems like a lot more traffic has been going down the left-hand tunnel," Valla said, coming to stand by him and looking at the two blood-spattered, horribly wounded bodies. "You're not fooling anyone with that."

"Yeah, I know," Victor said, turning to study the inside of the door. After he scanned it from top to bottom, he finally saw the little filigreed handle that was meant to lock it. He shifted it to the left and was pleased by the satisfying series of clicks. "Doesn't matter. No one's coming in after us, and anyone we run into is going to die."

"Unless they don't work for ap'Horrin," Valla said.

"Yeah, 'course." Victor concentrated a moment, and then his ghostly white-gold spirit hounds shimmered into being, and he willed one of them to watch the lesser-used hallway. "All right, down we go," he said, casting Inspiring Presence. Valla and his coyotes seemed to swell with the spell, standing taller and their eyes appearing more eager. Victor grinned as the shadows slipped away, and the complicated lock he'd been looking at suddenly seemed obvious.

"I love that spell," Valla said, nodding. Suddenly her heavy blue broadsword was in her hands, and she nodded. "You take the lead."

"Yep," Victor said, hoisting Lifedrinker and heading down the left-hand tunnel. His coyotes were quiet, only letting out the occasional yip, and he urged one of them to prowl ahead. After it had rounded a corner, Victor started forward, his other three coyotes and Valla keeping pace as they worked their way down the sloping, curving tunnel. Nothing seemed familiar to Victor, though he'd been pretty out of it when ap'Horrin had brought him here to break his Core.

Every dozen feet or so, another orange Energy-powered glow lamp lit up the shadows, and with his spell active, Victor could see through the gloom as if it was daylight. They'd traversed a hundred or so feet when he felt something from his scouting coyote—danger ahead. He held up his hand and whispered a warning to Valla, and the group continued to creep around the bend.

The passage leveled off and straightened out, and Victor saw his coyote ahead, lurking near a doorway on the left. The main tunnel continued deep into shadows, with a notable absence of glow lamps. Trusting Valla to see what he saw, Victor hunched low and crept toward the doorway. With a flick of his will, he urged his other companions to hang back and called his scout to join them.

When he got to the opening, he peered around the corner, just inching his head past the doorframe enough for one eye to see what lay beyond. It was an alcove with a square table and four chairs. Two men and a woman, similarly garbed to the ones he and Valla had already killed, sat at the table. One of them whittled a piece of wood with a tiny knife. Another seemed to be cultivating or meditating, and to Victor's surprise, the third was reading a book.

Victor pulled his head back, turned to Valla, who lurked behind him, and held up three fingers. He thought about it for a couple of seconds, then leaned closer to her and whispered, barely allowing air to slip past his lips, "I'll frighten them. Be ready." Her eyes widened, but she set her lips into a grim line, and she nodded.

Victor steadied his grip on Lifedrinker, visualizing his next move several times before he did it, just as he used to do before a match—or a pit fight. He pictured how he would step, how he'd cast his spell, and where he'd send Lifedrinker's edge. Taking a breath, he moved around the corner, cast Project Spirit, sending a wave of purple-black fear-attuned Energy into the small room, and then, as the guards' eyes widened in horror and they started to scramble, he cleaved the book reader's head from his shoulders.

The two remaining guards began to jibber and groan inarticulate, terrified sounds and Victor leapt upon the one in the middle—the cultivator—smashing him back with his heavy boot, so he tumbled out of his chair. He charged after him, kicking the table aside, and followed up with several brutal hacks. When he lifted Lifedrinker's bloody edge and turned to the third guard, he saw Valla standing over her corpse, wiping her sword on the fallen woman's cape.

Valla nodded grimly to him and held a finger to her lips. She cocked her ear, presumably listening for reinforcements, but Victor knew no one was coming—he could sense it from his coyotes. "Nothing's coming right now," he whispered, gesturing to one of his coyotes visible from the doorway. She nodded, and the two continued their descent into the depths.

"No worries from the beast you left up top?" Valla whispered.

"Nothing," Victor grunted. Before long, Victor saw a four-way junction ahead, brightly lit by three glow lamps. The passage they were in continued through it to a set of wooden double doors, and there weren't any signs of more guards in the open space.

He looked at one of his coyotes and willed it to scout out the junction. The shimmering, white-gold creature padded silently into the bright intersection, leading with its snout. Victor wondered if all of its senses worked—could it smell as well as see and hear?

No feelings of alert came from the scout, so Victor led Valla to the junction, and that's when he heard a low, vibrating chanting sound coming from the double doors ahead. To the left and right, he saw that the passage seemed to continue straight but sloped into darkness in both directions. Valla pointed to the doors and made an exaggerated shrugging motion.

Victor nodded and crept toward them, hugging the wall on his left. He felt Valla behind him and knew his coyotes were hanging back at the intersection, keeping watch. As he neared the door, Victor became aware of a heavy, thick Energy in the air. He wasn't familiar with its particular brand, but it didn't feel like pure Energy—it had a feeling of vibrance, a tang of copper, and he wondered if it was blood-attuned Energy. He looked at Valla, and she nodded—she felt it, too.

The chanting was louder, but the words were still indistinct, perhaps a language he didn't know, a language untranslated by the System's Language Integration skill. Was that a thing? Victor wanted to ask Valla but knew better than to start up a conversation while creeping outside a door that opened into a possible cult's summoning hall.

Valla's scouts had assured her that the Pyromancer no longer used the barn where Victor had nearly been immolated, and she felt sure they'd probably run into the coven of summoners in the oubliette—it was where Boaegh had been lurking, after all. Victor tried the door handle to see if it would move, and the little brass lever depressed at his touch. He gently tugged and pushed on it, hoping to open the door a bare sliver, but it wouldn't budge, seemingly barred from the other side.

Victor motioned for Valla to follow him back to the intersection, then he leaned very close to her ear and whispered, "I think the cult is in there. Maybe Boaegh and ap'Horrin too. I'm going to smash that door apart and go in swinging."

Valla frowned and tugged Victor's collar so he leaned closer and whispered into his ear, "We could search these side passages—try to find another entrance."

"I don't know. I feel a sense of urgency, like they're doing something I want to stop. Maybe it's all in my head, but . . ." he trailed off with a shrug.

"I did smell blood magic," Valla hissed. She shrugged in turn.

Victor looked at his coyotes and smiled at them, whispering, "Good work, pack. Time for me to call your big brother, though. Go get some rest." Victor dismissed the spell that held his pack on the physical plane and then looked at his Core; he'd already recovered all of the Energy he'd spent earlier.

Once again, he leaned close to Valla and whispered, "I'll berserk if there are more than a couple of them. My bear will also be enraged, so watch out for yourself." He shrugged and added, "I have good control of my berserking, don't worry too much."

"Your bear?" Valla breathed, her eyes growing wide. Victor grinned and nodded. They were standing near the wall, just around the corner from the double doors. He was getting himself geared up to make the attack when Valla touched his arm, and he saw that she'd put away her sword. She held a thick book in her hands instead.

"Victor," she whispered, "this encounter could result in one or both of our deaths. Will you allow me to send a message to Rellia so that she knows where we are? So she knows that I'm probably dead if she doesn't hear from me soon?"

"Seriously?" Victor was flabbergasted for two reasons—he'd assumed Valla had already snitched to Rellia about their movements, finding it hard to believe that she'd so literally honor his request to keep his actions between the two of them. Secondly, he found it hard to imagine she was pulling this now, right before he charged into a—potentially massive—battle. "If you're that worried, hang back! Guard my back and keep watch in case someone runs away from me."

He saw emotions warring on her face; he knew she wanted to go with him and didn't want to appear afraid. He wondered if her experience with fear in the woods played a role in her thought process—did she feel she needed to insist on fighting to prove something to him? He was about to remind her of her duty to Rellia when she finally scowled and nodded, replacing the book with her sword. She opened her mouth, but Victor beat her to it, whispering, "If shit looks really bad, just run for it. You have my permission to contact Rellia with the bad news if I bite it."

Valla nodded, and Victor grinned. He turned back to the double doors and walked toward them, then reached into his Core and pulled out a thick ribbon of rage-attuned Energy, getting it ready. At the same time, Victor cast Manifest Spirit again, this time calling for the fragment of his soul represented by the bear totem.

Red mist started to coalesce on the tunnel floor, luminescent and brimming with furious Energy. Victor felt it, felt the part of him that wanted to smash and destroy begin to manifest, gathering in a red, glowing cloud that rapidly resolved into an enormous bear. He tried to will it to be quiet, but the creature would have none of it, lifting its gigantic head toward the tunnel ceiling and roaring loud enough to bring dust and shards of stone showering down. The doors before the bear shook with the burst of sound, and Victor couldn't help it—he laughed.

He pointed to the door and urged his bear to attack, and then all hell broke loose. The massive bear, nearly too large to fit in the tunnel, bounded forward and shredded the door as if it was made of toothpicks. Splinters, planks, nails, and brackets burst forth as Victor's bear totem charged into the open space beyond, roaring again like thunder somehow bottled and released underground. Victor rushed forward, already reaching for his rage-attuned Energy again, readying his Berserk spell.

He almost stumbled, almost lost track of what he was doing, when he saw the madness beyond the splintered door. The room was large and square with stone walls that reached twenty feet to the ceiling. At the center of the room, which was probably a hundred feet on a side, nine figures in baggy brown robes were scattering from his gigantic bear's furious charge. Hanging upside down from silver chains at the center of the ceiling was a humanoid with bright green chitin where a human might have skin.

The insectoid person's arms and legs were held spread-eagled by the chains, and directly beneath him, an Ardeni man sat on a throne-like seat, tethered to the prisoner by a thick band of blood-red Energy—it was evident that the Energy was flowing from the bound insectoid to the man in the chair.

While his bear roared and pounced upon one of the brown-robed individuals, Victor had eyes only for the man on the throne—ap'Horrin. He narrowed his eyes and finished his spell, letting loose a roar of his own, not to be outdone by his bear. As the rage rushed through him, stretching his pathways to bursting and flooding his body with power, Victor screamed in a fury, remembering what this man had done to him.

He remembered lying on a stone slab while a tentacled monstrosity reached into his guts and broke up his Core. He remembered riding in a wagon, feverish and weak, near death from the disgusting wound he'd been left with. He remembered all the torment he endured fighting free of the Greatbone Mines. He remembered feeling lost and ruined because he'd executed the man this "lord" had sent to kill Victor in Persi Gables. Finally, he thought of the guards he'd massacred this night, and he roared again, and this time, it truly was as loud as his bear, for Victor had taken the form of his ancestors—he was a Quinametzin warrior bound for vengeance.

A brown-robed man stood between him and ap'Horrin, and he launched a series of rapid firebolts toward Victor. They streaked through the air like little missiles, flickering with intense white heat, and Victor laughed, charging right into them, head down, axe held high in one hand like a massive hatchet. The fiery arrows exploded off Victor's chest and helmet, and though the flames washed over him like liquid napalm, he laughed, shrugging it off. "Flames?" he roared, swinging Lifedrinker like a cleaver at the little man. "I've bathed in worse!"

Lifedrinker screamed through the air, and though the mage created a shimmering maroon shield of force, she burst it apart. Victor roared, and the mage screamed, and Lifedrinker took him in the chest, buried to the haft. Victor lifted him up, flopping limply on Lifedrinker's edge, and shook the little mage in the air, showering blood down on his shoulders, helmet, and face. Victor's gaze had never left ap'Horrin, and though the man seemed to be finishing his feast of blood-Energy, his eyes were wide with horror.

The room reverberated with the roars of his bear and Victor's own challenges. Victor didn't spare a glance for his companion, though—let the great bear fight his fight. He had to deal with ap'Horrin before he found a way to flee. Victor whipped his axe to the side, sending the mage's corpse flopping over the ground, then he bent his mighty knees and leapt the last twenty feet to come crashing toward ap'Horrin, his axe falling like a meteor toward the man's head.

As Victor descended, ap'Horrin either finished or broke off his feast of blood-red Energy. He made a sudden, perhaps panicked, gesture, and in a cloud of red mist, he streaked away from the throne, reappearing in the flesh, some twenty feet distant, stumbling toward the exit. Victor tracked his movement as he fell, and though the throne was empty, he still smashed it to bits with Lifedrinker. He bounded after ap'Horrin again, this time keeping his feet on the ground.

Ap'Horrin saw him coming, tried to pick up speed, realized it was fruitless, and turned toward Victor, holding out both hands. Red motes of Energy began to coalesce in the air between the two of them, and though Victor charged on, he felt it snaring him up, catching on his armor, on his skin, on his axe, pulling at him like quicksand. As the red mist grew thicker, ap'Horrin turned to run, shaky on his feet but slowly making ground on Victor.

A brown-robed mage came to Victor's attention because she'd started launching razor-sharp ice crystals at him. Victor held up an arm to protect his eyes as he strained and pulled against the blood mist, and most of the ice shards broke on his armored sleeve, his chest, or his helmet. A few found purchase in his flesh, but he ignored them—what were some puny stabs to him? Who was this tiny mageling throwing pathetic darts his way? He had a man to kill, and she was in the way.

Victor screamed, squatted down, bunched his enormous muscles, and charged through the rest of the mist, ripping it to shreds with his furious strength. Ap'Horrin cried out and nearly collapsed as Victor demolished his spell, and then he was free. He bisected the ice mage as he ran past, and as he caught up to his quarry, Victor gripped the back of his neck, lifted him off the ground, and smashed him into the stone at his feet.

Lifedrinker flashed with red Energy, humming in a high-pitched, war maiden's cry, and Victor planted her firmly in ap'Horrin's spine. Ap'Horrin shuddered and shook, and Lifedrinker took his Energy, dark, thick rivulets pouring into her. Victor looked around the room with a furious gaze, saw the corpses of half a dozen mages, and saw his bear roaring and struggling against the magic of the three remaining casters.

One held out his hands, creating bands of yellow-rimed ice that constricted the great creature, while another mage whipped at it with a putrid, sickly vine of foul Energy. The final member of the trio repeatedly launched bolts of yellow-white fire at the brave totem's flank, singing its ruddy fur and blackening its flesh. Victor felt his red gaze darken to murderous crimson and left Lifedrinker to do her work, charging to his companion's aid, screaming like the mad titan he was.

He smashed into the mage creating the yellowed, sickly ice cage, sending him sprawling as if he'd been hit by a motor vehicle. The caster bounced and skipped over the stone floor to crunch into the wall, and he lay unmoving, fluids leaking from too many orifices for there to be much hope for his recovery. With the cage gone, Victor and his bear made short work of the last two mages, and as they stood, heaving and growling, covered in gore, Victor surveyed the room.

Nothing stirred. Broken corpses lay in pieces and heaps, and Lifedrinker hummed in her high, trilling note, but, with his enemies slaughtered, Victor let his rage cool, let it fade from his pathways, and soon he was standing there, still bloody, still drenched in viscera, but back to his normal state of mind. His bear had faded with his rage, and he wondered if he'd subconsciously sent it away or if it had gone of its own accord.

He walked over to Lifedrinker, and as he pulled her from ap'Horrin's back, he saw the Energy motes of his Victory begin to gather over the corpses. He watched the golden Energy coalesce and saw that much of it was tinged with purple, though not as much as he'd hoped—none of the mages had been as strong as Boaegh. Ap'Horrin had surprised him with his abilities, but they hadn't been anything exceptional—the motes from his corpse were all purely golden.

The Energy surged into him, lifting him off his feet a few inches, but he felt that was more a reflection of the number of his vanquished foes than their power. Still, the flood of Energy was a strong one, and he felt the euphoria lift his mind fully clear of his battle-fevered thoughts, and he thought to look at the ruined doorway for Valla. Victor had expected her to be walking toward him by now, but she wasn't there.

As the Energy surge faded, he called out, "Valla!"

She didn't reply, but a weak cough above him caught his attention, and Victor jerked his head up toward the bound, green-chitined humanoid. Ap'Horrin had chained it upside down, and its mandibled face stared toward Victor and the doorway. "Are you alive, then?" Victor called up to the insect person.

"Yes!" it coughed, sounding like a man to Victor. "And I saw your companion—she pursued Boaegh as the coward fled," he coughed again, and yellow-green ichor dripped from his mandible to the stone floor.

"Fuck!" Victor turned and started to run, but the man called out weakly.

"I know where he's going! Help me down—I'm from the same world as that bastard!"

33

INTO THE FIRE

Victor ran his eyes over the insect-man's chains and saw a pulley leading to a winch on a nearby stone post. He hurried over to it and pulled out the pin, and the man started to drop through the air toward the ground as the wheel began to spin. Victor quickly reached out and grabbed the spinning wheel, saving his intended rescuee from smashing onto the stone floor by mere inches. "Shit, sorry 'bout that," he said as the chains jerked to a halt.

"It's fine—you saved me from much worse," the man said, grunting as he found his feet. He gestured to the chains and said, "I think that one, the one you cleaved through the spine, has the key." He gestured to ap'Horrin's corpse, and Victor ran over to it. Not seeing any belt pouches, he quickly pulled off the four rings he found on ap'Horrin's cold, gray-blue fingers.

As Victor walked back to the chained-up praying-mantis-looking guy, he trickled some Energy into one of the rings randomly and was pleased to find it was a dimensional container. "First try," he said, searching through the many contents with his mind. He smiled at the trove of goods and knew he'd need to spend a lot more time going through the valuables, but for now, he produced the only three keys he found within.

Only one key was a match for the silver padlocks, and Victor quickly unlocked them. As he was doing so, he gave the insect-man a closer look—he had no clothes or jewelry, and his bright green chitin was cracked in many places, oozing yellowish fluid. "Are you okay? Did you have some clothes or anything?" Victor hesitated to ask, not wanting to waste time when Valla might need some help, but he couldn't help putting himself in the guy's shoes.

"I had a belt and rapier, but they took them from me long ago. My name is Ksajik, and I owe you my life. Follow me, and I'll show you where the worm, Boaegh, has fled. Hopefully, he hasn't led your companion into a trap." With that, he started striding, with a pronounced limp, toward the doorway, and Victor followed, tucking ap'Horrin's four rings into a pouch on his belt. Ksajik had an interesting way of speaking with halting words and occasional clicks. His voice was clear, though, and Victor absently wondered if the System Language Integration skill was working overtime for him.

"What world are you guys from?" Victor asked in a hushed voice, pacing beside Ksajik, Lifedrinker held ready. The tunnel was sloping downward at a fairly steep angle, but it was straight, and he could see there wasn't anything lurking in the near distance.

"Zaafor," Ksajik said, green fluid spraying from his mandibles as he drew out the "zaa" sound.

"Never heard of it," Victor said and almost laughed at himself—how many worlds did he know the names of? He'd heard other names before, but at the moment, he could only think of Fanwath and Earth.

"It's distant from this one. The System has existed there for millennia, but it's a harsh place." He paused and leaned against the smooth stone wall for a moment, then said, "My apologies, I cannot speak and walk at the same time. That bastard took much of my Core. My recovery will take decades! We need to hurry before your companion is slain!"

"All right, shit!" Victor said, then stooped down in front of the insect-man and said, "Get on my back, dude."

"Er," Ksajik said, clicking his mandibles uncertainly, then he reached up his three-fingered, green hands to Victor's shoulders and mounted his back. "Yes, you're a sturdy fellow. This isn't shameful." Victor stood up, hardly feeling the man's weight, and started trotting down the tunnel.

"Not at all, man. No shame at all! Sounds like you've been through hell." Victor had a thought and then, despite the awkwardness of it, decided to ask, "You are a dude, right? I'd hate to be calling you 'man' or whatever, if not. God, sorry, that sounds terrible . . ."

"Heavens, but your mind is leaping to strange topics while we chase my mortal enemy! Yes, I'm a male—all of my caste are male. Now, when you come to the intersection, turn right." Ksajik's words were clipped and halting but firmly stated.

Victor grunted, taking the guy's point to heart—he should be more concerned about Valla. As he ran, Victor felt his Core, saw that his Energy reserves were good, especially his inspiration, and cast Inspiring Presence. He also tried to cast Manifest Spirit to summon his coyotes, but the spell wasn't quite off cooldown. He almost fell as he came to the intersection Ksajik had mentioned, and he slid on the dusty stone, trying to turn right at a near full-tilt run.

Ksajik clung to his shoulders with a vise-like grip, holding on while Victor regained his balance and started running down the new tunnel, occasional glow lamps showing him that it was long, descending, and very slightly curving to the left. He passed doorways, but Ksajik urged him to keep going each time, saying they were just storage or empty rooms. Victor had no reason to doubt the guy, so he charged ahead.

They came to a round, well-lit room with a circular stone stairwell at its center, and Ksajik said, "Down there. At the bottom of the stair, you'll find his portal room. Gods, but I hope he hasn't opened it yet. Is your companion a formidable fighter?"

"Valla's tough as hell," Victor said, starting down the broad stone stairwell, careful not to rely on the ancient-looking wrought iron balustrade. He believed what he'd said but also knew Valla wasn't him—she couldn't shrug off the kind of damage that he could, and he'd hate to find her fried corpse waiting at the bottom of the stairs. That on his mind, he began to hop down the steps, three at a time, and felt Ksajik cling more tightly to his back, grunting in strained wheezes with each of Victor's bounds.

After a couple of dozen hops, Victor finally landed at the base of the stairs and saw that he stood in a circular room, easily three times as wide as the stairway it housed. Smooth stone walls rose up in every direction except one, where a set of massive, bronze double doors stood.

"That's it. He's in there, I'm sure," Ksajik said, carefully letting go of Victor's shoulders and sliding off his back.

"Damn it!" Victor hissed, running up to the doors. They were near twice his height, and he could tell by how they seamlessly met in the middle that they were well made. He grabbed one enormous metal handle and gave it a tug and a push, not surprised when it didn't budge. "Looks like I might have to berserk again," he said, glancing back to check on Ksajik and maybe warn him to go up the stairs a few steps.

He was startled to see not only Ksajik standing by the stairwell but another shadowy figure emerging from behind it—an enormous, spider-like individual with a very familiar, smooth, featureless face with saucer-like, depthless black eyes. "You ugly motherfucker! I'm glad to see you!" Victor growled, his rage flaring to life without his urging.

Ksajik whirled to see the object of Victor's ire, and when his eyes fell on the Yovashi, he scurried up the steps. It didn't matter because the spider-like monstrosity had eyes only for Victor. He strode forward, huge legs spread out and long gray tentacles extending from the bottom of his torso, where Victor saw something like an octopus beak and gleaming red eyes. "You shouldn't have returned, System slave."

"The fuck did you call me, you ugly asshole? Which one of your faces do I talk to? The one with the beak or the stupid one up top?"

By way of answer, the Yovashi lunged forward a step, and his hidden beak coughed a horrible barking sound and snapped with a resounding *clack*. "I'll eat you with that one," the top mouth said.

"I don't have time to dick around with you," Victor growled, and then he cast Project Spirit, sending a wave of fear at the monstrosity. The Yovashi balked for just a moment, his enormous spider legs flexing and starting to scramble backward. Victor saw him begin to recover, start to bend his legs in the other direction, but it was too late—Lifedrinker ripped through one of those six gigantic legs, sending it flopping and twitching over the stone floor in a spray of black ichor.

"Fool!" the Yovashi screamed, stumbling back. Victor felt a massive burst of foul, filthy Energy pour out of the monstrous man, and a wave of nausea hit him like a ton of bricks. He almost threw up, feeling his guts roil as though he'd swallowed a bucket of worms. Stumbling backward, Victor dug deep into his Core and flooded his pathways with hot, rage-attuned Energy, but he didn't berserk; he just channeled the Energy into his body and Lifedrinker, and then he growled.

"You bastard! You think I don't remember the taste of your Energy? The way you dug around in my guts? I was a weakling back then, but you've fucked up, buddy. You should've hidden in a closet until I left." Victor wanted to berserk, wanted to go absolutely nuts on this guy, but he also wanted to have his wits about him—wanted to savor the feeling of thrashing this *pinche* motherfucker.

"Stop!" the Yovashi hissed, and Victor felt the power behind the words, felt them creep into his mind, worming their way into his brain, sending signals to his muscles to lock up and cease moving. He laughed, flooding the weird mental Energy out of his brain with a surge of rage, and, with eyes blazing, he strode forward and hacked off another of the creature's legs.

"Your will isn't strong enough to try that shit on me," Victor growled as the monstrous man pitched back, crying out, black ichor oozing all over the floor, making it slippery as Victor continued to advance, driving him back toward the curving, smooth stone wall.

"Listen to the voice of Tkelvic and obey! Drop your axe!" the Yovashi hissed through pain-clenched jaws. Victor felt a wave of that same slippery Energy, much heavier, denser than before, rush into his mind, digging at his brain but finding no purchase. Victor grinned and advanced, Lifedrinker held high.

"You dumb asshole, Tkelvic. Do you think I came back here to shut you guys down without improving myself? Are you strong for a Yovashi?" Victor asked, striding forward, slapping away a thrashing, chitin-covered spider leg, "'Cause I'm not impressed."

Tkelvic uttered a guttural snarl and drove with his remaining four walking legs, and Victor saw the huge red-eyed beak darting toward him from the nest of tentacles. He stepped to his left and brought Lifedrinker around in a baseball bat swing, and he knew, if he'd been in Yankee Stadium, he would have hit that fucker out of the park. Tkelvic screamed, and Lifedrinker shattered the beak, catching it on the underside of its "chin," carving deep through it into the gray abdomen of the Yovashi.

Tkelvic's tentacles thrashed and whipped, two of which were tipped in hard claws that clicked and scratched at Victor's armor. He shrugged them off, grabbed one, and tugged hard enough to jerk the monster to the side, and with his other hand, he began to hack in earnest, wielding Lifedrinker as he did when he was berserking—one-handed. Though he was his normal size, Victor was a big, strong man, and the axe whipped through the air without much difficulty, seeming to add to the momentum of his swings with her own vibrant will.

Before long, Tkelvic's gurgling, inarticulate cries began to die down to weak, wet gasps, and Victor was covered in the black ichor that was the Yovashi's blood. Bits of chopped, broken tentacles and chitin littered the ground, and Victor decided he'd wasted enough time—he stepped one booted foot onto the Yovashi's crumpled chest and brought Lifedrinker down in a killing blow, chopping through three-fourths of that stiff, gray neck, severing the spine, and ending his erstwhile tormentor's life.

"Enough," Victor growled, jerking Lifedrinker free and turning toward the massive bronze doors. He raised his voice, "Ksajik! I gotta get in there! Is there a trick to opening these doors?"

The bright green man haltingly descended the steps into view, glancing at the horrifying mess Victor had left against the wall and then at Victor's gore-covered figure, and said, "They're locked and warded from the inside. Perhaps you can smash them open in your giant form, but I wouldn't be sure."

"No time to dick around," Victor said, building the pattern for his new spell, the Inevitable Huntsman. He felt the magic draw from all of his Energy affinities, and then his vision became monochrome, and he had thoughts only for delivering justice. He looked around himself, noting the absolute lack of shadow and deception, nodded at the broken corpse of the Yovashi, and expanded his thoughts—who deserved justice?

When he'd cast the spell, Victor had been hopeful that he'd have some sort of control over who he hunted down or, failing that, that he'd seek out the person nearest, most deserving—he'd had reasonable confidence that Boaegh would top the list because that was who he'd stalked toward when he'd first cast the spell. His luck held up—he felt his gaze turn to the bronze doors, to the feeling of a presence beyond them, and he nodded; justice would be served.

Victor took a step toward the door and paused, staring at it as he felt the now familiar buildup of Energy in his gut. It wasn't quite ready, so he watched the doors, unmoving, unwavering, implacable. He heard a voice in the background, but it was of little consequence, some question about his actions from an innocent party. He ignored it, waiting. Then it was time; the Energy began to push at its bounds, and his urge to move toward his quarry grew almost unbearable, so he released it.

Victor stepped into another large round room. In his monochromatic vision, nothing could hide from him, and he saw his quarry, bright and scurrying on a raised dais. The other objects in the room were of no import—furniture lining the walls, books, tables, scattered papers, and a swirling doorway of brilliant Energy. It was all meaningless next to the need for justice. Victor stepped forward, and it wasn't until he was nearly upon him that Boaegh realized Victor had come into the room.

The Pyromancer wailed in surprise as Victor ascended the steps to the dais. He raised his hands, throwing out a sheet of fire that flared into a towering wall of crackling flames at the top of the steps. Victor stepped through it. The flames were uncomfortable and damaged his clothing, singed his hair, and reddened his flesh, but Victor ignored them—his quarry was three strides away; a few flames and some discomfort shouldn't stop justice.

Boaegh seemed surprised that Victor had stepped out of his curtain of flames, and he turned, panicked, toward his portal, abandoning the trunk he'd been digging through. With the patience of a glacier, Victor stepped toward him, saw the mage's intent to flee, and measured the distance. Unless he moved very quickly, indeed, the mage would escape. "No!" Victor said, his voice like grinding granite plates. He lifted Lifedrinker and whipped her toward the mage's back. She cut the air with a whistling shriek, a Valkyrie cry that echoed through the round stone room, shattering glass beakers and vials.

Lifedrinker struck the Pyromancer's back with such force that her entire metal head followed her blade into his torso, leaving nothing but her quivering axe haft protruding between his shoulder blades. The mage coughed in agony, blood following his utterance in a spray of gory liquid he stumbled through. His own momentum, coupled with the power of Lifedrinker's impact, sent him flailing headlong through the portal.

Victor continued on, unfazed—what was a portal in the face of justice? He saw it narrowing, saw the whirling bands of Energy begin to shrink, and knew that it would wink out of existence in seconds, so he simply pushed out another pulse of that implacable Energy and willed himself over the dais and into the swirling, shrinking disc of Energies.

Victor floated in darkness but kept his focus on his quarry, only to feel it fade out of existence. He looked around in the endless black, seeking some likely target for justice, but when nothing came to him, no heat on the horizon to stride toward, his spell began to unravel, and Victor came fully back to himself. Instantly he knew what had happened—he could vaguely recollect all of his actions in his Inevitable Huntsman form and knew he was traversing a portal—a very long one.

"Oh, fuck," he groaned, sudden memories coming back. He'd just stepped into his *abuela's* living room when he'd been sucked into a blackness just like this. How long had that taken? A few minutes? An hour? It had been hard to measure time then, just as it was now. He gripped his empty hands, hardly believing he'd thrown Lifedrinker. "Still, I fucking got that asshole. I better get his Energy when I get to the other side!"

He racked his brain, trying to remember the details of the portal room, trying to think about what he'd seen—had Valla been there? Had her corpse? "Shit!" he growled, knowing it was impossible to know; everything but his target had been a blur. The spell was undoubtedly useful for hunting down a creep like Boaegh, but it had some definite drawbacks. He hoped he'd gain more control as he continued to improve his will and the spell's rank. His mind snapped back to the present when he saw a pinpoint of light in the blackness.

The light expanded, just as it had when he'd been summoned to Fanwath. It grew to the size of a golf ball, then a basketball. It doubled in size several times until all Victor could see was a bleak, sandy landscape and a bright blue sky with a tinge of yellow. He felt solid ground under his feet, and, just like that, the portal was gone, and he was through it. Boaegh's body lay at his feet, and to his great relief, so did Valla—bound with silvery chains and thrashing, trying to work her hands free.

Victor reached down and jerked Lifedrinker out of Boaegh's body. He smiled at her, noting that her Heart Silver veins had grown thicker from his time in ap'Horrin's oubliette, and then he glanced down at the dead Pyromancer. "Just in case," he said with gritted teeth. He stepped to the side and hacked Lifedrinker through his neck, severing the mage's head and letting it roll down the gentle, sandy slope.

"Ungh!" Valla groaned through the metal chains wrapped around her mouth and head, staring at him with wide, furious eyes.

"Right, right! Sorry!" Victor said, kneeling at her side and pushing her so the chains holding her hands behind her back came into view. They were thin, delicate things, and when he reached for them, he could feel their Energy. He pulled at the end, seemingly hanging loose, wondering why Valla didn't just unravel them. It came away easily, and he kept unwinding until Valla jerked her hands back to the front of herself.

She reached up and tried to pull away the chain at her mouth, but Victor saw it wouldn't move no matter how she strained. "Let me," he said, reaching for the loose end of the chain and easily unwinding it. "Must be enchanted not to let the prisoner take it off. Makes sense," he chuckled.

"Not funny! Nothing about this is funny! Where are we?" Valla asked with storm clouds in her seafoam eyes.

"Um, Boaegh's world, I guess. I think it's called something like Zafer; no, it had a longer Zaa sound. Zaafor. That's it."

"Get this damn chain off my ankles, please!"

"Right," Victor said, unwinding the third chain. They were delicate but powerful things, so he slipped them into his storage ring. "Might come in handy." He dusted his hands off and looked to the horizon to take in the sights, but then an enormous surge of Energy poleaxed him. "Fucking hell!" he groaned as it lifted him off the ground with an orgasmic surge of well-being and euphoria. He howled and laughed as the purple-gold wave of Energy rushed through him.

*****Congratulations! You have achieved level 35 Spirit Carver, gained 10 will and 10 vitality, and have 8 attribute points to allocate.*****

"Hell, yes!" Victor crowed, lifting Lifedrinker into the air. He saw Valla staring at him from the sandy ground and smiled. "Level."

"Congratulations. Something tells me you're going to need it if we're going to get back to Fanwath in one piece," Valla said, standing up and pointing to something behind him. Victor turned, looking out over the desert landscape. Scrubs dotted the rough sandy ground here and there, along with strange cacti, similar enough to what he'd seen around his home to be identifiable as such.

Some of the cacti were thin with long spikes, others were short and shaped a lot like prickly pears, and still others reminded him of square barrel cacti. "They're called cactuses, er, cacti."

"Not the plants. That thing," Valla said, pointing to the right. Victor tracked the direction of her finger and sucked his breath through his teeth. A monstrous snake-shaped creature the size of a couple of city buses hooked together was gliding over the sand in the distance. Its back was covered with horned bone-like plates, and its head was maned with similar bony spikes. It didn't glance their way as it faded from view over the horizon, and Victor exhaled a breath he hadn't realized he'd been holding.

"Was that a fucking dragon?"

Status			
Name:	Victor Sandoval		
Race:	Human (Quinametzin Bloodline): Improved 4		
Class:	Spirit Carver: Epic		
Level:	35		
Core:	Spirit Class: Improved 1		
Energy Affinity:	3.1, Fear 9.4, Rage 9.1, Inspiration 7.4	Energy:	3041/3041
Strength:	135	Vitality:	140
Dexterity:	40	Agility:	63
Intelligence:	32	Will:	315
Points Available:	8		
Titles & Feats:	Titanic Rage, Flame-Touched		
Skills:			
System Language Integration	Not Upgradeable		
Spirit Core Cultivation Drill	Basic		
Cooking	Basic		
Animal Taming	Basic		
Unarmed Combat	Basic		
Knife Mastery	Basic		
Spear Mastery	Basic		
Bludgeon Mastery	Improved		
Axe Mastery	Advanced		
Grappling	Advanced		
Spells:			
Berserk	Advanced		
Sovereign Will	Improved		
Channel Spirit	Improved		

Inspiring Presence	Basic
Enraging Orb	Basic
Globe of Insight	Improved
Project Spirit	Improved
Dauntless Radiance	Basic
Heroic Heart	Basic
Spirit Walk	Basic
Tether Spirit	Basic
Manifest Spirit	Improved
Shape Spirit	Improved
Harsh Light of Justice	Improved
The Inevitable Huntsman	Improved
Aspect of Terror	Basic

ABOUT THE AUTHOR

Plum Parrot is the pen name of author Miles Gallup, who grew up in Southern Arizona and spent much of his youth wandering around the Sonoran Desert, hunting imaginary monsters and building forts. He studied creative writing at the University of Arizona and, for a number of years, attempted to teach middle schoolers to love literature and write their own stories. If he's not out enjoying the beach, you can find Gallup writing, reading his favorite authors, or playing *D&D* with friends and family.